Accidentally Yours

Jason Springer

Contents

Chapter 1

This, by far, was the stupidest day of my life. Not again.

"Cheer up, Eli! Haley is just another girl lost at sea."

That's one of my best friends, Preston Daniels. That smirk wearing joker was trying to bring up my mood, but it just wouldn't work. Not this time.

We both sat in Chaplin's Diner, a local and our favorite food joint. I sighed out of frustration in reply. It has been three months since my girlfriend, I mean ex-girlfriend, dumped me. If I had to recall Haley Jones' very words: I think we should start seeing other people.

It just had to be before summer vacation started — where I thought we'd be spending time together after being apart because of college.

She broke up with me for that guy everyone's been talking about.

Landon Clarke.

Scrunching up an innocent napkin into a ball, I threw it across the bar counter a little too harsh, making it drop to the other side. Betty, the longest hired worker here, noticed my doings. She picked it up, placing it right back in front of me. Betty wasn't a mean person at all — she's actually a very nice lady, and she already knew something was up.

Betty raised an eyebrow out of curiosity. Her lips lifted into a smile, making her wrinkles appear. "I never see you boys here unless you have smiles on your faces. What's going on?"

You would think I would be the one to swallow my pride and tell her. Instead, Preston decided to open his big mouth and blab away.

Preston ran his fingers to fix his golden brown hair styled up. He announced through a carefree tone, "Funny thing, Betty... but Eli here tried to get his girlfriend back but failed yet again."

The worst thing I could possibly do to Preston right now was kick him — he should be happy I see him as a trustworthy friend.

Still, I hated how desperate I sounded due to Preston's words. I just thought that if I went back to Haley and asked for another chance, we'd be back together. It was easy in my head. I haven't even done anything wrong! Yet her hazel eyes were only set for Landon Clarke.

This would be my — never mind, I'm not even going to mention how many attempts it has been.

Betty gave us an amused expression before sliding two cups of iced Coca-Cola on the house. It was perfect for this hot summer day and the anger boiling inside of me.

Betty shook her head. "Elliot, you're still young to give it another try. Maybe she wasn't the right girl for you."

Sighing, I nodded so it looked like I agreed with her. The thing was, I thought Haley was going to be that girl. I'm nineteen years old, living in the sunny shores of Santa Monica, California. Well, I was here during break or when I had time — back to the point — I would like to share this life with a girl sometime, you know?

"Yo, so I heard the news."

Enter my other best friend, Julian Cooper.

"Coops" was what we like to call him. He was more, let's say, serious than Preston's goofiness when it came to matters like this. Coops gave that smile of his at Betty causing her to admire his looks. It was like Coops had the ability to hypnotize people when he smiled. People call Julian Cooper "charming". Coops ruffled his medium length jet black hair before approaching the bar stool next to us.

"So, what exactly happened?"

Betty soon walked away from our emerging "man-to-man" talk.

I tried my best to appear unaffected. "It didn't work. I'm starting to believe she's actually in love with that Landon kid."

I didn't know why I kept calling Landon Clarke a "kid". He was actually two years older than me.

Betty jumped back into the conversation all of a sudden as she rang up a customer. "That handsome lifeguard on the beach, you mean?"

Betty, you're really not making things better.

My two friends laughed amongst themselves until they caught my aggravated look. You two were supposed to be on my side.

One thing for sure was: I hated, despised, loathed Landon Clarke.

Sure, I was probably being extremely immature, but it's not everyday your girlfriend dumps you for the lifeguard on the beach. I was actually in the swim team all my high school years — the captain at that — how was a lifeguard able to beat me? We're practically the same! I'll never understand girls. The three of us sat there silently until Preston had that light bulb moment.

Preston snapped his fingers as his emerald green eyes widened. "I just came up with an amazing idea!"

Coops and I exchanged smirks and waited for Preston to continue. This was going to be good — Preston and his impossible ideas.

Preston took a quick gulp of his cola. "That Landon dude has a younger sister, doesn't he? What was her name again? Lana! Yeah Lana, remember her? Anyways, what if you date Lana to get back for what Haley did to you?"

Lana Clarke.

I've completely forgot about her actually. But thanks to Preston's sudden memory boost, I remember all the things I've heard about her during high school. They weren't exactly good things — not like she was a bad person — but, people were saying how she was "out there". Lana Clarke had this job where she dressed up as those Disney princesses for kids' parties. Apparently, people around school said that Lana thought of herself as a princess living in her own fairy tale.

Lana didn't seem like that type of person — she kept quiet from what I could remember. But, I never thought of myself to date a girl who dresses up as princesses. That was something new.

Shifting my mind back, Preston's idea was quite genius. It wasn't going to hurt to try, right? I'm just going to show Haley that she made a huge mistake for leaving me. I know it's already been three months, but I never expected myself to be the "dumpee".

"Hello, anyone home?"

Coops waved his hand in front of my face to grab my attention. I muttered out a "what?", snapping out my thought process and found the two staring for an answer.

Preston crossed his arms, that cunning smile still on his face. "So, how about it?"

And this, everyone, marked the day I would get back for being dumped.

"And how exactly am I going to get Lana to go out with me?" I was stumped with this plan while the three of us were heading to our cars.

As far as I knew, Lana never saw anyone. She had this one friend, Olette Benson, that she would always talk to. Other than Olette, Lana Clarke was seen alone.

Preston also added, "Where are we even going to find her? Isn't she at one of those princess parties or something?"

While we were trying to recall what that place she works for was called, Coops so happened to remember. "It's... A Fairytale Come True, let's go there."

Preston stifled a laugh hearing the name, holding onto his stomach. Patting him on the back, I told Preston to get himself together before the people walking beside us thought he completely lost it.

A Fairytale Come True, here we come.

As we hopped into our cars, I thought about what I was about to do. It was crazy, but Haley and I had been dating for a while now. It was kind of irritating that all of a sudden she would leave me for Lana's older brother. I never personally met Landon. However, when the guys and I would chill at the beach, we would hear girls gawk about the "mature, hot lifeguard". Shoot me now.

Eventually catching sight of the place, I pulled over to the nearest parking space by the curb and met up with Preston and Coops. It was a small place with a girly sign that spat out A Fairytale Come True. Taking a deep breath, I glanced at them and their clever grins before walking in.

The glass doors slid across, and the three of us were soon standing in the reception area. The receptionist was speaking on the phone until she noticed our presence. She grinned wildly and slammed the phone down within a breath.

Readjusting her black-rimmed glasses, she smacked her lips in interest. "What can I do for you boys today?"

The lady's name tag was inscribed Maryann. She batted her brown eyes several times at Coops and he looked a little uneasy, judging by the hidden scared emotion in those hazel eyes.

Clearing my throat, I requested, "Ms. Maryann, we're looking for Lana Clarke. Is she here by any chance?"

Maryann cooed, waving that red coated pen in her right hand, "Well Handsome, it appears that Lana is running late at the - "

"Maryann, I'm so sorry! I came to pick up the dresses at the cleaners and it ended up being so traffic!"

That was when I heard Maryann reveal. "Speaking of Lana..."

Lana?

We all turned back towards the entrance and there was a girl catching her breath. My dark brown eyes readjusted and I couldn't believe that was Lana Clarke! Her shiny and straight light brown hair was very long, reaching her stomach. She was wearing a summer dress that complimented her petite yet nicely curved figure with a pair of sandals. Lana shortly realized we were there and her blue eyes widened.

How could I look past those bright, ocean blue eyes?

Lana seemed a little perplexed, adjusting those huge dresses she held onto. "You guys look familiar..."

Maryann chimed in, "They're looking for you, honey!"

Even more confused, it took Lana a minute or so to process and she eventually remembered who we were. Her face transitioned uncomfortably while the three of us continued to stand there, all frozen up. She placed the dresses onto the chair nearby her and didn't respond. How awkward was this getting? Coops quickly gave my left arm a nudge, signaling that it was "go time".

Walking over to Maryann to hand her what looked like a check-in card, Lana questioned, "What can I do for you three?"

This was the first time hearing her directly speak — it was so sweet sounding.

When I glanced over at Preston, his eyes seem to be stuck onto Lana as he gulped down. Was Preston impressed with her? Anyways, I just have to ask Lana and the rest will be cake.

Putting on my best smile that kills all the girls, I replied, "Hey Lana. I'm sure you remember me and the guys from school, right?"

Lana nodded her head in response as a friendly smile grew on her face.

"I was wondering if you wanted to go out sometime."

Lana stood there, and it was bothering me because I wish I knew what was going through her mind.

She then raised both eyebrows in disbelief. "Why are you suddenly asking me now, Elliot?"

Preston and Coops snickered softly in the back. It's not that I hate my name — but I prefer to be called Eli or El.

Before answering, I cleared my throat. "Feel free to call me Eli. I just feel like we should catch up sometime. It's been a while, don't you think?"

I realized how stupid of an answer that was.

Pursing her soft pink lips, Lana pointed out, "Unless I forgot, we never talked during high school."

Ouch.

Looking down at the floor, I couldn't find any words to say back. Maybe I should just turn around now. I didn't even want to see Coops and Preston's faces until I ended up seeing their rising grins from the corner of my eyes anyways.

"Well... okay. When do you want to go?"

Did my ears just hear that right? Immediately, my eyes widened at Lana's sudden agreement.

I stuttered, thinking of something quick, "How about this Friday? I'll pick you up."

Right now, it seemed like we both didn't know what we were getting ourselves into. Lana agreed so mission success, right? After exchanging numbers, I gave her my best smile once again, telling her that I'll see her soon. As she smiled back, there was something graceful about Lana Clarke that differed the quiet girl who minded her business in the classrooms.

The guys and I waved goodbye to Lana and Maryann and once we got out, I let out a big sigh of relief. That was the first time in a while since I've been that nervous.

"Very smooth, Eli."

Preston mocked my words: "Feel free to call me Eli" in a high pitched tone causing me to punch his arm. The three of us laughed in unison at my embarrassing actions.

Once I composed myself, I grinned. "I still got a date with her, right? Dude, I didn't know that was her for a moment... Lana is prettier than I remember."

Coops threw on a smirk and joked lightly, "What did you expect, Eli? Genes run in the family."

Touché. Even if it did feel like a punch in the face.

As much as that bitter feeling for her older brother started to reside again, I was satisfied with the fact that Lana Clarke considered going on a date with me.

I mean, a "catch up" outing.

Not that I had any doubts — maybe one or two — but, this was it. No turning back now.

Chapter 2

This had to be the worst day ever.

I was running late for little Rachel's 5th birthday, I still needed to pick up the dresses at the dry cleaners, my hair was a mess and now, I was stuck in traffic. What more could go wrong? As much as I loved my job, rush hour was killing me right now. How I got this job was kind of a long story, but to cut things short, my love for the beloved childhood classic Disney was what made me who I am today. I would become the roles of Cinderella, Belle, and everyone's favorite little mermaid, Ariel.

Could this traffic move any quicker? Finally cutting through the fish of cars, I ran out my parked car as fast as I could to get my newly cleaned dresses. It was a dream come true becoming a princess almost every day of the week, but even princesses get tired sometimes. Thanking Wilma for her reliable cleaning services, I ran back to my car for work, to change and head off again.

As I was driving, I practiced a few notes. Embarrassing as it was, I couldn't go to a party as a princess with a cracking voice. It would scare the poor children away.

I hoped Maryann won't attack me again for being late. It was really the swarm of cars' faults. Rapidly grabbing the two dresses and mermaid's outfit, I ran my fingers through my once tangled hair but ended up stumbling on the curb. I was lucky that no one saw and rushed through the automatic sliding doors.

Catching my breath, I managed to yell out, "Maryann, I'm so sorry! I came to pick up the dresses at the dry cleaners and it ended up being so traffic!"

Except, I didn't see Maryann in her usual spot. She was being covered by three tall figures. Those three athletic-built figures turned my direction hearing my voice, and that's when I got the feeling of familiarity. Blurting my thoughts out loud, Maryann revealed that the boys were looking for me.

And that "ah-ha!" moment happened.

They were from my graduating class: Elliot Wesley, Julian Cooper, and Preston Daniels.

What were they doing here? Not really in the right mood to be asking questions, my mind was trying to focus on getting to that party! However, I didn't want to appear as a messed up person — I already went through that during high school. What made me shiver was seeing them stare at me like that. It's like they've never seen me before.

Actually, that did sound reasonable.

Walking to Maryann to hand her my check in card, I asked polite as could be, "What can I do for you three?"

Instead of a decent reply, it was like a cat got all their tongues. Something was definitely wrong. Three guys, who were considered the "best looking" from your old high school, never show up at your work every day. Especially since we've gone our separate ways after graduation. That's when Elliot Wesley cleared his throat.

I remember his tousled short hair matching his deep brown eyes that all the girls would craze about. His sun kissed tan deemed his armor since Elliot was the swim captain of our high school and carried various trophy titles. At most high schools, basketball or football was considered the top sports, but leave it to Elliot Wesley to make swim popular.

Elliot soon stated the obvious that we all sure did go to the same school together a year ago. Still, I put on a smile and waited for whatever was about to come next.

He then asked through his strong voice, "Well, I was wondering if you wanted to go out sometime."

Let me make it clear. This was coming from the star athlete who — I bet — never realized I was in any of his classes. I was honestly confused.

Another thing that made me start to get uncomfortable was seeing Preston Daniels' eyes devour me. Despite being the class clown and ladies' man out of the three, Preston also played varsity baseball on the side. Even though he had such eye-drawing green eyes, that smirk of his was very unreadable to me.

Suddenly, Elliot goes "call me Eli" — a nickname that only his group of friends would call him — and something about catching up for lost time. At first, I thought he was pulling a prank. It wasn't my intention to come off as rude, but I ended up doing a guilt remark saying how we never even spoke at school to begin with.

Why now?

I watched as those dark brown eyes fell from embarrassment even though it was indeed true. Quickly sharing a glance with Maryann, she had this puppy dog face on. She was basically pleading me to just say yes. You owe me, Maryann.

Taking in a deep breath, I changed my past thoughts and told him I'd go along with this "catch up". If you only saw how fast his head flew up and how those eyes brightened. Was he really serious?

After that, we exchanged numbers and for some reason, "Eli" threw on this smile at me which I couldn't comprehend. He always had this award winning smile, especially since a dimple on his left cheek would appear when he did so. The three waved a goodbye to Maryann and me and off they went. That was definitely unexpected.

Maryann's voice escalated an octave higher. "Lana, I can't believe my eyes! You have a date — with a handsome young man too! Where can I get one?"

After correcting Maryann that it was not a date, I laughed sheepishly and sent a reminder about her fiancee, "You have Ricky, remember?"

She ended up clapping her hands together and gushed, "I know... but that boy next to Elliot was oh-so-handsome! Not like the other two weren't handsome, but you know — "

As she was praising on and on about Julian Cooper, I couldn't blame her. From what I witnessed during high school, not only was he praised for being an excellent soccer player, Julian has a good sense of appeal towards everyone.

Telling her that it was really time for me to head off — I'm so sorry, Rachel — I quickly headed over to the changing rooms. My other coworkers, who served as princesses as well, were all gone to their own fairytale parties. Changing into my costume as Cinderella, I adjusted the blonde wig and slid my feet into those lovely not-really-glass slippers.

I heard Maryann chortle as I made my way out. "It's about time you found your Prince Charming."

Shaking my head, I reassured her that I was in no need of a "Prince Charming" right now. I had other things to worry about.

Besides, all of this was nothing but catching up. Right?

Yet another successful day for A Fairytale Come True. There was always that accomplished feeling after the end of each birthday party, knowing that the kids still held onto their dreams and their little smiling faces to top it off. Taking off the flower I planted on my red wig as I played Ariel, I tossed it lightly into my bag and was ready to head home.

Going back out to the reception area, Maryann was also packing up her stuff. I told her and the rest of the girls I'd head out early and we all parted ways. Walking over to my car, I fished out my phone from my purse and dialed my best friend's number. Waiting for Olette to pick up, she greeted me with a lively hello.

"You won't believe what happened today."

Olette giggled. "Let me guess, a little boy confessed his love for you at the party today?"

How embarrassing. I knew she'll never let that moment go. When I was Princess Aurora at Sydney's 7th birthday, a boy who looked about twelve or so, told me that he was my Prince Phillip. It was sweet — in an adorable way — and Olette would never fight the urge of bringing that memory up.

I let out a laugh, shaking my head at the same time. "No way. I only have one Prince Phillip. Anyways, do you remember Elliot Wesley?"

Olette soon choked up, mentioning about his role as swim captain and a "natural born cutie". She was right, I guess.

I continued, "Him and his friends, Julian Cooper and Preston Daniels, were at my work today. Just when you think that's already random, guess what Elliot said to me?"

With the way I was going with the conversation, it seemed like I was tensing Olette with suspense. I already pictured my best friend twirling her long and wavy auburn hair anxiously on the other line.

Finishing it off, I sighed. "He asked me to go out with him sometime... to 'catch up', according to him."

All of a sudden, I heard what may be a phone dropping while Olette shrieked from a distance. When it seemed like she returned, Olette was completely animated.

"Oh my gosh! Please tell me you're completely serious? The Eli Wesley was at your work today - and he asked you on a date?! That is random but most of all, I'm so happy for you!"

Nervously laughing at her disbelief, I really couldn't believe it myself. Opening my car door, I sat down on the leather driver's seat.

"It's not a date though. He just wanted to catch up. What's bothering me is when did I ever appear in his picture perfect life?"

Olette's voice still projected excitement from the news. "Oh Lana, who cares! It's been forever since you've went out... wait, this will be your first time with a boy! You're always working, take this opportunity! I'm so excited for you!"

I wanted to tell her that I really didn't have time for that kind of stuff right now. However, Olette was too happy to take anything else in as she rambled continuously about how I had to go with Eli. Since I already agreed, I couldn't really back out anyways. Telling her I would and how I would call her back, I ended the call to head home after a long yet very interesting day.

Realizing what time it was, my older brother should be home right now. As I closed the garage door of our cozy house we grew up in and headed inside, I found Landon and his girlfriend, Haley Jones, together in the kitchen.

Haley was a bearable person in high school. I never really paid attention to her or knew her personally, but she was fairly popular with everyone. Come to think of it, I think she was part of Eli's group. But if Landon's happy, then I am. Haley's golden hair that reached past her shoulders shined under the kitchen light as I walked in. Her naturally full lips grew into a smile as she greeted me.

Landon waved. "Work, fun?"

I answered saying that it was the usual and noticed a tan forming on him after being a lifeguard for a while.

The two were both eating the dinner they cooked together and offered me to join them. Saying that I'd love to in a bit, I then asked Landon if I could speak to him privately. Hoping that it wouldn't cause any mishap, Landon still excused himself from Haley, and we were now occupying the vacant hallway. He ran his fingers through our matching light, brown hair. His similar blue eyes appeared concerned.

"What's up, Lana?"

Playing with the ends of my hair, I mumbled, "Is it okay if I go out this Friday?"

Being eighteen, I know it was unlikely to still be asking your older brother this type of question.

Landon raised an eyebrow, his expression now confused. "Yeah, of course. You don't have to ask me, Lana." He then saw the look on my face and a faint grin grew on his face. "It's a date, huh?"

Immediately shaking my head no, I tried to explain, "An old classmate asked me to catch up cause we haven't seen each other since graduation, I guess. I just didn't want you to think I'm putting — "

Lifting both his hands up, Landon immediately swerved in to stop me. "Whoa, Lana. Of course not! Don't ever think that, okay? He wants you to be happy too, you know? I'm actually happy for you. It's making me feel terrible seeing you always working."

My lips pulled into a faint smile. I corrected, "You're different, Landon."

"Just because you don't want me to be single forever, huh?" Landon tried to ease up the atmosphere.

We both shared a short laugh together until my heart suddenly tightened.

I asked, "I'm going to check on Dad. Is he okay?"

Landon nodded his head with a smile occupying his face. "Haley and I gave Dad some dinner. He should be resting upstairs."

Giving my brother a smile back, I told him that Haley was good for him and he chuckled in response. I wondered if Landon was thinking of being serious with her because like Elliot and them, Landon was popular during his high schools years as well. I guess you can say he was still popular now being a lifeguard. As harsh as it sounded, sometimes people could hardly believe we were siblings. It didn't really matter to me though.

As I headed upstairs, I spotted Dad sitting cozily outside the balcony — his favorite spot. His eyes were shut and my heart went back to normal seeing his even breathing. Trying to put on a strong smile, I still felt myself shutting down in the inside. Dad must have noticed the sound of my footsteps, and his eyes carefully opened. Once he took in the sight of me, Dad gave me his heart-filled smile that always made my entire day and those eyes I inherited glimmered.

Dad spoke softly, "How are you, sweetheart? Did you try the dinner Landon and Haley made? It was delicious."

I answered that I was the same as always except my voice unintentionally cracked. Holding his hand, Dad stroked the locks of my light brown hair.

His gentle voice asked, "Lana, is everything okay?"

I nodded my head, but truthfully, I realized that it wasn't. I wanted to tell him about my day, but what mattered most was wanting to know how he's feeling. Even if I sensed that Dad was getting weaker, he tried to not show or tell me like always. For the rest of the night, I ended up sitting with him. We stared up the night sky together with my head gently leaning on his shoulder for slight support. Things like this made me so happy.

Even though I live as a fairytale princess during the day, the fantasy stops when the parties are done.

More than anything, my only wish was not to find Prince Charming, but for Dad to get better.

Chapter 3

Briefly glancing at myself in the mirror, I wanted to make sure I didn't appear like a goof. I know the plan wasn't really to be with Lana, but I wanted to look somewhat interested. Throwing on a casual yet presentable gray shirt and a pair of dark pants, I hurried my way down the wooden stairs until I was pulled back from moving any further by my mom, almost slipping on my socks.

Mom was sitting in the suede L-shaped couch from our family room. "Heading somewhere?"

She had her chestnut brown hair tied in a ponytail as she peeked over her shoulder. As always, my answer would be that I was just hanging out — it's summer vacation after all. Before I could respond, Eian came charging right at me.

Mind you, Eian was our family dog. Our Siberian husky was jumping up and down, making all sorts of barking noises no matter how much I tried to calm him down. I ended up laughing at his joy and petted him. His frosty blue eyes continued to stare at me while his salt and pepper colored tail wagged non-stop.

Mom got up from the seat and was walking towards me. It's funny how small she was. Years ago, Mom was like a skyscraper. Not like her authority ever changed though. She folded her arms, giving me a slight frown.

"You never take Eian out for a walk anymore. Don't tell me you forgot your duties when you're here, Elliot Aaron Wesley."

This was bad. When she said my full, entire name, it was serious.

Chuckling lightly, I scratched the back of my head and explained, "You know I haven't, Mom. But today, I'm taking a girl out on a... date."

I couldn't believe I just said that.

Mom's pastel green eyes charmed with interest. With a smile, she asked who was the girl. After the break up with Haley, I guess Mom figured I had a hard time getting over it. Holding Eian down as he was yapping away, I revealed that it was Lana Clarke. Mom arched her right eyebrow, growing curious.

"I didn't know you talked to her, Ell. She seems like a very sweet girl."

Putting on my best shoes, I tried pulling Eian away. "Yeah. I ran into her with Preston and Coo — Julian not too long ago, and asked her to hang out sometime. And I'm going to be late if I stay here. I promise I'll take Eian for a walk."

In defeat, Mom eventually gave in and called Eian over.

After saying goodbye, I headed towards my black Honda Civic and checked the time. Oh man, I was going to be late. Checking the address Lana gave me, I managed to find my way through the streets and there it was. Seeing their house for the first time, it wasn't too bad. It was one of those Victorian-styled two story homes with sandy colored paint and white trimming.

Pressing the plated aged doorbell, I was expecting Lana to answer until... Landon Clarke was revealed behind the door.

Crap.

I was slightly taller than him which made me feel advantage. His face seemed puzzled until it looked like he remembered why I was there. That's right.

Landon gave me a closed grin. He commented as we shook hands, "Eli, right? Come on in."

Or the ex-boyfriend of your current girlfriend — choose your pick. I was standing near the guy who took Haley's heart away from me. Just imagine how I felt right now. Expecting to find Haley there, disappointment appeared finding out she wasn't.

"Hey, so you're taking Lana out?"

Snapping out of my thoughts, I took a brief look at him and noticed the resemblance between the two. Of course, Lana — being a girl — was definitely prettier, but the two had the same hair and eye color.

I nodded. "Yeah. You don't mind, right?"

A smirk appeared on Landon's face until he retorted jokingly, "If I did, then you wouldn't be here."

It took everything I had to hold it in and just laugh along at his sly joke.

Looking around their home awkwardly, I noticed how small it was compared to mine yet it had similar things — those family portraits taken in the past, stuff to show off your kids' achievements and all those things that make it your home. As I was examining the Clarke household, there was one important someone missing.

Where was Lana?

Landon had turned on the T.V. and that's when I asked where his sister was. Thinking that she was getting ready upstairs, Landon knew otherwise and was looking at the clock. He expressed an apologetic look.

"She's... probably at the party still, but I'm sure she'll be home soon. Sorry, my sister's been pretty busy."

Completely understanding, at least I wasn't the one late. I nodded with no offense.

"I've noticed ever since high school, she's always been the person to commit herself to school and work."

There was a sad grin that appeared on Landon's face. "What can I say? Lana is one of the very few girls to know what she really wants."

"Landon, is Lana home?"

Following Landon's gaze, my eyes reached the stairs and found a middle aged man making his way down. He looked just about my dad's age. Slightly younger, maybe. This was probably Mr. Clarke. Where was Mrs. Clarke? She was in the family pictures — I assume she was at work or something.

When the man caught sight of me, he paused before questioning, "Is this one of your friends, son?"

Landon shook his head in reply and reminded him that I was Eli Wesley — the boy taking his daughter out tonight. A friendly yet cautious grin rose upon Mr. Clarke's lips. He soon offered his hand out to me.

"Nice to meet you, call me Mr. Clarke."

Giving him a solid handshake, I mentioned, "The pleasure is all mine, Mr. Clarke. I'd like to introduce myself formally. I'm Elliot Wesley, but you can call me Eli."

Mr. Clarke let out an impressed laugh, slapping my back right after. He seemed like a really friendly guy and I noticed those ocean blue eyes came from him. Mr. Clarke then looked around the room.

"I didn't know Lana was home already... Is she getting ready?"

Landon quickly headed over to his dad which made me question why. It looked like he was assisting his father down the stairs. Mr. Clarke looked pretty strong to me though.

Landon answered after an embarrassed chuckle, "No Dad, she's not home yet... probably soon though."

Knowing that Lana was now late, Mr. Clarke quickly offered me a drink or something to eat, but I politely declined his generosity.

That's when we all heard.

"Landon! Please tell me he isn't here yet!"

What caught our attention was a girl barging in the front door wearing a humongous yellow dress. It looked like from that one Disney movie — was it Snow White? It must be. I remember her wearing something yellow.

Landon and Mr. Clarke began laughing heartily making Lana's round blue eyes widen, finding us by the stairway this whole time. Despite her hair looking a little out of place, Lana managed to look like a princess. She looked great in that overly huge dress. I noticed Lana was embarrassed since her cheeks turned red.

Lana laughed unsteadily. "Sorry Eli, I didn't mean to be late. The celebrant's mother offered me cake and when you sent me the text, it reminded me that this was happening today."

Honestly, I didn't know how to react. She barely remembered? In the end, I smiled and told her it's alright. I guess.

Seeing her face fill with relief, she quickly made her way — huge dress and all — to her dad. Lana gave him a gentle kiss on the cheek and asked through concern, "Dad, shouldn't you be getting some rest?"

Mr. Clarke chuckled. "Just because I'm getting old doesn't mean I can't meet the boy taking my daughter out."

Lana made a face, but I caught the worried look showcased in her blue eyes. I wondered what Mr. Clarke meant by that.

Suddenly, Landon teased his sister, "Isn't Cinderella supposed to be the late one? Since when did Belle ever end up like her?"

That's the one!

The two exchanged their sibling interaction with one another before Lana glanced back my direction. She smiled, her voice sounding rushed. "I'll be back down in a bit."

As we all waited in the bottom steps, Mr. Clarke began coughing out of the blue. It sounded coarse which made me grow a little concern seeing him like that. Landon returned with a glass of water and two medicine pills.

Mr. Clarke must have seen my worried expression and began to wave his hand to indicate that he was fine.

"I just have a common cold, son. No need to worry."

Grinning in relief, that's why Lana said he should be getting some rest.

A few minutes later, Lana was heading down the stairs. She still looked a princess without the need of a fancy dress. She wore a light pink dress that flowed above her knees. Moving her very long and straight, light brown hair all over her right shoulder, she had a shy expression on once she noticed I've been staring at her. However, her attention rapidly whipped towards Mr. Clarke who was holding in his coughs.

Her voice grew alarmed. "Dad, are you okay?"

Mr. Clarke simply nodded his head, giving her a reassuring smile. His voice was a bit hoarse as he told me, "Now Eli, don't be back too late, alright? Make sure Lana has a good time."

Saying with all respect that I would do everything I could to make sure she does, both Mr. Clarke and Landon gave me a grin in return. Though Lana's tensed expression had softened gently, I couldn't help but feel like she was still bothered by her dad's coughing incident. As we headed out the door, Lana looked back at her family one last time before we left.

I decided that we should eat at Tuscan Bistro, a decent restaurant. Not too cheap and not over the top. During the whole time — from the car ride to as we are sitting face to face in our table — Lana's mind was preoccupied with something else.

Clearing my throat, I started up a conversation. "So, how's work?"

Lana snapped back to reality and replied honestly, "I like it... it's nice being able to make kids smile and be a part of their childhood even if it's just for a day."

I wanted to say how nice it was of her to do that, but everything got awkward soon after. What was I doing wrong? Trying to catch eye contact with Lana, her blue eyes were gazing somewhere else. Growing a little aggravated, I ended up staring down at the menu.

"Did you ever accept the scholarship to Auburn?" Lana surprisingly broke the silence this time.

She knew about that? Well, our school did say it loud and proud during the usual morning announcements. That scholarship... funny story.

Shaking my head, I grinned. "Actually, I didn't."

Lana had given me the look of disbelief.

Chuckling from her expression, I nodded. "Don't get me wrong, I love to swim but, it wasn't the direction I wanted to head into. I go and dorm at USC right now."

Lana grew a small smirk. "Living on the high road, aren't you?"

I cracked a smile and said in my defense. "Thanks to the other scholarships I managed to get, but I'm thinking of transferring out. I want to get into the aerospace program at the California Institute of Technology."

That school was ranked best for that type of field.

Lana grabbed the cup of iced water and nodded in interest once she finished taking in a sip. She stated lightly, "You were an excellent swimmer I heard... Don't take offense, but I didn't see you as the type of person to be interested in that stuff."

Giving her a grin, it was quite of a stereotype. Instead of pursuing a full scholarship to swim for Auburn, I wanted to deal with space and life surrounding it.

I shrugged. "It doesn't seem likely. But ever since I was little, exploring what's up there or the technology behind spacecraft seems interesting to me."

Getting a little conscious, I wondered if I sounded like some nerd. It was hard talking about this with other people since they all thought I'd continue swimming. Oddly enough, I liked how I was able to talk about this matter openly with Lana. She listened attentively and for once, she was the first girl that knew what I meant.

Lana smiled. "It's not a bad thing though. I think your choice is amazing. I never pictured a talented athlete wanting to go to outer space. Too bad you can't swim up there."

Of course, she was joking.

I ended up laughing in surprise before she joined in. This whole time, I was definitely proven wrong. Lana Clarke was a good person to talk with. Our conversation was put to a stop when the waitress came for our orders. Once she was finished and gone, we continued talking about what we've been up to since graduation.

Tracing the outline of her ceramic plate, Lana revealed, "I'm still working at the same old place... I haven't really looked into college yet." A sad smile was pushing to show on her lips. "I guess I could say I'm still the same."

I asked, hoping I wasn't prying, "So the money you're working for... is that for college?"

She shook her head. "It's... for other things." Her tone was blunt.

Once the food came, the silence grew between us again. As I stared at my plate, I smoothly sneaked a glance at Lana, who was busily gazing down at her food as well. Growing a bit uneasy, I couldn't help but feel bothered.

Speaking up, I suggested, "Hey, I'm not really much of a restaurant kind of person, how about we hit up the pier after?"

Lana gave me a soft smile, nodding her head in response.

And now, a way to capture her heart.

Winning a stuffed animal at those game stands.

We walked side by side at the Santa Monica pier with the ocean present before our very eyes and shouts from people riding the attractions above us. Lana was smiling brightly seeing everyone have a good time as they strolled along the wooden planked floors. Feeling content with my suggestion, I was looking for a particular game stand I'd win for sure at.

"I was just wondering why — I mean — out of all the people from our school, how come you wanted to spend one of your summer days with me?" Lana suddenly asked.

How was I going to respond to that?

Fixing the bottom of my shirt, I answered as casual as I can be, "Well, why not? It's not hurting us both, right?"

Luckily, Lana ended up agreeing before gazing off the opposite direction.

Sighing from the not-so-smooth excuse, my mood boosted up seeing the stand I had been looking for. It was the basketball one and if you made it through the far hoop, you'd win a huge teddy bear as a prize. It was just calling me to win!

Suggesting to head over there, Lana shook her head at first, telling me that she's fine with just walking around. That was when I put on a confident smile, saying that it wouldn't be a problem. As we walked over to the booth, Lana slipped in a cheerful good luck as I handed a five dollar bill to the crabby guy behind the stand who looked in his late twenties.

This was going to be easy.

Rolling my head from side to side, I held the basketball at — what I assumed — the correct position and tossed the ball with — what I assumed — the right precision. Except something went wrong. It completely missed and bounced right off the rim.

Consciously looking around, there wasn't much of a crowd around me. Not only was I surprised, but I caught Lana's eyes widen for a moment. When she noticed my gazing, she quickly threw on an encouraging grin.

Alright, this was nothing.

Just try again.

Toss after toss, I felt my pride and confidence being crushed every time I missed.

Pulling out the last bit of cash in my wallet, the stand guy jeered as he snatched the bill away, "You sure you want to try that again, champ?"

Ignoring his lame taunt, I threw the basketball — my last chance — but once again, it missed.

This couldn't be happening.

"It's probably just an off day, huh?" Lana's voice gave me a calm sensation.

Even if I tried to nod, it killed me with shame walking away from that stupid stand, knowing that guy's cocky grin was plastered on till the very end.

In disbelief, I muttered, "I don't understand how that happened..."

But, it didn't seem to bother Lana as much as it was bothering me.

She was walking down the steps towards the shore and chuckled. "I can see why you stuck with swimming."

Following her down the pier, I scoffed a laugh as she stuck her tongue out. Normally, I'd be pretty bitter, but Lana was able to tame the fire that was once growing inside of me. When she turned around to face me, her ocean blue eyes glowed from the fading sunset.

A tiny smile appeared on her porcelain face and she shrugged. "You don't have to impress me, Eli."

Then, she paced over to the waters. I found myself in this state of confusion. There was something about Lana Clarke I couldn't put my finger on. She wasn't like Haley or any girl I met before. Lana's personality ran its own unique track. It made her so fun and carefree.

"Hey champ, come here. The water is very cool," Lana teased, pulling my attention.

Just my luck. I just had to be wearing shoes. Taking them off anyways, I rolled up my jeans slightly — not really caring how weird it looked — and joined Lana by the waters. It was cool and refreshing to the touch. Lana turned to look at me, her hair whipping along, releasing this faint sweet smelling perfume.

Her thoughts must have poured out unwillingly as she beamed, "It's amazing, huh? Nothing beats the ocean — the sound of the waves — the feel of the sand — the movement of the waters. It's just so beautiful."

With the way Lana spoke and presented herself, this entranced feeling was starting to appear within me. I was literally being engulfed by her. Not realizing it was sun down and nothing burned the sky but the soft moonlight and the pier's carnival lights, I was staring at Lana without notice. She didn't seem to see since her attention was out to the ocean.

"You know, this is when the ocean looks the prettiest. You see how the moon shines on the waters right there? It almost looks like glitter — it's so mesmerizing."

Observing what she was looking at, I agreed with complete interest. By that, I mean, I wasn't just nodding my head to make it seem like I was paying attention.

For some reason, something overcame me as we stood together, staring off at the ocean. I suddenly forgot what my main objective was. The whole reason why I was with Lana tonight. When we shared eye contact again, I leaned in towards Lana — without even thinking — with my lips out for a kiss.

Someone hand me an award for being an idiot.

As a result, I felt — not a kiss back — but a slap in the face.

Chapter 4

Even if I promised Olette I wouldn't throw my guard up tonight, Elliot Wesley just tried to kiss me!

Call it a natural reflex, but once I opened my eyes, my right hand already flung itself across Eli's cheek.

This outing was good so far. I enjoyed the dinner we had, the small talk, seeing Eli try to win at that pointless game stand — I think that was my favorite part — but I wasn't expecting this sudden attempt to kiss me! Who did he think he was? I was here, just trying to tell him what I thought and liked about the beach we shared, and he decided to throw his lips at me once I turned to look at him.

So much for a day "to catch up from high school".

Was this what he told all the girls?

Letting my hand drop, my eyes were held wide open. "What was that about!"

Eli immediately held onto his slapped cheek, making a light hissing sound. Guilt suddenly ran through me and I sighed. Followed by my outburst, I slid in an apology, but he shook his head. Eli was still holding onto his cheek.

"No. It's all on me. You're right — that was completely uncalled for and it won't happen again."

I didn't know if he said that because he realized he was wrong or if he was scared I'd slap him again. Did I even slap him that hard? I couldn't forget the fact that it was different. Ever since we've been at the pier, I felt like I was the one doing all the talking and Eli was just spacing out — I know he wants to study aerospace, but this wasn't the right time. Was he still upset about losing? It really didn't matter. Maybe that slap was a good wake up call. Eli continuously rubbed his cheek until it appeared to look okay. His dark brown eyes gazed up at me and shook in panic.

"That — I didn't mean to do that. Can we forget what just happened?"

Good idea.

Nodding my head, I told him that I was sorry for the sudden outburst — even though he shouldn't have showcased those lips of his near my face like that. Eli never even answered my first question to begin with. When he eventually seemed to have shaken the whole incident off, he laughed sheepishly. We both stood by the shore as the soothing waters gently touched our exposed feet.

Through this moment of silence, the question never left my mind. Why, of all things, did Eli decide to kiss me? Eli never — I repeat — never looked my way during high school. He was one of the star athletes at our school, he had all the girls going crazy for him, he had friends that circled around him all the time... it was driving me a little nuts.

Shouldn't Eli be spending his summer with them — not me? Even though we "pretended" this never happened, I knew it was bothering us both. We just didn't have the guts to mention it again. Letting those thoughts go, I realized it was getting late and began to worry if Dad and Landon ate some dinner yet.

Running my fingers through my hair, I suggested, "Hey Eli, it's been an... interesting day, but it's getting pretty late."

Eli turned to face me, but he held those dark brown eyes somewhere else as if he couldn't look at me in the eyes anymore. Understanding my hint, Eli grinned loosely.

"Sure, I'll take you home. What happened earlier... I just want to say sorry again."

"What happened?"

Eli did ask to forget what happened — why should he bring it up again?

Realizing what I did, Eli gave me a smile in return. And seeing that smile and the way that dimple on his cheek appeared, threw me off. I was positive that all the girls would claim Eli Wesley as the best looking at our school. I think it was mainly because of his smile that won girls over.

We found our parking spot in the 3rd street promenade and got into his car. This day of "catching up" wasn't what I expected. I didn't know if I should say that went well or completely flopped. Maybe in the middle. For the majority of the car ride home, we shared another awkward moment of silence.

Ever since I stepped foot out of my house with Eli, I kept wanting to know what was going through his head. I guess my thoughts got the best of me.

"What's on your mind?"

His attention was stuck on the road yet his body language seemed alarmed. Eli spilled out. "I was just thinking if you had a good time."

Truthfully, what was I going to say? That everything went well until he tried to kiss me? No. That wouldn't end the night well.

Coming up with a conclusion, I answered sincerely, "It was fun. I think... we should catch up again."

Biting my tongue right after, I grew conscious. What if my reply came out sarcastic to him? Instead, Eli answered back saying that he'd like to and next time, no surprises. I was definitely fine by that. Something told me I wouldn't be hearing from Eli anytime soon though. Asking him if he had a good time in return, Eli gave his attention to me once the spotlight hit red.

He smiled, dimple showing. "I did. I'm a little disappointed I wasn't able to snag you something though."

"Not all girls need a stuffed bear, you know."

Before I knew it, we were in front of my house. It was like those moments you'd see in the movies when the guy driving didn't know what his next move was after parking his car on the curb. But, this wasn't like the movies right now.

Giving him a smile, I took my seat belt out. "I guess it's time for me to go."

Instead of an "okay, see you later" kind of reply that I was thinking he would do, Eli took off his seat belt and told me to wait. Watching him get out of his car, I was surprised to see him make his way just to open my door side. What a gentlemen move that was. Maybe to redeem himself from his failed attempt earlier? Yes, I know I'm being mean. Oddly enough, I couldn't grasp the concept why I was so amazed by this.

Eli grinned sweetly and motioned his arm out. "My fair princess, your castle awaits your return."

I had a feeling he'd say something like that.

As cheesy as this moment was, Eli should know that I'm off duty right now.

His actions still managed to make me laugh. I shook my head. "Those don't work on me, Romeo."

Eli looked away momentarily, before shrugging his shoulders with a closed smile on his face. "It was worth a try. I'll be seeing you, Lana."

Telling him the same, we both parted ways and I was now opening the door to my house. Glancing over my shoulder, Eli was walking back to the driver's seat. He must have caught my gaze for he waved shortly before completely driving off. I found myself smiling until my older brother opened the front door before I could get the key to turn.

Landon raised his eyebrows, almost amused, as he towered over me. I always thought Landon was so tall, but Eli was an extra two or three inches taller than him.

Landon took in my smile and teased, "Turn out good?"

Dropping my expression, I nodded my head casually while saying it went well. And that was it. Quickly bringing up the question if they already ate dinner, Landon automatically noticed my plan of diverting his attention about my night with Eli. Lifting his arms up in defense, Landon played "innocent".

"Hey officer, I won't ask anything else. I just want to know if my little sister is being treated right the way she should be."

Smiling, I replied that Landon didn't have to worry about me. My whole mood gradually changed once I focused back on Dad.

Landon gave me a comforting grin. "He already ate and took his medicine. He's getting some rest now."

I gave him a faint nod, feeling some kind of relief.

"You know... he's breathing a lot better than before."

"Landon, but." I sighed. "Will he ever be the same?"

There was a long pause and I knew my question had an unknown answer to it. In fact, Dad's cure was still unknown to all of us. Landon gulped down hard as his eyes wandered the darkened front yard, but before he could answer, I shook my head to disregard my silly question.

Once I stepped inside, Landon stopped me from walking away. "Lana, he's always here for you — I am too."

Gazing over my shoulder, I forced on a smile. "I know. It's just hard how something like this is changing him."

His blue eyes stared into mine as he walked towards me. Landon placed his hand on my shoulder and continued to grin, hoping it would ease me up. My brother always had such a kind aura to him.

"Dad's strong, Lana. Lung cancer isn't changing him. Don't you worry."

I hated when those two words slip through my ears.

Sometimes, I couldn't even say it outloud to myself.

Landon pulled me into a hug causing me to embrace him back. He then whispered that I should catch some sleep for the next day. That's right — three parties, playing all the princesses — who's tired? Then again, I'm half joking.

Bidding good night to Landon, I made my way upstairs and peeked in the slightly opened door of my parents' room. From what I could see, Dad was sleeping soundly and I walked in — as silent as I could be — to gently kiss his forehead and wish him a good night's rest. Heading over to my own room, I realized after a long day from parties filled with Disney loving children to Eli Wesley, I was in need of some sleep.

"Lana! Aren't you going to pick up your phone?"

Olette continued to press on, holding that insisting look of hers. Instead of doing her errands like she was supposed to do, she was killing time and encouraging me to answer my ringing phone.

I told Olette everything the following day about the so-called catch up event with Eli. She was more thrilled about it than I was. I still remember her jumping almost ten feet in the air, reminding me of a basketball player about to make a slam dunk — that was not a reference to Eli's fail at the prize stand which Olette and I both laughed about. What caused Olette to reach maximum glee was when I mentioned about Eli's "kiss". She commented how romantic and fairytale-like that was, but why did I ruin it by slapping Eli in the face?

One, I didn't fall for those kind of things.

And two, yes, my job was being a princess. But, sudden kisses from boys never worked for me especially when it was that sudden.

To sum it all up, reality was far from a fairytale even if that moment was something you'd probably see in a film and the two characters automatically kiss. But, let's face it. It just doesn't work out that way.

It has been a couple of days now, and I thought that's all what was going to happen between Eli and me. Yet I've been getting occasional calls from him and I ignored practically all of them. This wasn't intentional though. When he would send a text, I'd reply saying that I was busy — which I really was! Eli seemed to not give up and ended up trying to contact me again the very next day like a routine.

Olette and I were both sitting in the lobby of my work before my princess transformation happening in an hour. Olette continued to give me that glare to pick up Eli's phone call. Her usual delicate hazel eyes managed to pierce through me. The torture! I shook my head no in reply.

I didn't purposely mean to avoid Elliot Wesley — I just wasn't expecting that "see you soon" to happen, well, soon.

To be honest, I couldn't comprehend why he was still putting in all this effort. I'm positive Eli could just handpick anyone from his crowd of friends. Why did he still want to contact me?

"That boy has some puppy love for you, girl! Just pick up the phone already!" Maryann hollered over the counter.

Olette nodded in agreement as her locks of wavy, auburn hair followed along.

Puppy love, I held in my laughter.

Making up an excuse, I stood up from the comfy wine colored seat. "Looks like I have to get ready now."

Except only my closest friend and coworker would catch I was using that as an escape.

Olette questioned through suspicion, "You still have plenty of time to get ready! What's the rush?"

A memory of Mom always telling me to never run away from whatever life throws and to face it no matter what, ran through me. Her smiling face appeared through my eyes as she would say, "because in the end, those are possibilities that may take you places you never expected".

Gulping down, I felt my heart beating sadly at the thought. Even though Eli wasn't exactly a problem, he still fell under that category where I shouldn't run away. Sighing in defeat, I took in Mom's words — along with Olette and Maryann's persistence — and headed over to my phone. It started ringing again which caused Olette to nearly throw it at my face. Luckily, my hand managed to catch it on time.

Clearing my throat, I picked it up. "Hey Eli."

His husky voice flowed to my ear drums. "Hey Lana. I've been trying to get a hold of you. I'm guessing things are still pretty hectic?"

How would I be able to make him believe I've been busy when I'm a girl who wasn't even occupied with college — let alone, it was summer vacation! Olette noticed my frantic vibes and gestured me to say something quick.

Letting out a loose laugh, I mentioned, "Yeah. Work has been piling up lately."

Eli seemed like he understood my situation on the other line, but then, he bought up about seeing each other again. Hesitant, I tried to see it as Eli just wanting to get to know me better. There's nothing wrong with that, right? And he did seem like a good guy.

Remembering that Dad wanted to know Eli a little more himself, I wondered if it would be too soon to invite Eli for dinner. As I cupped the receiver, Olette was making all signals to go for it.

I then asked, "Alright. Would you like to join my family and me for lunch or dinner sometime? Your choice on time."

For some reason, his response to this was completely stunned, but he quickly fixed himself. I ended up hiding the smile that was growing on my face.

Eli cleared his throat. "Yeah, I'd love to. I'm free anytime actually. What day is good for you?"

Pursing my lips, I told him I'd get back to him on that because honestly, we haven't had guests over in such a long time. And that was the end of that. After saying goodbye and clicking the end button, I glanced over to find Olette giving me that utter look of disapproval.

She exhaled. "I'll let you know? Lana, Eli's going to think you're avoiding him in every way you can!"

Messing with a loose strand on my top, I answered carefully, "Is that a bad thing? I just don't want things to happen."

Maryann suddenly hopped into the conversation. "What are you so afraid of, Lana?"

Letting my eyes drop, I mumbled out, "Losing him if anything serious did happen."

I decided to snap my mouth shut soon after. I shouldn't have said anything - how weak and miserable did that answer make me look? Even though it was unlikely about anything "serious" to happen, it was no joke or lie to say that I was afraid of things like that.

Hearing my response, I regretted my words even more seeing their faces transition sadly. The entire place grew quiet and I ended up clicking my tongue. It really wasn't a purpose to create such awkwardness.

Something distract us!

All of a sudden, Olette's phone beeped. I figured it was a text — and maybe the distraction we needed. She glanced down at her phone and pursed her lips.

"Oh man, my mom thinks I'm heading home already. I haven't even bought Angeline's food yet."

Angeline was Olette's baby sister, by the way. She's absolutely adorable.

Soon, Olette flashed her phone screen before my eyes and shook her head. "Can you believe my mom knows how to text? It's crazy, right?"

Olette's disbelief caused me to slowly forget my past thoughts and made me laugh.

I grinned slightly. "Remember when we had to explain to her what 'LOL' means?"

Maryann shouted in their defense, "Give us some credit, girls!"

We all laughed together and this was always a great reminder to me why I was so grateful to have them in my life.

I gestured that I was leaving as well. "I need to get ready now too. I'll see you two later. Tell your parents and Angie I said hi."

She stood up from the seat, ready to take off. "Definitely. And Lana?"

When I looked at her, Olette gave me a warm smile. "Don't be afraid to open up... not just to Eli, but to other people too."

Nodding my head, I said that I would try and she returned an encouraging smile before pulling me into a tight hug. As I headed over the dressing room, I smirked.

"Besides. Maryann does still owe me for giving Eli a chance."

Maryann started to giggle from the counter and shook her head. "Oh sweetheart, you never know. Maybe you're the one who'll be owing me." She added a wink and the three of us shared another laugh.

In the company's dressing rooms, I rummaged through the hangers of dresses and found the needed dress. I began to question why in most — if not, all — Disney princess movies, the Prince always has to be the one doing the rescuing. I mean, why couldn't it be the other way around sometimes? I was sure a princess could be able to save the day. Grabbing the short jet black wig, I always thought I looked funny when I was playing Snow White.

Another day being a princess, it was good to dream at these times.

Chapter 5

I still couldn't let go of how idiotic it was of me to do that.

Preston and Coops died of laughter when I revealed my attempt to kiss Lana. No matter how I tried to play it cool, it was too obvious with the way my voice sounded. Not taking their reaction as a warning already, I wanted to tape my mouth shut when I mentioned about that prize stand. I swear something was wrong with it! Right when they finally composed themselves, they burst into laughter once again. I still remember Preston wiping his eyes while he held onto his stomach — his signature laughing style.

Coops shook his head and smirked. "Seems like the Wesley lost his touch."

In denial, I didn't want to talk about how I saw Lana different that night. Just being around her pulled me in naturally.

That wasn't the plan. And I had to stick to the plan.

As if Preston read my thoughts at the time, he reminded, "Bro, you don't want anything to happen or else both of you will be in trouble. Just keep it — what is it? Oh... laid back, nothing serious."

I told him I had everything under control. That's when Coops flashed me a look, hoping that I really did. Julian Cooper was reading past me. But, I knew I wasn't going to fall for Lana.

Haley was the one on my mind. Right?

"Mom told us you went on a date!"

"Finally getting over Haley?"

What a surprise to head downstairs to.

That, to whom it may concern, was my two younger sisters.

And let me add how they're twins. "Double Trouble" was what I always called them.

Abigail, "Abby", was the older one and much more mischievous compared to Alyson, "Aly". Twelve and extremely dangerous on top of that. Both of them had the same dark hair like me from Dad except they got Mom's green eyes. The only way I could tell them apart physically was by their hair. Abby always kept her hair shoulder length while Aly loved her hair all the way to her back which she braided ever so often.

Abby had this scary grin while investigating me like a cop. "So, aren't you going to tell us about her?"

I shook my head no.

Aly chimed in, "It's a good thing you're finally seeing other girls. You looked so miserable when Haley dumped you! We were scared you would turn into a hermit crab."

The twins giggled and I shook my head in annoyance. All of this was normal though. These two — ever since they could breath — loved snooping about every detail in my life.

Abby then continued on asking me who the girl I took on a "date" was.

I sighed. "It wasn't a date. We went to high school together and decided to catch up for lost time. You two don't even know Lana Clarke."

Aly's green, round shaped eyes widened as she gasped. "The one that dresses up like princesses?!"

Abby nodded continuously, all excited. "Oh my gosh! Tommy likes her!"

Well, turned out I was wrong.

Curious about the mentioned name, I asked, "Wait... who's Tommy?"

The two looked at each other, shaking their heads in unison as if I lacked the knowledge of life.

Aly answered a matter of fact, "Only the cutest boy at our school! He was telling all his friends how a pretty, older girl was at his little sister's party. He was saying how she was his princess! We were all so, so jealous!"

Abby let out a dreamy sigh, becoming trapped in this fantasy with that Tommy kid. A little twelve year old thought Lana was his princess?

Letting out a laugh, I shrugged. "Don't worry. Tommy is all yours."

All of a sudden, Abby wrinkled her nose. "Wait a second. Isn't Lana... too pretty for someone like you?"

The twins shared a laugh together again. My loving twin sisters — what would I do without them?

Crossing my arms, I smirked in return. "Why wouldn't she? If you make fun of me, it's like you're making fun of yourself — we're related, remember?"

It was all jokes, but the two stopped their laughter and ended up sticking their tongues out in unison, saying how that wasn't nice. Letting the conversation drop, I gave them a content grin and gently messed with their hairs.

"Stop that, you giant!" Abby fidgeted. "Anyways, food's ready. Let's go eat."

Laughing to my amusement, I nodded along and we walked towards the dining area. Ahead of the two, I soon heard my name being called out. As I turned around, it was Aly. Abby also had a faint grin growing on her face.

Aly admitted through a genuine smile, that Wesley dimple appearing. "You know Ell, even though we're mean to you — like any little sisters are — we really do miss you."

Giving them an appreciative grin back, I waited for my sisters to head in first before following behind them. Greeting Mom and Dad who were waiting for us, I sat in my usual spot and ended up checking my phone. Throughout these past days, I tried getting a hold of Lana. It was like she suddenly disappeared which kind of worried me. Did I mess up that bad?

The girls I've taken out before dating Haley were nothing like Lana. They would only bat their eyes furiously when talking with them. There was even a time I grew annoyed and asked if there was an eyelash stuck in their eye. Moving on. Why was it that I was able to catch those girls in a heartbeat? All I needed was for Lana to take me over when Haley was there — coincidentally somehow — and there, I would prove to Haley it was a huge mistake to leave me.

Yet that seemed like the hardest thing to achieve.

"Why are you so stuck on your phone these days, son?" Dad interrupted my train of thought.

Quickly sliding my phone into my pocket, I shook my head as I shoved a mouthful of Mom's tender beef stew.

Abby's gossiping self spilled. "Maybe he's talking to the girl he went on a date with!"

This caused Dad to get all interested and he asked who. Throwing a look at Abby for making stuff up again, I then remembered how I told Mom that I actually did have a date with Lana. Looked like I had to go with it. I answered Lana Clarke, and Dad's dark brown eyes widened.

"Liam's daughter?"

I guessed yes.

When Dad saw my half response of a shrug, he added, "She has an older brother, doesn't she? What was his name again... starts with an L as well. Oh! Landon, Landon Clarke."

Bingo.

Nodding my head completely, I tried to hide the resent I felt. Dad smiled — we got that signature dimple from him.

"Their father used to work in the auto shop with me a few years ago."

That was something I didn't know. Dad's current job was at a dealership, so his past jobs were something rarely bought up about.

"Yep, but just before I left the shop, Liam asked for vacation. He was never one to leave though. I remember how dedicated he was fixing up those cars. And he never came back even after his vacation was done. After hearing some news about the Clarke family, I figured it had to do with his wife." Dad's eyes slowly saddened.

Wait, what happened?

Dad was leaving me in suspense!

Mom put her fork down. Her usual, upbeat face seem to have fallen. "Cathy was such a sweet person. It was so unfortunate of her passing."

No wonder Lana's mom wasn't home the time I came over.

Holding a still position, I couldn't even comprehend what I just heard. I also noticed the solemn expressions on Abby and Aly's faces.

Dad gave us a small nod. "I rarely see Liam around anymore, but Mike told me that Landon asked to take his father's place not too long ago."

This was opening so many doors.

My head jolted up and I stated, "Landon is a lifeguard though."

Dad nodded his head once more. I got it — double jobs. Even though it was very weird talking about Lana and her family, I never expected my parents to know that much about them. What surprised me most was their mom. There wasn't a time I remember hearing anything about that during school. There was a lot more to the Lana Clarke I use to share the classrooms with.

Once we were done with lunch and I finished washing the dishes, I headed back to my room where I couldn't help but stare at my phone wondering if I would get a reply any time soon. Realizing how anxious I've become just to hear from Lana, I plopped onto my comfy bed to clear my mind. As I was reaching some sort of peace, my phone beeped. Almost falling from getting up too fast, I checked my inbox but it was Preston asking if he wanted to chill today.

Not what I expected, but why not?

Still, I scrolled through my contacts to find Lana's number and called it. After a few ringing, it went to voicemail. I sighed, contemplating if I should give it another go. Fine, last try. Holding my breath as the phone rang, I became litterally breathless hearing a "Hey Eli" come from the other line.

Get a hold of yourself, Eli.

"Hey Lana. I've been trying to get a hold of you. I'm guessing things are still pretty hectic?"

It's kind of evident since she hasn't been picking up your calls or answering your texts these past few days, the obvious mocked me.

After some small talk, I soon went straight to the question asking if she wanted to meet up again. Things weren't going to move if I stood here and waited. Eli Wesley was always known for being bold.

She eventually replied, "Alright. Would you like to join my family and me for lunch or dinner sometime? Your choice on time."

Would Haley be there? This may be the chance that I've been waiting for. Sooner than I thought. A little too excited than I wanted, I quickly answered saying that I'd love too, and when.

Yet, those dreadful words came: "I'll let you know".

I just hope that didn't actually translate to "never want to speak to you again". But, I needed to keep my cool.

Going back to Preston's text, I ended up calling him and suggested that we meet up at Chaplin's with Coops.

Maybe I shouldn't have headed downstairs to grab a drink of water. Should have known better after being attacked by the twins two days ago.

Mom was occupying the kitchen, chopping away some vegetables until she noticed my presence.

She asked over her shoulder, "Before we eat, why don't you take Eian out for a walk?"

Great. I already did what I promised though.

It's not like I hated walking Eian. It's just — every time I did — Eian would get extremely excited and would start jumping, running, chasing. And that was something I tried to avoid as much as I can.

Picking up a chilled water bottle from the fridge, I hinted, "Abby and Aly hasn't walked Eian."

As if they were magnets, the twins came running in. Abby crossed her arms as Aly shook her head side to side.

Abby shouted, "Mom! El is lying! We've been walking Eian more than him even when he was still here!"

Well, that wasn't entirely my fault. I was so busy with swim practice.

However, Mom sided with the twins. "The girls are right. Look, Eian misses having you around. Go on, please."

There was no possible way to say no when Mom says "please" in that tone. Calling out to Eian, he jolted in. His tail was wagging like crazy. Chuckling, I attached the leash onto his collar as I stroked his fur.

Playing a grave expression as I looked at him, I reminded, "Let's go out for a walk, boy. Control yourself this time, okay?"

He barked in response, making me laugh.

So far, so good. Nothing was distracting this silly dog. Glancing around my neighborhood, everything was pretty much still the same — it did lose much of its coolness. I'm kidding. I couldn't help but miss the place that made me feel at home.

Suddenly, Eian started barking and my eyes widened, seeing his tail wag 100 miles per hour. This couldn't be good. Looking for what was getting him so worked up, I noticed a party going on at the house across to my left. There was a bunch of pink streamers, pink balloons — just pink everything! On the lawn, there was a pink sign posted with a crown on it that said: "Princess Kimmy's 6th birthday".

Seeing all of this made me think of Lana and that's when I started to wonder if — somehow — she was there.

Eian was barking up a storm and no matter how many times I told him to be quiet, he wouldn't contain his joy. Eventually, he hurdled across the street towards the house, bringing me along. I didn't understand why he wanted to go there, but my stomach flipped seeing a familiar someone walk out the door.

It was Lana.

She was actually there!

Slowing Eian down, I watched as Lana was smiling happily at the parents — Mr. and Mrs. Parker — and I recognized "Princess" Kimmy and Lana wearing matching dresses.

It looked like Cinderella. She had long blonde hair from what I remember, and I think she wore that pink dress during the movie.

Lana soon turned away from the family, bidding one last goodbye. She was a total princess yet it seemed so natural for her. It was only then, I took notice how freaky it must be for me to just stand here watching Lana do her job, with Eian jumping like a frog. Sometimes, I wondered if Eian was even a dog.

Once the door was closed shut, it looked like Lana was heading over to her car and this signaled Eian to drag me towards her. Was this an instinct?

Slightly alarmed at the hyper dog coming her way, Lana's widened blue eyes seem to have grown bigger seeing the dog's owner was actually me. Her face was in complete shock — I bet mine was even worse.

"Eli? It's you! What are you doing here?" Lana asked.

Her voice just as surprised as her current expression. A smile was slowly appearing on her face.

"Funny story, I live in this neighborhood actually. My dog... bought me here..."

Another forehead slapper! I was blaming my own dog for crying out loud. Eian started jumping happily, forcing himself towards Lana and she laughed.

Lana ruffled his hair as she cooed, "Who's this happy guy?"

It was a little surprising since Eian was the type of dog to be aggressive to people he first meets. I still remembered the time he jumped at Haley and she screamed for her life. But, it was like he knew Lana and listened to every word she said.

"That's Eian, our family dog. Eian, this is Lana. Be nice."

Lana smiled brightly at Eian and then glanced up at me. "He's a real sweetheart. Hey Eli... don't take this as bad or anything, but it's a little funny how we stumbled across each other like this, don't you think?"

Running a hand through my hair, I let out a laugh. "Tell me about it. I'm kind of glad to see you though."

Her blue eyes flickered momentarily hearing that, but she smiled before nodding her head in agreement. I found myself gazing at her with her blonde wig. She manages to pull of any hair color.

Confident, I stated, "You're Cinderella, aren't you?"

In the end, Lana shook her head as she softly chuckled.

"Very smooth, Eli." Words of Preston Daniels.

She politely corrected, "Close. I'm actually Aurora from Sleeping Beauty."

Sheepishly joining her laughter, I played it off saying how it's been a long time since I watched those classic Disney movies.

"It's okay, Eli. I don't want to take my wig off just in case someone from the party sees me — so much for being a princess, you know?"

Blurting out unintentionally, I wasn't able to stop myself. "You make a beautiful princess either way."

Stunned by my words, Lana stared at me for a moment until we were both approached by a kid who looked younger than us.

The red haired kid had his green eyes on Lana and interrupted, "Excuse me, P-princess... may I take a picture with you?"

Lana took her gentle, blue eyes off me momentarily and gave her full attention to the young boy.

"Princess Aurora" gave the boy a sweet smile and soon replied, "I remember you from the party. Of course you can."

The red head grew a wide grin and soon called three of his friends — from who knows where — over. Then, the kid had the nerve to ask me to take the picture for them! Lana threw me an apologetic glance before she transitioned into a smile for the picture. The four guys all thanked "Princess Aurora" and waved goodbye with their overjoyed faces. Once they were gone, Lana apologize and I shrugged, telling her it was no big deal. At least those kids saved me from what I said earlier.

Giving Lana a smile, I said, "It was nice seeing you, Lana... or should I say Princess?"

A laugh escaped from her momentarily and I felt satisfied making her smile like that.

She shook her head and teased back, "I believe I'm off duty for now, kind sir. Oh yeah. About that dinner, you should come over Friday night if you can."

For some reason, happiness went through me and I couldn't find an explanation why. Was it because I'd actually be a step closer from proving

Haley wrong or was it because I was actually looking forward to this? I shook myself mentally from those thoughts, coming back to reality.

Nodding my head, I replied, "Sounds good to me. Just let me know what time and I'll be there."

Lana seemed relieved hearing my answer and said that she will.

Before parting ways, I playfully bowed and she let out another cute laugh, curtsying as a reply back. Eian and I walked Lana to her car and she soon greeted Eian a goodbye. He barked in return and as a result, she kissed his nose lightly.

Lana's blue eyes were bright as could be. "I'll see you soon, Eli. Take care."

Wishing her the same, I waved goodbye to the fairytale princess as she drove off. Eian was happily trying to stand up like a human.

Shooting him a look, I joked, "Hey now, Eian. Paws off."

Chapter 6

"Ms. Clarke, I'm sorry to say but your father's medical bill still needs to be paid off."

Sighing sadly, I was next to Dr. Hamilton as we were heading down the hospital corridor.

Dr. Hamilton gave me a sympathetic look. "Your father has been very responsive though. He is a strong willed man."

Hearing this felt assuring, but what still needed to be paid off haunted my thoughts. It was either I had to work double time, or find a second job. Going to college and other dreams I planned for would have to be put aside because Dad needed this money most. I'm sorry, Mom.

"Doctor, I'm sorry for the delay but is there any way we can be given more time?"

Dr. Hamilton's gray eyes dropped onto the clipboard before stating, "I'll see what I can do. We all wish the very best for you and your family."

Thanking Dr. Hamilton, we soon went opposite directions and I headed to the pharmacy to pick up Dad's required medicine. After doing so, I grabbed my phone from my purse and dialed my work.

Maryann picked up with her perky yet business-approached voice. "A Fairytale Come True, how may I assist you today?"

Walking out the doors to the parking lot, I answered, "Hi Maryann, it's Lana. Can I open my days off? I remember you telling me that people have been wanting me booked for their parties."

Her voice seemed puzzled. "Yeah, your position here is well known but Lana, are you sure? Your only days off are Wednesday till Friday."

I replied that I was aware of that yet if it was still possible if I could work all week besides Friday.

Maryann's confused voice then grew with concern. "If you'd like, honey. But what happened to starting college or pursuing that dream you and Cathy shared?"

The last part killed me, but that would have to wait. Assuring Maryann that I was fine, I made up a white lie saying that it was only a minor setback and working extra days would really mean a lot. In the end, Maryann opened my schedule. Before hanging up, she reminded me that I mustn't forget to take care of myself. There was nothing to worry about when it came down to me. I would be fine.

It was just another way to work a little harder for the better.

I never pictured myself cooking dinner for someone besides my family.

In the kitchen, I was pacing back and forth thinking of what to make before Eli arrived.

"Lana, you okay?"

Stopping myself, I completely straightened myself out and nodded with a smile for Dad. Eventually looking back at the empty pots and pans, I explained how I couldn't decide what to make. A grin grew on Dad's weak face. Every time he did smile though, relief would flash my way.

"How about one of your mother's delicious recipes? I love her chicken Parmesan."

Whenever Dad always talked about Mom, he never made it sound like she wasn't here any more. He never used past tense when he mentioned her.

"What a great idea." I smiled, giving him a hug.

Dad chuckled in return, messing with the bun I lazily fixed for my hair. "Cathy's recipes always wins my heart every single time."

Playfully rolling my eyes in return, I wasn't trying to win any hearts over.

"You know, Lana, you're looking tired. Maryann mentioned that you've been working a lot lately. Is there something you'd like to tell me?"

Keep a strong smile on, I shook my head. "No, everything's great. I just wanted to work a little extra. I know Landon has two jobs, but I thought it'd be good to help him out. No need to worry, Dad."

Staring at me momentarily, Dad was trying to comprehend what I was hiding through my eyes. He eventually sighed, going with what I said.

"Alright. You're still young, Lana. I really would like you and Landon to go to college too."

Dad added how that was what he really wished for. It bothered me. Why didn't he say he wished to get better?

Keeping that smile, I looked away momentarily until Dad asked if he could help me with dinner. Gazing back at him, I felt unwanted tears forming in the rim of my eyes, but ended up swallowing harshly to rid them away.

"I'd love that, Dad."

After an hour, we managed to finish a three course meal and honestly, I was very proud of what we accomplished together. Dad was always a good cook. Cooking with him bought back so many memories when my parents would do this together. As much as it bought joy to me, my heart wouldn't stop aching.

"Wow! Smells good in here!"

As Dad and I turned around, we found Landon walking in with his work jacket over his left shoulder. It must have been a long day for him at the auto shop. It's always amusing how Landon would be covered in dirt and grease from the auto shop and could easily transition into a clean-cut lifeguard.

Greeting Landon a welcome home, he then plopped on the wooden stool and grinned.

"Special occasion?"

Did he forget? Maybe I forgot to tell him. Through his speaking, Dad slid a glass of cold water and Landon smiled warmly in a thanks.

I shrugged, taking the dinner rolls out of the oven. "It's nothing big... Eli is coming over."

Landon's eyes widened as he gulped a large amount of water. He wiped his mouth. "He's coming over? Oh man, if I only knew I would have asked Haley to come, but she's hanging out with her girls. Did you know about this, Dad?"

"Sure I did. I wanted to know more about Eli."

Churning Mom's house soup, I commented, "He's really not that big of a deal, Dad."

Landon remarked out of amusement, "Lana! That's cold."

Dad nodded in agreement and we all laughed lightly. It wasn't meant to sound rude, but I didn't want Dad to think anything serious was happening between us. I didn't even really know Eli. The best thing to say about this was we're just friends.

Dad took a stretch from all that cooking and announced in a joking matter, "I'm going to fancy myself up for tonight. It's been a while since we had a guest in the house."

We laughed again before Dad headed upstairs to complete what he said. Landon shook his head, giving me an amused smile.

"Same ol' Dad. Hey Lana, Maryann called me at work today and said that she was worried about you. Is there something you need to tell me?"

I'm going to get you for this, Maryann!

Shaking my head, I covered my emotions by turning back to the cooking pot. The thing was, Landon knew me way too well. He could see and interpret my moves like a simple picture book.

Landon pressed on with a stern voice. "Lana, I know you went to the hospital today to pick up Dad's medicine. Did Dr. Hamilton say anything?"

In defeat, I fidgeted with my jean pocket to pull out the folded medical bill and showed it to him. I watched as his blue eyes scanned through the paper. Just as expected, his eyes soon widened when he reached that dreaded spot. Running a hand through his short brown hair, he looked up at me.

"Lana, listen. You have nothing to worry about. You don't need to work more. I got it all under control."

Landon's not the only one — I knew my brother very well too. Through his blue eyes, I sensed hidden fear. Turning the stove off, I took the paper and placed it back in my pocket.

"No, that's not right. Landon, you've been working even way before me just to make ends meet. I need to do this to help us. I can't always rely on you to save the day because I know you've been dreaming to go to school and get that engineering degree. Let me do this."

As much as I knew he wanted to resist, Landon eventually gave in. His blue eyes saddened until he nodded.

"Lana, I want you to promise me that if it's too much for you, stop. Don't push yourself, okay?"

"I promise," I replied with a stiff smile.

That tensed expression soon disappeared as my brother grinned. "Okay. Now, does my sister have to be all 'fancied-up' as well for tonight? I'll get everything prepared for you."

"You too, grease monkey."

Chuckling contentedly, I playfully threw the pot holder at him and the atmosphere became a little better. Landon soon got up from his seat and threw the pot holder back at me. Before I could return it back, he was already jolting up the stairs. Didn't he say he would help me get things prepared?

As I was rummaging through my closet, I spent the next hour deciding how to do my hair, what to wear and nothing looked right. It was so girly of me, but I couldn't help it, nor did I have a reason behind all of this. I ended up putting on a collared short sleeved coral dress that flowed a little above my knees. After curling the ends of my hair, it managed to balance my whole outfit together. It was casual, but presentable.

Heading back downstairs, I found Landon living up to his words as he finished setting up the table, looking his best. Landon caught me there and showed off his presentation.

He smirked. "So, what do you think?"

Giving him a thumbs up in reply, I went to the kitchen to make sure the food was all ready. Even though it was just dinner, I think the part that made me most nervous was how this would be the first time someone came over for dinner in a while.

Before we knew it, Dad was also heading downstairs and like he said, he looked ravishing — if that's the right word to put it. He was wearing his white long sleeved polo along with a pair of slacks. His hair was combed nicely and he was adjusting his tie. Landon whistled once Dad reached the bottom step.

"Dad, you trying to outdo Lana here?"

We laughed once more which made me love this kind of mood.

"Oh no. It's not my night tonight. You two are always the kidders," Dad corrected as he pulled us into a warm embrace.

Suddenly, the doorbell rang.

Leaving them in the foyer, I headed to the front and took a deep breath. Everything would turn out just right.

Opening the door, I found Eli quickly turning back to face me since he heard the doorknob moving. As we locked eye contact, I was pretty surprised by his appearance. Eli always looked amazing — I must say — but there was always something about a boy who cleaned up effortlessly. Eli grinned, showcasing that dimple.

"Hey Lana, you look great."

I said the same back to him — it was true. To my shock, a car honked from behind him. Peeking past Eli, I then heard him let out a sheepish laugh.

"That's just Julian and Preston. My car wasn't working earlier, so they took me here."

There was a tint of embarassment being exposed on his face as he explained.

"Oh, you should have told me. It wasn't a hassle, right?"

Eli shook his head and smiled. "Of course not. They don't mind and plus, I didn't want to miss this."

Preston was looking out from the car window and waved, smiling brightly at me. I waved back — less enthusiastic — but managed to par up the smile in return. Julian also gave me a short wave before driving off.

Bringing Eli inside our house, he soon caught Dad and Landon's eyes. I couldn't help but notice those dark brown eyes wandering off like he was in search of somebody. But, that was just a silly thought.

Dad gave Eli a welcoming smile. "Good to see you again, Eli."

Eli held out his hand first saying how the pleasure was all his. After all the greetings, it was time for dinner. Anxiety was slightly taking over because I was always conscious when it came to sharing my cooking. As I bought out Mom's homemade soup to the table, I ended up stumbling in a middle of their conversation.

I heard Eli say, "Yeah, sports was something I did all four years, but I focused on swim mostly."

The three took in the soup well and I let out a sigh of relief, taking in a few sips as well. Dad then nodded in amazement.

"That's incredible. You were swim captain, weren't you?"

Eli nodded, and I smiled unintentionally at their interaction.

Landon added, "Not going to lie, but you were kind of a legend ever since you were a freshman. My friends mentioned what a great athlete you were."

Hearing this, Eli looked a little surprised. I didn't realize all this attention was too much for him to handle.

Dad continued with interest, "So, I heard you go to USC? Do you swim for them?"

A little nervous, I hope Eli didn't think Dad was interrogating him.

Eli shook his head, after gulping down a spoonful of soup. "I do go there, but I... decided I wanted to go out for the aerospace program."

Dad grinned, joking. "What a daring choice. It's kind of unfortunate you can't swim up in space though."

Eli laughed back. "It's funny because Lana said the exact same thing to me."

We joined Eli's laughter around the table as Dad winked briefly at me. My dad and I were similar in many ways.

During the whole dinner, everything went smoother than I thought. Dad and Landon appeared to be getting along with Eli. Eli was always polite and answered all questions with no hesitation — he even wanted to know about my family and this just caused Dad to go on and on with stories. Even though Dad seemed so happy speaking freely, there was sadness appearing in his blue eyes when he spoke about Mom.

"Lana, why don't you share that red velvet cake you made?" Dad's voice broke my thoughts.

Smiling, I got up and headed back to the kitchen. That missing feeling for Mom grew stronger as I sliced the red velvet cake — the cake we use to bake together.

"Hey, you need any help?"

It was Eli. His eyebrow arched with concern from the slight shaking as I sliced the cake.

Quickly shaking my head to indicate I was fine, I grinned faintly. "I hope you're enjoying."

"Of course I am. Thanks again for inviting me over."

"No, thank you for coming. Here. I hope you like it."

Handing him the other two plates, we both headed to the dining table to finish the meal. When everything was all eaten, Dad and Landon both showered me with praise. Eli even added a compliment saying how it was the best dinner he's had. It made me feel heat on my face, but he's probably just being nice. Soon after, Dad decided that he should be getting some rest. Landon shot me a look, signaling that he would take care of everything and I returned with a thankful expression.

Once the dinner table was clean and Eli said his goodbyes to both of them, we decided to spend the rest of the night sitting outside the front porch. The summer weather was perfect tonight. The breeze left gentle kisses on our faces.

"You're a really good cook, you know that?"

Laughing quietly, I shrugged. "I have to thank my mom for that."

"That red velvet cake you made was so good! You should sell those, it'll sell like crazy!" Eli complimented with a huge grin.

Normally, one would respond back with a modest reply, but I kept silent. I know Eli's compliment meant no harm nor did he know, but what he said just bought me back to that moment.

"Lana, one day everyone will enjoy all these cakes and pastries we make together."

"Sorry, did I say something wrong? I didn't mean to." Eli sounded uneasy, probably noticing my blank expression.

When I gazed back at Eli, his soft brown eyes glowed in the porch light. I never imagined a guy to have such gentle looking eyes like Eli's.

"It's not your fault. My mom liked to bake a lot. That was her recipe." My voice was quiet.

"I can tell you really miss her... your whole family does."

To avoid any tears, I stared up at the night sky and admired the stars shining so brightly.

For some reason, I spoke without a thought, "The moment she left until now. It was the worst years of my life being in high school. A life without your mother, who took care of you since the moment she held you in your arms and said 'welcome to the world'... it was just so hard for me and my family. The pain it put on my dad was worse. He couldn't even look at Landon and me for months."

Letting out a shameful chuckle, I admitted, "I don't even know why I'm telling you all of this, Eli."

This feeling gradually lifted from me — that bottled up emotion I've tucked away for so long. Was it all this stress that was making me reveal this to him? Why was it so easy to talk to Elliot Wesley?

"Your mom sounds like a wonderful person. I'm sure she's very proud of you, your father, and your brother."

I felt myself smiling. "You think so?"

Eli smiled with comfort as that dimple of his showed. "I know so."

After a slight pause, Eli questioned, "I don't know why, but I've been wondering about this for a while. Why did you choose that kind of job — to be a princess?"

Hesitant for a few seconds, I replied honestly, "It makes me feel invulnerable to the world, like nothing could ever go wrong."

What left me confused was how Eli grew quiet all of a sudden. I wanted to ask what was wrong, but the moment broke off when Eli's phone made a beeping noise. Eli soon said something, but it was too low for me to hear. His brown eyes jumped at mine momentarily before he reached for his pocket. His attention was stuck on the screen before he mentioned that it was from Preston.

He turned back to me apologetically. "I'm sorry, Lana. They just told me they're a block away. I didn't know they would come —"

Before Eli could finish, I politely intervened saying that he had nothing to be sorry about. I shouldn't have spoke so freely with him in the first place. Why didn't I regret it though?

"Lana, I'm glad I came tonight."

"I am too... you helped me in ways that probably wouldn't make sense."

Eli's face grew puzzled, but he took the compliment. As he ran his fingers through his hair, Eli cleared his throat.

"So, we'll be seeing each other again?"

Without even processing the question, I ended up nodding my head and a pleased grin appeared on Eli's lips. Just like Eli said, Julian's car appeared by the curb once again. We stood up and said our goodbyes and good nights. Before heading off to his friends, Eli turned around and that smile of his surprisingly took me away at that moment.

Even though it was dark, I knew it was Preston hollering a good night to me so I waved, knowing they'd see me. After they drove off, I took a deep sigh and closed my eyes.

There was something about Eli tonight that I couldn't point out, but I liked it.

Chapter 7

"I can tell you really miss her... your whole family does."

Ever since dinner, I've been having a nice time with Lana and her family. I didn't have much to say about Landon, but Mr. Clarke was a nice guy. When he talked about Mrs. Clarke though, I couldn't help but notice the pain on his face. Now that Lana and I were sitting outside the front porch, she seemed to be able to talk to me more comfortably. It was a little surprising, but there was nothing wrong with that.

Already feeling guilty seeing how Lana was affected by this topic, she gazed up the sky and blinked her eyes several times. Was she trying to stop herself from crying?

You're doing a great job, Eli — I meant that with complete sarcasm.

She confessed, "The moment she left until now. It was the worst years of my life being in high school. A life without your mother, who took care of you since the moment she held you in your arms and said 'welcome to the world'... it was just so hard for me and my family. The pain it put on my dad was worse. He couldn't even look at Landon and me for months."

It left me speechless.

This was the real Lana Clarke.

The girl who was constantly putting a strong front for everyone.

Lana chuckled softly, saying how she couldn't believe she was telling me this. Still, I was glad. Lana probably never opened up to matters like this and I couldn't blame her for it. At this moment, I wanted to comfort her — to make her know that everything would be okay.

"Your mom sounds like a wonderful person. I'm sure she's very proud of you, your father, and your brother."

She gradually gazed her attention back at me. Those sad eyes brightened hearing that.

"You think so?"

"I know so." I grinned

A relaxed expression started to appear on Lana's face and it was satisfying to see. I didn't want to see her sad.

The plan was suddenly forgotten because right now, more than anything, I wanted to be there for Lana.

I found myself asking, "I don't know why, but I've been wondering about this for a while. Why did you choose that kind of job — to be a princess?"

"It makes me feel invulnerable to the world, like nothing could ever go wrong." Her voice was completely honest.

My stomach flipped. Everything about her — just like when we were at the beach — was taking its toll on me.

Suddenly, a familiar muffled noise came from pocket. Hearing this reminded me how the guys would text when they were coming. Such bad timing.

I muttered out softly before reaching for my phone. "You're really different from the rest."

Lana stared at me with confusion and a part of me was glad she didn't catch that even if I meant it in a good way.

After telling her that we should see each other soon, Coops' red Mustang — once his father's and newly restored — was now occupying the curb. My car just had to break down on me last minute which was making me look like a complete loser in front of Lana. To be honest, I didn't want to leave yet and I felt horrible having to cut our conversation short.

Before heading to the guys, I turned around and gave her a smile, hoping she would be okay.

Closing the passenger door shut, everything that happened tonight left me in a daze. Seeing the guys again, my mind recalled back to this afternoon when we were driving over here. The two were telling me to be as "charming" as I could be.

Preston was throwing in all these "tips" like: look interested when her family is talking, be polite and well mannered — things that every human being should be doing genuinely in the first place.

But, that's Preston for you.

And, I didn't have to look interested. I walked into the Clarke household already interested.

"Dude, you just going to sit there all quiet?" Preston joked as his body shifted to face me.

Coops then added the question about how tonight went. I wasn't sure where to start or what to say. Instead, the "plan" shifted back into gear and I let out a sigh.

"Haley wasn't there."

The two looked at each other shortly before sighing also from expecting too much.

Coops now had his eyes stuck on the road. "Is that all that happened?"

"Well, dinner with her family wasn't bad. Lana's a great cook. When we all talked, I made sure nothing would end up awkward. But, there was something I didn't expect."

"What?" They asked in unison.

Thinking about it, should I even reveal about what Lana told me? It seemed kind of personal to her. Sighing again, I ran my fingers through my hair.

"I discovered a hidden side to her."

Preston's eyes widened, his thoughts running wild. "I knew it! She's a secret agent!"

"What? No!" Coops and I started shaking our heads while Preston laughed to himself.

"You know how we see Lana as that quiet type of girl? She really isn't like that. We talked outside and she kind of opened up to me about her feelings. Lana lost her mother and if you guys only saw their faces when they would talk about her..."

The guys were oddly silent which confused me.

"I don't blame them, Eli. Mrs. Clarke died in an accident. It was bad from what I remember on the news coverage. I think it was during freshman year." Coops' hazel eyes jump shortly at the rear view mirror. "You didn't know?"

Preston murmured, "Yeah man. I had Lana in my English class and she wouldn't stop crying. She left school for a while too."

Taking in their words, something hit my gut.

"Dude, you keep spacing out back there." Coops sounded like a mixture of concern and worry because I was never like this.

"Don't tell me... you actually like Lana?" Preston suddenly accused.

At that instance, I shook my head and told them that this was all part of the plan to get close to Lana. The closer I get to Lana, the more likely I would be able to "coincidentally" bump into Haley.

Everything felt so confusing though.

"Remember Eli, you shouldn't get too attached," Coops reminded me.

I wasn't going to get attached to Lana Clarke — I was almost chanting that in my mind.

Preston angled his head through curiosity. "Hey Eli. Why do you even like Haley that much? She's hot and all, but when it comes down to this, is she that worth it?"

Asking myself that, a few weeks ago I could name so many things right off the bat. However, I couldn't even answer the question in my head right now.

Haley Jones was my first girlfriend — I thought we were serious. As old fashion as I was sounding right now, I wanted Haley to be my first and last. We started dating before the end of senior year, and it felt like something that would last. Haley never gave me a legitimate answer why she chose Landon over me.

Was it only closure that I needed and not to be together again?

"I'm going to start calling you space cadet. You're creeping me out, bro." Preston continuously waved his hand across my face.

Shaking that all off, I thought of something quick. "Haley means a lot to me and after all we've been through, I don't want to let it go just like that. But —"

"But, what?" Their voices collided once more.

Not finishing my sentence, I shrugged to indicate that was it. What I meant to say was if Haley really didn't want us together again, I would be officially fine with that. Maybe.

This option was bothering me.

Unconsciously messing with the window button, I was making it open and close non-stop. I kept contradicting myself. This wasn't who I was.

"Seriously? You're going to break my windows. Stop that," Coops yelled, turning the steering wheel to make a right.

Preston chuckled. "This guy needs something to wake up his system. Chaplin's?"

Coops smirked before nodding. "It seems like Lana Clarke put some kind of spell on you."

And that may be it.

Even if the guys forced me to chug down the usual malt from Chaplin's as a wake up call, I still wasn't in the right state of mind. Once Coops took me home after Preston, he warned me again to get my head in the game. I knew that, but Coops was always the wise one.

Secretly, I was starting to care too much about Lana than I intended. I spent an hour or so, surfing the web to see if I could get more information on what happened to Lana's mom. Chills run up my spine. Late night. Bus. Car. The bus driver wasn't paying attention. After scrolling through, I exit out the browser.

I rotated my computer chair, finding my mom by the door with a basket of laundry. She looked surprised, probably similar to me. Her free hand was on her chest.

"Oh, I didn't mean to startle you, El. I just came with your laundry." Mom then placed the neatly folded clothes onto my bed while I thanked her.

"You didn't have to do that, Mom."

I always felt bad when she does the laundry by herself. When I still lived here, I would help her out with all the folding since the twins would only wear their clothes once — assuming it was already dirty — and tossed it into the basket. Mom ended up smiling as she shook her head, motioning that it wasn't a problem.

"Mom... did you know Lana's mother well?"

Her small lips pursed until she nodded. "Yes, I did. Cathy would always help the girls and I during the fundraisers. She was so sweet and made the best red velvet cake I've ever tasted. She's a magnificent baker in general!"

Happy at first, her eyes soon drop to the floor momentarily. "It still hurts me that I never got to thank her for all she's done."

Biting my tongue, I wasn't sure how to respond.

"How was dinner with the Clarke's by the way?"

"It was great. Her family is really nice and Mr. Clarke is very welcoming. I have to agree with you on the red velvet. It's amazing. I told Lana she should sell those," I replied.

Lana's gloomy face when I suggested that appeared before my eyes causing me to wince.

Even though Mom smiled back, her eyes still looked sad. "I'm glad to hear. I remember seeing Lana around your school and she reminds me of Cathy in so many ways. Cathy told me before her passing that she was planning to open a bakery in town. The girls and I were so excited for that. but then..."

Mom didn't finish her words. She was holding her emotions back.

It made more sense.

That's why.

I didn't know my compliment actually backfired at the time.

"Lana did look upset when I said that... I didn't know."

Mom gave me a faint smile. "It's not your fault, El. You should have Lana over one day. I would love to formally meet her."

Saying that I'll do so, I then asked myself if this was starting to get too far. Was it? This would be nothing more than introducing Lana Clarke as a friend to my family. And I felt content with that thought.

Mom nodded before grabbing the laundry basket from the ground. "Well, I'm going to go finish this. It's late, El, get some rest. Good night."

I grinned. "Good night, Mom... I love you."

Don't laugh.

Mom seemed slightly taken back with my last words — in a good way. Saying she loved me too, Mom turned around and headed out my bedroom door.

I was thankful to have her here.

"Guess what, bro!" Preston rejoiced from the other line.

Pulling the phone away from my ear briefly, I answered with a what.

Preston replied with his renowned joking tone of a voice, "There's a fair happening this week in town! It's going to be as big as the LA and OC county fair! Did you hear that? Once in a lifetime opportunity over here! You ready to ride unreliable rides that look like they're about to break down and eat some chocolate covered bacon?!"

That's Preston Daniels for you.

I laughed at his excitement. "I sure heard you the first time. Yeah, sounds good to me." Looking off to the side, I ended up asking, "Can I bring Lana?"

"Sure, but I really thought this was going to be a brotherhood day though. Just kidding. Maybe Lana could bring some girls along with her. Or what if she brings Haley? Oh man, that would be good!"

Chuckling halfhearted along with Preston, I wanted to make it seem like I was agreeing with him. Truthfully, I actually didn't want to see Haley at the moment.

Tapping my fingers against my desk, I asked, "When are we going?"

"Friday. You down?"

Even though it was summer, Preston decided to be ahead of the game and take some summer classes. Preston's always finding ways to get out of school quicker. Fridays are Lana's day off. It'll work out then.

"I'm down."

"I'll tell Coops to drive us!"

"No, I'll drive this time. He's been driving your lazy self around for a while now."

Preston mocked me back and jokingly countered how this was Coops' way of returning the favor Preston once did for him — that was indeed true. Telling Preston I'd catch him later, I soon dialed Lana's number. Instead of thinking whether to text or call, my finger automatically hit the call button.

To my surprise, she picked up. We talked back and forth how everything was since our last encounter even if it was only a few days ago. Lana laughed when I told her how Eian didn't want to go to the groomer's yesterday. The silly dog almost jumped out of the window when he saw that Pet Co. sign mocking him. It was satisfying knowing that Lana has been doing well, along with her family. I just hoped she wasn't just saying that though.

Getting to why I made the call, I asked casually, "I don't know if you heard yet, but a fair is happening in town. Want to go with me and the guys on Friday? You could bring some of your friends if you want to."

As long as they weren't a boy, I regretted not adding that in.

Lana answered with interest that she was up for it and she might bring her close friend if she was free that day too. I unusually felt relief when Lana said her close friend was a "she". Probably Olette Benson. Telling her that sounded good, we ended the call and I grinned to myself, looking forward to this Friday.

"Spill the beans, mister."

"Spill what?" I groaned, turning around.

I already knew it was the twins poking through my business yet again. Both of them had their hands on their hips as they stared at me with mischievous grins.

It was scaring me a bit, and it was pretty difficult to scare me.

Aly gave me the nod. "You know what we're talking about. What happened at the dinner?"

They still didn't let that drop yet? Since when did these two obsess with the events of my life? Oh yeah. Since the moment they were born. Playing around with them, I acted out a naive face. Inside, I was trying my best not to laugh.

Abby threw her hands out. "Seriously, Ellie! Tell us what happened! Are we ever going to meet her?"

Aly snickered in the back, hearing Abby call me that stupid nickname.

There were only two nicknames I only approved of - "Eli" or "El" - but never, ever "Ellie".

Do I look like a girl?

No.

Was I a girl?

Of course not!

"Okay Abigail and Alyson. I'll tell you. It went great and yes, maybe sometime soon," I returned with a playful smirk.

They cringed hearing their full names being announced by me, but eventually disregarded it. I watched them suddenly cheer in unison.

"Mission success!"

Abby had a huge grin on her face. "It's about time you bring another girl to the house. Haley was as boring as a wall. I can't wait to meet Lana!"

Aly gushed out, "And to make things better, she's a princess!"

Shaking my head, I said in defense, "Nothing serious is happening between us, okay? Lana is just a friend."

Abby scoffed, waving her hand. "Either way, you're bringing a girl home — that's what matters to us. Bring her soon, okay?

Turned out they only wanted company the entire time. The twins walked off to their shared room and that was when Eian appeared, coming towards me. Running my hands through his fur, I chuckled.

"See what we have to go through each day, boy?"

Eian barked in reply in agreement, or he's probably siding with my sisters to bring Lana over soon.

Chapter 8

"Santa Monica fair, here we come!" Olette clapped her hands with joy.

As we were waiting to be picked up by Eli at my house, I wasn't sure how to feel right now — excitement or nervousness? The thought of being with his friends was having me all over the place. Thank goodness Olette was here with me.

Olette adjusted her floppy, summer hat in the mirror from our living room until it suddenly lifted up from her head. Catching that, Landon let out an amused chuckle, walking off with it.

Landon looked down at the hat and teased, "You going to Paris, Benson?"

Olette flipped around and raised her arms to grab her hat. However, she was three inches shorter than my 5 foot 6 which gave Landon a better advantage.

"Give it back, Landon!"

Even though Landon did have a girlfriend at the moment, I couldn't help but notice the constant flirting whenever the two are together. It didn't bother me for some odd reason. I've always thought my best friend and brother would look cute together. Olette always denied this. With Landon, I never asked.

Landon eventually stopped and softly plopped the hat onto Olette's head. "Where are you two going? The beach?"

I shook my head. "Did you hear about the fair? We're going with Eli and his friends."

"Yeah. Similar to the one that happens in Orange County, right? Make sure to get those deep fried goods." A grin grew on Landon's face.

"Are you planning to go?" Olette tilted her head.

Landon's smile fell into a goofy smirk. "As much as I know it wouldn't be as fun without me, I'm probably not."

Olette's cheeks turned red despite looking a little mad. It made me hold in my laugh until my phone started ringing. Putting off my attention from them, I took a glance momentarily at the screen and Eli's name was blinking.

"Hi Lana, you two ready? We're waiting outside."

"Oh, you are? Okay, we'll be out in a bit."

Eli let out a small laugh. "Take your time. See you soon."

After ending the call, I turned back to Olette and Landon. "Olette, they're outside. I guess we'll be going now, Landon. You and Dad will be okay, right?"

"Lana, you worry too much... I feel like I'm the younger sibling sometimes. We'll be fine. You two have fun, alright?"

Laughing at my brother's joking persona, I punched him lightly in the arm even if it had no effect on him. Before leaving, I quickly walked upstairs where Dad was taking an afternoon rest. I noticed how much he was resting lately.

Carefully opening the door, I found him sleeping peacefully while observing his constant breathing. Looked like Dad wasn't struggling, that was a good sign. Kissing him on the forehead, I didn't want to wake him, so I headed downstairs already.

As Olette and I walked out the front door, I whispered playfully, "Don't worry, I could tell Landon liked that hat on you."

Olette slapped my arm gently in return as she shook her head. "That's not true! Come on, Lana. Your prince is waiting for you."

She winked and I rolled my eyes to not laugh.

Something I wasn't expecting to find was Eli, Julian and Preston all outside of his car. They were all talking — maybe even joking with one another since they appeared to be laughing — and eventually noticed we were walking over to them. The three waved and we gave them a smile, waving back in response.

I murmured as we crossed through the lawn, "I'm kind of worried today will be awkward."

Olette slipped me an encouraging smile. "Don't worry, we're going to a fair. I'm sure we'll have fun, Lana."

Giving her a smile back, we soon reached Eli and them. Just like Olette and me, the hot weather seemed to affect their choice of clothing — the three resorted to wearing monochrome v-necks and shorts instead of the usual jeans and trendy jackets.

Preston removed his sunglasses which revealed his bright green eyes. "Hey girls, ready to have some fun? What's up, Olette?"

Olette smiled as they exchanged a small hug. During high school, Olette was the more sociable one. Her cousin, Tyler Benson, was also co-captain of the football team. Their social standing, in general, fell into place.

My eyes drifted towards Eli and I caught him gazing at me. His deep brown eyes sheepishly glanced away for a moment before he gave me a warm smile.

"I never got to introduce myself to you. I'm Preston Daniels."

Realizing that Preston was talking to me, I saw his hand out and a genuine grin on his face.

Taking his hand, I smiled in response. "Nice to meet you, I'm Lana Clarke."

"And I'm Julian Cooper." Another voice came from beside me.

Looking over to my left, Julian also had his hand out with a friendly smile occupying his face. Shaking his hand, I ended up introducing myself again. Never did I think I would associate with the "kings" of my old high school. I guess the past was in the past.

After all the introductions and greetings, Preston cheered, "Who's ready for some deep fried madness!"

Eli chuckled as he politely opened the car door for Olette and me. "Preston, don't scare them with your weird cravings."

His friend guffawed before he mocked him back. Everyone laughed together soon after. Hopefully it would stay like this.

The fair was, if I had two words to describe it, incredibly huge. I couldn't even take in everything because of the way it stretched in every direction. All sorts of rides, concessions stands, and tons of people were crowding the area. You could only imagine all the heat everyone was adding to this usually hot weather. Various smells from the food made at the fair wafted towards my nose. Cotton candy, kettle popcorn, grilled meats, you name it! It all smelled so good causing my stomach to rumble with curiosity. In amazement, the five of us walked to the entrance gates.

Sneaking a short glance at everyone, Preston was stretching his arms before placing his sunglasses back on. Standing beside me, Olette waved her hands in front of her face. Looked like her hat wasn't helping much. To my left, Eli was talking to Julian and before he turned his head towards my direction, I looked straight ahead like nothing happened.

"You'll like the fair, there's a lot to do."

"And a lot to eat!" Preston added in, sounding like a kid in a candy store.

Shaking his head, Julian joked, "You'll be hearing a lot of food remarks about Preston. He's like a dumpster always eating all kinds of trash."

We began laughing again at Julian's comment. It was relieving because Eli and his friends has been very kind to Olette and me. Preston's cheeks started turning a light shade of red and that couldn't possibly be from the heat.

"It's not my fault fair food is so good!"

"Good but unhealthy. Remember last time?" Eli countered back.

Preston's green eyes widened and I saw his Adam's apple bob down and up — maybe he was recalling back to that memory? Not a good one, I guessed.

Eli opened his mouth to speak again except Preston immediately jumped in. Preston started to wave his arms around, his voice becoming uneasy.

"Come on man, we don't have to talk about that. We're almost at the entrance. Let's go!"

Chuckles drifted off from us again. As we continued on, Julian turned his attention to Olette and me.

"Don't worry, there will be an opportunity to reveal about Preston. It's a funny story actually."

"Not that funny!" Preston shouted, being a few steps ahead of us.

Olette soon whispered to tease me, "You were worried about these three?"

Giving her a small shrug, a smile grew on my face. Going through the entrance, I realized that Eli already paid for our tickets. No wonder he was walking a little quicker to the entrance. Even though I tried saying that it was best if I pay him back, Eli insisted that it wasn't necessary causing me to frown. However, he grinned at me with that dimple showing.

"Don't worry about it and just enjoy, okay?"

Nodding my head in defeat, I soon heard Preston take a deep inhale of the fair's variety of smells.

"Just like the OC fair! I smell the chocolate covered bacon! You all have to try it! Right. Now!"

An amused look appeared on Eli's face. "Hold on, Preston. We haven't even taken one full step in the actual place."

My eyes surveyed the entire area. There were so many rides that ranged from the usual Ferris wheel, spinning rides, even small kiddie rides. Screams of joy or terror were scattered all over the place. Rows and rows of concession stands selling all kinds of food — like the wide selection of deep fried choices Landon and Preston have been talking about — and prize stands occupied the area. Hundreds, maybe thousands, of people were walking all over the place.

Olette suddenly squeezed my upper arm in excitement. "What ride should we ride first?"

Upon overhearing Olette's question, Preston let go of his food craving. He snapped his fingers. "I like your thinking, Olette! Well guys, which ride?"

Eli looked at Olette and me. "Any ride okay for you two?"

We both nodded. I absolutely loved amusement rides! Even if the rides seemed a little worn down. Julian pursed his lips as he glanced around from place to place.

"Well... what do you girls want to ride?"

I noticed Olette's eyes stuck on a ride to our right that signaled me the answer.

I gave them a challenging grin. "Let's start with that one."

The boys followed my direction, having shocked expressions at first. Grins soon rose on their lips. As we headed over there, Olette nearly squealed with joy and I tried my best to get a hold of myself. Thrill rides were always our favorite.

Ride after ride, the entire afternoon was filled with fun. I admit, I was worried about spending time with Eli's friends. Since I spent more time with Eli, it was safe to say that I was somewhat comfortable around him. This was my first time associating with Julian and Preston. And so far, it was great.

I was probably wrong, but throughout the day, Eli looked more at ease seeing us all get along as well. Then again, I was usually the one worried.

After the rides, we stopped by the farming area with all kinds of farm animals. This part of the fair wasn't exactly pleasant smelling, but it was very entertaining seeing all the pigs and cows, even goats. There was so much to do here from watching the circus acts and animals to walking through a twisted fun house. Though I was standing by Olette most of the time, I would exchange glances and smiles with Eli.

Through it all, Preston finally got his wish to buy all sorts of interesting yet completely insane food being sold here. I glimpsed over as Preston and Julian were waiting in line at the deep fried foods stand while Olette made a stop to the restroom.

"Having fun?" Eli decided to wait with me at the funnel cake stand.

Nodding my head, I smiled. "Yes, it's incredible. Thanks for taking us."

"It's no problem, I'm glad you are."

"Are you having fun, Eli?"

"Of course. Couldn't have asked better people to go with."

It was hard to understand what he meant by that, but I was glad hearing his response.

Holding that smile, the young worker soon took my order of the funnel cake with glazed strawberries, whipped cream, powdered sugar and vanilla ice cream on top. This reminded me of the ones sold at the Santa Monica pier, but Preston insisted that there was a "difference".

All of us met at the eating area and Olette nearly attacked me for the funnel cake. My eyes landed on Preston and Julian who were carrying a bunch of food in their arms. Preston presented each one for sharing as if it was a commercial.

"Okay, this one is the deep fried Oreo's, S'mores, Twinkies, my all time favorite — the deep fried Klondike bar. Oh! I wanted to try the donut chicken sandwich... and here's the super sized corn dog, the special onion fries, some nacho fries, the jumbo hotdogs and..."

The list went on and on as Julian and Preston were laying the food down onto the table. I wasn't entirely sure if that should sound appetizing or a little frightening.

Satisfied, Preston started chomping on the chocolate covered bacon in his hand and offered, "Let us feast. Feel free to take anything!"

"Don't talk with your mouth full," Julian pointed out.

We laughed, taking seats around the massive amount of food on the table. After trying some and with the use of force by Preston to continue eating, I was completely stuffed.

How we were able to finish all of it, I may never know. Never mind.

The answer was because of Preston. Most of the time, our eyes were stuck watching him eat everything with no hesitation. Where did all that food go? Preston was completely fit from what I could see.

Hopping out of his seat, Preston was even more energized. "I could run a marathon right now! Ready for round two?"

Eli hinted for all of us, "How about we just walk it off first?"

As we gathered the trash to throw away, we nodded in agreement. Walking around the fair was difficult especially with people wanting to go from one place to another. I ended up bumping into Eli several times causing us to give apologetic smiles to each other. Once we managed to get out of the rush of people, the five of us literally let out a sigh of relief.

Julian wrinkled his nose before becoming relaxed with the open space. "I understand everyone is psyched having the fair here, but it is way too hot for all these people."

I couldn't agree more.

"Hey Eli! Want to try that game over there?"

All of us followed where Preston was pointing at and a specific memory came my way.

Preston was suggesting the prize stand very identical to the one Eli had tried winning me a teddy bear at the Santa Monica pier.

Laughs were held in by Julian and Preston as Eli's ears transitioned a shade of red — I didn't think it was due to the heat. I even heard Olette giggle beside me, using her hand to cover her mouth. As much as I wanted to laugh, it wouldn't help Eli's embarrassment at all.

Eli lightly punched Preston in the upper arm. "Yeah, yeah. Laugh all you want."

I was fighting into a smile watching all of this.

"Eli! Preston! Julian!"

The atmosphere around us shifted as we turned around to find two girls waving their hands. I squinted my eyes at the blonde with a bob cut along with a brunette, having her hair tied up in a bun, trying to figure out if they were familiar.

As they moved closer, the girls were definitely from our school, but I couldn't recall their names. They were smiling brightly at the sight of the three. The girls practically jogged to hug them and the boys returned their hugs with less effort.

The blonde rejoiced, "It's so good to see you guys! Oh my gosh! How have you been?"

The three answered with the usual "good" or "fine", asking the two girls the same thing after. I found out the blonde's name was Tess and the brunette was Irene.

Irene's large brown eyes lit up, filled with joy. "We haven't seen you three since, like, forever!"

Julian nodded his head, having a friendly smile on. "It's been a while. You two having fun?"

As Eli and them were all reconnecting, I threw a look at Olette and she was feeling the same way. She mouthed the word 'awkward' to me and I shrugged slightly. Didn't you dislike those moments where you would just standing there while a person was talking to a friend of theirs?

"Is that you, Olette? Hey!" Tess chimed, approaching Olette.

Olette threw on a closed smile. "Hey Tess."

For some reason, it seemed like none of them looked happy seeing Tess and Irene. Well, if I compared how the two girls were acting.

"Who's this?"

"Are you new here?"

Finding out they were referencing me, the boys and Olette abruptly explained how I was Lana Clarke and how I went to school with them as well. I really didn't like how I wasn't able to talk for myself, but it was too late to react anyways. Tess and Irene gave me a tiny grin in response, and I simply returned what felt like an uncomfortable grin.

Irene tapped her chin. "Oh! Your last name is Clarke, right? Are you related to Landon in any way?"

I had a feeling I'd get this question.

"He's my brother actually..." I muttered out. My eyes shifted from left to right.

Tess suddenly burst out, "Oh my gosh! Really? That's, like, so funny! Is your brother dating Haley?"

I nodded my head. So what?

As much as their random outbursts were confusing me, Tess looked like she wanted to say something to Eli except our undivided attention was suddenly pulled by a —

"Trash can!"

Tess stopped by clamping her mouth shut, and we all found Preston running to the nearest trash can. All the food he took in went upstream and I felt my body wince, hearing him.

Julian's hazel eyes widened. "And this... is the memory that Preston wants to hide so much."

Oh.

Chapter 9

It was all too close.

Way too close.

If Tess said another word, I would have been done for. Tess and Irene were — and would always be — the gossip girls that would butt in our group. They poked their noses in our business during high school and it was annoying. The only two girls I was able to tolerate their nosiness were my twin sisters. That was it.

This entire time I was sweating like a day's worth of walking through the Sahara Desert, knowing Tess and Irene would see before their very eyes that I wasn't with Haley anymore, and ironically, I was spending the day with Landon's sister. That was the kind of stuff they hunted for and that would have been a mess I wouldn't want to explain.

So, I give thanks to Preston. Even though throwing up all the food he ate was embarrassing for his part.

Our attention was on Preston, who already ran to the nearest trashcan. Irene and Tess' reactions were pretty much horrified. Looking over at Lana and Olette, they both had wide eyes as Lana's face dropped to concern. Coops appeared completely speechless and his hazel eyes shifted back to mine.

We were thinking the exact same thing.

If it weren't for Preston, the plan would have fallen because of Tess and Irene's over-curious minds.

I knew eating all that junk would bite him back. Heading over to Preston, I patted his back. "Let me get you some water."

Preston shook his head. A small smirk appeared that no one from our group could see except me. "You owe me, bro. My acting skills got you all, didn't it?"

My mouth dropped. Preston was acting? He was actually using it as a diversion! I got to hand it to him, he really fooled me.

Preston complained quietly, "I'm literally about to puke having my face this close to the trashcan, but let's continue on. I swear, out of all people, why Tess and Irene?"

Holding in a chuckle, I patted his back once more. "You saved me, man. You deserve an Oscar."

Preston scoffed a laugh. "Whatever Eli. Now get rid of those girls while I play sick."

Walking back to the group, I looked at Coops. "Hey, you think you can get Preston some water?"

Coops nodded his head sternly, still believing that little actor was really sick to the stomach. Olette offered to come with Coops which left Lana, Tess and Irene. Lana's concerned blue eyes were still stuck on Preston.

"Is he alright, Eli? He should go to the restroom before it gets worse."

Shaking my head, I smiled to hopefully relieve her worried expression. "No, he's okay Lana. Preston told me he's feeling a lot better now."

"We should go to him. We can all sit and wait for him to get better." Lana was having a hard time buying my words.

Growing guilty, I hated seeing Lana worried. She was supposed to be having a good time. On the other hand, Tess and Irene were looking uncomfortable from the situation. Tess twirled her short blonde hair as her pink lips forced into a smile.

"Um, Eli. Irene and I are going to go."

Irene nodded several times. "Yeah. It was nice seeing you... I hope Preston will be okay."

Looked like Preston scared them away for me. Giving the girls a closed grin, I nodded.

"He'll be fine. Nice seeing you two as well. See ya."

Lana and I waved as the two walked away, disappearing in the crowd of people and that was the end of Tess and Irene. We approached Preston, who still had his head close by the trashcan.

When Coops and Olette returned with some water and napkins, Preston continued playing things off so well as he wiped his mouth with the napkin. Preston breathed heavily, taking the bottle from Coops' hand — if only Coops knew! He thanked Coops and Olette before taking in a huge gulp. After drinking, Preston chuckled loosely, seeing everyone's concerned expressions.

"Should we get you some medicine, Preston?"

Preston's eyes jumped at Lana. He grinned despite playing a hurt expression. "No, it's cool. After getting all that out, I feel better."

Did Preston secretly take drama class during high school? He was fooling everyone! If he didn't tell me, I'd be insisting that we go home already, so he wouldn't go on puking everywhere — that's what really happened when Preston was actually sick to the stomach.

Coops suggested from Preston's past experience, "Preston, you sure you're going to be alright? You don't need to go home... right?"

Preston held a strong expression which worked perfectly so he'd appear tough in front of Lana and Olette. "Yeah, I'm okay. The day's not over yet! Let's all live it up, okay?"

Despite the uncertainty in everyone's faces, they eventually nodded. Lana glanced towards my way and she still wasn't convinced that Preston was alright — even if he wasn't serious at all. When I gave her a reassuring grin back, her face eventually softened. The five of us ended up sitting down so Preston could "recover" and the girls wouldn't worry so much about him.

After a while, Preston's acting changed to show his "normal" state. It was hard going along with this because seeing Coops' serious expression was pretty hilarious. It looked like any moment Coops was expecting Preston to throw up again, and it was worrying him despite trying to mask it.

"How you now feeling, bro?" I was sitting beside him.

Preston finished up the water bottle. "Doesn't feel like anything happened. Now come on, let's move the spotlight away from me and enjoy the rest of the day."

Everyone gradually went at ease seeing Preston act like "Preston". He began showing off his recovery in front of Lana and Olette, and the two laughed in entertainment. Preston grinned that sideways smile of his and winked at them.

Shaking my head at the sight, I caught Coops giving me that look. The kind of look where he was doubting if Preston was really sick or not. Was he catching on? But in the end, Coops had a tiny grin on his face seeing Preston better. Yeah, he cared. Having an older brother himself, I guessed Coops wanted to be the role of an older brother towards us. That was the kind of brotherhood we shared.

For the rest of our time, we continued walking around. The fair was lit up with all the bright, colorful lights. The best part of ending this eventful night would be riding the Ferris wheel. After suggesting that, Preston had this mischievous smirk on, mentioning the Ferris wheel was only a three seater. There were five of us — how was this going to work out?

Even though I didn't want Lana to leave Olette, Olette suddenly insisted that she would be okay with Preston and Coops. Lana threw a confused glance at Olette. If I was right, it looked like Olette winked at Lana. Was she trying to get us two together? Coops and Preston also realized what Olette was indicating and grinned from ear to ear. Could they make the situation any more obvious?

The "re-energized" Preston then placed his arms around Olette and Coops' shoulders. "So looks like we figured out who goes with who! Ready?"

Olette and Coops began fidgeting from Preston's actions causing Lana and me to start laughing.

Coops warned, "Don't do anything stupid when we're up there, Preston. I want to stay alive."

"Seriously. I'll push you off if I have to," Olette added.

Preston let out a pout. "What! Just a few moments ago, you two were so worried about me! Now, you want me dead?"

We laughed together, and seeing Lana's face light up was definitely a great sight. It relaxed me seeing her enjoy this day with my friends. I was worried Preston and Coops would scare her or treat her differently, but I shouldn't have doubted my bros.

Realizing that I would be riding with Lana, I didn't know why I started to get all nervous. I was supposed to be the confident Eli Wesley! Getting myself together, I had to prove to the guys that I had everything in check. The five of us stood in line and before we knew it, we were boarding onto the Ferris wheel.

Lana and I got on first and waved to the rest, even though they would be riding the next cart beside us. Sitting next to each other, I took in a deep breath. Should I start a conversation? I had to do something!

"You're not afraid, are you?"

Gazing at her, her blue eyes were on me and there was something about the smile she had on that expressed she was teasing me.

Letting out a laugh, I shook my head. My voice held confident. "Me? Scared? Of course not."

"You're awfully quiet though, Champ."

Champ.

Looked like that name stuck onto Lana — but it didn't bother me. Would it be weird to say that I was okay with her calling me that? But if I see that stand guy again, that would be another story.

I smirked. "Are you sure you're not the scared one? You can hold onto my arm if you are."

Lana let out an amused grin before glancing off to admire the view. "You're funny, Eli... You know, even though Preston got sick from all that food, today was really fun."

Hearing her words were very soothing — I didn't mess up this time! Well, our day wasn't over yet. I shouldn't jinx my words.

"It's been an honor to spend this day with you, princess," I teased even though it was all true.

"You're never going to stop with those cheesy lines, are you?" She countered with a smile on her face.

Sharing a laugh as the Ferris wheel made its rounds, we continued to look out at the fair and city night life. My eyes gradually made their way towards Lana. Just the way she looked, the way she simply stared off was just... beautiful. I couldn't get my eyes off of her.

What were these feelings I have towards Lana Clarke? The plan was to get Haley back, but I haven't thought about Haley since that day the guys and I were at Chaplin's and created this plan.

"Why are you looking at me like that, Eli? There's nothing on my face, is there?"

Realizing how close our faces were, I inched away to stop myself from doing something stupid again.

Feeling my face heat up, I quickly blurted, "There w-was a bug!"

Her bright, blue eyes grew in shock. "A bug! Is it still there?"

Lana was consciously touching her cheeks, searching for that non-existent bug. What was the matter with me?

"Oh. It... flew away."

She gave me a relieved smile and continued to stare at the fair when we reached the top. That was close.

When the Ferris wheel ended its rounds, Lana and I got off to wait for the guys and Olette. Soon, the three all hopped out of the cart and had these wide grins on their faces. Preston flashed me that look and I instantly shook my head. What were they expecting during the ride? Since we decided the Ferris wheel would be the last thing on the list, we exited from the fair to head back from this hot yet entertaining day.

Once everyone got into my car, I started up the engine and drove away. The car ride home was quiet with Coops resting his head against my car window while Olette had fallen asleep with her head on Lana's shoulder.

Preston let out a yawn. "Man, today was a blast!"

"At least you know now not to eat so much," Coops reminded.

Oh yeah, Coops still didn't know.

Having to drop off the closest home first, oddly enough, Lana would be the last one. After taking Olette and the guys home, I pulled up to the curb of Lana's house. She moved up to the front seat after Preston left.

Lana's voice was full of gratitude. "Thank you again for today, Eli."

"As long as you had fun, I'm happy. So no need to thank me."

"I hope you had fun."

"I already knew I would have fun even before the day started. Thanks for joining us."

"Your friends are great by the way. The fair was really fun... I kind of wished my dad got to experience it too." Her words soon trailed with laughter, even though her eyes appeared embarrassed.

"I could tell they like you too. You know... there's still the LA and OC county fair that happens during the end of summer. Let's take him then, yeah?"

Lana nodded in agreement yet her blue eyes were telling me something else. I couldn't be wrong, but it looked sad — as if she believed it wouldn't happen.

When Lana said she was going, I quickly took off my seat belt to get out of the car. Opening her door, her face flushed slightly again. I guess she never thought I'd be a gentlemen about these kind of things. I could be rather "princely", if I say so myself.

I gave her a promising smile. "I really meant what I said. Let's take your dad to the next fair, okay?"

"Thanks. I'd love that. Good night Eli," Lana replied happily before heading into her home.

There was just something I liked whenever I knew I could make Lana Clarke happy.

"Aww Coops! Don't deny it, you couldn't help but worry about me!"

Our main highlight to bring up constantly this weekend was Preston's little stunt during the fair on Friday. We wouldn't let it down and would laugh about it every minute or so. This Sunday afternoon, the three of us were sitting around the usual table at Chaplin's Diner after surfing some waves at the beach. No sign of Landon there fortunately. Coops jokingly rolled his eyes for the millionth time as he called Preston an idiot. He was in denial that Preston tricked him.

Coops took a gulp of his soda float. "I just didn't want to see you puking everywhere especially with Lana and Olette there. You know how embarrassing that would be?"

Preston guffawed, fixing his damp golden brown hair. "That's what you tell yourself. Admit it!"

"Admit, what?"

"That you care about me!"

I barged in, making fun of the two. "Okay... I didn't order a side of bromance over here."

They quickly composed themselves, dropping the topic soon after. Preston nodded before grabbing some fries from the basket.

"Yeah, yeah, lover boy. Anyways, what's the progress with Lana? You kiss her yet? In front of Haley? Did you even see Haley yet?"

"Preston, for the thousandth time — No. Lana and I didn't kiss yet. There is progress and no, I haven't seen Haley or kiss Lana in front of Haley."

Preston smirked, completely ignoring what I just said. "Hey, what's that Disney song where that red crab with an accent sings something about kissing a girl?"

"Wow. You seriously have an attention span of a fish." Coops shook his head, dipping a fry in ketchup.

Preston then snapped his fingers as if he discovered the lost city of Atlantis. "Ah-ha! Kiss the girl! Eli, if you don't hustle I'm seriously going to sing that song to you as motivation!"

Without a choice, Preston started practicing — more like mumbling gibberish — while Coops and I just watched in amusement or in disturbance. Whichever was more logical to you all.

Coops groaned, cupping his ears after ten seconds of Preston's gibberish. "Eli, hurry up before Preston drives me crazy."

We started laughing until our server, Rachel, came with our orders of Chaplin's famous burgers. Rachel's chirpy voice matched her playful blue-green eyes.

"Here you go, boys."

Before leaving, Coops gave her a wink in thanks causing Rachel to giggle bashfully before whipping her long dark brown hair with her. Rachel was a year or two older than us, but age never stopped Coops from catching girls' attention.

"One day, the ladies will start to think something's wrong with your eye," Preston joked, sliding the tray with his burger closer to him.

Coops turned his attention back at Preston, angling his face up as a challenge. "Jealous, bro?"

"There's nothing to be jealous about. Unlike you, girls will never get tired of my charm."

"You mean, being a smooth talker?" I corrected, holding a smirk.

Coops took his burger and shrugged. "Hey Preston, you know what they say though... actions speak louder than words."

I hissed from Coops' comeback which caused Preston to throw a balled up napkin at Coops.

"I hope you know what I mean by that action." Preston mocked.

Coops and I joined his laughter — it was just one of those good days with the guys.

Through our laughs, my phone started to vibrate against the counter top. Halting my laughter, I placed my burger down and almost didn't believe that Lana was the one calling. I told the guys it was Lana and they became quiet, focusing on their burgers. But, I caught their growing grins.

"Hi Eli, I hope I'm not bothering you right now."

"Me? Nah, I'm just grabbing something to eat. What's up?"

"It's just..." Lana's tone sounded unsure causing me to wonder. She finally continued, more confident, "You wouldn't be busy this coming weekend?"

Lana wanted to hang out? I blinked.

"Nope, I'm free this weekend. You have something planned?"

The guys were looking at me with curious faces.

"It's not really my plan or anything... you know my brother's girlfriend, Haley? Well, it's her birthday party this weekend and I was wondering if you wanted to come with me." She suddenly added, her shyness clearly showing, "It's okay if you don't want to though."

The look on my face could only explain minimal to what I was feeling right now. Coops and Preston raised their eyebrows with suspicion as I gawked on the phone.

"Eli?"

Shaking my head, I heard myself say through impulse, "You say you want me to come with you to Haley's birthday? Of course I'll go with you. Fill me in with the details and we'll go together."

She sounded relieved after hearing my response. "Thanks. I'll call you back, okay?"

"No problem. I'll hear from you soon then. Bye."

As soon as I ended the call, Preston scoffed from what he overheard. "You better not be joking around right now. Did Lana just call you to go to Haley's party?"

I nodded, a little unsure myself. I couldn't believe I forgot Haley's birthday was this coming weekend. Have I lost track of time?

Coops' grin of victory appeared. "This is it, Eli. You're almost there."

"Looks like I don't have to sing anymore." Preston actually looked pretty upset.

"That, my friend, is a good thing," Coops praised.

Preston darted a look back at Coops, causing the two to start laughing in the end. I soon joined them before they thought something was wrong.

The moment I've been waiting for was about to come, but why was my heart beating more in anxiety than excitement?

Chapter 10

"I'm so excited for my party! Thanks for helping me out, Lana."

The two of us sat by the granite counter top island of our kitchen. Haley came over to talk about her party plans with me. She needed a girl's perspective to back up her ideas, so Landon wouldn't be much of help then. Even though I thought Haley had her girlfriends to help her decide, it was a little too late to object since she showed up our porch steps this morning when Landon left for the auto shop.

She twirled her soft, blonde hair between her fingers, focused on the pictures she printed out. "This is going to be the party of the summer! It's perfect that my parents own a beach house, right?"

I nodded, hoping to show some kind of enthusiasm successfully. "You don't have to thank me. I'm glad to help."

Haley giggled before deciding which Tiki torch would be a better choice. She settled her crisp, hazel eyes on me.

"I just thought I'd give you a heads up, but Landon was telling me he's worried about you! He said that you wouldn't feel — how should I say this — comfortable at my party? He's so silly!"

The sad thing was, Landon was actually right.

Putting on a smile, I went along with it. "Yeah, he worries too much. I'll be fine."

Shaking her head, Haley suggested, "You can always bring someone along and don't worry, I'm not expecting gifts from them." She giggled once more as her lips curved with interest. "Landon also told me you're seeing someone! You should totally bring him!"

Bring Eli to Haley's party? They were friends in high school, weren't they? That might not be a bad idea. As I thought about it, Haley then asked who exactly was this "someone".

"It's Elliot Welsey from our high school," I admitted nonchalantly.

The moment I revealed it was Eli, there was something that changed in Haley's expression. She was smiling like always, but her eyes flickered intensely, hearing the sound of Eli's name. That was what it looked like. Then again, I was probably observing things way too much. She must have noticed me studying her expression.

Haley broke the silence, becoming back to herself. "Eli, huh? I haven't heard from him in a while actually. Anyways, you should definitely bring him, girl. It'll be fun."

"Are you sure? It's your party after all. I'll really be okay," I insisted politely.

It was unnecessary for people to have to worry about me.

"Lana! Of course I'm sure. If you still don't believe me, do it as a present and so Landon doesn't have to worry, okay?" Haley batted her eyes, showing her bright smile at me.

In defeat, I nodded in agreement and Haley appeared happier than usual. Did she want me to bring someone along that badly? It was true that I didn't really socialize during high school, but that didn't mean I didn't know how to! I guess it was fine though.

It would be nice if Eli could come. But, that was if he could. Wait a second. What was I thinking?

After three hours of party deciding, Haley made up her final decision and soon headed out to get everything prepared for this weekend. Wishing her the best, Haley gave me a big hug for the help even though I wouldn't say I really helped. I gave my opinion once or twice. Most of the time I just agreed with her choices. Not like her choices were bad in the first place.

Once Haley was gone, I went upstairs to see how Dad was doing. Instead of him taking a rest, I felt relieved finding him in his usual spot by the balcony. When Dad heard my foot steps creak against the wooden boards, he looked over his shoulder. Dad grinned and motioned me to take the seat next to him.

Before sitting down, I questioned, "Dad, are you hungry?"

He shook his head. "I'm fine, honey. Just a little tired is all. Did Haley head home already?"

"Yeah. She said bye... You should take a rest, Dad."

Taking the chair next to him, he held my hand tightly and shook his head once more. "I already feel more energized having my wonderful daughter here."

Giving him a smile back, we sat there quietly for the meantime. The summer heat actually cooled down from Friday, making it much more relaxing. My eyes gazed over at Dad and these buried worries of mine got the best of me to ruin our serene moment.

"Dad."

When our eyes locked, I pleaded, "Tell me how you're honestly feeling. I've noticed you've been looking weaker. Is the medicine not helping? How about the treatment? Should I talk to Dr. Hamilton about this? I'm so worried."

Seeing how my sudden outburst startled him, Dad's blue eyes abruptly widened. He stroked my light brown hair to calm me down momentarily.

"Lana, I'm alright. What makes you think that?"

"B-but Dad, I haven't been able to see how you're doing lately because of work... and instead of spending time with you on my day off, I hung out with my friends. I'm sorry."

Holding the unwanted tears in, I swallowed that invisible lump in my throat.

"Sweetheart, when I say I'm okay, I mean it. And why are you sorry? It's not a crime to spend time with your friends. I will always be here, you understand? Don't cry."

Dad comforted me as he pulled me into a hug. I hugged him back tightly, trying to compose myself.

"Dad, I don't want to lose you."

He chuckled, hoping to lift up the mood. "Who says I'm going anywhere? I'm right here, aren't I? And I'm going to stay here."

Getting a hold of myself, we gradually pulled away from our hug and I saw the heart warming smile Dad had on his face.

"Lana, I don't want to see you upset, okay?"

As I nodded my head slowly, Dad reached in to kiss me lightly in the forehead.

"Now, let's talk about you. Landon told me that Haley is having her birthday party this weekend. You're going to, right?" Dad swiftly changed the subject.

"Yeah, I am." I added openly, "Haley wants me to bring Eli."

A grin rose on Dad's lips. "I like Eli. He's a good kid."

"He is, Dad... but I don't know, we're so different."

Suddenly, Dad raised his eyebrows in confusion. "Is it because of high school? That's all in the past, Lana. All those 'popular' kids during high school, they are really just the same. Everyone moves on from that. Between you and Eli, you're just two growing teenagers."

"I guess. I just don't want anything to happen."

"Lana, is your heart telling you that or your fears?"

Taking Dad's words into consideration, I remembered all the times I've been with Eli. He was different from what I expected. There were times where he surprised me. I even surprised myself when I was with him. However, the fact I opened up to Eli so quickly worried me. Was I just trusting people too easily? Or was Eli different?

"It's hard to say right now, Dad."

Dad nodded, his blue eyes settled on me. "I know you'll find the right decision to make you happy in the end."

I hope he was right.

After accompanying Dad and eating lunch together at the balcony, I assisted him to his bed and wished for a peaceful rest. I left his door slightly open, just in case.

Walking to my bedroom, I sighed from mild disappointment recalling back that I didn't have any parties to do today. I wasn't regretting it much though. At least this gave me an opportunity to spend the Sunday afternoon with Dad.

Suddenly, that instant shot that reminded me to call Eli about Haley's party hit me. Biting my lower lip, I stared at my phone for the longest time, debating if I should really ask him. Would it be weird or would it be too much to ask? Haley did know Eli and she wants me to bring him along. Finally, I found myself picking up my phone from my bed and dialed his number.

It had only been two days since I heard or saw Eli yet this odd feeling in my heart fluttered hearing him speak. Was it because of what he said to me Friday night? I found Eli wanting to take Dad to the county fair very sweet in a way. Disregarding those feelings, I quickly answered back hoping that I didn't bother him.

"Me? Nah, I'm just grabbing something to eat. What's up?"

Taking a deep breath, I finally summoned enough courage to ask, "You wouldn't be busy this coming weekend?"

"Nope, I'm free this weekend. You have something planned?"

Hoping that I could keep things casual and he wouldn't think anything else, I finally cut to the chase and invited him to come with me to Haley's party. Clutching tightly onto my phone, I waited for a response. The silence felt like forever.

Glancing around my pastel colored room, I called out to him from the other line, "Eli?"

"You say you want me to come with you to Haley's birthday? Of course I'll go with you. Fill me in with the details and we'll go together." His voice sounded slightly rushed but honest.

My knotted stomach was long gone. "Thanks Eli. I'll call you back, okay?"

"No problem. I'll hear from you soon then. Bye."

As we ended the call, I thought having Eli with me at the party would make it a little more fun now. That was what I was hoping for.

A part of me was scolding myself to ask such a thing. What led me to do this?

"You really don't mind helping me figure out a gift for Haley?"

Haley's party was tomorrow!

Because of all the back to back parties I had this week, I didn't have time to find Haley a present. Since it was conveniently my day off, this was the perfect time to figure something out. Luckily, I have Eli here to help me too. The both of us were strolling around the 3rd street promenade of Santa Monica beach.

Eli ran a hand through his dark brown hair and chuckled briefly. "I may not be the best gift finder... but I'll try my best."

Giving him a smile at ease, Eli suddenly added a comment that perplexed me.

"And I wouldn't miss the opportunity to spend time with you."

Giving him an amused look, I almost didn't believe what I just heard. I shook my head and joked, "Now you're making me question if I chose the right person to go with."

Catching Eli's ears turn slightly red, I smiled softly in entertainment. As I glanced around the crowded promenade, I spotted several stores — and many performers on the side which was very distracting — that seemed like good options. But, which one to choose?

I sighed. "Where should we start? I really don't know Haley that well."

There was something peculiar whenever I said Haley's name in front of Eli. Just like Haley, the two reacted oddly. Those deep brown eyes would suddenly cloud up at the sound of her name. As much as I thought about it, it just sounded silly to assume. Eli was looking around the promenade as well. Watching his eyes search around, I swiftly glanced off before he caught my gazing.

"Don't you girls like clothes or jewelry... something like that on your birthday?"

"I was thinking that too, but I have no clue what Haley's style is. When I see her, she's usually just wearing a tank top and shorts. But, jewelry sounds like a good option. I noticed her ears are pierced... maybe earrings?"

"Earrings it is then." Eli soon flashed me that dimpled smile of his.

As we headed to the nearest store with reasonably priced jewelry, I noticed how comfortable I became with Eli. I was shopping with Elliot Wesley of all people!

When I asked him if he could help me today, Eli instantly offered that he could pick me up so we could go together. It hasn't even been a month since that random day Eli and his friends came to my work. And now, it felt like we were friends. We were though, weren't we?

Eli opened the glass door for me and after thanking him, we were happily greeted by the employee managing the front. Dressed up in professional attire, a lady in her late twenties with her raven black hair curled clapped her hands seeing us walk in. She had very deep make up which emphasized her faint blue eyes.

Approaching us, she chirped, "How I love when couples go buy jewelry for each other! What will it be today? Rings? Necklaces or bracelets for the lady? Pearls? Diamonds?"

Quickly stopping her wild imagination, I corrected, "We're just looking for a birthday present for a friend."

The lady's eyes widened, realizing the awkward situation she put Eli and me in. Glancing over at Eli, I found him completely flushed in the cheeks even though he nodded his head in agreement. Putting her hand over her mouth, the lady let out a tiny laugh and nodded. She introduced herself as Diane.

Diane smiled, her cherry red lips contrasted her pale white skin. "Oh, I'm sorry! I just get so excited, don't mind me. Anyways, what are you looking for?"

"May we see your selection of earrings?" I smiled.

She nodded, motioning us to follow her lead. "It will be my pleasure."

Diane took us to a showcase with a bunch of earrings to choose from. My eyes glanced from row to row to find something that Haley would possibly like. Or what appeared "Haley-like". Even if all the earrings were beautifully made, none of them really popped out to my interest. This was harder than I thought.

I turned to Eli. "Would you happen to know what Haley would like?"

Eli abruptly shook his head. Clearing his throat, he had this weird grin on. "I wouldn't say... so. She seems like a person to like flashy things."

Pointing at a pair of chandelier styled earrings, I questioned, "You mean, like that?"

Eli briefly took a look over my shoulder and I completely froze up having him so near to me. A faint masculine scent came my way. It was very pleasant smelling and not over the top. It always gave me a headache when boys pour cologne like a bucket of water. When Eli realized that he was just inches away from me, his deep brown eyes widened and he took a step back. The two of us let out an awkward laugh before he nodded.

"That one is nice, but it seems a little too... formal?"

I laughed it off. "It does look like something you'd wear to a grand ball or something."

Continuing on the search, my eyes soon caught these stud earrings that were star shaped. As cliché as it sounds, there was something about it that resembled Haley. Whenever I see her, she always seems so bright, and stars are bright. If I told that to Eli, he'd probably laugh. My reasoning wasn't so creative at all.

"I think this one is pretty cool." Eli broke my train of thought.

Finding out which one Eli was looking at surprised me. It was the same one I had been looking at!

I smiled. "I thought about that one too actually."

"Great minds think alike, right?"

"So, do we have something?" Diane's enthused voice popped in as she stood from across the counter.

After showing her which one, she picked it out of the case and handed it to me. Diane described the star-shaped earrings and how it was made of sterling silver and studded with crystals. She had this convincing tone, mentioning that it was "top quality" with a great price. Diane wiggled her eyebrows.

"You'll never go wrong with a choice like this!"

Giving her a small nod, I already knew this would be a perfect gift. "I'll take it."

Joy spread all across Diane's face. She took the box with the earrings from me and told me to follow her to the cashier. I figured Eli was walking behind me until my eyes gradually landed a beautiful locket shown in its own glass showcase.

The silver heart shaped locket with an intricate, engraved design reminded me so much of Mom's. It almost looked identical.

Pausing shortly to examine it, I almost felt Eli running into me, but he reacted quickly.

"What's up, Lana?"

Shaking my thoughts away, I shrugged. "It's nothing."

Eli gave me a confused look, but believed it for a short moment. Once Diane charged the earrings and placed them neatly in a gift bag, she waved us a happy goodbye as we headed out. Looked like we finished quicker than I thought. Putting my attention to Eli, I gave him huge thanks, but he shook his hands out and motioned that it wasn't a problem.

Eli added after he smiled, "I told you I'd help, right? You don't have to thank me."

"I appreciate it though. I hope I didn't take time away from you." I couldn't help but feel guilty.

He shook his head once more. "You have nothing to worry about. It's no big deal, Lana. Can I ask you something though?"

I nodded.

"You were looking at that necklace for quite a while..." Eli revealed his observation.

Flushing red in the cheeks, my eyes wandered around the promenade. "It's just... my mom had a similar necklace like that. My dad had given it, but we decided that she should keep it with her. Seeing that locket reminded me so much of my mom, that's all."

Eli's face softened hearing that and he gave me a nod, understanding. After a moment, Eli lifted the mood and tore me away from the pain.

"Lana, have you ever been to Chaplin's?"

"The diner? No, I haven't." A laugh eventually escaped from me. "I remember that was your spot during high school."

Eli joined my laughter. He scratched the back of his head, almost showing me a shy side to him.

"The guys and I practically live there. How about I treat you out?"

I raised an eyebrow. "Are you sure? Wait, why?"

He nodded, his lips stretching that soon revealed his dimple. "Even if it sounds kind of lame, it's a special place to me. You'll love it, trust me."

"Well... I did hear they have good ice cream shakes."

Eli smiled, causing me to feel this sudden warmth. "The very best."

Chapter 11

"**W**ell, well. If it isn't Elliot."

I was immediately greeted by Betty once I held the door of Chaplin's open for Lana. The crew in the kitchen all greeted me afterward from the open window, and I waved back with a bashful grin on my face.

There was something about the look Lana had on when we were at the jewelry store that worried me. That locket reminded Lana of her mom and I could already tell she was missing her. Lana needed something to cheer her up. And I knew taking her to Chaplin's — a place I considered my second home — would be the perfect place.

"You weren't kidding about living here." Lana let out a soft chuckle as she walked into the diner.

As I laughed along with her, Betty soon approached us with menus in hand. Her grayed eyes glanced over at me and then to Lana.

"I see a new face here. What's your name, honey?"

"Lana. Nice to meet you." Lana followed with a friendly smile.

"Gorgeous, aren't you? I'm Betty. Welcome to Chaplin's Diner! Elliot, no Preston and Julian?"

I nodded. "I wanted to show Lana how amazing this establishment is... and I can't forget about the people working here."

"Oh dear. You're more charming than Julian." Betty hooted through amusement.

Lana giggled quietly beside me as I winked.

"It took you that long to realize that, Betty?"

Betty released a laugh before looking over to Lana. She smiled. "You're actually the first girl Elliot bought here... where will it be? The bar or the booths?"

Even though it wasn't much of a spilled secret, Betty was actually right about that. Haley was never the person to like these types of food. She was those healthy, organic kind of girls. The complete opposite from the greasy, satisfying goodness Chaplin's offers.

When I asked Lana which she preferred, she replied that anything was fine. I ended up choosing the booths. We'd be able to talk more freely without anything or anyone surrounding us. Going along with my choice, Betty guided us to an empty booth and laid the menus down. She grinned warmly.

"Call me when you're ready. I'm sure Elliot can tell you about our menu inside and out, Lana."

We all laughed and I jokingly shooed Betty away before she embarrassed me more.

"The atmosphere here is really nice." Lana had a pleased smile on her face.

Chaplin's Diner was your typical 50's styled diner. Bringing you back to that era, the whole retro feel bought all ages from our community here. Of course, it was dominated by us during high school, but we still give space for families and the elderly to relive those memories.

I chuckled. "I can't believe it's your first time here. Okay, these right here are pretty good."

Showing her the menu, we both ended up looking at the shakes and malts selections. It was the perfect choice of refreshment for the summer. Lana's ocean blue eyes scanned through the menu.

"Which one of these are good?"

"Cookies and cream, you can never go wrong with that," I stated after a proud grin.

After calling for Betty's attention, she got our orders — I ended up getting the root beer float and waffles fries to share — and left us alone.

As we waited, I tapped my fingers against the tabletop. Since the beginning of the week, I've been trying to forget that I'll be seeing Haley again. Even though Coops and Preston honestly liked Lana after meeting her, they knew that this coming Saturday was the perfect opportunity to follow through with the plan.

When they mentioned this and caught my inattentive mind, the guys began questioning me again if I had any interest for Lana. Avoiding the question, I told them that I had everything under control and they eventually respected my answer.

Being with Lana at the moment was very refreshing — even though I was with her because she needed help finding a present for Haley. This suddenly caused me to start doubting what I was doing with Lana.

At first, I needed to be with Lana to get back at Haley. What was going on now? My mind started twisting itself with all these "what-if's" and "maybe's" like it has been doing these past few days.

Stopping this thinking madness, I wanted to spend these moments with Lana.

No plan. No Haley.

"Hey Eli... is it true what Betty said?"

I blinked. "That I know the menu inside and out?"

She laughed. "Um. Not that... the other thing."

Lana was nervously messing with the ends of her long hair and I eventually caught on.

Nice one, Eli.

I replied sincerely, "She is. I mean, I'd go with my friends all together as a group. But, by myself? Yeah, you're the first one."

"I have a hard time believing that." A sly grin grew on her face.

Of course she was joking, but I said in my defense, "Hey! I'm really not that kind of person."

Stopping myself, I didn't want to mention it was because I had a girl-friend for a year or so.

"I'm kidding. Anyways, I'm a little surprised that you bought me here."

"Don't be. But... you should be honored."

I gave her a little wink, laughing after. Lana smiled back before joining me.

"Here you two go."

A plate of freshly fried waffle fries appeared with a side dish of Heinz ketchup. Putting our laughter to a pause, our eyes glanced up and Betty was there carrying our drinks as well. She placed them gently onto the table and smiled.

"Enjoy! If you need anything else, let me know. "

Once we thanked Betty, she walked off to attend other customers and I handed Lana her order.

"Hope you like it."

After taking in a few sips, Lana nodded her head in approval. Her blue eyes brightened, looking back at me.

"You were right, it's very good!"

"Don't tell me you were doubting me," I teased.

Her cheeks tinted right after. Lana shook her head. "Oh no. Thank you for the wonderful suggestion."

Before turning her attention back to her drink, she let out a giggle which made me happy to see. I was glad that her mood was much more cheerful than earlier. Getting to my drink, I quenched my thirst from the summer heat. For a little bit, we both picked at the waffle fries until I found myself asking.

"You know, last time you and me went out, you never really told me what your dreams were."

"My dreams?"

"Well, what you wanted to do in the future — I felt like I was talking about myself most of them."

Lana grinned faintly as her eyes wandered. "I'm not sure. I haven't really thought about my future, but if we're talking about dreams, I want — I want to open the bakery my mom always wished for. Maybe go to college to get a business degree."

Lana stopped before continuing on.

"But right now, I just want to focus on the present and live it to the fullest. I know it's bad not to plan ahead, but the most important things to me are what I have at the moment."

Her last sentence was very puzzling to me.

"Can I ask what that is?"

There was a shy smile forming on her face. "I can't really say right now."

Chuckling, I nodded my head, respecting her answer. "You know, if you go for it... I think that bakery will be a huge success."

Lana stirred her drink with the red straw and shrugged. Her expression seemed to have change. Despite the smile she had on, the sudden change in her blue eyes were already revealing her hidden feelings.

"It would have been better with Mom still here... but thanks Eli."

"You know, I'd love to meet her."

Lana gazed back at me and I licked my lower lip in hesitation. That sounded weird. Hoping she knew what I meant, her eyes had shifted. Lana seemed a little taken back, but her soft cherry colored lips soon lifted.

"I think she'll be very impressed to meet the Elliot Wesley."

Trying to cover up the embarrassed emotion I was feeling, I answered smoothly, "Elliot Wesley isn't that great."

"Actually, I might say otherwise."

Hearing the compliment, I felt my face heating up. Good thing Lana didn't seem to notice. I quickly grabbed my drink and took in a few sips, hoping it will cool me down. The carbonated liquid stung down my throat, but I eventually was able to tolerate it. It took me the whole drink to finally feel at ease again.

"Eli, is it okay if we head home? I still need to make some dinner," Lana's voice hinted bashfully.

Turning my attention back to Lana, she also finished her drink and I gave her an impressed grin.

"Yeah, that's fine with me."

Calling Betty for the check, I paid which caused Lana to insist she would pay me back. It was cute seeing her expression, but it's always a rule for me to pay — especially since I was the one who suggested to stop by Chaplin's in the first place.

After saying goodbye to the employees, Betty threw me a look of approval and I grinned to myself. Once we found our parking, we hopped into the seats and before I knew it, I was soon pulling up to the curb of the Clarke residence.

"Thank you again Eli, for today. I appreciate it."

Walking with Lana to the front porch, I shook my head. "It's really no problem."

Not sure if this would be a right time, I blurted out, "Hey Lana... My family — especially my younger sisters — have been kind of asking if they could meet you. If you don't mind, maybe you could come over sometime."

Her face seemed to express disbelief. "They do? Yeah, of course. I'd love to meet them."

I nodded. "You really don't know how many times a day my twin sisters ask about you." Letting out a laugh, I continued, "So, whenever you're free?"

She smiled. "I'll let you know... and Eli?"

"Yeah?"

"I want you to meet my mom too."

For some reason, this exclusive feeling went through me knowing that Lana wants to introduce me to her mom.

"I wouldn't miss the opportunity." I grinned happily.

Once we said our goodbyes, I stopped Lana before she headed in.

"So, I'll pick you up tomorrow then?"

Lana raised her right eyebrow slightly until she let out a giggle, remembering why. Her eyes gazed down at the bag with Haley's present.

"Yeah, that sounds good. Thanks."

Shrugging, I couldn't help but smile. "Tell your dad I said hi."

Lana nodded her head in return. Waving goodbye, I headed back to my car as she closed her front door.

Once I took a seat, I let out a deep breath. Reality got the best of me. I shouldn't be doing this — to Lana. I couldn't stop myself from wanting to know her more. Being around her was different. And I liked it.

Coming to a conclusion that everything's changed, I once told Preston and Coops I wouldn't get attached to Lana Clarke, but I finally realized I already had.

And I didn't want to let go.

8:38 P.M. Preston - Tell me the look on Haley's face when she sees you!

8:44 P.M. Coops - Hit us up when everything's over.

Sighing from the texts, I slid my phone into my front pocket. After picking up Lana, we walked over to Haley's humongous beach house. Memories of when Haley and I would just hang out here appeared, but my heart didn't pound at the thought. Instead, I was growing nervous having Lana by side.

Lana wore a strapped navy blue dress with floral prints. Her long hair was curled to perfection. To sum it all up, Lana looked beautiful. Lana soon caught my involuntary staring, and she gave me an amused grin.

"You're going to be okay wearing shoes, Eli?"

Being me, I ended up wearing shoes which was something you never wear to a party by the beach. The funny thing was, I was wearing a navy blue shirt too. It wasn't intentional at all, but we were kind of matching — color wise.

Giving her a laugh, I nodded. "Don't worry about me. It's my fault."

Lana's blue eyes glowed from the sunset, and she smiled warmly. Even though I grinned back, my palms were sweating up a storm. In just a few seconds, Haley was going to open that door. As I was spacing out from all the possibilities, a familiar voice appeared.

"You're here!"

My eyes shot at the voice's direction. The birthday girl was making her way towards Lana with open arms. My body winced. Haley's golden hair was all wavy and she wore a crimson red strapless dress that flowed down her ankles. Haley hugged Lana tightly, and that was when Lana handed her the gift bag after.

Haley's hazel eyes grew. "Oh my gosh! You didn't have to get me a present!"

"I hope you'll like it... Eli helped me out," I heard Lana announce shyly.

Once my name was mentioned, Haley took in that I was standing just a few feet away. Our eyes met and all these flashbacks were flung at me. When

Haley and I would hold hands, kiss, laugh together to when she told she didn't want to be together anymore, the rejection. I took in a deep breath, knowing that I had to get myself together.

Haley twitched into a smile — a forced one. I knew when her smiles were real or not. Haley and Lana walked over to me and I put up a good front.

"You both... are matching," She observed as if she didn't know what to say.

Lana looked over at me before she released a short giggle, and I threw a smile at Lana. Looked like she noticed it too.

"Happy birthday, Haley." I gave Haley a closed grin.

Haley tilted her head up me. "Thanks Eli. Good to see you."

Past her smile, Haley's eyes were darkly deciphering me.

She told us to follow her inside and once I stepped foot into the huge beach house, familiar faces were there as the music bumped loudly. I heard so many drunken "Hey Eli!" "What's up, man?" "I've missed you, Eli!" "How have you been?" as I walked by, giving the guys handshakes and girls my best smile.

Feeling my forehead glisten with sweat, I uneasily gazed around my surroundings. I was hoping no one would speak up about my past relationship with Haley. Good thing everyone was focused on the party.

"Eli, you okay?"

Shaking that all off, I grinned to make sure Lana wouldn't get uncomfortable vibes.

"Absolutely perfect."

An hour or so into the party, Lana and I were outside of the beach house where the shore line was just a couple steps away and these fancy Tiki torches lit up the night. I introduced Lana to people I used to talk to during high school earlier. The majority were pretty much out of it already.

Embarrassing, but as if luck was on my side, no one bought up about Haley and me.

When my eyes gazed off briefly, I caught Haley speaking to her close friends from inside. Her eyes also looked away towards the glass doors, and we unfortunately locked eye contact. I cursed under my breath as soon as she started walking over to Lana and me as we sat in the comfy chairs.

Haley smiled brightly. "You two having fun?"

We both nodded our heads except Lana was more enthused about it.

"A lot of our friends were asking about you, Eli. They say you've changed," Haley revealed.

What was she doing? Lana now had her attention on me, her eyes all confused. Placing my plate down, I shrugged.

"Well, it's been a while."

"It's okay, you weren't really close to my circle of friends anyways."

Nor were you, I wanted to say.

She swiftly changed the subject. "Thanks for coming Lana. You too, Eli."

Even though I was pulling myself together in front of Haley and Lana, I was literally cringing inside. Haley's eyes gradually landed at Lana.

"By the way Lana, Landon's here. He's looking for you actually."

Lana's blue eyes were still perplexed with the current situation, but eventually nodded her head. Once Haley pointed out where he was, Lana turned to me, saying that she'll be right back. I smiled at her, mentioning that I'd be waiting here. Lana stood up from her seat which left me with Haley. Right now, this side of the party was pretty secluded. Everyone was either inside or by the beach.

Once Lana was gone, Haley sighed while folding her arms. Yet, my heart didn't skip a beat being alone with her.

"What are you seriously playing, Eli?"

That invisible mask Haley seemed to be wearing was lifted off.

Arching my eyebrow at her, I stood up so we'd reach eye contact. I was very much taller though.

"Nothing. Lana asked me to come with her."

She scoffed with doubt. "You don't expect me to believe that. Face it, you're using Landon's sister to get me jealous."

"You're wrong." I frowned, hearing those words come out of her mouth. Guilt was growing within me.

"Don't give me that look, Eli. I've known you for a long time now. For goodness sake, we dated! You still haven't gotten over me, have you?"

"Why do you think everything's about you?"

"Because for the past three months, you've been asking me to get back with you! Don't tell me that you haven't been thinking about me." Haley's lips twitched. "Lana doesn't know, does she?"

Growing aggravated, I ran a hand through my hair. "That doesn't concern you, Haley."

"Please. You probably didn't know she existed until you found out she was Landon's sister." Suddenly, Haley tapped her chin, finding amusement in all of this. "I wonder what will happen if I tell her the truth..."

"You wouldn't." My voice grew cautious.

"Why not? It's my birthday after all."

Taking a short pause, she acted as if she knew everything. We continued to share harsh gazes. I sighed.

"I never even understood why you chose Landon over me."

Haley's coral colored lips parted. "There was nothing else left between us, Eli. No spark whatsoever."

"Have you ever thought how I ever felt though?"

"You left first, Eli! You went off to go to USC last minute or whatever. Imagine how that made me feel!"

"I still wasn't far from here, Haley. I went to see you as much as I could."

"It wasn't enough!" She glared at me as if I was stupid.

I was speechless. I almost couldn't believe that was the reason that came out of Haley's mouth. For the past three months, I was so determined to win Haley's heart back but this whole time, she left because I couldn't give her the attention she wanted.

During the last months of our relationship, I remember clearly always trying to make things work, but Haley seemed to have given up already. I shouldn't have bothered because it turned out, I was the fool thinking I could fix it.

The truth came out. "I'm sorry I couldn't give you what you needed. Since we're talking, I guess we should end it right. I'm over it too."

The moment I said that, Haley's expression fell. There was no taking anything back anymore. Haley's eyes became oddly hurt as they studied my honest expression. Haley gasped slowly.

"You're telling the truth... aren't you?"

When I nodded, Haley tried to rid the glassy effect from her eyes away. Was it wrong of me to say all of this on her birthday?

"Whatever." She huffed.

"You have Landon and I've learned to accept it."

She ignored my words. "Don't tell me you actually like Lana."

Frowning, I held a stern gaze with her. "Why... would it matter to you?"

Haley shook her head and didn't answer. Haley couldn't possibly care about us, right? She blinked her eyes a couple more times until it looked like she regained herself. We stood there in silence which felt like a lifetime. Did I even need an answer from her? So what if I may like Lana? Haley was dating Landon after all. I didn't want to think about this anymore, we were officially done.

What caused us to break away was when Haley's eyes jumped at something else. Glancing over my shoulder, it was Lana and Landon. They were coming our way, but I was positive they were too far away to even hear our conversation. Fully turning, I waited for them to approach us at a reasonable distance, but what frightened me was seeing Lana's worried face. Even Landon looked worried.

"What's wrong, Lana?"

"Something's happened with my dad. He's at the hospital right now. I'm sorry Haley, but I have to go." Lana's blue eyes shook with discomfort.

My stomach flipped hearing that. Landon glanced at his girlfriend sadly, but I quickly insisted that I'd take Lana to the hospital.

"We'll go first. Don't worry Landon, we'll keep you updated."

Landon's identical blue eyes gazed at me with thanks. He looked at his younger sister, telling her not to worry too much and he would follow later. Haley nodded her head, yet I knew her mind was still on the track of our conversation. She soon glanced at Lana and smiled, thanking her for coming. When Haley looked at me, it was hard to read her tinted hazel eyes. However, Haley told me the same.

After saying goodbye, I never looked back at Haley and our conversation. I wasn't thinking about how to tell Coops and Preston that right now — I focused all my attention on Lana.

Going to the hospital, everything happened in flash. Lana kept silent the entire time. My heart pounded with wonder. What was going on with Mr. Clarke? Worry was becoming contagious because of Lana's panicked expression and body language. I found myself reaching out to grab Lana's shivering hand. She stopped walking, turning around to react to what I just did.

"Lana, he'll be okay."

Lana returned with a faint grin and we continued to walk to the emergency room. I've always hated hospitals — the smell, the stale and bright lights, just the whole atmosphere about it.

"Dad!"

Snapping out of it, I found Lana rushing over to her dad. He was lying in the hospital bed with a weak smile on his face. Despite the smile Mr. Clarke had on, his blue eyes were expressing sadness. I gulped down. This wasn't the same Mr. Clarke I remember.

Lana nearly cried out, "You said you were going to be okay... w-what happened?"

"I just want to focus on the present and live it to the fullest. I know it's bad not to plan ahead, but the most important things to me are what I have at the moment."

As I watched them, it soon became clear to me what Lana was talking about this whole time.

Chapter 12

What happened when a nightmare actually came true?

I panicked.

Everything that occured earlier washed away as I speed walked in the bright, odd smelling hallways of the hospital. My heart raced as I tuned out the world — Eli — everyone — to set my mind on Dad. What if he wasn't okay? I bit my lower lip, letting my feet take me to the emergency room.

Suddenly, I felt something warm reach for my hand. Pulling to a stop, I realized I was shivering before I settled my eyes on Eli. Giving him a vacant stare, Eli smiled to calm my nerves. His lips stretched kindly that soon revealed his dimple.

"Lana, he'll be okay."

Eli's assurance had given some relief, but I could only give him a closed smile in return. We soon reached the Emergency Room and I asked the front desk where Dad was. It turned out Dad was occupying the room just across the counter. Heading over, I found him lying on the hospital bed. He had his eyes shut and was connected to a monitor with an I.V. My heart was clenching as I prayed that it wasn't anything serious.

My voice shook. "Dad!"

Dad's eyes opened slightly at the sound of my voice. At first, he looked at me with disbelief — like he didn't want me here. Dad smiled weakly in return. His eyes momentarily glanced over at Eli, who was standing behind me.

Rushing over to Dad, I nearly choked. "You said you were going to be okay... W-what happened?"

Before Eli picked me up earlier today, I recalled Dad promising me that he would be completely okay by himself and we wouldn't have to worry. "Have fun at the party", his words to Eli and me before we left repeated through my head. As Dad was about to answer, someone interrupted.

"Are you the daughter of Mr. Clarke?"

Turning around, Eli had been staring at me until he looked over his shoulder at what appeared to be the doctor. The doctor gave me a friendly grin even though his face was slightly worn out, having dark circles under his eyes. The doctor then asked Eli if he had any relations with us. Eli shook his head which made the doctor instruct him politely if he could take a step outside. Giving Eli an apologetic look, he indicated that he understood the situation and smiled faintly at me before leaving.

Once Eli slid the curtains for privacy, the doctor introduced himself as Dr. Welsh.

"Dr. Welsh, is my dad okay?"

Dad tried to calm me. "Lana, I'm fine."

Dr. Welsh looked at us before he glanced down at the clipboard. "It was just a mild attack, Ms. Clarke. It was a good thing that Mr. Clarke went to seek medical attention immediately. You have been receiving treatment for your cancer... Am I correct?"

I nodded for Dad.

He informed, "After treating Mr. Clarke, he's much better. Just more rest. We'll have him transferred to a different room since I would like him to stay in the hospital so I can check for progress for a few days. Dr. Hamilton is your primary doctor?"

"Yes. Will my dad get better though?" I hoped, holding onto Dad's hand.

Dr. Welsh pursed his lips momentarily. "As of now, he is better after the attack. But, I will have to make sure."

After the doctor asked Dad if he was comfortable or feeling any kind of pain, Dr. Welsh soon departed to attend other patients. Now that it was just the two of us, I looked at him and he sighed, taking in my expression.

"Don't look at me with those eyes, honey."

"Dad, tell me what happened."

Dad was hesitant at first, but he ended up answering, "The coughing wouldn't stop — it reached a point where I had a hard time breathing."

"You had me so worried, Dad. I thought that — that –"

"Of course not, Lana. I'm always going to stay right here," Dad interjected, holding a smile. He reached out to wipe the tear that rolled down my cheek. "My daughter shouldn't be crying right now. You should be at the party having fun."

"I don't care about the party, Dad. If I only knew this would happen, I would have never went."

"These kind of things happen, Lana. I'm sorry."

"But not to you, Dad. Not to you." I emphasized the last words.

In the end, Dad pulled me into a hug and I tried to wipe the tears that flowed from my eyes. I hated falling apart like this. Trying to get myself together, Dad was the one who's going through this. I shouldn't be selfish and helpless about this situation. Dad needed all my support. It shouldn't be the other way around. When I managed to stop crying, Dad had a comforting smile on his face. I kissed his forehead lightly and insisted that he should be getting the rest he needed.

Dad reminded before closing his eyes, "I'm not going anywhere, Lana. Eli is still outside?"

I forced a smile. "He is, Dad. I know... Let me know if you need anything, okay?"

Dad nodded his head in response before falling into a deep slumber. Making sure he was comfortable, I took a deep sigh. As I was about to leave, I wiped my eyes first to make sure I didn't look like a complete wreck.

Opening and closing the curtain, I was immediately approached by Eli. He presented a water bottle before me and I took it in thanks. Eli was holding a concerned expression, making me mention that Dad was going to be alright.

All of a sudden, a beeping noise appeared. It wasn't coming from my phone, but Eli reached for his pocket and glanced at his screen — I guessed it was a text message. What confused me was seeing a small frown appear on his face. When I asked if he needed to go home, Eli shook his head.

"It's nothing," was all that he said.

I nodded shortly before the two of us sat on the plastic chairs aligned against the wall.

After taking a few sips of water, I murmured, "I'm sorry, Eli."

"Sorry for what, Lana?"

"For everything. I didn't mean to drag you into this."

"Lana, it's not your fault."

After a moment, Eli stated with hesitation, "When I first came to your house, Mr. Clarke didn't have a cold. Didn't he? It's something more serious..."

Taking a deep breath, I only responded with a small nod. Things like this was just so hard to admit — so hard to accept. Eli called my name soon after. Pulling my attention to Eli, I found his dark brown eyes staring into mine so warmly. The aura he gave was comforting for some odd reason.

Once we locked eye contact, Eli encouraged, "I know he's going to make it through."

I revealed through frustration, "I'm... just scared and seeing Dad go through this is difficult."

Eli nodded his head, understanding. His voice was soft to keep me in a calm state. "It's okay to be scared, Lana. Things like this are scary to go through. But I have a strong feeling he's going to be fine because I know he doesn't want you to worry, so he's going to get better. You understand?"

There was something reassuring about Eli's words.

I let out a soft chuckle. "It's funny how you're more confident than I am."

"If you ever need someone to turn to... to give you that extra motivation, I'm your guy." Eli had that signature smile on.

Surprised, I didn't know how to react. Even though Eli knew nothing about what was going on with Dad specifically, he was willing to help. What shocked me was getting this sense of sincerity from him. Eli was being honest with his words. Smiling faintly in return, I nodded my head in thanks. Fear was still hidden beneath me.

Eli continued to stay by my side for another hour. He tried getting my mind off things asking what I thought about the party. Now that I thought about it, Eli looked completely uncomfortable when he was there. The party was interesting, I have to say.

"Were you like them during high school?" I referred to our old classmates who drank a little too much.

Immediately, Eli shook his head. "Honestly, no. I've been to parties like those, but I never drank. Being an athlete, it messes you up completely — in general. Plus, I wouldn't consider myself a captain if I was like them... I would always lecture my teammates about that." He chuckled. "They would joke and call me the old man."

Joining his laughter shortly, I was a little amazed hearing that. "You're quite the responsible one, are you?"

Eli ran a hand through his hair. "Well, I wouldn't say that. I make mistakes too. But thanks."

Raising an eyebrow, I noticed Eli seemed bothered especially with that answer he just gave me. Even though we talked, something was distracting him.

Biting my lower lip, I wanted to ask, until I heard Landon's voice. He was here?

The two of us broke off our conversation. Landon's face was filled with worry, reminding me of myself an hour ago. Standing up from my seat, I went to meet him.

"How's Dad? Is he alright?"

"Yeah, it was just a mild attack according to the doctor. He's sleeping right now, but they're going to transfer him."

Landon let out a sigh of relief before nodding back.

"Hey Eli, thanks for doing this."

Eli stood up from his chair too and said that it wasn't a problem. Since it was getting late, I suggested for Eli to head home. I didn't want to keep him here any longer. Besides, I was sure he had other things to do. Even though Eli insisted that he was fine staying with me, I assured him we'll be okay. Landon soon headed in to check on Dad, leaving me with Eli.

"I hope your dad will get discharged soon." Eli said softly.

"I hope so too. Thank you again, Eli."

"No need. I'm glad to be here for you." His words managed to confuse my heart.

What did he mean by that?

Leaving me speechless, Eli greeted me a good night and see you soon. It took a while to register that, but I quickly waved before he walked away. Those deep brown eyes were so puzzling. They were filled with regret and sorrow, making my mind twist at whatever possibility it may be.

Every 26th of the month makes me miss you even more, Mom.

Preparing a small amount of baked goods I made, I was planning to visit Mom. Maryann always gave me the day off every 26th of the month. Dad was discharged from the hospital just yesterday, but he needed the rest. I told him I'd assure Mom that he was doing much better. Unfortunately, Landon also had work today. So I guess it'll just be you and me, Mom.

Dad was sleeping soundly this afternoon, and I promised him I wouldn't be long. I didn't want to risk anything even though Dad would show me that he was fine. He lost a lot of weight by the day which worried me even more. He looked so frail, but I tried to keep my head up.

Checking the clock from our kitchen, it was already two in the afternoon. As I was heading over to grab my car keys, the door bell suddenly rang. Confused, I walked over to the front door thinking that it was those door-to-door people.

My eyes widened seeing Eli.

Eli took in my expression and grinned. The way he smiled hinted that he was embarrassed.

"Hey Lana."

Fully opening the door, I was still in disbelief. "Eli?"

His eyes wandered. "I know I should have given you a call. I don't know why I ended up driving to your place. I've just been wondering how everything's been."

Still taking his sudden appearance in, I quickly shook my head to get back into reality. I gave him a smile. "I'm a little surprised that's all. But, everything's been good. Dad just got out of the hospital yesterday."

Pausing, I figured this was actually a perfect time to ask. "Since you're already here... did you want to come with me to visit my mom?"

His brown eyes widened before he nodded. "Yeah, of course. Will Mr. Clarke be okay?"

I smiled from his concern. "He's doing much better than before. We won't be long."

Did you bring Eli here, Mom?

Once again, Eli insisted that we carpool. I was starting to feel bad that I was always getting rides from him.

Eli commented the small plastic carrier I was holding as we walked over to his car, "You made all of those?"

I nodded my head, mentioning that they were Mom's recipes and he could try some if he'd like. Eli grinned in return.

As we were heading over to the cemetery, Eli questioned as he drove, "What's your mom's favorite flowers?"

Stunned, I answered slowly, "Tulips... why?"

"Any color?"

"She loves pink tulips actually."

I was wondering where Eli was going with this, but I should have caught on sooner. Eli pulled over to a nearby florist on our way there. He told me he'd be quick and before I could say anything, he was already gone and making his way inside. Sitting in his car, I was fighting into a smile from Eli's actions. It was surprising yet very sweet — like how he's always been since he entered my life this summer.

Eli walked back to the car, with a pretty bouquet of bright, pink tulips in hand, in a matter of what felt like a minute. He opened his car door and sat down, showing me the bouquet.

"You think she'll like these?" He flashed a smile.

I chuckled, taking in the beautiful scent of the flowers. "She'll be more than happy."

As we reached the cemetery, I told Eli to follow me. My heart raced as we headed up the hill. I never bought anyone to meet Mom before — only Olette. This was really personal, and I was scared at whatever was going through Eli's mind right now. When I glanced at Eli briefly, he had such a tender expression on his face which made me feel a bit more confident.

I smiled sadly at the sight of Mom's gravestone a few steps away.

"Mom, I'm here... I bought someone for you to meet."

Eli took in Mom's gravestone, probably reading her birthday and the day she left Earth. Putting on his captivating smile, he introduced through a respectful tone, "Mrs. Clarke, it's a pleasure to meet you. I'm Eli Wesley."

He then bent down and placed the bouquet into the holder. At the moment, a mild breeze surpassed us. I gasped lightly, remembering how Dad would always tell Landon and me that the wind was Mom. As silly as it sounded, I thought it true.

I revealed through amazement once Eli stood right beside me, "Eli, I think Mom just said hi back."

He turned his attention to me, his warm eyes looking into mine. "I think so too."

Going over to Mom's gravestone, I smiled. "Hi Mom, another month has passed, and I still can't help but miss you. I know you're watching us up there... but it's still a little hard."

Clearing my throat, I had my back towards Eli and I was happy to have it that way. I didn't want him to see me vulnerable.

Touching the cold marble with my fingertips, I continued, "Everything's okay with us, Mom. You don't have to worry. So far, summer has been more than what I expected. Landon and I have been working, but we're completely fine. Dad just got out the hospital and he really misses you — all of us do."

I whispered, almost pleading, "Mom... please help Dad get better. Landon and I would be even more lost without Dad."

For a while, I continued to stare down at Mom's gravestone. My mind going blank. There were many times when I would just go here to free my mind. Closing my eyes, I put on a smile for her to see.

"I love you, Mom. Forever and always."

Turning back to face Eli, he was quietly standing there with a calm expression on. When we locked eye contact, he smiled causing me to smile in return. The two of us ended up sitting down on the lush grass. I opened the container I bought along with me and offered some of the pastries I made.

"It may not be as good as Mom's, but I hope you'll like it."

Taking it from my hand, Eli encouraged, "I'm sure it's amazing." He took a bite and nodded. "You know, Mrs. Clarke, I think your daughter inherited your wonderful baking and cooking skills."

I laughed. "Pulling the flattery card... Are we?"

Eli held an innocent face. "Flattery? I'm just telling the truth."

Being with Eli and Mom right now was very relaxing. I've been stressed out these past few days, but having them by my side at the moment created such a carefree atmosphere. Eli's eyes roamed around the scenery, the mild wind rushing past his dark brown hair.

Taking in his facial structure, I quietly observed that strong nose to his lips and chiseled jawline. His dark eyebrows framed his set of deep brown eyes nicely. Eli has captivating physical qualities, but those looks seemed to disappear.

All that I really saw was what's hidden beneath that shell.

"Don't tell me there's a bunch of crumbs on my face." I heard Eli say, laughter following after.

Snapping out of it, Eli caught me staring. I immediately shook my head, looking away before he noticed my cheeks turning red. It was so embarrassing. I hope you didn't see that, Mom.

"Hey Lana... it's really none of my business. But —"

"You're going to ask about my dad, huh?" I interrupted with a whisper.

His eyes widened, thinking that I was offended. Eli grew cautious. "Oh no. I mean — if you don't — that's not..."

I gave him a short laugh, shaking my head. "It's okay, Eli. Don't worry."

Taking a deep breath, I couldn't decide if I should tell Eli or not. But instead, my mouth slipped.

"My dad... he has lung cancer." I focused my attention on the grass, running my fingers along it. "It's to a point where treatment may or may not help."

There was a moment of silence, and I couldn't blame him. Something like this was hard to take in or even comment on. I still remembered the first time the doctor told us Dad was diagnosed seven months ago. It felt like someone shattering a mirror right at you. Painful — sharp — broken.

"The treatment he's getting will help, Lana. Don't worry." Eli let out a deep sigh. "I know I have no right to say because it's difficult, but you have to stay strong, okay?"

I bit my lower lip. "Sometimes it's hard to stay strong though. Dad never smoked or did anything yet he has to go through this. It's so unfair."

My heart pounded, and I gulped down that harsh lump. Suddenly, Eli reached for my hand. My first reaction would probably be to pull away, but I held on. His grasp was so heartwarming, and I was growing calm because of it. His soft eyes searched mine for connection. Eli grinned faintly.

"We're going to help him make it through. We're going to give him all the support so he can get better quicker. We're going to be there for him, okay Lana? And when you feel like it's too much for you to handle, I'm going to pick you right back up. You don't have to be afraid anymore — I'm here and you should always know your dad is going to make it through. I'm sure your mom feels the exact same way."

A tear rolled down my cheek hearing his words, but Eli managed to wipe it off before I could react. I felt my eyes shake, unsure of this moment. Was this really happening?

"You'd really do that, Eli?" I gasped.

He nodded. His words ever so sincere. "I promise."

Chapter 13

From the confrontation with Haley to Mr. Clarke ending up in the hospital, all that mattered to me were the Clarke's. After coming home from the hospital, I was sure of my decision. Those feelings I had for Haley were long gone.

The next afternoon, I spent it with the guys. I wasn't able to think of a way to tell them. They still didn't know.

Preston continued to nag at me while we were racing at his place — with a game console and controllers, of course. This was the usual thing to do when we're too lazy to drive anywhere. Right now, I was owning Preston.

During Haley's party, Coops and Preston scored dates with these girls we met during spring break at a USC frat party. I helped them get in despite coming from different schools. There was a third girl, Kate, but since I was with Lana, they ended up asking Tyler Benson. A horrible replacement, if I say so myself. Not really responding to Preston's question due to my focused mindset, Coops grunted.

"Tyler wanted to get in her pants the entire time."

Coops hated hormonal crazed guys like Tyler. Make that two of us. Preston peeked over his shoulder for a quick second and laughed.

"And Francesca seemed more into you than you were, bro."

I stifled a laugh — not only because I was close to the finish line — but, Coops also had to add that Francesca O'Henry was a complete psycho.

As my car passed the finish line, I threw my fist up and grinned in triumphant at Preston. Coops whooped in the back while Preston rolled his eyes, saying that I was just lucky. I doubt that.

Handing the PS3 controller to Coops, we switched places. Coops plopped onto the black bean bag couch beside Preston, and I sat on the gray suede futon against the wall. Preston's bedroom was bigger than ours combined. This was the ideal place to chill. We were always jealous of him since middle school. He even had a fully furnished one bedroom loft back in Boston where he goes to college. The perks of being a single child.

As they started another round, I blurted out my thoughts. "Couldn't you have picked someone better? Tyler, really?"

Coops' attention was stuck on the flat screen TV as he teased. "We told Kate that Tyler was just like you, so it wouldn't make much of a difference. She's probably scared out of her mind now."

The two burst into laughter. I ended up throwing my plain black snapback at them even though Kate's opinion about me didn't matter. Preston tossed my hat back, and it was only then they asked about the party. The only thing I told them last night was that I would tell them everything tomorrow — which was now.

There was no way I could avoid this. I glanced down at my hat and felt my mood slowly drain out. The feeling of victory beating Preston was no longer there.

"Yesterday was... complicated."

All of a sudden, Preston paused the game. There was only one thing that would cause Preston to ever stop a game. If a zombie apocalypse happened. Last time I checked, there were no flesh eating monsters outside, so it surprised me.

He cursed before he said, "This whole time you're acting like everything's okay! What went wrong?"

Preparing myself, I stared at their worried eyes. "Hear me out, guys."

They set down their controllers and turned to face me, giving their undivided attention.

"I got to talk to Haley — alone. We finally got some closure and apparently she left because I wasn't by her side as much as she wanted."

As the guys were rambling how stupid and lame that was, I soon revealed, "Haley was suspicious about Lana too."

The guys grew horrified and I shook my head. I knew they were thinking Haley told Lana and that was what was "complicated".

"She didn't say anything. Lana and her brother came to us while we were talking. Their dad ended up at the hospital, so I left with Lana."

Preston asked through a wave of confusion, "Rewind. What did you tell Haley?"

"Is her dad okay?" Coops cocked his head to the right.

Unsure myself, I eventually answered, "I don't exactly know what happened to him... but Mr. Clarke should be alright. I hope. About Haley, this was what I needed to tell you guys."

I gulped down. "When Haley and I talked, I told her the truth... that I was over her. For a while guys, I haven't been honest about how I feel about Haley. It's really Lana that's been on my mind."

Silence was shared between us causing me to grow nervous. The only sound was the upbeat track coming from the video game.

"How long?" Coops asked.

"What?"

"How long?" He repeated.

"Answer the question, Eli." Preston insisted.

"I would, but I have no clue what you two are saying."

Why did they have such creepy smiles on?

"How long were you feeling this way?" Coops changed it more specifically.

Were they referring to Lana? Blinking my eyes, I answered slowly, "For a while."

"Like when?" Preston poked at the topic more.

Giving them a look, I sighed. "Okay, look. I'm sorry for not telling you two sooner, but after I took her out the first time." I finally admitted, "There was something about Lana that changed my feelings about Haley. It's been so confusing, but I realized I was over Haley."

All of a sudden, Preston grinned ear to ear. "Pay up, Coops."

You could only imagine how confused I was. Coops then reached for his pocket and grumbled words I couldn't make out before he handed Preston a bill that looked like a twenty.

I pointed. "That. What is that?"

The two shook their heads at me.

Coops explained, "Eli, you call us your bros yet you didn't even admit to us that you liked Lana?"

Preston finished. "We knew, man. Coops and I have been trying everything to get you to finally admit it. We could see it in your face when we would talk about Haley and the plan, but you still kept going along with it."

Turned out I underestimated them the entire time. I scoffed a laugh and couldn't help but grin.

"That still doesn't explain the cash."

"Since you kept being an idiot, we made a bet." Coops gave Preston a glare before continuing, "When you finally told us, we would ask how long it took for you to fall for Lana. Preston said it was right after you went on a date with her. I thought that was too soon... I thought it was right after you had dinner with the Clarke's."

Preston guffawed as he waved the crispy bill. "But, look who won?"

The three of us laughed. Starting now, the plan didn't exist. Haley wasn't on my mind, and it felt so good getting that all off my chest.

Embarrassed, I ran a hand through my hair. "You guys suck... So, you didn't mind this whole time?"

Coops gave me a funny look. "And you're an idiot, Eli. Of course, we don't. If you like Lana, go for it."

Preston nodded with enthusiasm before joking. "Aw, look at Julian Cooper, being a good sport even though he lost."

Coops shot Preston a deathly look, and I watched the two in amusement. As the two were battling it out, I checked my phone. I told them everything, but there was one thing that was still bothering me.

Opening my inbox, I frowned again at the sight of Haley's name. She sent me a text — a horrible reminder — when I was at the hospital with Lana.

11:04 P.M. Haley - Deny it all you want... I know, Eli. I won't tell her because I'm so much better than that. Just know, the truth will come out whether you tell her or not, and we'll see the outcome with Lana. Best of luck.

"I promise."

At that moment, Lana Clarke trusted me with her life — the real deal. There was still a lot to know about her, but when we sat in the grass by her mom's grave, there was that push to do everything in my power to make sure she would be happy. The more time I spent with Lana, the more I became absorbed by her.

She was like an addictive book I couldn't put down.

Lana's relieved face the moment she heard my promise, knowing that someone would be there for her, was etched into my mind. I was going to be that person.

Suddenly, I felt something wet and slobbery hit the left side of my cheek. I was outside my backyard with Eian, who was licking my face to get my attention. Ridding my thoughts away, I gave Eian a smile before petting his fur.

"Stop playing around and get up! Lana's coming over, isn't she?" One of the twins screeched out of nowhere.

I released a faint groan from my younger sisters' torment. It was true though. When I took Lana home, I asked her to come over this Friday for some lunch. I was actuallyextremely nervous especially with my double trouble sisters. However, even though Lana and I weren't serious or anything like that, I was looking forward to introducing her to my family.

A light bonk abruptly hit the backside of my head. Reaching for the impact, I hissed and turned around to find Aly, who giggled mischievously. The twins were standing by each other. Both wore these frilly matching dresses that differed their usual t-shirt and jeans. Throwing them an exasperated glare at first, I then raised my eyebrows from their attire.

"Why are you two so dressed up?"

Abby rolled her green eyes as if I forgot how to breath. She smirked.

"You're saying you don't want us to look nice for Lana? Fine, let's go Aly. Let's change to our soccer uniforms which is dirty and stained with grass and mud. You like the sound of that, Ell?"

Shaking my head, I chuckled. "No, it's not that, but I don't ever remember you two dressing up for someone... not even Haley."

Aly raised her right hand up and corrected. "Who said we wanted to dress up for Haley?"

Abby nodded and Eian barked.

Giving them an amused grin, I checked the time on my watch. Lana would be over in an hour. I spent the whole morning cleaning the house from the inside to outside — I felt very accomplished about that too. Mom was inside cooking lunch with Dad helping her.

"Today will determine if we accept Lana or not." I overheard Abby remark to the younger twin.

Turning around, I folded my arms. "What's that?"

Aly sighed and moved her hands to motion me to go inside. "Nothing! Now go inside and fix yourself, mister!"

Could you see why I was so troubled? A part of me was regretting this because of my sisters.

Cooling myself down, I walked in and felt the rush of the A/C seep through my skin. Eian followed behind me, and our noses sniffed out the savory scents coming from the kitchen. My stomach growled, but I resisted the temptation and headed upstairs to take a quick shower.

Stepping out of the bathroom, I picked out a short sleeved striped shirt with black jeans. Rubbing my hair dry with the towel, I checked my phone. Lana had already sent me a text that she was on her way. After making sure my hair was done right, I rushed down the stairs and found my family all in kitchen.

Joining them, I smiled seeing how joyful they were. Mom and Dad were quite excited to have Lana over. Who knows what the twins were cooking up though. Once my parents realized I was there, I went over to the dining table to see what Mom made. Her signature dishes — baked lasagna, the special house salad and traditional bread sticks — were laid neatly onto the table cloth.

"Mom, it looks great. Thanks."

Mom's kind green eyes brightened up. "Don't worry about it, Ell. I hope Lana will like it."

Not believing Mom's lack of confidence, I was about to reassure her until Dad jumped in, "Honey, who wouldn't love what you make?"

My parents became all mushy, leaving the twins and me with sour expressions.

And that moment came — our doorbell rang.

Within a blink of an eye, Eian charged at the door as if his life depended on it. Silly dog. He wasn't even barking. Instead, he was making these huffing noises while wagging his tail. Leaving my family in the kitchen for the moment, I walked to our front door. Taking a deep breath, I put on a confident expression before opening it.

The first thing I noticed was Lana's bright blue eyes gazing up at me. She gave me a shy smile and I took in her usual light yet sweet smelling perfume. It was always a mark that made me know she was there even with my eyes closed.

However, my dog got to react first and nearly jumped at her. Lana flinched back from surprise before she took Eian's paw and shook it. She giggled as she pulled her straight brown hair behind her ear. Lana wore a black blouse that she tucked in with a faint blue skirt. It made her eyes more vibrant. When Eian finally calmed down, we shared glances again.

I motioned Eian to go inside before I stepped out. "Hey, sorry about that."

Lana shook her head and I used my right arm to direct her in my house.

"Come in, my family is looking forward to meeting you."

Lana's cheeks tinted a light shade of red, but it became more evident when I mentioned that she looked pretty. She then moved her embarrassment aside and lifted a container for me to see.

"I made some red velvet cake I hope that's fine."

"More than fine." I assured her with a grin, and we both walked in.

What surprised me was finding my parents and sisters already waiting just a few steps away from the door. Way to surround Lana. Lana greeted my family respectfully before I finally introduced her. Mom and Dad had inviting smiles on their faces as they shook Lana's hand. When Lana reached the twins, their identical eyes stared into Lana's before they finally nodded and took her hand. I released a breath.

"How about we all have some lunch? I hope you're hungry, Lana." Mom smiled.

Lana nodded. "I'd be glad to. Thank you for having me."

All of us were sitting around the dining table. Mom and Dad took the opposite ends of the table, the twins sat on the left side while Lana and I occupied the right side. As we ate, I noticed that Lana appeared to be enjoying Mom's dishes. Everything had been running smoothly. I grew at ease.

"So Lana, may I ask how your summer vacation's going?" Dad gave her a friendly smile.

Lana put her fork down and grabbed her napkin to wipe her lips. She nodded.

"It's going well, Mr. Wesley."

When Dad asked about how her first year of college went, her eyes fell to the plate momentarily and I gulped down.

Lana made eye contact back with Dad. "I didn't attend college actually. I've been working."

"As a princess!" Abby pointed out with a proud tone.

Dad looked embarrassed from his question until Mom added, "You've been working since high school, right? You're very hardworking. Do you enjoy it?"

The attention seemed to be getting to Lana — her cheeks were flushing.

Lana said politely, "Thank you, Mrs. Wesley and yes, my job's treating me very well. I really like making people smile."

My parents both smiled hearing that, and I grinned. Dad mentioned after that not a lot of people would care to do those kind of things nowadays — I couldn't help but agree. Lana Clarke was different from the rest.

My family got all excited when Lana asked about them. The twins went on and on about how they play soccer and nearly bombarded Lana with questions about being a real life princess. Even though I was worried Lana would get annoyed, she seemed to not mind at all.

Dad then revealed to Lana how Mr. Clarke and him worked together at one point. Just like the first time I heard myself, Lana looked surprised.

"How is Liam doing? I haven't seen him around." Dad asked about his old friend.

My stomach flopped all over the place. My family didn't know — I didn't tell them. How was this going to hit Lana? When I frantically gazed over at Lana, she still had a cheerful smile on her face.

"He's doing good. I'll be sure to have him make more appearances." She chuckled softly which caused my family to laugh from her light humor.

Though I joined along, watching this was painful. Lana managed to cover up the truth so well. If she never told me or if I never witnessed Mr. Clarke at the hospital, I wouldn't have suspected a thing.

What got my family happier was when we bought out the cake Lana made. The twins licked their lips as they saw the smooth cream cheese frosting over the deep red, soft looking cake. My parents looked completely impressed by Lana's manners and baking skills at that.

Dad was on his third slice. I hoped that Lana didn't think anything wrong about him. "Absolutely amazing! Made from scratch?"

A smile grew on Lana's pink lips. "I'm very happy you like it, Mr. Wesley. And yes, it's my mom's recipe."

Becoming cautious, I was worried that Lana would grow uncomfortable speaking about her mom. First Mr. Clarke, now her mom? I knew it was normal to ask about your parents, but it was difficult with Lana's situation. However, the atmosphere stayed the same throughout the lunch.

As soon as everyone was done eating and we — Lana and I, not that I wanted Lana too — offered to help Mom clean up the table, Mom still insisted she could take care of it herself. Dad accompanied Mom, saying that he'll help. There was a saddened smile that resided on Lana's face seeing my parents together which hurt to see.

"Your mom is such a talented cook, Eli."

Snapping out of it, I grinned. "She'll be very happy to hear that. Want to go outside?"

Once she nodded, we headed out back. Our backyard was huge, but that was really because we managed to fit a pool and a garden for Mom. I wasn't saying the pool was for me. My family enjoyed it just as much. Lana gasped, taking in the green life and the pool equipped with a diving board and a small waterfall Dad installed himself.

"This is beautiful," she praised.

Soon, I heard extra footsteps coming from behind us, along with some barking. Lana gave the twins a friendly smile. Eian was immediately right by Lana's side, wanting her attention as well. The twins quickly started up a conversation with Lana.

As I tried picking out what the twins were saying, I suddenly had this urge to use the bathroom — I was talking about my bladder, by the way.

Debating whether I should leave Lana with the twins, it would be a very risky choice. In the end, I ended up telling Lana that I would be right back. Before heading back inside, the twins' eyes jumped at me momentarily with cheesy smiles on their faces. They would be good, I told myself.

Right when I turned off the faucet, my phone started to ring from my pocket. Drying my hands with the towel, I reached for it and was confused at the unrecognized number. I picked it up anyways.

"Eli! If you're with Lana at this very moment, pretend I'm Preston, got it?" The voice screeched.

Not understanding the situation, I replied slowly, "Olette, is that you?"

"What did I say! Don't tell me Lana is there!"

So, it really was Olette.

I laughed. "No, it's just me right now. I'm in the bathroom."

Why did I just tell Lana's best friend that?

"Eli, gross! You're not exactly peeing or doing whatever, right?"

Luckily, Olette was matching up to my weirdness.

Giving her another laugh, I answered, "Of course not. Um, so what's up? How did you even get my number?"

"That doesn't matter right now. I need you to help me, Eli."

"What's wrong?" I was still completely confused.

"It's Lana's birthday in less than two weeks! Did she tell you? If not... now you know. Being her usual self, she doesn't want to do anything special. Want to help me throw a surprise celebration?"

Blinking my eyes, I was still taking in that it was almost Lana's birthday. She dropped no hints at all about that.

Blurting without notice, I agreed, "Definitely. I can help."

Olette squealed. "Perfect! Expect more calls from me, okay? And you better be treating my best friend like a princess right now. Thanks Eli. Bye!"

I thought getting a drunk call from Preston when he thought he called a girl named Elaine was random, but this topped it off. Still, I smiled at the idea of surprising Lana on her birthday. She would never see it coming.

Looking forward to it, I was in the backyard where Lana and the twins should be. Hoping that the twins haven't scarred her or anything, I was definitely not aware of what was coming my way.

Within a flash, a bright colored blob was thrown towards me.

A huge explosion erupted, and water soon splattered onto my clothes.

You have got to be kidding me.

As this moment was happening, my mind began to add this all up. Water balloons. That was the blob. Where was the source? My eyes gazed up and found the throwers. The twins. That was no surprise. They've been itching to have a water balloon fight the moment I got home from college. Even though they had satisfied grins on, they were still equipped with those deathly water bombs.

Which left me with Lana. Her lips curved into a smile before she giggled, revealing soon enough that she was the one who threw it.

No way.

Twitching into a smile, I — Eli Wesley — would put all things aside and declared the start of the water balloon war.

Chapter 14

"He likes you! That's all to it." Olette stated a matter of fact as she carried her sister in her arms.

I stopped by her house after work since Olette was alone babysitting. At least this gave us some time to catch up. I told her everything that happened when I visited Mom with Eli. That moment still seemed surreal to me. Flashbacks would always appear causing my mind to drift off. Eli was so sincere with his words and the way he wiped my tears off made my heart skip a beat. That kind of feeling never happened before — never did I expect it to happen so soon.

"I promise." Eli's words would echo in my head.

Angeline was cuddled in Olette's arms and let out a coo. She was too adorable. Despite taking care of her soon to be one year old sister in the fall, Olette continued to stare at me for a response.

Occupying her sofa in the living room, I mentioned, "He's just being a friend, Olette."

Olette looked down at Angeline and noticed the baby fidgeting. Quickly, I grabbed the bottle and handed it to Olette to avoid the hassle. Olette expressed gratitude and adjusted the bottle gently for her sister to take. Angeline looked like a mini version of Olette — I guess I should say her mother since Olette looks exactly like her too. The only difference was Angeline inherited Mr. Benson's blue-green eyes and dark brown hair.

When Angeline's eyes were slowly fluttering, Olette's voice was hushed as she slowly swayed her arms. "A boy would not do all those things and want to be considered a friend."

"You make it sound like boys are uncaring in every possible way," I countered.

We giggled, but quickly stopped because it was too loud for Angeline's liking.

After a few minutes of silence, Olette placed sleeping Angeline into her crib in the living room. We both walked to the kitchen where we could talk in a decent speaking level and still be able to hear Angeline, if anything.

Pouring a glass of cherry limeade for me, Olette also poured herself one as I took a seat on the bar stool. After thanking her, I took in a sip of the lemonade as the refreshing tangy taste danced on my taste buds. It was our favorite drink of all time.

Olette continued to press onto the subject. "It's different though, Lana. I have this huge feeling that Eli likes you! Think about it, he's been showing you around and taking you out, he introduced you to his side of friends, he was there for you at Haley's party, he's showing signs that he wants to be part of your life and your family's and... let's not forget, you're going to meet his family this Friday!"

Absorbing Olette's words, this was actually the first time I thought about this. Was it something more? Most of the time, I would find myself with Eli and not even think about it. He was someone I naturally went to. His actions throughout these past few weeks could be seen differently, but I was sure he was just being nice. Why would a guy like Eli Wesley be interested in me? It just didn't add up right.

Olette leveled her hazel eyes at me. "I know you're not going to say anything, but Eli is a sweet guy from what I could see. You just don't see guys like him everyday."

I shrugged, bringing the glass cup to my lips. "I don't know, Olette. Can we not talk about this right now?"

Olette nodded her head, but a new found smirk grew on her face. "Fine. How about we talk about your birthday then?"

"Olette, no."

"Lana, yes!" She clapped her hands. "We have to do something!"

I frowned. "No. Besides, I'm working."

She gave me a stare as if I've gone insane. Olette, of all people, knew that celebrating my birthday was never a big deal to me. I hated being the center of attention. It was something I had little tolerance for, as crazy at it sounded. I could deal with the attention when playing a princess, but this was different. Sometimes I wished Olette actually forgot about it.

Olette placed her glass down and insisted. "Oh no, you're not. Lana, let's celebrate! You didn't want to do anything for your sweet sixteen, you completely blew off the fact you turned eighteen, can you at least acknowledge your day of birth this year?"

Her little pleading made me release a laugh, but I wasn't going to budge.

"Another year isn't going to change anything. It's actually going to make me feel old."

"How about a small, tiny celebration then? Maybe we could invite Eli!"

Gasping, I completely objected such thoughts. Olette placed her hands on her hips and pouted.

"Why not! Eli is your friend, right? So why wouldn't he want to celebrate your birthday too?"

Seeing how Olette was using my words against me, I still wasn't going to go along with a birthday celebration.

I reminded, "I'm working though, remember?"

"Until what time?"

Her hazel eyes were demanding an honest answer. My eyes wandered her bright, white kitchen and I slowly answered.

"Not sure yet."

Olette threw her hands out. "You're going to drive me nuts, Lana!"

Her voice was projected loud enough it seemed to have woken Angeline up. That wasn't good. Olette groaned from her unintentional outburst, and I hid the smile of amusement growing on my face.

As I followed Olette back into the living room to help, I carried the crying Angeline in my arms. The light baby scent wafted as I rocked Angeline gently. Angeline's big, round eyes continued to stare at me and her crying slowly ceased.

I smiled warmly. "Your big sister being too loud for you?"

Olette scoffed a laugh. "Whatever, Lana."

Seeing how I managed to put Angeline back to sleep, Olette was left in amazement. "I still love you though."

Taking my eyes off Angeline, I smirked. "Still not changing my mind about a birthday party."

"Let the operation begin. You ready, Lana?" Abby looked up at me with devious green eyes.

What was going on?

Eli left me with his twin sisters and his adorable dog, Eian, since he had the use the bathroom. His younger sisters were very cute and a friendly duo, but their current expressions were somewhat misleading.

Meeting Eli's family for the first time was nerve wracking. As I drove to his house, my fingers continuously tapped against the steering wheel. All these possibilities would circle around my mind. What if Eli's family didn't like me? What if I leave the wrong impression on them? What if everything just turned out bad? Most of these thoughts were negative, but I managed to pull myself together.

If I could easily adjust to people being a princess, I would be able to do it in real life as well.

And, so far, I was enjoying company with the Wesley family. Eli's parents were very charming. It made me happy taking in how much love was happening in their family. Seeing Eli's parents together made me miss Mom even more, but I tried to keep a smile on. This wasn't a time to be selfish with my thoughts.

My train of thought vanished when I saw Aly reel in a deep blue colored cooler. Eian trotted along side of her. Raising my eyebrows with curiosity, it made sense when Aly opened the lid. The cooler was filled with chilled, colorful water balloons. Aly whipped her long dark brown hair behind her shoulder and grabbed one.

"Lana, you like having fun?"

Smiling a little, I was unsure how to respond.

Abby accompanied her younger twin and grabbed a water balloon herself. "We've been wanting to have a water balloon fight with El for the longest time. He's kind of a wuss, just to let you know, but today is the perfect day! What do you say? Want to be the first one to attack?"

I bit my lower lip. "You don't think he'll get mad? And what about your dresses?"

The twins both looked down at their clothes and shrugged.

Abby then gave me a thumbs up. "These don't matter. And if Ellie gets mad, then that makes him even more of a wuss! So, are you up for it Lana?"

Would it be rude to do this?

The twins stared at me with their eyes hinting "it wasn't a problem at all, Lana".

To be honest, I didn't know if I should. Eli invited me over to his house, and here I was, deciding whether or not to throw a water balloon at him. Coming up with a decision, I walked over to the cooler and picked one up.

The twins flashed a bright smile, both showing dimples just like Eli. Eian headed towards me, and I smiled to pet him.

Abby rejoiced, "You are awesome, Lana! Okay, get ready."

"Why is he taking so long?" Aly scrunched his nose, becoming impatient.

"Probably putting some more makeup on or something, but whatever, he's going to get drenched!"

His little sisters were too funny — yet cruel at the same time.

I still had doubts, glancing down at the water filled balloon. "You two sure everything will be okay?"

The twins nodded.

And suddenly, the backyard door was sliding open.

This was it! Make your choice, Lana.

Hesitant, I waited for the perfect time. Eli looked completely oblivious as he stepped his foot outside. In fact, his attention looked preoccupied. There was even a faint grin stuck on his face.

Taking a deep breath, I decided to be spontaneous and threw the water balloon right at him. Whatever was going to happen next, I was going to go with it.

The three of us watched as the launched water balloon splattered all over Eli's clothing. I winced, hoping he wouldn't get mad. The horror of this backfiring wouldn't leave my mind.

Everything felt like it was happening in slow motion, and Eli definitely didn't see any of this coming. He blinked his eyes several times, taking the whole situation in. When it looked like he understood what was going on, his brown eyes soon glanced over our direction.

The twins were laughing loudly as they tossed their water balloons in hand up and down. An overjoyed Eian barked, circling around Eli. Seeing Eli's shocked and blank expression was amusing. I didn't know why I started laughing myself. This was too much, wasn't it? Eli eventually caught on that it was really me who threw it, and his lips pulled into a smile.

"I knew you guys were too scared to ask me first... that's why you did a surprise attack, huh?" His tone full of tease.

Eli was moving closer. His eyes searching for where we held the water balloons, I bet.

Abby motioned Aly to throw the balloons as she screamed, "It's on, Ellie! Show us what you got... if you have any! Lana, reload now! He's going to get the balloons!"

Within a blink of an eye, everything became madness.

Every second, a balloon would be launched — whether it'd be for us or Eli — that it became blinding. Shouts scattered all over the place as we ran around the Wesley's backyard. I hoped us girls wouldn't get submerged, but Eli, being the athletic guy he was, managed to grab as much as he could from the cooler and threw the balloons like no tomorrow. However, it was hilarious because Eian appeared to be on our side. The siberian husky would come out of nowhere and bite the water balloon causing it to pop already in Eli's hands.

Eli then looked at me briefly, as if he was cautious to throw one at me. I assumed there was one thing Eli was worried about. That I was one of those girls who were scared or would get mad if their hair got wet or clothes messed up, but I wasn't like them. Giving him a shrug, I saw this as an open opportunity to throw one right at him. I kept a challenging grin on.

"Eli, don't blank out! You're losing so far!"

The twins giggled at my words, running towards the back, and this reassured Eli that I didn't mind anything. I never pictured myself ever doing something like this, especially with Eli Wesley. My mind was too busy having fun. Eli let out a chuckle, his damp hair dripping and sticking against his forehead.

"I just wanted to make sure, princess."

"Right now I believe this princess is close to getting you completely drenched."

"Three against one? Is that even fair though?" He laughed.

"Ellie! Enough with the talking and stop showing off! This is war!" Abby roared.

The more we got into the "war", the more competitive my mindset became. A little competition never hurt though. Eli and his sisters were having the same amount of fun I was getting. Unfortunately, it only lasted minutes, and the amount of water balloons decreased dramatically. The twins managed to grab the last one and tossed it towards Eli yet he managed to dodge it. The last of it popped onto the lush, perfectly cut grass.

Everyone let out a huge breath, and we took in the mess we made. Random water puddles were all over the concrete, but it only took minutes before the summer sun dried it up. The worst of it were the broken balloon pieces that colored up the ground with all its various bright colors. When I looked at the damage we had on, our clothes had a few water spots, but not as bad as Eli's clothes. He looked like he hopped in the shower with clothes on.

Without even realizing it, Aly came towards my right and handed me a baby blue towel. She grinned. "You can use this. We totally dominated Ell."

Abby joined in. "We are the champions! Good job, Lana. You really impressed us back there."

Carefully wringing my hair dry as I sat down in the plastic chairs, the twins were doing the same. Their smiles were expressing so much joy, it was such a sweet sight to see. I gave them a friendly grin back.

"Thanks, you two. It was fun."

"Rematch. We definitely need a rematch." Eli's voice entered.

My eyes jumped off from the twins momentarily and found Eli walking towards us with Eian alongside him. Eli was rubbing his hair dry against his towel with a smirk on his face. The twins continued to mock their older brother, making me laugh along with them. Eli still had a grin on his face before he glanced down at his drenched clothes which stuck against his skin. I felt bad about the sabotage, but he didn't seem to mind.

What completely shocked me was when Eli turned sideways to pull his shirt off, revealing his body — like it was nothing!

His body. Exposed.

My eyes widened, and I immediately glanced the other direction.

I heard the twins teased.

"El, have you been getting lazy at the gym?"

"Look at your stomach, it's so flabby!"

What were they looking at though? From the millisecond I saw of Eli's exposed body, he appeared toned. Feeling my cheeks heat up, I focused on getting my hair dry until his sisters appeared close by my side.

Aly's eyes reached mine as she whispered, "Why are you turning red, Lana?"

"You're blushing, aren't you?" Abby squealed before she covered her mouth.

Hushing the girls, I quickly looked past their shoulders and hoped that Eli didn't hear anything. He was busily wringing his shirt dry by the pool. Eian was with him, and Eli splashed a little water from the pool at his dog. Eian let out a joyful bark before nearly tackling Eli, causing him to break out into laughter.

It was cute to see, and I was right about what I saw. Definitely had that tanned swimmer's body. The girls at my school weren't joking when I would overhear them talk about the "swim meets" which actually translated to "watching Eli".

The twins completely noticed when I gazed back at them. Abby and Aly had the most cunning smiles on their faces. How embarrassing was this getting? Abby gave me a wink before turning around to call her brother's attention.

"Hey El, we're going to get clothes. Any shirt sounds good for you?"

Eli's dark brown eyes landed on the twins, and he smiled crookedly. He stopped wringing his shirt to face us, but my eyes were stuck on the twins to avoid contact.

"That better not be a trick question. The last time I said yes, you two gave me a hot pink shirt."

Aly's voice played innocent. "We would never do such a thing like that."

Finding myself smiling at their interaction, the twins ended up agreeing to Eli's words and both skipped inside the house, bringing Eian with them.

Without having an excuse to look at something, I gradually set my attention to Eli and his exposed self. Eli must have noticed my uneasiness, and he ran his fingers through his hair from embarrassment as well. Definitely not helping, Eli.

"Sorry... swim got me use to it." Eli grabbed the nearby towel the twins left and placed it over his shoulders.

My brain also reminded me that we do live nearby a beach, it was normal to see shirtless guys. Why was it different with Eli? And was I that easy to read?

Blushing, I glanced away and lied, "No... it's not that."

He chuckled softly and changed the subject to save me from humiliation. "You were pretty good during the water fight."

"You too, champ."

"I still demand a rematch though," Eli teased.

"Anytime. But I'm positive that I'll win again."

We both laughed together. The comfort level between Eli and me was very surprising. I was able to joke around with him so freely. My clothes were attacked from water, my hair was probably a mess, yet it didn't bother me at all how I looked in front of him.

As the laughter subsided, I took a look at the backyard and suggested, "We should start picking up the mess, huh? I don't want your parents to get mad."

Eli saw the mess of popped water balloons and nodded with a smile on his face. "Sounds good. I bet the twins are taking a long time so they wouldn't have to clean up."

And, at least I wouldn't have to look at Eli.

Taking the spare black hair tie I always keep on my wrist, I pulled it out and tied my slightly dried hair into a bun. My clothes were pretty much close to drying since Eli didn't have much of a chance to cause as much damage as we three — including Eian — had done on him. The two of us went around the backyard and managed to clean up within minutes. As if nothing happened. I realized how quick this clean up was than expected.

"Hey, Lana."

Turning around, I stared Eli right in the eyes.

"Thanks for doing this with my sisters. I saw how happy they were." Eli smiled with his dimple showing.

I smiled back and confessed, "I thought you would be mad at first... but it was fun. I actually never did something like this before."

His dark brown eyes widened. "No way! Good thing you said yes then." He laughed. "Just kidding, I wouldn't get mad. Most girls wouldn't like things like this..."

"I guess they don't know what fun is then." I grinned, followed by a small shrug.

"El, please tell me the twins didn't do anything."

Following where that voice came from, our eyes found Mrs. Wesley by the backyard door. Her faint green eyes were filled with concern. Eli raised his eyebrows and I was just as confused.

"Mom, what do you mean?"

Mrs. Wesley let out a sheepish laugh, seeing the two of us okay. "The twins came into the house, completely soaked in water, and said they needed to get clothes for you all? I thought something serious happened. I mean, I heard a bunch of shouting, and your father and I just thought you all were just —"

"Mom, don't worry. We were having fun," Eli interrupted with a smile on his face.

I gazed at Mrs. Wesley with honest eyes and a reassuring smile.

She took in our expressions and nodded with relief. "I'm sorry. You know me. What exactly did happen though? The twins ran off before answering."

"Hey! What happened to the mess?"

Speaking of them, the twins came back. As Mrs. Wesley stepped forward to let them through, Abby and Aly were holding a stack of dried clothes in their arms. Aly frowned playfully.

"Aw man. We were going to blame Ell for the mess."

The twins giggled, and Eli groaned despite holding in a chuckle.

Mrs. Wesley was still puzzled about what exactly happened and assumed, "What mess? What did I say about jumping in the pool? You even bought Lana into this?"

Abby shook her head and corrected. Her lips lifting into a genuine smile. "Mom, we were just having a blast with our new friend, Lana. Thanks for letting us meet her, Ell."

Chapter 15

You know the feeling when everything just felt great?

Yeah that.

I was having that feeling this very moment.

My family loved meeting Lana. Coops and Preston both knew about Lana all along, while I was "playing a game with denial" — according to Preston. The plan to get Haley Jones back was officially dropped and forgotten between us three. So much could change within a month.

Weeks ago, I was a bitter person. Well, that was done and over with.

"El, you just going to stand there grinning and not tell your old man why?"

Snapping out of it, I dropped my grin and gave my undivided attention back to Dad. We were both outside by the drive way this morning, changing the oil of my car. Noticing the wondering expression on Dad's face, I shook my head and reassured him that I just remembered something funny. Dad shrugged and continued on with the process. Ever since I was crawling, Dad taught me just about everything when it comes to cars.

Even though I could change the oil myself, Dad always insisted to help. He would always say this was the only opportunity to have some "father and son" bonding time. It made me feel guilty whenever he joked about it. Wiping my hands with the cloth, I wanted to hear his opinion since we were close.

"Dad, how do you know when a girl is the one for you? When you know it's real?"

"El, how old are you again?" His voice almost joking. I didn't get to see his expression since he was busy attending the car.

"Nineteen." I laughed. "Come on, Dad. My birthday was in January... it wasn't that long ago."

Dad joined my laughter, revealing an entertained expression from my question. He shook his head. "Of course I wouldn't forget my boy's birthday. My point is, you're still young. You're acting like tomorrow is the last day you'll experience love."

"I know that, but there's a huge difference between liking and loving a girl. How will I know?"

"Hand me the container right there, Ell."

After handing it to him, it took a few minutes before Dad turned his attention to me. Dad wiped his forehead using his forearm.

"To be honest, there's really no direct explanation to feeling love. You'll just know, son." He continued, "For example, when I first met your mother, my world made a complete 360. She was the only girl I saw in my eyes. Every other girl were nothing but blobs... Now El, don't give me that look."

Dad was referring to my wrinkled nose, hearing him talk cheesy.

He chuckled before his dark brown eyes seemed to be drifting off. "Loving a girl is when the looks that attracted you are no longer there. What matters to you and what makes your heart yearn for her are her inner qualities. To love someone is when you're willing to do anything and no matter what, you two will make it through the ups and downs in life. Remember, love isn't meant to be perfect. People say love is a complete fairytale, but they are wrong. What makes love real are those bumps in the road — the trials of life."

"If I want to make a girl happy all the time... does that mean I actually love her?" I was still unsure.

Shaking his head, Dad pointed out, "That's different, Ell. Love isn't about mending a broken soul — it's when two souls become one."

"Wow, Dad. You sure you weren't Aristotle in your past life?"

We shared another laugh. Once the laughter died out, I let out a sigh.

"I don't think that's the case, Dad. I don't feel that way because I feel sorry for her. Being with her makes me happy, and I want to be able to make her feel that way too. When I'm with her, I don't have a care for the world because that's how comfortable I feel around her."

"Hm, I think you just answered your own question then, Ell." He then smiled. "The girl you're talking about... it's Lana Clarke, right?"

Glancing back at Dad, he had the look of knowledge on, and I nodded my head sheepishly.

He then placed his hand on my shoulder and encouraged, "She's a great girl, Ell. There's something genuine in Lana that your mother and I both like. I know your relationship with her will go a long way."

My eyes widened, realizing that Dad got it wrong. "Oh, we're not together, Dad."

Immediately, disbelief scattered across Dad's aged face. He let out a short laugh. "You're kidding me! What are you thinking, son?"

Giving him a grin, I didn't really know how to respond to that.

"What if... I made a mistake though?" I reminded myself.

That nothing-can-ruin-this-day feeling was gone. Ignorance was bliss sometimes. I've been too happy to even look deeper at the possibilities if Lana ever figures out about me and Haley's past. Haley suspected what I planned to do before everything changed. Even though Haley said she wouldn't tell, I wouldn't rely on it. My question caused confusion towards Dad.

"Mistake? What do you mean, Ell?"

I gazed off, staring at Mom's growing flower garden from the front lawn."It's nothing. Forget what I just said."

Dad still spoke up, "Whatever this mistake may be, I trust you will figure out a way to fix it. That's the Elliot Wesley I know."

I knew talking with Dad would help me a bit. His words made me more confident. I wanted to be with Lana — more than anything — but because of my past with Haley and that stupid plan, it seemed like we couldn't be together.

"Eli, just be yourself around Lana. That's all to it!" Preston advised as he scanned the aisle of our nearest party supply store.

Here we were, shopping.

This was something I never expected to do with Coops and Preston — ever.

After getting a text from Olette earlier today, it was a shopping list to get a few things for Lana's surprise party.The guys were down to help out for her birthday. When it comes to surprises, they'll be first in line. Of course, this wasn't a prank of some sort, but it was along a similar outline.

I couldn't believe when Olette told me that Lana never wanted to celebrate her birthday. I thought this was something all girls look forward to. Lana deserved a celebration, and I was happy that Olette asked me to be a part of it. Her birthday was just a week away, and Lana wasn't expecting a single thing since. I looked at the list on my cellphone screen and right back up at the guys.

Finally, I answered, "I have been. The thing is, Haley was suspicious about the entire thing with Lana. What if she tells Lana? What will do then?"

Preston tossed a bag of streamers into the cart. "It's not entirely true though. You do like Lana, that's why you were with her. Look, did you think Landon ever knew that Haley was dating you before breaking it off? Think about it, Eli... she was fooling around with Landon!"

"So, Haley and I are practically the same, huh?" My eyes fell to the floor, hearing Preston's explanation.

"Not helping, Preston." Coops jumped in before he landed his hazel eyes at me.

Coops then nudged my side. "Eli, you're not like Haley. You never did follow through with the plan. Yes, you did ask Lana out because of wrong intentions at first, but you grew to like her in the end. We saw it coming — heck, even Haley noticed it too. Haley's happy with Landon and she told you that she's moved on. She's not going to say anything. No one's going to speak up about it. You need to stop worrying and focus on Lana and her upcoming birthday."

"Yeah! That's what I meant to say!" Preston nodded in agreement. "It just didn't come out right."

"Uh huh. Right." Coops made us laugh.

Coops' words were reassuring which made me finally let the thought go right now. He was right after all. I shouldn't worry about Haley spilling the beans. Instead, I needed to focus on Lana. Everything would be okay. There were only a few more things left to get. As I glanced up, I overheard Coops and Preston ranting to one another.

"You see that girl right there? Talk about looking her best." Coops murmured sarcastically.

Preston was chuckling. "For real. I don't understand why girls have to dress up to go to a store. This isn't the place to be picking up guys. Look at the girl right next to her. She's just wearing a shirt and shorts, and she's looking good!"

"Well, most girls don't realize it," Coops stated a matter of fact.

Figures. They would be checking out girls.

When I pushed the cart closer to them, I took a look at whoever they were observing. The girls were a blonde and a brunette. The blonde was wearing a pink haltered dress with nude heels and had her hair curled. On the other hand, the brunette looked comfortable with a t-shirt and shorts with flip flops on. Even if their faces weren't visible, the guys were right. Sometimes, girls who didn't even try could outshine those who actually do.

The more I unconsciously stared, the more the t-shirt the brunette was wearing looked familiar — I just couldn't pinpoint where exactly. Suddenly, I heard Preston gasped, but I didn't think any of it.

As the two girls turned to face each other, their side profiles revealed Lana and Haley.

"That's Lana." I said it like reading a book out loud.

It was that moment where my mind was obviously not working at the time.

Preston and Coops gave me the weirdest stare.

My eyes widened and realization hit me — that's why Preston gasped.

"Oh crap. It's Lana! What are we going to do?"

What were they doing here?

Preston did an air clap. "Wonderful observation, Captain Obvious."

Giving them a glare, they stifled their laughs before motioning to quiet down. We huddled around each other, facing the opposite direction. Maybe they would walk the other way, and we wouldn't have to bump into them. Talk about coincidence! Olette chose the wrong time to make us do the shopping. The three of us gazed at each other with frantic expressions.

Coops quickly whispered instructions, "I'll buy the stuff and wait in the parking lot. Stall them, okay? Since Preston's such a good actor, he'll stay with you."

We nodded.

"Aw man, sorry dude. We were checking out Lana." Preston groaned, disregarding the fact Coops complimented him.

Shaking my head, now wasn't the time. I gave Coops the nod, indicating it was go time. "It's fine, Preston. You weren't exactly checking her out anyways. Okay, we'll meet you then."

Coops grinned, pushing the cart the other way. "Turn around when I'm gone. See ya."

As Coops was heading down the aisle, my heart pounded wondering what exactly was happening behind me. Was Lana and Haley still there? Did they see us? Once Preston caught my eyes, he mouthed to follow him.

Nodding back in response, Preston then reached for his front pocket and magically pulled out a piece of paper. The wonders of Preston Daniels. As Preston "read" the paper, he then searched around the aisle before sighing.

"Nothing we need here. Come on, bro." Preston waved his hand to motion we move along.

"Eli?"

We slowly turned around in unison, and right before our very eyes were Lana... and Haley.

Gulping down at first, I immediately focused my attention on Lana. No way did I want to make eye contact with Haley. Lana's ocean blue eyes widened. She was just as surprised as we were. Giving Lana a grin, she happily smiled, seeing some kind of reply from me. I loved how she looked completely comfortable. Her casual style made her effortlessly stand out. And that shirt she was wearing? It was our senior shirt with the whole graduating class' names in the back. That's why it looked so familiar.

My eyes unintentionally jumped over to Haley. Moments ago, Coops and Preston were comparing the two. How awkward was that? Haley's eyes were wide from surprise before her lips fell into a frown. This wasn't going to be good.

Preston, being him, was as casual as could be. "Hey Lana! It's good to see you!"

Did he forget to mention Haley on purpose?

"What brings you two here?" Haley suddenly coughed out.

Preston and I glanced at one another, and we both knew he pissed off Haley for not acknowledging her. Gazing back at the girls, Preston took the lead.

"Just finishing up a list for my mom. Eli here decided to help me."

Haley looked completely unconvinced while Lana gazed around the aisle. Her long brown hair was tied into a pony tail, and it whipped from side to side.

"Celebrating something?" Lana asked.

As I was about to comment on that, a sudden "there you guys are!" appeared.

Wasn't this situation getting better and better?

The girls turned around to — who I knew — was Landon. Preston got a peek on the incoming figure and gave me the complete "we are done for" look. I returned with a stern "we got this" expression.

Landon was wearing his lifeguard attire, and he cracked a smile once he caught sight of us. Who knew I would be cool with the guy whom I so called declared "despised"? Waving shortly at Landon, he eventually reached his sister and girlfriend.

After introducing Preston to him, Landon grinned.

"You guys planning to throw a summer party or something?"

"Preston's mom sent him out shopping... at a party store." Haley mumbled under breath.

Preston guffawed. "Oh Haley... Haley Jones, you are such a funny girl! Who says my mom can't party? She's quite the party animal... maybe that's where I got it from."

I seriously wanted to slap my forehead at that moment.

There were entertained expressions that grew on Lana and Landon's faces until they started to laugh full on. Haley narrowed her eyes momentarily for Preston and me to see before she forced out a giggle.

Landon had a smirk on his face. "Speaking of parties... shouldn't we be preparing for yours, Lana?"

"We are not having a party, Landon." She abruptly reminded as her eyes grew cautious.

Preston continued to act oblivious. "Party? Is it almost your birthday, Lana?"

Lana's cheeks turned a light shade of red before she nodded. "In a couple of days... but, don't listen to Landon."

"Hey, that's something worth talking about. You have anything planned?" I followed Preston and his naive tone.

Lana smiled and shook her head in response. "It's just a birthday, Eli. It's something I'll always have."

Why did she act like it wasn't a big deal? Once I took in her last words more thoroughly, my stomach twisted. I caught on what she meant by that. Landon gave his younger sister a small pout. We ended up going along with it, laughing at his insistence. I was unsure if Landon knew about the surprise party though.

As this was all happening, the corner of my eyes caught Haley deeply observing Preston and me. She was probably trying to figure it all out, but with the rate this was going, Preston was doing a good job with the distractions.

Preston lightly suggested with a wink, "Let us know if you change your mind about that, Lana. So... what brings you three here?"

Lana giggled through a bashful expression. "Haley needed to return something she bought here from her party. Landon took care of it, so Haley and I were just looking around which brings us here."

"Almost as if we were supposed to bump into each other..." Haley continued to mutter again.

My body tensed up hearing that.

Landon gave his girlfriend a funny look before Lana spoke up, "Not a bad thing though. It's kind of funny that we always manage to bump into each other."

"Well, I don't ever mind seeing you, Lana." Preston stated with a sideways grin.

If there was one person good at pushing someone's buttons, it would be Preston. Haley looked like she was about to blow up any minute.

"Shouldn't someone else be saying that?" Landon coughed.

Preston grew a sly grin and immediately agreed with Lana's brother. I knew Landon was referring to me. Both shared a chuckle with each other as Preston nudged my side and even wiggled his eyebrows — way to make it obvious.

A flushed look appeared on Lana's face, and I felt myself heating up too. Lana threw a playful glare at Landon for embarrassing us. Preston was going to get it later. Despite the joking atmosphere we all had, Haley was at the end. She was almost scowling at the fact we were having a good time without her.

"We should get going, right?" Haley interrupted.

The Clarke siblings went to seek their attention back to Haley. Landon appeared concerned at his girlfriend's unsteadiness.

"Is something wrong?"

I gulped down, not anticipating what she was going to say.

Haley made sure I was watching and placed her hand over Landon's chest lovingly. She shook her head.

"It's nothing, honey. It's just... we don't want to keep your dad waiting, right?"

A saddened look spread across Lana's face. "You're right. We should get going... Sorry guys."

Preston complained in a low enough tone for only me to hear. "Way to kill the mood, Haley."

Giving them an understanding nod, I ran a hand through my hair. "No, it's cool. We should get going with that list, right Preston?" I grinned. "It was nice seeing you."

Lana specifically.

Haley soon wrapped her arm around Landon's and motioned that they should go on first. If she was trying to prove something, it definitely wasn't working. It was actually good that she wanted to leave. The look on Landon's face seemed slightly annoyed, but he went with his girlfriend's request. Preston greeted only Landon a "see you later", but he eventually added Haley's name when it looked like her nails were about ready to dig into his skin.

I played it cool. "You never told me your birthday was coming up."

We've been talking a lot throughout the week, and I thought Lana would bring it up, but she never did. If Landon never mentioned it or if Olette never told me, would I have ever known?

"Um... I don't really like people knowing." She admitted with guilty eyes.

Preston playfully placed his arm around my shoulder. "Eli's just trying to tell you that he wants to spend that wonderful day with you."

I tried move away from his grasp, but Lana laughed at the sight. She blushed before mentioning that she was working that day.

Lana immediately changed the subject, "I should get going now. They're probably waiting. I'll see you two around."

As we nodded our heads, I could only picture the look on Lana's face when the surprise party happens. Even if she didn't want to celebrate it, I had a feeling the party would make her day.

Before walking off to find Landon and Haley, she looked over her shoulder one last time before sharing a smile with me. We watched until Lana turned around the corner. Once that moment happened, Preston and I let out a sigh of relief.

Mission success!

Preston made a gagging face. "I wanted to throw up when Haley was all like..." He changed his voice to match Haley's. "It's nothing, honey."

Trying to stop my laughter, it killed me every time Preston would copy Haley. As perfect and similar it was, it could be pretty scary at the same time. I quickly suggested that we get out of here to meet with Coops. He was probably wondering what happened to us.

Exiting out the store, we walked towards the parking lot and found Coops leaning against his car. He was searching around the lot until his eyes spotted us.

As we headed over, Coops commented through a smirk, "Took you long enough."

Preston mentioned, "Hey, you didn't have to deal with Haley. Okay?"

"True enough."

Pulling out my phone, we hopped into Coops' car while I dialed Olette's number. She wanted to meet up once we were finished. After a few rings, she picked up.

"Hey, we got the things and guess what? Lana happened to be there."

Olette gasped. "No way! Tell me she didn't find out... tell me she didn't!"

"Nope, we pulled it off."

The guys and I all smiled as Coops pulled out of the parking space.

"Oh, good. I knew I could rely on you guys."

"I'm just glad Landon and Haley didn't figure it out too."

That was way too close.

"Well, I'm planning to tell Landon... Haley was there too?"

I blinked, catching her bothered tone. "Yeah. You don't sound too happy about that?"

"Who says? I was just asking, Eli!" Olette became defensive from the other line. "Besides, it's not like I care or anything."

Laughing a bit from her mumbling at the end, I wondered, "Wait a sec, something's up."

She sighed. "Don't tell... but I really don't like her."

Olette doesn't like Haley? I couldn't remember Haley associating with Olette before. All these questions spurred around my mind, but all I really needed to do was just ask.

"I won't." I promised. "Is there a reason why though?"

"I can't tell you, Eli. It's a little personal."

Respecting her words, I was suspicious into thinking that it had more to do with Haley's relationship with Landon.

Shifting topics, I asked. "So, where exactly do you want to meet up?"

"At my place, we have to talk about what we're going to do."

Chapter 16

This birthday was much different from my past ones. More specifically, I dreamt of Mom.

The dream was so vivid that it seemed authentic. In my dream, Mom actually stood there in front of me and greeted me a happy birthday. I cried and told her how happy I was that she was alive. When she stroked my cheek, the warmness from her hand still resided. That was how real it felt.

There was something Mom was trying to tell me that I couldn't figure out. Her mouth would move, but no sound would come out. Her face looked bothered, but she tried to put a smile on. My reaction to that was hard to tell from the dream's perspective, but I felt confused. There was an urge to say, "Please speak up, Mom", but the only words that I did hear from her the moment I woke up was, "Never forget how much I love you".

The moment I opened my eyes, I felt my pillow was damp from tears. Instantly, I reached for my eyes and realized they were soak. It has been years since I cried in my sleep. Heading to my bathroom, I washed up and took a deep breath.

Then, it hit me.

Today was my birthday.

Usually people would be happy, ready to hop out of bed and anticipate what lies ahead. Why did I felt the complete opposite? Those moments I spent with Mom filled me with happiness, but disappointment was all that I felt after, reminding myself that it was only a dream. I didn't like this bittersweet feeling.

Shaking my head, I was going to enjoy today — like any other day.

I just wish I knew what you were trying to tell me, Mom.

Sitting back onto my bed, I reached for the reason of my sudden awakening. My cellphone. There was a missed call from Olette, and I saw that I received multiple text messages. My heart suddenly raced at the sight of Eli's name from the inbox. He sent me a message right on midnight.

12:00 A.M. Eli - Happy birthday, Lana! I didn't know whether to call, but you're probably asleep right now. I hope you have a great day! I know you said that celebrations aren't a big deal, but just know that today is worth being extra happy about. Don't overwork yourself today. Happy birthday again!

It was that moment where your cheeks immediately heat up. Reading the last few lines of Eli's text caused me to fight a smile. Making a mental note to thank Eli, it was only then my phone started to ring with Olette's name flashing on the screen. Picking it up, I was soon flooded with Olette's variations of "happy birthday".

Thanking and laughing from her unique greeting, my best friend wished me a wonderful day before we hung up. I'm glad Olette didn't have a clue that I would end work early today — she would have insisted on a silly celebration.

My family must have heard that I have awaken because two knocks were made on my bedroom door. I called in whoever to come in. Right before my eyes, Dad and Landon came barging in. Okay, maybe not barging in, but their excitement for today was overwhelming. My mouth dropped seeing Dad carry in a tray of who-knows-what while Landon carried a small birthday sign.

As they moved closer, they sang the happy birthday song, and I saw a candle on that tray of who-knows-what. There was me just sitting in bed, watching my wonderful dad and older brother greet me a happy birthday. You could only imagine my shocked expression, even though I should have expected something like this. Dad settled the tray onto my bed and it was a waffle.

I held in my laughter. It was Landon's infamous "birthday waffle".

According to my brother, it was not your typical waffle because it was covered with a mountain of whipped cream and strawberries along with a candle on top. There was a huge difference.

"Happy birthday, our Lana! Happy birthday to you!" They clapped and sang.

Giving them a thankful smile, I closed my eyes momentarily and made a quick wish. Once the candle was blown out, Dad and Landon both threw their hands up in the air. Carefully getting out of bed, I hugged them tightly in an instance.

Dad kissed me on the forehead. "Another year older, you've grown beautifully Lana. I really wished you didn't have to spend your day at another party."

As I pulled away from the hug, I looked at them with grateful eyes. "Thank you, Dad, Landon. I appreciate it. You didn't have to wake up so early."

Landon interrupted me from continuing on, "Lana, we did this because we wanted to. It's your birthday and you're working! You have to start the day on a happy note."

I did dream of Mom; that already made my day.

I shook my head. "It's what I love to do though, but thank you both. Dad, you should be getting some rest and here you are making me breakfast."

In the end, Dad gave me his usual 'everything is fine' look and motioned that it wasn't a problem.

Dad soon added, "This isn't your real birthday cake, but Landon insisted on making you his waffle cake or something."

Grinning, I complimented, "This is perfect. We don't need a cake."

However, Landon pleaded, "Just a real cake between us, okay? When you get home from work."

Looking at the two, they really did want an actual cake, so I sighed and gave in with a nod. After finishing the waffle, Dad and Landon let me go to get ready for work. After taking a shower and getting prepared for the day, I honestly didn't feel any different. Has it really been a year? The more I thought about it, time has been flying by.

Ready to head out, Dad and Landon greeted me one last happy birthday before I drove out of the garage. Today was going great so far. Nothing extravagant, just the way I liked it.

However, the first thing to happen when I walked through the doors of my work was —

"Happy birthday, Princess Lana!"

Suddenly, I was showered by confetti, and my ears took in the sounds of party poppers.

Blinking my eyes, I took in my surroundings and found Maryann, along with my four coworkers. They were filled with smiles and huddled around to give me one big hug. Letting out a surprised laugh, I thanked each of them.

My raven haired coworker, Remy, and blonde coworker, Pauline, handed me three gift bags. My cheeks flushed as I insisted that they shouldn't have. Instead, Remy and Pauline shook their heads and shoved the bags towards me with excited smiles on. Giving them a grateful hug, Maryann and my fellow brunettes, Josie and Quinn, followed after with a small chocolate cake.

All five of them started singing "Happy birthday" as I watched in amazement. Everyone was so kind to me. It bothered me at the same time because I knew Josie and Pauline weren't working today yet they still took the time to come and celebrate. As soon as they were done, I immediately blew out the candle, and the girls let out screams of joy.

Sharing the cake — even if it was a little too early in the morning — we gathered around the reception area. I couldn't help but feel gratitude towards them. Every year, they would do a celebration, but it seemed to be getting bigger as the years go by. Last year, I made sure they knew that presents weren't ever needed, but looked like no one got the message.

That was when they urged me to open the presents. Hesitation hit me because of all the attention, but I went along with it after seeing their excited expressions. Opening each one, I was shocked to find what was inside.

My eyes grew when I unwrapped the familiar boxing of Maryann's gift. Leave it to Maryann to remember my favorite perfume in the whole world. Daisy by Marc Jacobs.

Lifting it up, I beamed, "You got me this!"

Maryann winked. "I'm going to take that as a thank you."

Our circle of six laughed and I soon opened the gift bag from Remy and Josie. Taking out the tissue paper, I pulled out a navy blue, polka-dot, strapless dress. The dress could be worn formal or casual and wasn't too girly for my taste. Remy and Josie were very fashionable and high-end shoppers, so getting a dress from them would make my closet a little happier.

The next present was from Pauline and Quinn and they gave me something I've wanted for a while — just never thought they knew.

My eyes widened for the third time. "The camera!"

It was a white tiny instant polaroid camera. There was this one time we went shopping, and I caught sight of this particular camera. They must have noticed me staring at it. The two giggled before Remy and Josie joined along.

"Which brings us to part two of our present!" Josie grinned brightly.

Bringing the box down to my lap, I tilted my head. "Part two?"

Remy nodded before taking out a wrapped box from her leather purse. A little taken back from the excess present, I carefully opened it and found five containers of film refills for the camera. Gazing back at them in awe, I threw on a grateful smile before getting up from the chair to give them all a hug in thanks.

Pauline explained, cheerful like always, "We knew how much you wanted these things. It's the least we can do for our favorite princess!"

Hugs and thank you's wouldn't be enough to show how blessed I was to be surrounded by people like them. Unfortunately, the celebration only lasted half an hour since I had to get ready for the first party. It was all good laughs and smiles, but there were parties that needed to attend to. Thanking my coworkers for all coming by to celebrate, it was only then I magically transformed into Cinderella and headed off to party number one.

Luckily, the day seemed to be in my favor. The parties all ran smoothly, and everyone looked happy throughout. No cranky kids and the parents were all filled with relief. My last party of the day was being Belle. It surprised me how fast these parties came and went.

"Thank you, Princess Belle!" The seven year old, Sarah, shouted with glee.

As I waved her a goodbye, I wasn't expecting the birthday girl to run over and hug me. Her little arms wrapped around my huge dress so I knelt down to hug her back. Her parents soon got over and apologized for her chasing me, but it was absolutely adorable. That was all I needed for me to enjoy my birthday or any day — seeing all the young celebrant's smiles stretch miles with happiness. When little Sarah was taken back to her party, I headed over to my car and called it a day.

What sounded good was a nice, long rest, but I remembered how Dad and Landon insisted to have cake when I got home.

Parking by the curb of A Fairytale Come True, I changed back into my regular attire even though Maryann acted a little odd. She suggested that I try on my new dress from Josie and Remy. Though I told her that I was only going home, Maryann pleaded to see me in that dress. Giving her a look, I went back into the dressing room anyways to try it on. Maryann and her influence.

Glancing at myself in the mirror, the dress was a perfect fit, and I loved the sweetheart neckline.

"Can I see the dress?" Maryann hollered from the outside.

Laughing quietly, I stepped out of the dressing room to show her. She clapped her hands and complimented the dress. However, before I could head back to the dressing room, she rushed inside and grabbed my clothes.

My mouth formed into an O. "Hey! My clothes!"

She waved my shorts and shirt. "You look so pretty, Lana! The dress needs to stay on. I'll keep hold onto these."

Not believing this, I asked why, but she gave me a little shrug and pleaded me to keep the dress on. Well, I was only going to go home. Nodding along, I gave her a small smile. Our receptionist's expression was the perfect example of ultimate joy. As I was about to head out, I thanked Maryann again for the present while she greeted me one last happy birthday.

Maryann blew me a kiss. "Enjoy the rest of the day!"

Once I made it to my house, I still needed to thank Eli for the birthday greeting. He probably thought I've been ignoring him this whole day!

Growing guilty, I pulled out my phone as I walked into my house. It really didn't alert me that the house was quiet and dark at this time. Dialing Eli's number, I let the phone ring as I walked around the first floor of my house. Where were they? The phone continued to ring, but my attention was taken away when I noticed lights coming from the backyard.

Curiosity got the best of me, so I followed the light source. As the phone continued to ring, I wondered why Eli didn't pick up, but once I opened the sliding door of my backyard, my heart jumped out from the sound of —

"Happy birthday, Lana!"

My once bare backyard was now decorated with party streamers, balloons, and icicle lights to light up the place. A huge sign was hung between two trees and there was a table with a two tier cake on top. It was absolutely beautiful. What surprised me most was seeing everyone — Dad, Landon, Olette, Preston, Julian, and Eli all there.

This had to be a dream.

Was I still dreaming?

They all noticed how surprised I was, and Dad approached me to bring me closer to the group. Pushing the end button on my cellphone, I dropped my phone to my side as Dad held his hand out to me. He smiled once I took his hand and I walked over to everyone, completely speechless. This surprise party was for me?

Olette and Landon got to me first, and the two had such mischievous grins on. Olette giggled while I still had a look of disbelief across of my face.

"Surprised, aren't you? I couldn't go another year not celebrating my best friend's birthday. You deserve this! Happy birthday!" Olette chimed before she hugged me.

Feeling my eyes water up as my best friend held me, I returned the hug before she moved off to the side for Landon. My older brother looked down at me and grinned warmly. He reached to wipe the few tears that have fallen.

"So... I kinda lied. You forgive me?" He followed with a chuckle.

Playfully sticking my tongue out, I nodded before giving him a hug as well. Today was definitely filled with surprises, and the shock eventually subsided. After Landon and Olette, Preston and Julian came towards me. Eli's close friends were here. They grinned from ear to ear.

Preston rejoiced, "Oh man, you looked so surprised! Best surprise I've ever done. Happy birthday, Lana!"

"Hope you don't mind us celebrating with you. Happy birthday!" Julian added through a grin.

Shaking my head, I beamed, "Thank you guys, I was definitely surprised. Thanks for being here."

Preston and Julian opened their arms, and I gave them a hug. My stomach soon fluttered at the sight of Eli. He was waiting patiently at the end and smiled with that dimple on his face. I noticed Preston and Julian gave their best friend a grin before walking off to join Landon and Olette.

Eli came towards me, and his dark brown eyes stared deeply into mine. I immediately blushed. It was a chilly night, so the heat coming from my cheeks weren't normal with this kind of weather.

I gave him a sheepish smile. "Eli, I-I really didn't expect any of this."

Eli chuckled lightly, before having his arms out. "Happy birthday, Lana."

For the first time, I found myself in Eli Wesley's arms, and the warmth scattered. My heart wouldn't get a hold of itself. I wasn't sure what to make out of it.

Before I knew it, I was still trying to take in everything and closed my eyes. Once I opened them, I wasn't in Eli's arms anymore, but everyone was around me, still there. This wasn't a dream then. My family and friends were all smiling until Preston announced that it was "party time". Dad was highly amused by Preston's enthusiasm.

Landon lit my birthday cake with nineteen candles. I couldn't believe I was already nineteen. Olette linked her arm around mine and pulled me closer to the table. As everyone gathered around, I was hearing the birthday song once more as everyone sang. Mom, I'm glad to be around wonderful people like them. When everyone hit the final note, Eli and his friends started waving their arms around and that signaled me to make a wish.

I would tell you what I wished for, but maybe it wouldn't come true.

One by one, the flames on the candles disappeared leaving a low lit ambiance once again. All of us clapped and I could feel my lips stretching into a big smile.

After cutting the cake, I gasped when I saw that it was white cake with strawberry filling. My favorite cake ever. Looking up at Olette, she gave me a little wink, and it was no surprise my best friend knew. Handing out a piece for everyone, the surprise party was all smiles and laughs, and I managed to get a little side talk with everyone.

As I sat with my best friend, I wondered, "How did you plan this?"

A sly grin appeared on Olette's heart shaped lips. "You shouldn't under-estimate Olette Benson!" She giggled. "Okay, I asked Maryann to tell me your schedule since I knew you weren't going to tell me."

That's why Maryann was persistent about wearing this dress! She want-ed me to look nice for the surprise.

We laughed, and I gave her a tight hug. "Thank you Olette."

I felt Olette shaking her head. "Don't thank me. You always told me you didn't want a party, so a surprise party was my only choice! It wasn't all me though, Eli and everybody helped."

Glancing around, I saw Dad talking with Eli and his friends. I felt my-self smiling, seeing how Dad enjoyed their company. Whatever they were talking about, it looked a little serious before all four of them broke into laughter. My eyes soon travelled over to Landon, who locked eye contact with me. He chuckled before walking over to us.

When he reached us, I couldn't help but notice. "I'm kind of surprised to not see you with Haley."

The blue in Landon's eyes seemed to haze a little. Was something wrong? As I studied my brother's face, he must have noticed and quickly shifted his expression. His eyes glanced from Olette to me before giving me a faint grin.

"It's your day, Lana. Having fun so far?"

I nodded. "Yeah, you guys really know how to surprise. Thanks for all of this."

Landon smirked. "We knew you'd go along with this surprise, so really, the pleasure is all ours. Now go have some fun!"

The three of us laughed before I remembered the present my coworkers got me. Getting my purse that was laid onto the table, I pulled the camera out of the box. Olette's hazel eyes grew in excitement and asked what it was. Landon knew and was amazed by the fact my coworkers bought me this. Taking the camera out, I placed film in and smiled.

"I want to remember this moment. Let's all take pictures?"

All of a sudden, we heard a, "Did someone say picture?"

It was Preston, of course.

And that started the picture taking. The tiny polaroid spat out all sorts of pictures we took. These polaroids were credit card size, so they were portable and adorable. Taking pictures with everyone, from group to in-dividual, was a blast.

These weeks of summer have been so much fun, and I was glad I finally caught some of those memories on camera. Showing Dad the picture of him and me together, he was completely astonished and pointed out the kind of polaroid he had back in the day.

He grinned at me. "At least it was my good side."

Dad never failed to make me laugh.

The small get together was slowly reaching an end, and it was almost midnigh.! This was probably one of the best birthdays I've had. The company, the surprise, just everything about it. Everyone all helped clean up the small party, and we were now standing outside the front of the house.

Preston and Julian were the first to head off. Before leaving, the two teased how they wished today was longer. They approached Dad, and I watched them do — what I guess was — a unique handshake with him. It was a guy thing, I guessed. Dad laughed, being bought into the world of teenagers once again. Preston and Julian gave me one last hug and greeted everyone else a good night. We all returned by wishing them a safe drive home.

Olette then announced happily, "I think I'm going to get some more cake. Would you like to join me, Mr. Clarke? Landon?"

"Sounds like a great idea." Dad smiled.

I frowned a little. "Dad, you shouldn't eat too much sweets."

However, Landon sided with Dad. "Aw Lana, don't worry about Dad. He has a high tolerance for sugar. And I'll take that offer, Olette."

As the three headed back inside the house, Eli and I were left together.

Looking at him, there was an amused expression lying on Eli's face before he noticed my gazing. His brown eyes blinked away before I offered if he wanted to come join inside. I wondered why Olette didn't invite Eli. Or even me.

In response, Eli ran a hand through his hair before he stuck both hands into his pockets. It was the first time I've seen extreme signs of nervousness.

"Did you have fun, Lana?"

Fun would be an understatement.

I smiled. "Of course, thank you again for being here."

"I'm glad I got to celebrate with you... I actually have a present for you," Eli soon revealed.

My heart skipped a beat. I repeated. "A present?"

I wasn't sure why I was acting like a complete space cadet at the time. Eli then reached for his back pocket and pulled out a small, rectangular velvet box. It looked like a jewelry box. My stomach started to tie itself into knots as I wondered what it could possibly be. There was a pleasant grin on Eli's face, and I watched him slowly open the box to reveal yet another wonderful surprise.

That locket.

Just like Mom's.

Gasping, I placed my hand over my mouth. Speechless. That was what I was. Seeing the necklace bought me back to the time Eli and I went to that store together. I couldn't believe Eli got me the locket! My eyes gradually made their way back up at Eli, and his dark brown eyes were twinkling from the moon light.

"I remember you telling me that this locket reminded you of your mom's. I wanted to get you something that will bring you closer to her somehow." Eli gulped down, his eyes were concerned that he made a mistake. "Do you like it?"

When I finally got a hold of myself, the only response was this sudden rush from my face. Eli was so considerate and his words were dancing around my mind.

He wanted to bring me closer to you, Mom.

Realizing that my silence was worrying him, I gave Eli a huge smile and nodded my head several times in thanks.

"Eli, this — you — I love it. Thank you," I managed to jumble out.

A content expression spread across Eli's face and he smiled, revealing that dimple. He offered kindly, "Here. Let me put it on for you."

Hesitant at first, my body ended up turning around for me. Goosebumps ran over me as Eli gently pushed my hair over my shoulder. Within seconds, the cold white gold touched my skin, and I immediately gazed down to observe the beauty of the locket. My heart raced, and it felt like it wouldn't stop beating this fast any time soon. I wasn't sure why I was feeling this way towards Eli. He has been a wonderful friend, but the more I was around him, the more my feelings would confuse me.

I eventually summoned enough courage to share eye contact with Eli again. My body froze when I watched him carefully move my hair back since it was covering me. I couldn't stop myself from blushing, but I couldn't blink away. Eli smiled warmly at me.

"You're absolutely beautiful, Lana. Happy birthday."

A part of me wanted to do something more, but whatever this feeling was, I was happy with it. I couldn't have asked for a better birthday.

Chapter 17

"Is it possible to over swim?"

I managed to hear Preston as I swam laps around my pool. The feeling of refreshment ran through me. Reaching the end, I pushed myself back up and ran a hand through my face. I blinked, only to find Coops and Preston floating in the middle with astonished eyes. They realized it was my "no mercy" swimming and gave up.

Coops cracked a grin. "I thought we were just swimming, not training for the Olympics."

Preston joked along. "The last time he swam like that was when he couldn't figure out the concepts of limits during Calculus."

As the two of them laughed, I rolled my eyes before joining in.

Taking a break, I got out and grabbed my towel. They followed after and we sat around the chairs on this typical summer day. I had the house today since Mom and the twins took Eian to the groomer's while Dad was at work. Rubbing my hair with the towel, I scoffed a laugh.

"Thanks for bringing up that nightmare."

"Something wrong?" Coops wondered.

I shrugged, tossing the towel to the side. "Nope. Just wanted to take a swim."

"I'm going to pretend I believe you for a moment," Preston mumbled, checking his phone. After a few seconds, he groaned.

"You guys see the invite to Tyler's? I swear, that kid throws parties every week."

"That's nothing new." I gritted my teeth.

As much as Tyler Benson could be a bigheaded jerk, his mid-summer party was infamous in its own way.

There was always — always — something worth remembering each year.

"Wonder what the main highlight is going to be this year." Coops sighed. "Anyways, pretending's over. Preston has a point. You don't swim like that unless you're preparing for a swim meet or something's bugging you. Last time I checked, you're done with swim."

Preston took a guess. "And judging by the look on your face, it's Lana. Her surprise party was a success, bro! I'm telling you, all you got to do is officially make your move."

I narrowed my eyes slightly. "How does the look on my face tell you guys it's about Lana?"

"Come on. After all our years knowing you, it was some new facial expression. You look like some lost puppy."

When you get compared to a puppy, of all things, that was never a compliment. However, these two weren't my best friends for nothing.

"Lana likes you too, you know." Coops stated lightly.

I gazed up at my black haired friend. "What?"

"I may not know her well, but I know enough to tell you that she's comfortable around you. Have you ever thought the possibility that break up with Haley was meant to meet Lana?"

Sharing that moment alone with Lana before her birthday ended, sur-passed the happiness when I placed first during my last swim competition. I never thought my trophy of four intense years of swim would ever take the back seat. Then again, that was just a trophy.

Seeing Lana's face light up when she saw the locket, to when I put it onto her, tugged my heart in a way that I wasn't sure what exactly Lana has done to me.

As much as I wanted to agree with Coops, I couldn't tell if Lana even had the slightest bit of interest in me. Lana had her dad to worry about and other stuff to focus on. The best thing to do was to keep my promise and be by her side when she needed someone.

Coops and Preston waited for an answer until, what sounded like, my phone ringing appeared in the background. Saved by the ring, you could say. Preston quickly tossed it towards me. I expected it to be Mom's usual calls, hoping that I didn't tear down the house. Once I checked the caller ID, my mouth dropped.

"It's Lana."

My lips twitched into a smile.

Amused expressions appeared on their faces as they said in unison, "Seriously?"

I realized that Lana should be at a party this time. It was Tuesday and only two in the afternoon. Letting it ring, I looked up at them.

"She's working though."

"Then why's she calling?" Preston whispered.

"I don't know — A mistake?"

Coops frowned, cutting in. "Why aren't you picking it up?"

"What if she gets into trouble? Maybe it's just an accident." I thought.

Preston gasped. "Or... what if it's some kid from the party who stole her phone and wants to check if she's really the princess she says she is?" He sounded serious. "This could ruin her!"

Coops gave us the look as if we've completely lost it. "Are we really having this conversation right now? Eli, just pick it up."

Preston added in, "And if it really is her, we're not here right now. Maybe she wants to go out on a date."

He stressed the word "date" mischievously. Stopping myself from laughing at Preston, I cleared my throat and quickly picked it up before the call was missed.

Getting up from the chair, I walked off. "Lana?"

"Hi Eli. You... sound a little scared. Is everything okay?"

"Oh no. I'm good. Nothing's okay — wait, I mean it's okay."

Lana sounded slightly amused. "I'm not bothering you, am I?"

"No, it's all good. I just thought you were at work."

"And you thought I accidentally called, huh?"

I smirked, even though she couldn't see it. "Not going to lie, but yeah. Are you doing anything right now?"

"Actually, I was going to ask you that."

Suddenly, I found myself saying, "Awesome. Let's be together."

Record scratch.

That came out wrong — or frank.

Preston released a whoop in the background loud enough for Lana to hear. When I sharply turned around, Coops already punched Preston in the arm, yet both were trying to stop themselves from bursting into laughter.

"By going to the beach!" I quickly added as my face heated up.

There was a slight pause until Lana answered that she was up for it. "By the way, what was that?"

I laughed it off. "That was just the T.V., sorry about that. You want me to pick you up?"

"I appreciate it, Eli, but I think my car of mine needs to be driven." She giggled softly, "So, the beach?"

"Alright, I'll see you at three?"

As soon as we ended the call, I faced the two, and Preston was already crying from laughter or pain. Walking back closer, I tried to play it cool. It didn't help that Coops chuckled along.

Preston wiped his eyes, holding his hand over his stomach. "When I said make a move, I didn't mean that straight to the point."

I stared at the still water from my pool. "That was embarrassing. You guys are definitely helping."

Coops attempted to clear his throat. "I'll cut you some slack and say that was a nice save. Preston and I will head out soon."

Looking back at them, I felt bad. The whole "No Bro Left Behind" rule was flashing before me. As they took in my expression, they knew. After what felt like nonstop laughter, Preston and Coops calmed down. Coops got up from his chair and Preston followed, grabbing his towel and cellphone.

"Don't worry about it, but just know, this is going on your record," Preston remarked lightheartedly.

Coops mentioned before his voice shifted dryly, "I hope you're taking my question into consideration. Plus, Nathan's coming to town and I was given the opportunity to pick him up."

Preston's eyes widened, along with mine. Our blonde hair friend gasped.

"No way, dude. You never told us! Remember the pranks we used to pull on him?"

"And remember the better pranks he pulled back on us?" Coops was slightly bitter.

In the end, we knew Coops admired his older brother. All of us did actually.

Throwing my towel over my shoulder, I grinned. "Tell him I said hi. It's been ages since we last saw him."

Coops nodded. "Will do. And apparently, he finally proposed to Wendy."

After congratulating Coops' brother indirectly, Preston faced me and smirked. "Your princess awaits."

As I headed down the pier, I looked around to find Lana. She mentioned that she was already at the beach. The ocean breeze and the smell of sea salt wafted towards me. The soft sand sunk my toes every time I took a step. The beach was pretty crowded around this time, so I carefully searched around. There were a couple kids from my old high school that I bumped into, but we only exchanged smiles and waves.

Before I knew it, I turned around when I heard the sound of Lana's voice calling my name. She waved shyly once we locked eye contact. A smile automatically grew on my face. Going towards her, she wore a black top with denim shorts. Despite it being mid-afternoon, the weather was chilly, so she wore a grey hooded jacket and tied her hair into a ponytail. I liked seeing Lana wearing casual clothes like that.

What got me to break into a bigger smile was the locket I gave her hanging around her neck. The locket winked from the soft sunlight and suited her well. Once I reached Lana, her blue eyes were brighter than ever, and she smiled. Since I figured we were pretty close, I opened my arms to give her a hug.

That was a normal thing to do, right?

At first, Lana looked a little surprised. Once she realized it was simply a hug, she proceeded. Her petite body felt snug in my arms, and I couldn't stop myself from grinning like an idiot before letting go.

"Thanks for meeting up with me. It turns out today marked the first day in six months we didn't have any scheduled parties."

I raised an eyebrow in disbelief. "You're kidding!"

Her laugh sounded melodious in my ears as she moved her hair that was partly in her way. "Or Maryann probably just got lazy."

I joined in her laughter. "How have you been? Your dad?"

A smile appeared on Lana's face. "Great actually. Dad's doing better from what the doctors said. He didn't want me to stay home today. I... hope I didn't ruin any of your plans today."

Relieved to hear about her dad, I felt lucky Lana chose to spend today with me. That meant something to me. I wasn't sure why she felt the need to apologize for. I was the one who blurted out "to be together" so bluntly.

Looking back at that, I wanted to slap my forehead. I've left Lana so many wrong impressions, I need to make it right. Shaking my head, I gave her a smile.

"No, you really have nothing to worry about. It's probably going to be on the next blue moon this happens, so let's make today the best."

Upon hearing that, Lana smiled before nodding in agreement.

Coming back to this place with Lana again reminded me when we first went together. It was the "catch up". I wanted to make up for that day — especially when I made that stupid mistake of attempting to kiss her. There was so much temptation now, but I couldn't just yet. Lana wondered what we should do, and I glanced around.

"Is Landon working today?"

Even if I had nothing against him — anymore — it would still be pretty awkward.

"Oh no, he's with my dad right now."

A little relieved, I threw in a suggestion. "Since we're already here, you want to go by the waves?"

Her blue eyes quickly jumped at the moderate waves. It was only a second before her lips pulled into a smile, and we went. Families and people of all ages were by the shoreline, making it packed. We went around it though and let the waves touch our feet. The cold sensation tingled for a bit before I got used to it.

I faced towards her. "When you were a kid, did you ever play that game where you go near the waters and run as fast as you could away from it?"

She let out a giggle. "Who didn't? Want to give it a go?"

"Bet you I won't get wet." I teased with a challenging grin.

Lana arched her right eyebrow with doubt. "You sure about that, champ? We should bet on that. Loser buys funnel cake."

"Oh, it's on."

The childhood memory was soon revived. It was a blast with Lana. We couldn't stop laughing, and I didn't care how silly we probably looked. The waves weren't that bad, and we managed to stumble away before getting attacked. The only damage would be the water hitting my calf, but I was taller than Lana.

Realizing that a huge tide was coming our way, I was ready to jet off until Lana managed to pull me back. Surprised from her strength, she took this opportunity to make a run for it, and that made me say hello to ocean water. My shorts were drenched half way and some of the water splashed up on my shirt. Once again, Lana got me.

After the wave receded back, I glanced up at Lana who covered her mouth with her hand. She was chuckling, and that gave me the greatest idea. Lana cupped her hands.

"I guess I won, right?"

Shaking my head, I lightly mocked. "You sure about that?"

Instantly, I carried her in my arms effortlessly, and her blue eyes widened from shock. She shouted that I put her down, but at the same time, she was flushing out red. Of course, carrying her saved herself even more because I ended up getting hit by the waves. Once I put her down, she stuck her tongue out when she saw that my plan didn't work at all. Still, the moment was fun.

Accepting defeat, I laughed. "Your expression was priceless, so I won. I guess funnel cake's on me."

Lana's face grew even redder, but I knew she wasn't the type to take it to heart.

Heading back up to the pier, I ended up making a stop to the restroom. Lana nodded, mentioning the same. As soon as I was done, I waited by the seating area. Today was going great.

Sitting on the bench, I looked back at the conversation between the guys. Coops asked me if I thought it was meant to be with Lana. Was it?

"Look who it is... Elliot Wesley!"

Putting my attention to that voice, I couldn't help but jump a little once I caught sight of Tyler Benson. We were just talking about him hours ago. He carried a surfboard in his arms and gave me a short wave. Not really surprise he'd be surfing, I got up before giving him a handshake.

Tyler whipped his damp auburn hair to the side. "Dude, about time I see you! What are you doing here?"

I shrugged lightly, putting on a grin. "I'm with Lana right now. You going back for a swim?"

His brown eyes jolted momentarily as if he couldn't understand what I said. Suddenly, Tyler's sideways smirk appeared.

"Oh yeah, you're not with Haley anymore. Yep. You know me, king of the waves. So, you going to my party?"

That was Tyler Benson and his ego running loose. Even though I was unsure myself, I answered, "Most likely. Thanks for invite."

He scoffed a laugh. "I better see you there. You know, I only invite the best. The ladies are probably waiting, so I'll see ya, bro."

Keeping a calm temper, I gave Tyler a brief nod before we greeted each other a goodbye. Tyler wouldn't be a bad person if he wasn't so arrogant. Minutes after the encounter with Tyler, Lana emerged from the restroom. My mood shifted happily seeing her, even though I lost the bet.

"Hope you're hungry for funnel cake."

She smiled. "Trust me, I am."

Suggesting Lana to save a table for us, the line was absolutely ridiculous as I waited. The funnel cakes here were completely worth it though. Also, as long as I was with Lana, I didn't mind at all. Ordering the one with strawberries and ice cream, I found Lana and placed it before her. Handing her a plastic fork and knife, I grinned.

"One fresh funnel cake for the fair maiden."

Lana released a light giggle. "Thanks for being a good sport, Eli. Come on, you deserve it too."

As we poked at the funnel cake, Lana looked up at me and ask if there was anything new.

I wanted to tell you I had feelings for you, my mind replied quietly.

Instead, I gave her a slight shrug.

"Nothing much. Do you know Tyler from our old school? I saw him earlier."

Even though Lana smiled, her eyes expressed discomfort. "Tyler, meaning Olette's cousin, right?"

"That's him. He has this party every summer. We should go together."

Her blue eyes dropped momentarily to the plate before she murmured. "Thanks Eli, but I'm not exactly Tyler's favorite person."

My fists clenched slightly, and I felt this sudden need to know why. "Did he do something to you?"

Immediately, Lana's head shot up, and she abruptly shook her head. "No. He's just..."

"A jerk." I finished her sentence for her.

As much as Lana didn't want to admit, I could already sense we were thinking the same thing.

I nodded. "Yeah, Tyler's the complete opposite from Olette, but I'll make sure he won't bother you."

She teased gently. "My knight in shining armor."

We shared a laugh, and I asked Lana if there was anything new with her. Lana bit her lower lip for a moment.

"Well... more like a shocker, but my brother isn't with Haley anymore."

Was I hearing things?

When Lana noticed my expression, her eyes still looked shocked. My mind was still putting it all together. Landon and Haley broke up? A part of me wanted to start asking questions why, but it wasn't really my place to ask.

She nodded. "I don't blame you for being surprised. I really thought they would stay together."

My curious side got the best of me. "Do... you know what happened?"

Lana picked at the glazed strawberry with the fork. "Not really. You're probably wondering why I told you this, but Landon was acting pretty weird during my birthday. I thought maybe you knew since you guys were together before I came."

Honestly, I had no clue. I really didn't know what to feel. Running a hand through my hair, I sighed.

"I don't. Sorry. Is your brother doing alright?"

There was a confused expression that grew on Lana's face as she confessed freely, "See, that's what's bothering me. Landon's okay. He told me he never wanted a serious relationship and called it off."

I gulped down harshly hearing that. Landon broke up with Haley. The back of my mind started to question if Haley told Landon about us. If she did, then Landon would have told Lana. Coming to a conclusion, Haley still kept her mouth shut. As much as I wanted to wonder why, I wasn't going to question it anymore. I remembered waiting for the day to happen, but it didn't affect me in that kind of way.

I eventually broke the ice. "Winner gets last piece."

Her eyes went down to the plate, and even if she offered it back to me, I shook my hands out and insisted. Lana popped the last bit of funnel cake into her mouth, and we both stood up to throw away the trash. Things did get a little quiet between us, but I wasn't going to let the day end like this.

Garnering her attention by grabbing her hand, Lana's sky blue eyes grew. Smiling, I squeezed her hand slightly.

"It's going to be okay, Lana. Landon wouldn't want you to worry about him and Haley."

Though she did appear doubtful for a while, Lana soon nodded her head. "You're right, Eli... I don't know why I worry too much. Thanks."

Even though I didn't want to let go of her hand, I casually loosened my grip and asked her if she wanted to hit up the stores. The atmosphere between us became more happier when we messed around, trying on all those ridiculous hats and sunglasses. Lana eventually looked more at ease, and I was glad to see her mood much better.

As soon as we finished walking through the gift shops, the sun was already setting. The sky was just magnificent with powerful, bright colors taking over. Lana and I walked side by side by the pier. Good thing we avoided the amusement park with the game stands. I already went through that humiliation.

"The view is so pretty." Lana's voice broke my thoughts as she praised the glittering ocean and colorful sky.

When I agreed with her, Lana settled her focus on me. Her eyes stared into mine so gracefully and I gulped down.

"Thanks for today, Eli. It was really fun."

"I had a fun time too."

All of a sudden, Lana started to play with the ends of her ponytail. Her voice was shy. "You know, I feel very happy when I'm with you."

Hearing that, it was that moment where you felt like busting out into a happy song and dance. But, I didn't have a group of people waiting to join nor a band ready to start playing. Lana was happy when she was with me. That was all I needed to hear.

Clearing my throat, I thought this would be the right moment. The sunset, this somewhat romantic atmosphere before us, I should really tell her now, right?

"Lana, I —"

Her eyes gazed right at mine. "Yes?"

"Well, I've been meaning to say —"

Right when I was about to tell Lana everything, her eyes momentarily unlocked with mine and gazed past my shoulder. Her expression looked completely in disbelief.

Lana asked with a hushed tone, "Eli... is that Landon and Olette over there?"

Chapter 18

As much as I wanted to listen to Eli, seeing the honesty in his warm brown eyes, my attention was torn away when I caught sight of a familiar person. It was my brother, Landon. He stood right outside the seafood restaurant on the pier with a girl faced away from me to see. At that instance, my mind registered that she wasn't Haley. They officially separated two days after my birthday though I was uncertain what the reason was.

Instead, the girl had auburn hair that was straight to perfection. I squinted my eyes, taking in the physique and soon enough, the familiarity made sense.

Olette.

My best friend was with my older brother.

I couldn't help but blurt out my discovery, "Eli... is that Landon and Olette over there?"

At the time, I wasn't paying attention to what was coming out of Eli's mouth. He cut his sentence and turned to follow my gaze.

Eli's tone was unsure as he spoke, "That does look like them. Why are they here?"

"I'm not sure." My lips fell slightly. "I'm sorry, what were you saying earlier?"

Once Eli faced me, a sheepish expression surfaced. His brown eyes were still bright from before as his lips grew a tiny grin.

He changed the topic, "How about we do some investigating?"

Though there was an adventurous approach to Eli, I felt a little horrible. I shouldn't have interrupted him. Now, he wouldn't tell me what he was about to say which was going to haunt me for a while. Letting it go momentarily, I eventually nodded and Eli's dimple appeared as his smile increased. Unsure on how to advance at Landon and Olette, I thought all these possibilities about them.

Keeping a straight face, maybe a little surprise from us would get some answers. Still, that little voice in my mind tried to push me away and not bother them. However, it was too late to turn back.

The girl was laughing along with Landon. I could tell right off the bat when it's Olette's laugh. As she turned around, Eli and I were put to a stop when she exchanged glances with us. Landon soon joined. They froze.

Judging by the looks on their faces that moment, they definitely weren't expecting any familiar faces. Olette straightened her wavy hair as she wore a beautiful black dress while Landon wore a dress shirt and black slacks — that couldn't be a simple outing.

Olette widened her eyes, but she waved. Her voice quivered a little. "Lana, Eli! Hey, what are you two doing here?"

Looking over at Eli momentarily, his eyes shown awkwardness, but he gave a taunting grin over at Olette. The two were exchanging glances, almost like Eli had a sense of knowledge about the two.

"I was kind of going to ask the same thing," I returned with my eyebrows slightly raised.

My older brother soon hopped into the conversation. He greeted Eli and the two swapped brief nods. Landon ran a hand through his light, brown hair.

"I guess we should tell them, Olette."

Olette flashed a glance at Landon as if she wasn't ready. My mouth dropped a little as my mind came up with a conclusion.

Instead, I asked from the worry building up inside me, "Landon, I thought you were with Dad."

"He's okay, Lana." Landon's voice was filled with confidence. "About - "

"I'll tell her," Olette interrupted.

Before I had time to react, Olette locked her arm with mine and dragged me away from Eli and Landon. Being forced along, I looked over my shoulder shortly and found the boys with dumbfounded expressions. Once we reached the railing of the pier, the two of us overlooked the darkened ocean. Olette broke the silence by letting out a laugh.

"This is a little awkward..."

"Is this something I shouldn't know about?"

She shook her head and reassured, "No, of course I want you to know. Not like this though."

To be honest, I didn't have the slightest feeling to be upset. I was more curious how it happened. Looking back, Olette and Landon showed signs of mild flirting, but Olette always denied any feeling towards my brother. Does she think I would be mad at her? My best friend's hazel eyes then stuck onto mine.

She admitted, "While I was planning your surprise party, we met up one time so I could tell him about it. And... I don't know how this happened, but we ended up kissing! I'm so sorry for not telling you any sooner! I was just confused and the fact that he was dating someone... I..."

Olette sighed and I could see the mixed emotions through her eyes.

"Olette, I get it that you weren't ready to tell me," I guaranteed calmly, "but, I don't think you were the reason why Landon broke up with Haley. Do you happen to know why?"

To my surprise, she nodded. "It happened that same time. We were talking about stuff and then Haley came up. Landon told me how she was getting clingy and jealous over the littlest things. He mentioned that he was getting tired of her immaturity."

I felt my eyes widen to my dismay. "Really? He did look a little bothered when I asked about her." Suddenly, an amused grin stretched on my lips.

"Hold on a second. So, you and Landon had this going on during my birthday? I never expected a thing!"

An ashamed expression appeared on Olette's face as she became red in the cheeks. Olette let out a wail from my teasing voice.

"I'm sorry, Lana! Like I said, I never wanted you to find out like this."

Giving her a comforting smile, I shook my head. "No, it's okay. I promise you, I'm not mad. The funny thing is, I'm not that surprised. You know I was envisioning this ever since sixth grade."

Olette stuck her tongue out at me before she pulled me into a hug. Embracing her back, all that really mattered was seeing the two happy. I didn't have to see them for more than two seconds to know how much they enjoy each other's company. When we broke off from the hug, Olette appeared more at ease.

"We should head back to them." I suggested, trying to search where Eli and Landon was.

However, Olette questioned, "Not just yet. Were you on a date with Eli?"

Compared to the formal appearance Olette and Landon had, we were just wearing casual clothes and having a fun time at the beach. Was it a date? I shrugged a little, playing with my hair.

"You're playing with your hair. It's so a date," Olette gushed.

As we giggled about it, I recalled back to when Eli was on the verge of telling me something.

Growing guilty from my actions, I revealed to Olette, "Before I found you and Landon, Eli was going to tell me something." I glanced off onto the ocean. "It sounded like he was going to - "

Instantly, Olette grabbed my cheeks with her hands. Her mouth forming into an O and shouted, "Confess his love to you! Lana, how could you stop that moment from happening?"

"I wasn't going to say that... I couldn't help it," I murmured while my face immediately flushed.

Olette nodded her head, understanding. "I know. Come on, let's go back to them."

Walking back, Eli and Landon were still by the front of the restaurant and appeared to be stuck in a conversation. When I ask Olette if we interrupted them, Olette mentioned that they already finished dinner. This caused curiosity to build up within me and I wanted to know how it went. Olette would always squeeze out every possible detail from me, it would be interesting to switch for once. Olette gave me a little wink and promised to spill everything later. We agreed on a more appropriate time.

Once the boys noticed we were close by, they turned their attention to us. Eli gave me a wave and I smiled back. Even though his hair was a little disheveled by the waters, he still looked good. The thing was, I probably looked like a mess, but it didn't bother me at all. Was I that comfortable with Eli Wesley?

Throwing Landon a look, he does this thing where he squints his eyes at me with an awkward grin on his face. I figured he thought I'd be mad, but I played along saying that we'll talk later. It was funny how I felt like the older sibling at the moment. As Olette approached Landon's side, I then looked over at Eli.

I suggested gently, "We should get going, huh?" Eli nodded in agreement.

Turning back to the incoming couple, we dismissed the once awkward encounter and said our goodbyes. Olette signaled that she'll call me later and I grinned, returning that she should just enjoyed her time with Landon. Eli and I walked off toward the parking area to call it a day.

Today was rather eventful. I always find myself surprised whenever I'm with Eli.

Breaking the quiet atmosphere, Eli chuckled. "That was unexpected. Did you have any clue about it?"

Looking into his brown eyes, I answered sincerely, "Yes and no. The two would always flirt and all, but I never knew it would happen this soon. I'm happy with them though."

Eli nodded. "I knew Olette was crushing on Landon for a while too."

My eyes widened. "You did?"

"Yep." He grinned. "Interesting way to end the day."

If Eli could see that Olette has feelings towards my brother, was he able to tell that I was growing feelings towards him too? Shaking my thoughts away, I let out a small laugh.

"It was. Hey, Eli?"

Eli gave me a curious look as he reached for his keys in his pocket.

Pulling an extra strand of hair behind my ear before placing my hands in the pockets of my jacket, I revealed, "Before we bumped into Olette and Landon, you never finished what you were about to say."

An embarrassed look spread across Eli's face. He finally responded to what felt like forever, "That I really like being with you."

As I finished dinner with Dad and Landon, I was actually relived that this Friday deemed a regular day. For a while now, I felt like so many surprises came my way. Maybe I just wasn't use to it, but it was nice to spend time with Dad today and have a nice supper with the family. Dad told his usual jokes, causing the overall atmosphere to liven up.

The moment I closed the kitchen faucet shut, Dad then asked, "Is it true that Landon and Olette are dating?"

Landon nearly choked on his water, hearing Dad gossip. We shared another laugh as I nodded for Landon. As if Dad couldn't transition the mood any more awkward, I was put into the spotlight when he asked about Eli.

I felt the heat in my cheeks. "Dad, you don't want to tire yourself out. Remember what the doctors said?"

Dad chuckled softly. "Asking a question isn't going to hurt me, honey. It seems like you two want me living under a rock or something."

We laughed with Dad's humor until our doorbell rang. Telling them I'd get it, I headed towards our front door. Turning the knob, I found no one there. Looking left to right, I thought it was the neighborhood kids playing a joke even though it never happened before. When I glanced down, I found an envelope on our doormat.

Even more curious, I knelt down to pick it up. Opening the ivory envelope, I pulled out the piece of paper. The letter was similar to one from a Disney movie. Chuckling at the fact I was addressed "Princess Lana" and that a "grand ball" was approaching, I noticed there was no time, place, or any information present. No one even signed it. Maybe this was a joke.

Closing our front door shut, I walked back to my family and they looked at me with interested expressions. Telling them that no one was there, I showed the letter.

"This was left instead."

"A letter?" Landon raised his eyebrows.

When Dad asked who it was from, I shrugged. "I'm not sure. It's some invitation to a grand ball or something." Laughing, I mumbled, "Suddenly, my life has turned Disney."

Dad tapped his chin and wondered, "A grand ball, huh? Where's the fairy godmother?"

Thinking Dad was joking around, I laughed again. To my dismay, Olette emerged to our kitchen. I nearly shrieked in surprise. A giggle escaped from her as she walked over to my side. Her auburn hair was wavy once again as she tied it half up. She wore a flowing yet casual white dress that danced above her knees and, correct my vision, was she holding a wand?

Then, it occurred me.

My voice probably didn't par up to my confused face, "Fairy Godmother?"

Olette nodded, instructing me to follow her. "We have to prepare! Come along, dear."

Quickly shooting looks at Dad and Landon, they seemed completely aware that Olette popped in all of a sudden. Another weird dream? My dad and brother told me to just go along with it. Confused, I sighed and followed. Olette was humming happily and took me to the downstairs bathroom.

I stopped on my feet and questioned, "Was that you by the doorbell? How did you get inside?"

Olette was too much in the role. "With magic, silly. Go inside and you'll find something beautiful to wear. Let me know when you're done."

Looking at my best friend as if she grew two heads, I couldn't believe this was happening. Instead, Olette disregarded my scared face and motioned me inside my bathroom. Getting a little tensed, I wasn't sure what to expect. Flickering the lights on and shutting the door behind me, I gasped again.

One of the dresses I owned was hanging by the shower. It should be in my closet. Not here. Taking it down, it was my sleeveless, polyester turquoise dress that ran above my knees. Putting it on, I looked at myself in the mirror and let out a tiny laugh.

I announced to my reflection, "I don't know, but I'll go along with it."

Opening the door, Olette was waiting outside and her hazel eyes brightened at the sight of me. She nodded approvingly and just when I thought we were done, I was now sitting down on a stool as she curled my hair at the ends. Even though I attempted to talk to her, she simply replied that I was getting prepped up for the ball. And from the looks of it, she wasn't kidding. When my fairy godmother did her magic, Olette then announced that my carriage awaits.

"Olette, this isn't a dream, right?" I asked with nervousness than excitement.

In return, she gave me a tiny slap in the arm. That was enough to reassure me it wasn't and enough to make my arm a bit red. Dad and Landon were waiting by the foyer with pleased smiles on their faces. Something was telling me they knew what was going on. Seeing how they weren't going to give me any answers, I said my goodbyes. They teased gently that I shouldn't be scared. But, who wouldn't be?

And when I walked out of the door, there was Preston standing outside by a red mustang with Julian driving.

Preston waved, all dressed up. "Good evening, Princess!"

I immediately blushed. Turning around, the front door was already shut and I was the only one outside. Taking a deep breath, I followed my words and went along with it. My heart wouldn't stop beating the more I walked closer to them.

The green eyed blonde grinned and opened the door for me. "You look beautiful tonight, Lana. Are you excited?"

My shyness was taking over. "I actually don't know what to feel."

Julian and Preston laughed, telling me to hop in. Getting all embarrassed from this current situation, my mind started to come up with some conclusion.

Did all of this had to do with —

"Well, off you go. Coops, take care of Lana!" Preston hollered with his hands cupped while Julian drove off.

Since it was the two of us, I anxiously tried to find a perfect time to ask what Julian knew. Maybe he would tell me. Unconsciously playing with the hem of my dress, I looked out the window to see if I'd get a hint of where we were heading to.

Julian's calm voice entered my mind. "Don't worry, we won't be late."

Looking over at Julian, his crisp hazel eyes shined from the moonlight as they focused on the road.

I chuckled nervously. "I think I would be more okay if I knew where we were going."

Julian turned the wheel and a smile appeared. "Take a look."

Giving my attention back to the window, Julian stopped at the community park. It was just minutes away from my house. This park was well known for the huge lake in the middle. Suddenly, I noticed that Julian had gotten out of the car and opened the door for me.

"Well Princess, we'll have to separate from here."

Not ready, I tried not to panic but luckily, Julian instructed me where to go. Thanking him for everything, Julian simply returned a warm grin. I just wished I knew why this was happening. Everything felt so fast paced. It felt like reality pushed me into a dream. Heading to the beginning of the trail that circled around the park, goosebumps appeared. I've been here several of times before at night. Why was I panicking?

As I followed the path and searched around, I felt like the only person in this park which was probably the main reason why my heart was racing crazily. That's until I found something lying on one of the benches. Something like this could be part of a horror movie.

Ridding those thoughts away, my eyes caught sight of an elegantly engraved metal mirror with a red apple next to it. When I reached it, I lifted the mirror and there was a note under it. Picking it up slowly, I unfolded it and found a handwritten note. It wasn't messy, but it didn't appear like a girl's handwriting. It read:

"The mirror made a mistake. Snow White isn't the fairest of them all..."

Reading this caused my heart to get even more jittery. I felt myself smiling and noticed that the end of the note mentioned to continue on walking. The more I walked around the path, I past another bench and there, a "glass" slipper. Another note was there as well:

"Because I've been looking for a girl that fits this slipper."

I giggled at the cheesy words. Going around the park, there were more surprises that were left on the benches. The next one had a crown on top of it that was identical to Aurora's from Sleeping Beauty. In the middle was another note:

"This girl is very familiar. Did we meet once upon a dream?"

Even though I was scared moments ago, all of this was shocking me in a positive way. My heart was thumping every single time I read a note and found something new. Seeing how I almost circled the entire park, I was put into another stop when I spotted Flounder from The Little Mermaid lying on another bench. The plush toy was next to a couple seashells with a note by it. Picking it up, the note read:

"And out of all the fishes in the sea..."

From the beginning, I grabbed all the stuff from the benches. I didn't want to leave any of it, so my arms were getting full. Smiling happily, I noticed that I was close to the end. And there, a red rose laid on top of the bench with a note beside it:

"You seem to have broken my spell."

I could feel my entire body heating up as I read the last note. The park was silent and I glanced around even though I wasn't sure what to look for. However, there was something I spotted. On the lamppost near the exit, there was a paper taped onto it. Going closer to it, I wondered if that was another letter. Being careful, I reached for the paper and removed the taping that enclosed it. My eyes widened at the note:

"If you give me a chance, I can show you the world on a magic carpet ride."

Gazing off to the parking lot, there was nothing in sight. Becoming a little confused at first, my attention was soon taken away when I spotted a flying carpet.

Or was it?

Right when I thought my heart would calm down, it started to beat heavily once more. My jaw dropped in amazement when I saw Eli.

He was sitting on top of a car — that was covered in the sides with a black blanket — but he was sitting on a carpet similar to the one from the movie, Aladdin. A flying carpet, how clever. The "flying carpet" was moving and I couldn't believe my eyes or my ears. Eli Wesley was singing "A Whole New World" as it moved. One of my favorite Disney songs. This moment was unbelievable and I almost dropped all the things I was holding. Immediately, I felt my eyes getting all watery at the sight.

Eli did all of this for me?

There was no sign of embarrassment as Eli sang and to be honest, I never expected him to sing so well. When he reached a reasonable distance to me, the "flying carpet" was put to a stop. Was someone driving the covered car? Eli finished the last note and looked down at me with a bright smile on his face. That dimple appearing on his cheek. Knowing that it was impossible to hide the red growing on my cheeks, I couldn't find any words to explain how I was feeling. I wasn't sure why I felt tears rolling down. Does being treated like a princess naturally make you more emotional?

Soon, Eli carefully hopped off and came close to my side. His brown eyes looked slightly concern that I was crying, but I shook it off and laughed to lighten up the mood. It was hard to believe that star athlete Elliot Wesley would put in all this effort for a simple girl who plays as Disney princess.

Eli smiled, gently wiping the tears from my face. "I probably scared you for a moment, huh?"

Looking at all the things Eli left on the benches momentarily, I gazed up at his princely appearance. "This is... amazing. Thank you, Eli. You really know how to make a girl feel special."

"Well, there's only one girl that matters."

"Should I watch out for Jasmine, Aladdin?" I teased and we chuckled together.

Eli motioned to hand him all the things I was carrying and he set them aside onto a nearby bench. We were standing under the same lamppost I grabbed the last note moments ago. All of a sudden, Eli took my hand and his touch seemed to have warmed me.

His gentle brown eyes stared deeply into mine. "There's something I've been meaning to tell you for a while now."

I waited patiently, heart fluttering.

"You're special to me, Lana, and all I feel is happiness when I'm around you," Eli paused and his voice showed confidence and sincerity, "Will you be my girlfriend?"

Chapter 19

No one wants to face the interruption of a confession.

I was so close. So close. All the courage to tell Lana how I felt was going to take over like a surfer riding a huge tidal wave. Except that tidal wave got the best of that surfer, and that surfer just had to be me. Was it just bad timing? The moment Lana's bright blue eyes shifted away from mine, I knew something was up. The thing was, I wasn't expecting Olette and Lana's brother to be the reason why. That actually shocked me too, so I couldn't exactly blame the world for ruining the moment. To be honest, I was just as curious.

Suggesting to play investigator, we sort of interrupted the two. I could already tell that both weren't just meeting up as friends. Their clothes were way too polished. After the slightly awkward confronting, Olette had dragged Lana away from Landon and me. The shocked expression on Lana's face told me she didn't want to leave us behind, but I was positive Olette need a place to explain — privately — especially with this kind of case.

It's funny how Lana and I went through a day of just having fun to unraveling an unintentional mystery.

Would it be weird to say that I sort of figured this was coming?

As much as Olette tried denying it to the guys and me during the time we were prepping up Lana's birthday surprise, there were too many obvious hints that indicated she liked Landon more than a best friend's brother. I felt like some detective, but I had to stop myself from prying. I didn't even know Landon or Olette that well to begin with.

Being stuck together at the moment, Landon had decided to start some small talk. The guy was all dressed up and ran a hand through his light brown hair that was styled up. I couldn't believe my blood use to curdle just hearing Landon's name mentioned. Now, I was there standing right by him. A sideways grin grew on Landon's matured face.

"Wasn't really expecting to bump into you guys."

"Lana didn't tell you she was going to the beach?"

Landon shook his head a little. "No. Well, I don't think she did unless I wasn't paying attention."

We shared a laugh shortly until it eventually died out, leaving us both to silence. Tess and Irene's gossiping selves must have rubbed onto me the time we ran into them during the carnival.

I spat out unconsciously, "You and Olette, huh?"

Good job keeping things subtle, Eli.

"Yeah." A closed grin appeared before Landon murmured, "I know what you're thinking."

My eyes widened. "You do?"

I wasn't thinking of anything, really.

Landon released a sigh as the same colored blue eyes the Clarke's shared settled towards my way. "I know I was dating Haley, but before you think I'm moving too fast, you have to hear me out."

Cringing mentally at the thought of Haley, I felt hot and nervous all of a sudden. Did Landon know about Haley's relationship with me? The last time I saw Landon and Haley together was when the guys and I almost got caught at the party store. That was only a few weeks ago. However, I kept a straight face and pointed out that there was no need to explain even if a part of me was curious about how Haley and Landon decided to split. My past self would have been jumping for joy hearing this.

I waved my hands out. "It's cool. If you're going for Olette, you'll make her happy."

Lana's older brother stared at me, almost a little perplexed at my beaming confidence. That's what triggered my palms to reach a sweaty state. Why did it seem like Landon was staring into my soul? It's a little creepy, if you ask me. After a pause, Landon's face grew at ease and he released a smile.

He confessed freely, "I don't know why I'm telling you this, but I really like Olette. You ever had that feeling before? Yeah, Haley's a great girl and all, but not the one I would get serious with. I'm tired of jealous and immature girls. Olette is the opposite of that."

"I see what you mean," I replied in a low tone. "So... you broke it off with her?"

"In a way, I guess." Landon's lips fell into a tiny frown. "Things weren't working out for a while to a point where it was the best thing to do. Last time I heard from Haley, she's at the Bahamas."

Not surprised, Haley would go on a trip to the Bahamas.

Even though Landon and Haley did look happy together, I was relieved that she was currently out of the picture. Casually looking around the crowded night life of the pier, I kept things casual.

"I respect your decision."

Suddenly, Landon freed a laugh of amusement. At the same time, he punched my arm lightly which surprised me. Giving him a bewildered look for a quick second since I thought he had lost his mind, I soon dropped the expression once I found Landon smiling.

Landon acknowledged, "You're a little mature for your age, you know that? I'm going to keep this short, so listen up Eli."

Gulping down, reality hit me remembering that this was Lana's older brother I was talking to — the guy who I stated I would hate for the rest of my life, the guy who once dated my ex-girlfriend even though Haley and I were still together during the same. It was true that Landon didn't exactly know that. Landon's blue eyes glared at me with such intensity that it was borderline seriousness or ready to kill.

"I'm not only saying this because I'm her older brother, but if you plan on asking my sister, make sure it's because you really care about her. The last thing I want is for Lana to get hurt."

I would never want to hurt Lana. She seemed to have changed my thinking so easily just by spending time with her. My reaction was to nod obediently. For some reason, I felt tongue tied. Why was I feeling intimidated? After a few seconds, Landon's face dramatically softened and another soft chuckle escaped from him. Relief took over, seeing his lighthearted attitude.

He smirked. "Don't worry. What I'm trying to say is, do something that Lana would never forget. She's different from most girls, and she deserves the best."

Before I could respond back, Landon's eyes jumped off shortly. His eyes were staring right past my shoulder. Glancing over, we watched Lana and Olette walk their way back. The two looked completely fine and were even laughing heartily with one another. Everything went well then, but I knew it would. Lana wasn't like those girls who cringe at the whole "best friend's brother" deal.

Settling my eyes at Lana, we exchanged glances before she broke into a shy smile. Seeing her and absorbing every detail made my heart beat like never before. I already knew that Lana was different from most girls — Landon didn't have to tell me that she deserves the best. Any guy would be the luckiest guy in the world to be with her.

And with that, I would make sure I would be that guy.

"El, why are you rummaging through the cabinet like a mouse?"

The twins snickered from behind me.

You see, I had a plan.

As I searched around our cherry wood cabinets by the left side wall of our family room — not like a mouse — common sense invaded knowing that my plan wouldn't work if I couldn't find the source. Looking over my shoulder, the twins were standing several feet away with curious eyes and smirks plastered on. That was something I should be already used to. Usually, I would think they would have something else better to do, like soccer, but I actually needed them. I walked towards them as my height towered over.

"You two happen to know where the collection of Disney movies are? Like the princess ones?"

While I was asking, Abby was sipping on a chilled glass of fresh lemonade. She must have choked from disbelief and nearly spat the beverage out. Aly and I looked at her with concerned looks, but Abby wiped her lips with the sleeve of her neon blue shirt and indicated she was cool.

Aly then looked back at me with raised eyebrows. "Say that again."

I sighed, preparing myself for the parade of embarrassment. "Where are the Disney princess movies?"

There was a long period of silence in our family room with Eian occasionally barking from whatever adventure he was having outside our backyard. Suddenly, Double Trouble burst into laughter. I was waiting for that to happen — just two seconds off. After telling them once more that I was serious, Abby scrunched her nose.

"You're such a weirdo. Are you that bored with your life, El?"

Even though this request was weird, I resisted not telling them why I needed them and the movies. I wanted my plan to be a little secretive, but maybe, they could provide some insight. Scoffing mentally at the thought, I couldn't believe I was considering twelve year olds' opinions.

I offered, "If you find me the movies, I'll tell you why."

The twins huddled and began whispering to one another as if they needed the time to think about it. It was silly to watch, like they were going through the process of the Pythagorean theorem. In the end, I knew they would agree. Their curiosity was their biggest weakness.

Abby stretched her arms while pointing out, "Fine, but first, you're looking in the wrong place. That's where we keep all the photo albums, you big dummy. The videos are in the other cabinet."

The short girls jokingly pushed me aside to create a walk way towards the cabinets. Just one cabinet down, the gold of Treasure Island was revealed. All those bright colors and frilly fonts of the Disney movie names popped out as Abby swung the cabinet door. Instantly, Aly and Abby began picking through the stacks of DVDs. One by one, I saw the movie titles of Cinderella, Beauty and the Beast, and the rest slowly rise up in Aly's arms. My eyes grew at the total. Even though the twins mentioned we were missing some, there were six to watch!

"There," the twins announced with proud smiles.

Taking the stack of movies from Aly's hands, I pursed my lips. "You guys know the order of these movies?"

A knowing look flashed before their faces, but Abby questioned anyways, "Wait a second, you're not actually going to watch all of these..."

There brown eyes shifted side to side as they asked in unison, "Are you?"

It always scared me how they would always say stuff at the same time. Was it twin telepathy? Ever since we were younger, I sort of wished for a twin myself. Shaking myself mentally at my wishful thoughts, I nodded.

"Yeah, I am. So, you know?"

The expressions on their faces were priceless. Huge eyes, jaws dropped — if I only had a camera, I would capture this moment and never let it down. The twins looked at each other confusedly until grins grew on their faces.

Aly folded her arms. "Tell us why first."

I knew they would bring up the question soon enough. For some reason, I felt all shy telling this to them. My younger sisters, of all people!

"I'm planning to ask Lana to be my girlfriend. I thought it'd be pretty cool to use the Disney princesses somehow as inspiration, cause you know, she plays as the princesses."

Before I could finish my explanation, excited expressions lit up the twins' faces. Abby threw her hands up.

"Say no more!"

The two grabbed the stack of DVDs from my arms and proceeded in sorting them out. Thanking them, the first movie was Snow White and the Seven Dwarves. The twins insisted in watching the movies with me, so they could provide their opinions. I figured they would, so I went along with it.

We all gathered around the L-shaped sofa in the family room and Eian appeared to join us. For the most part, it was quiet as the movie played. I was taking mental notes with every movie we went through. It was around noon when I popped in Snow White's movie and we watched continuously. The only thing I ate was the handful of popcorn Aly made during Cinderella.

As we were watching The Little Mermaid, our house phone started to ring. Seeing how no one was going to move, I heard Abby grunt and she took one for the team. By the time she hung up the phone, my ears caught Aly ask who the person was. The twins started to whisper and giggle to one another, but I thought nothing of it and returned to watching the movie.

As Ariel was adjusting to her human life, I realized that I didn't have my cellphone on me the entire time. Was it today that the guys wanted to hang out? Thinking about that, our doorbell rang and I suspected it to be Dad and Mom even though it was odd that they didn't go through the garage. Abby jumped up from the sofa again and announced happily that she would get it. A little confused from her sudden enthusiasm, I shrugged it off. The movie was on the scene with the singing red crab Preston loved so much.

However, I knew I should have known better.

"Hey bro, you feeling better? We bought — hey, what's this?" A familiar voice remarked.

Stunned, my eyes shifted away from the screen to the voice. It was Preston with Coops standing by the family room. Coops held a box of pizza while Preston carried a plastic bag. The smell of the pizza made my stomach churn. Their eyes went on the T.V. before hopping back onto mine.

Coops' expression was confused. "We thought you were sick."

Getting up from the sofa, I shook my head, but then all pieces came together. The twins were eyeing the pizza box.

"What'd you tell them, Abby?"

Abby's expression was held innocent. She always used this tactic, but I always looked past it.

"Well, Julian called wondering where you've been cause you haven't been picking up your phone. I told him you were sick and we were all alone in the house. We were hungry and you couldn't take care of us — which is true!" She giggled. "So Julian said Preston and him would come over to bring some food."

The twins were masterminds at this. Frowning slightly at them, I warned them not to do it again, but the guys indicated it was okay. Abby and Aly cheered in unison and grabbed the box of pizza from Coops' hands.

"Thanks!" The twins beamed.

While the twins were busy eating away, the guys waited for an explanation. I guess it's rather shocking to find that your best friend has been missing your calls because he's been busy watching Disney movies. But, I had a good reason behind all of this. While the song "Kiss the Girl" was playing faintly in the background, Preston's face contorted with seriousness that I thought he was actually upset.

"I can't believe you're watching this movie... without me! You know too well this song originated from me. What's the deal, Mr. Sick guy?" Despite the expression on his face, a joking tone projected off Preston's voice.

Coops teased, "We even got you the soup you liked so much from that Chinese restaurant."

Looks like the twins managed to fool us all.

Chuckling, I ran a hand through my hair. "Sorry about that, guys. The twins are crazy and I didn't have my phone on me."

"We figured after the fourth call," Preston snorted, "so, what's going on?"

I soon revealed, "Well, I'm planning to ask Lana... to be my girlfriend. And don't laugh, but I wanted to ask her using the Disney princesses. I thought maybe watching the movies would give me some ideas how."

A part of me was waiting for the guys to laugh at my face, but they nodded their heads as grins appeared before me.

Coops and Preston noted in unison, "About time."

The twins were nice enough to leave enough cheese pizza for the guys while I was stuck eating the soup — not like it was entirely a bad thing. Preston requested to rewind the scene again, so he could sing along even though he made up lyrics for ninety-nine percent of it. When Coops asked what exactly to look out for, I really didn't know how to answer. So far, I picked up that Snow White and Sleeping Beauty both had their princes kiss them to wake them up — not really a good idea to do — while Cinderella was known for that glass slipper.

There were things that happened this summer I thought I'd never do with the guys. First shopping, now watching Disney movies? Well, it was for Lana and I wanted to make sure everything went well.

About eight hours passed, and I kid you not, we finished watching all six movies. The twins got tired after The Little Mermaid and would join in periodically. After the credits of Aladdin started to roll, the guys and I stood up from the sofa and stretched.

Coops check the time on his watch. "Dude, it's already eight. Did we seriously just spend the day watching this?"

I nodded. "Can't believe it either."

Mom and Dad got home during Beauty and the Beast and were surprised to see everyone in the family room watching our childhood movies instead of being out like usual. Mom made dinner and left the food for us since we promised we would eat after watching. While we sat around the dinner table, Preston asked what the plan was before devouring Mom's home cooked meal. Taking in a few bites, I had to think about it first. All of the movies had different aspects, I wasn't sure how to make use of it.

"Why don't you do the glass slipper thing, that's cute!" The twins suddenly joined in the conversation.

Preston snapped his fingers. "Or! Three words. Magic. Carpet. Ride."

The five of us let out a laugh before I countered, "How in the world is that even possible?"

We continued on exchanging ideas while throwing some out. I admit, most of them all sounded good, but I felt like it just wasn't good enough.

While the twins and the guys started lightly arguing whose idea was better, that invisible lightbulb on my head appeared.

"Guys, I got it." I broke the atmosphere.

"Finally! Someone who understands." Preston added.

Shaking my head, I corrected after a laugh, "As much as your idea about slaying a dragon sounds awesome... I think I have a way to combine everything, but I'm going to need your help. And possibly Olette and Lana's family."

As I explained the plan from beginning to end, looks of approval surfaced on everyone's faces and I never felt so confident yet nervous about pulling it off.

A little contradicting, wasn't it?

So far, tonight was going as planned.

Standing around the park's front, I received a text from Coops saying that Lana was now going around the park. With the help of everyone, including the twins who prepared the elements of each princesses on the benches, I hoped Lana was enjoying. "Fairy Godmother" Olette and Preston were also with me. This was it. This was going to be the day I ask Lana. Would she say yes? We've been planning this for three days now and I never thought time would pass so quickly.

The part that was worrying me was her answer. And believe it or not, I — Eli Wesley — was going to sing. Olette suggested it and everyone jumped in the pool of agreement. The twins even had to bring out that I was in choir during middle school, and it was time to wake up my vocal chords. I didn't mind, but I had to make sure I didn't choke or anything dumb like that.

Olette was pacing around, a little more anxious than myself. "Oh my gosh. She's almost here. How are you feeling, Eli?"

"I'll be fine." I gulped down. "You think she'll say yes?"

Preston and Olette looked at each other with smiles on their faces. They both nodded.

"Dude, don't worry about that. I'm going to start up the car," Preston announced as he reached for the keys in his pockets.

This was another thing I was worried about.

I half-joked, "Make sure to go slow. You're a speed demon, you know that?"

Olette offered, "You sure you don't want me to drive?"

Preston shook his head and reassured both of us, "I got this!"

We all laughed shortly and knew Preston definitely wanted to make a contribution. Once I felt my phone vibrate, that was Coops' signal for Lana was reaching the very end. I motioned the two to head inside Preston's car which we covered the side and back with a black blanket. On the roof was the carpet prop Maryann let us borrow from Lana's work. This was the closest thing to a "magic carpet ride".

Taking a deep breath, I wished for the best and carefully made my way on top of the car's roof. Preston and Olette had closed their door sides while I was searching for Lana's arrival. I soon spotted her as she was reaching the very last lamp post by the park's front sign. This was the last message I wrote which referenced Aladdin. Lana appeared to be reading the note and once she finished, she dropped the note to her side and began glancing around.

I gave the car window on Preston's side a light tap which signaled that it was go-time. The magic carpet ride began its take off. Waiting a few seconds for Lana to face our direction, I cleared my throat and began singing the first verse of "A Whole New World". Yes, it was cheesy and I may have looked like a fool, but I admit it was fun. Getting this expression of happiness from Lana was all worth it. After finishing the chorus, the "magic carpet" was put to a stop and I carefully hopped off from the car's roof top.

Lana looked absolutely stunning like always. That sweet smile on her face managed to make my heart skip a beat. Her blue eyes were glistening from joy and probably surprise. From what I could see as I stepped closer, her cheeks were slightly stained with tears. Why was she crying? I couldn't help but become a little concerned.

When we met at a close distance, Lana gazed up at my trouble face and let out a soft chuckle. Reaching out to wipe the tears away, I gave her a smile.

"I probably scared you for a moment, huh?"

Lana carried all the little things I left at the benches and it left an impact on me. Even though it's only been two months, Lana was the first girl I've met to ever show me this sincere personality. Her eyes gradually made their way back to mine.

"This is... amazing. Thank you, Eli. You really know how to make a girl feel special."

To be honest, this wasn't enough. Lana deserved more and I only hoped that I would be the lucky guy that would have that opportunity. My heart started to race. I liked Lana Clarke. She wasn't just that quiet girl in the classroom I once knew. She wasn't just the younger sister of Landon Clarke.

"Well, there's only one girl that matters."

Lana's cheeks turned a darker shade of red which caused me to smile at the sight. Still, she managed to tease, "Should I watch out for Jasmine, Aladdin?"

After sharing a laugh, I gently grabbed all the objects from Lana's arms and set them on the nearest bench. The both of us stood by the last lamppost of the last note and as we gazed at each other, I grabbed Lana's hand. Her hand always felt perfect when I held it. I wasn't sure how to exactly explain it.

Summoning enough courage, I confessed, "There's something I've been meaning to tell you for a while now."

Her blue eyes were indicating for me to continue on.

I let my heart do the talking. "You're special to me, Lana, and all I feel is happiness when I'm around you... Will you be my girlfriend?"

When I finally asked, it felt like a million years passed through the span of seconds. The anticipation was killing me or I was going completely insane. Lana's facial expression transition in a way that it appeared like she was taken back. Instantly, I thought she didn't feel the same way as me. My heart thumped, but eventually paced in ease when a smile grew on Lana's pink lips. I felt my fists tighten at my side as I eagerly waited for an answer.

Her voice was filled with disbelief before she broke out into a small, happy giggle. "Eli... yes. Of course!"

The tension in my heart officially subsided and honestly, I wanted to break out into a song and dance. But, we heard enough of Eli Wesley's voice for one day. I felt my face lift up with joy and all of a sudden, my arms just moved for me and pulled Lana into a hug. Her arms made their way to embrace me back and this nothing-could-ruin-this-moment emotion was all that I felt. She laughed happily as we hugged and I gazed down at her, giving her a huge smile.

We were soon accompanied by Olette, Preston, and Coops. Olette was on the brink of tears while Preston and Coops had wide grins on their faces. Lana and I both looked at each other before I kissed her forehead gently. Her smooth skin managed to make my body tingle all over.

While this was all happening, I felt the back of my pants pocket vibrating. It was my cell phone. Of course, I didn't choose to pick it up and was too busy celebrating this perfect moment.

But later did I realize that this phone call would change everything.

Chapter 20

Why was I feeling more nervous than ever?

Fixing the hem of my ivory lace dress, I then looked at my left and right where Dad and Landon stood. The two wore pleasant smiles but had almost questionable eyes seeing how I was hesitant reaching for the doorbell.

The Wesley's doorbell.

You see, tonight the Clarke's were having dinner with Eli's family.

Eli told me that his parents found out that we were officially together only a day later. His mom excitedly suggested a dinner — if we were okay with it. We saw how that wasn't a bad idea, and she soon called schedule.

This would be the first time all of us would spend time together. I was very excited to have my family meet Eli's kind parents and sisters, but I was worried about their reaction when they see Dad. Mr. Wesley mentioned that they were once coworkers.

Lately, I've noticed how weaker Dad was getting. His face constantly looked tired, even if he smiled with every chance he got. His breathing pattern would change to a point where he would have to receive daily breathing treatments. This worry wouldn't escape the back of my mind, no matter how many times I told myself that Dad was going to get better. Dad currently puts on a confident attitude whenever we would have appointments at the hospital. However, I grew to realize that, sometimes, Dad did this to keep us from worrying.

And those actions were what were scaring me the most.

"Do you and Eli communicate telepathically, or should I ring the door-bell?" Landon joked with a wider grin growing on his face.

Shooting Landon a playful glare back, he laughed quietly when I finally pushed the doorbell. Dad tried putting me at ease by squeezing my left hand lightly while we were waiting. Giving Dad a meekly smile back, my heart jumped once I heard the door knob rummaging.

Before we knew it, Eli appeared before us, and all this tension and anxiety soon melted away. Eli wore a white dress shirt along with a black tie and slacks. He looked handsome all dressed up. What got me was seeing that smile of his. The way that dimple appeared every time was contagious. Eli opened the door fully, and we shared a few seconds of eye contact before he also turned his attention to Dad and Landon.

"Hi, come on in. Was the drive here alright?" Eli questioned, having his hand out for handshakes.

"Hey, Eli," Landon took his hand and pulled Eli into — what he told me — a "man hug".

Dad shook Eli's hand strongly and grinned. "Good to see you, son."

While the three were exchanging greetings and small talk, Eli managed to make Dad and Landon laugh before heading inside. Already, I could hear the enthusiastic commotion from what was probably Eli's parents. Being the last one outside, Eli grinned at me. His dark brown eyes gazed sincerely into mine.

"You look beautiful," he complimented.

"Thanks. You're not so bad yourself," I returned honestly, trying to rid the rapid blush appearing on my face.

Eli chuckled in thanks before he reached for my hand. He whispered into my ear, taking me by surprise, "Don't worry too much. I'm sure tonight's going to go well."

Giving him a look at first, I let my surprised expression disappear once Eli flashed me an encouraging grin. Eli tightened the grip of our hands momentarily, and I liked the feeling of warmth he always gave me.

After greeting Eli's parents and being squeezed by hugs from Abby and Aly, I introduced Dad and Landon personally. It was no surprise seeing Eian trot his way towards me. The whole atmosphere was very inviting — just like the first time I met the Wesley's.

Mrs. Wesley fixated her attention to all of us and suggested, "Should we all have dinner?"

"That sounds like a great idea," Dad represented our thoughts with a grin.

As we all walked towards the dining room, I watched Dad and Mr. Wesley reconnect with one another. Mr. Wesley commented how happy he was to see Dad after so long. Their laughs bellowed through the hallway. Gulping down, I noticed how Dad looked rather frail compared to Mr. Wesley.

My attention was torn away when I realized we were by the table. Mrs. Wesley prepared a meal that was fit for a king.

"This looks amazing," I blurted from awe.

Mrs. Wesley released a bashful smile. "Thank you, Lana. I may have gotten carried away, but I do hope you all like it."

Mr. Wesley soon had his arm around his wife's small body frame and complimented, "Just by looking at it, we all know it's going to be good."

My family and I took in the caring interactions and smiled delightfully at the sight. The Wesley family were very loving. Before we sat down, the twins acted like ushers. Everybody laughed as Abby and Aly sat us in pairs around the table. Dad was with Landon, the twins were together, Mr. and Mrs. Wesley sat by each other, while I was with Eli. Eli exchanged glances with me, and relief also appeared before his deep brown eyes.

Mrs. Wesley kindly offered us first the dishes she made. I remembered eating her cooking the first time I visited the Wesley household, and my stomach was filled heartily. Sneaking peeks at Dad and Landon, they were also enjoying. For the most part, dinner went smoothly. The adults talked about daily happenings while the twins entertained Eli, Landon and me with their upbeat personalities.

Abby chortled. "And, there was this one time where Eli thought he put sunblock on and went for a swim. Once he got out, he was screaming to our mom that his skin was burning. He ended up looking like a lobster for a week. It was hilarious!"

While everybody was laughing amongst themselves, I carefully glimpsed over at Eli. He ended up transitioning into the lobster Abby was telling us. I never thought I'd see the confident athlete react like that. I could already see how Eli dreaded this moment once he looked at me. In the end, Eli was a good sport about it and laughed along.

I whispered, "It happens all the time."

"Remind me why I always wished I had an older brother instead?" Eli replied in a hushed tone with a joking grin.

We shared a smile before focusing our attention back to eating. For the mean time, I was glad that the atmosphere was never awkward. Eli's parents' didn't seem aware or bothered by the fact that Dad may have looked different from before. However, they did wonder what Dad has been up to lately. Dad casually replied that he was taking a break after experiencing chest pains during his old job — which really did happen when signs of his cancer started to take a toll on him.

Mr. Wesley had a pained expression. "Liam, you were always a hard worker. Before I left, everyone was honestly missing you. How are you doing now?"

A saddened smile appeared on Dad's face hearing that. "I do miss working at the shop. I'm feeling a lot better now. Thanks for asking, Nick."

Once I heard Dad's reply, my body stiffened momentarily. Eli probably noticed this as he was wiping his mouth with the napkin. Dropping the napkin to his lap, Eli's hand then gently grazed over my back, and I looked at him with hope that Dad really was.

Abby hopped in the conversation and encouraged, "Mr. Clarke, I hope those chest pains go away. I play soccer with Aly, but I get tired more easily because of my asthma. I know how that feels."

Seeing our families interact as one was such a heartwarming sight to see. Eli's parents both looked over at the twins with proud smiles. Dad thanked Abby for her motivating words. I really loved Eli's younger sisters.

All of us soon finished the wonderful dinner, and after thanking the Wesley's for the meal, the adults soon shooed us away as they were cleaning up the table. Even though we all wanted to help, it was no use. Pushing in the chair towards the table, I noticed that Landon disappeared, just like the twins. Eli and I gazed around until he asked if we wanted to head outside for a while. Nodding in agreement, we both headed over to the front door but soon found where Landon and the twins were.

The three were all in the living room playing with Eian. Landon appeared amused by the twins and Eian's company. Abby and Aly looked over their shoulders and fully turned around to acknowledge us.

Abby's face twinkled mischievously. "Oh hey, El! Guess what? We were just telling Landon how much of an awesome older brother he is."

The twins giggled, leaving Landon and me with wide eyes.

Landon soon came in for a save as Eian was jumping to grab his attention. "I'm sure Eli cares a lot about you two, just like I care about Lana."

As a result, the twins nodded their heads in agreement. Abby added through a sweet smile, "You're right. He does. We just like messing with him. Where are you two lovebirds going?"

Once I glanced over at Eli, he was — once again — flushed out red which made me chuckle quietly. Eli's eyes made their way towards mine, and he smiled crookedly.

"We're just going outside for a while," Eli soon replied.

The twins placed their hands over their mouths.

Aly whispered loudly towards my brother, "Landon, you should watch out."

Despite Eli shaking his head side to side, he joined in our laughter once more. Landon got up from the sofa and folded his arms.

"Hmm... I don't know. I think I trust Eli." Landon carried a smirk.

Eli and Landon exchanged grins before we walked towards the front porch. Before opening the door, Eli quickly asked if I needed a jacket in case it was chilly out. Shaking my head, I smiled from his concern, but I knew I was going to be okay.

Being alone with Eli felt different. We've sat in the front porch steps together before, but my heart was beating at such a fast pace having him near my side. His subtle masculine scent always wafted towards me when we were at close proximity.

"Lana, thanks again for bring your dad and Landon over." Eli pulled my attention. He ran a hand through his brown hair and chuckled a bit. "Even though the twins enjoyed making me the center of attention, it was nice seeing our families together. I felt like they were having a great time."

When I turned to see Eli, he was grinning happily as he gazed up at the stars. Breaking into a smile myself, I completely agreed.

"I noticed that too. I would love for this to happen again. Thank you and your family for inviting us."

Tearing his attention from the sky, he gradually settled his eyes on me. My heart palpitated, realizing that our faces were so close to one another.

"You don't have to thank us." Eli paused for a moment until he confessed, "You know Lana... Being with you, I haven't felt like this before."

Biting my lower lip, I lightly teased, "Is it a good thing?"

Eli let out a chuckle, and I followed along. He nodded his head several times, soon placing his arm around me. Being in his arms right now, I couldn't help but release a full smile.

"Of course," he admitted.

"I hope you know I feel the same way too."

"And that's why you make me the luckiest guy in the world," Eli hinted through a bashful grin.

Sticking my tongue out, I joked, "I'm glad that even up until now, you still haven't dropped your cheesy lines."

"Never, my fair maiden," Eli played a hurt expression.

The two of us laughed before sitting there quietly for a few minutes. Honestly, it wasn't awkward or anything. Usually, silence was a killer, but when I was with someone who I was close with, silence was just a moment where we could enjoy being together.

"Lana." Eli called to my attention.

Shifting my head to gaze up at him, Eli's eyes were on me. "I know you were a little hesitant from before but," he requested, "Did you want to come with me to Tyler Benson's party? He called me a few days ago, and it turns out that Preston already RSVP'ed for the party."

My eyes widened. "He did?"

Eli looked slightly in discomfort, but he nodded. "Yeah. Tyler may not be everyone's favorite person, but he really knows how to throw parties. I assure you that nothing bad happens at his parties, and you'll have fun."

Thinking about it, I wasn't sure, yet a part of me was telling me that Eli was right.

I smiled, "Sure."

"You sure?"

"I'm sure."

"Really?"

"Yes Eli," I repeated, on the verge of giggling at his brightened expression.

Eli then continued, "I really want you to enjoy this summer. There's still the OC county fair coming up. We should really take your dad there and Landon, if he wants."

Becoming speechless, I couldn't believe Eli remembered from a while ago. Looking back, Eli was so determined to bring Dad and let him experience the fair. I felt touched by that. Eli was not only caring towards me, but to my family as well. That was one of the many reasons why I liked him.

"That would be great. We should do it as a surprise."

I saw a smirk growing on Eli's lips. He noted, "I do like throwing surprises."

After another laugh, our gazes met once again. This time we were stuck. I was taking in every detail of Eli's face, from eyes to lips. My heart was racing again. For some odd reason, we were inching closer and closer. Was this going to be my — our — first kiss?

If time gave us a second more, it would had happened.

"Oops! This is bad." A familiar voice appeared out of nowhere.

Eli and I abruptly inched away from each other and gazed over our shoulders to see who that was. It was the twins with stunned expressions on their faces.

Abby gasped. "We're telling!"

The twins quickly ran inside, leaving us alone once again.

Eli sighed. "Yep. Got to love my sisters."

I laughed quietly, letting my head rest against Eli. "They're still adorable though."

"You look happier, you know that?" Dad voiced his observation after we shared a few moments of silence with Mom.

Gazing back at Dad, I smiled bashfully and shook my head in denial. Maybe it didn't seem believable because Dad just chuckled softly in return. The two of us stood by Mom's grave this morning since we've been wanting to pay her a visit to start the week. Unfortunately, Landon had to open the auto shop. Dad already placed Mom's favorite pink tulips into the flower cup.

"Dad, you know that you all make me happy."

Even though I was positive Dad was only kidding, I never wanted him to forget that.

Dad nodded, placing his arm where his clothes seem to hung loosely around my shoulder. "Of course I do."

We shared a smile together before turning back to Mom.

All of a sudden, Dad mentioned, "I'm sure Cathy likes Eli too. Don't you, honey?"

Turning a bit red, we did update Mom about the news with Eli and how we had dinner with the Wesley's. While Dad was spending a few moments alone with Mom, I unintentionally started to observe him.

The way Dad knelt down and grazed his fingers on Mom's gravestone caused me to swallow that huge lump in my throat. Sadness ran through me. Forcing on a smile, I knew it was because it hurt to see Dad like that. He missed Mom so much. All of us did. Every time we came to visit Mom, I always tried my best to stay strong.

Because, you wouldn't want to see us upset, right Mom?

"Lana, you ready? I don't want you to be late for work." Dad's tender voice reminded.

Snapping away from my thoughts, I almost forgot that I had work today. Dad noticed how I blanked out and flashed a worried face towards me. Reassuring him that I was okay, I walked closer to Mom's gravestone. Settling my index and middle finger to my lips, I then placed my kissed fingertips onto her stone.

"See you soon, Mom. I love you," I whispered, longing to hug her.

Getting up from my knees, I soon accompanied Dad, and we walked back out. Having my arm hooked with his, I asked him if he was alright once we made it to my car. Being Dad, he gave me a smirk like I shouldn't have doubted him.

"Don't you worry about me. As long as I see you and Landon happy, that's all I need."

Giving Dad a tight hug, we both headed inside and placed our seat belts on before driving back home. Telling Dad to get some rest and to call me if anything happens, he did his usual "wave of assurance" and countered back for me to be safe. Making him a quick cup of his favorite green tea, I kissed Dad on the forehead before driving off to work. Every time I left the house, I always spoke to Mom to watch over Dad for us.

Once I parked by the curb of A Fairytale Come True, I grabbed the newly-dry-cleaned dresses of Aurora and Rapunzel along with my shoulder bag and made my way inside. Maryann was dealing with an interested couple in the front, and I greeted them a good afternoon. After the exchanged greetings, Maryann gave me a quick wink, and I hid the laugh that tried escaping.

Walking in the dressing room, I found Pauline and Quinn already dressed as Cinderella and Belle, respectively. The two were busy applying their makeup, but turned to see who arrived. Smiles appeared on their bright faces.

"Hey girls." I waved happily, placing the dresses carefully on the chair closest to me.

"So..." Pauline's eager expression was quite puzzling until her green eyes traveled to the locket I always wore off-duty. "Aren't you going to tell us?"

I figured Maryann would spill the beans about Eli and me. Having a bunch of girls as your fellow coworkers, it was almost mandatory to share details with them. After telling them a detailed yet quick as possible explanation, the two both clapped their hands and sighed in unison. Being hopeless romantics, the two commented how adorable Eli was for asking me like that. The entire time I felt my cheeks burning red which has been happening quite often lately.

Quinn as Belle batted her eyes and praised, "That is too precious. I swear, where can I find a guy like that? Does Eli have any single friends?"

All of us giggled together. I couldn't believe I was actually thinking if Preston and Julian would be interested. Luckily, I still had time to get ready for Bianca's 5th birthday. About ready to head into the separate curtained room, Pauline called out my name.

"Has your Prince Charming kissed you yet?" Pauline, or Cinderella, questioned politely.

Quinn gasped, changing her voice all soft and princess-like. "Oh, that's right! Has he?"

Chuckling at the two who transformed into their princess roles, I shyly shook my head. With looks of disbelief appearing before me, I reasoned with them that we've only been together for a few days. However, I looked back at the night when we had dinner with Eli's family. We were close.

Quinn and Pauline both joked how Eli should hurry up. My face flustered upon hearing that, and I quickly bought up that I had to get ready. The girls giggled before I moved the curtain closed.

Carrying the dress in my arms, I thought about it, and I was really in no rush for a kiss. However, I wondered if that moment would happen sooner or later.

Once I finished the last birthday party, I was just about ready to head home. A little exhausted, I ran a hand through my hair that was all knotty from wearing the wigs. Setting my hair into a bun, I got out of my car to clock out from work. The glass doors slid open, and Maryann gave me a welcoming wave.

"Long day, sweetie?" Maryann asked from the counter.

Giving her smile, I tried to rid the exhaustion away. "Today was eventful, but fun for the most part. I'm ready to hop into bed."

Maryann started to wave her trustworthy black pen around. "There's actually something in the dressing room for you."

Thinking of a worst case scenario, I walked over to the dressing room with fear. What could it be?

Once I opened the door and flicked the light switch open, there was a bouquet of elegant pink orchids on top of one of the vanities. The one I prepped myself up in. A surprised gasp escaped from me, taking a step closer. Carrying the bouquet, I admired the beauty of the flowers as the delicate scent welcomed me. The pink orchids were absolutely beautiful. There was nothing attached to the flowers, but I only thought of one person who could possibly leave this for me.

Quickly dropping off the dresses and making sure that the dressing room was prepared for the next morning, I grabbed the bouquet before shutting the lights off and made my way back outside to the reception area.

Except this time, an additional person was waiting there.

My eyes couldn't believe it for a moment. "Eli!"

Dressed up in casual attire, Eli was standing by the reception area. He gave me that dimpled smile, having his hands in his pockets momentarily. Eli soon approached my side and saw that I was holding the bouquet.

"A bouquet... Who gave you that?" Eli questioned jokingly.

I played along. "Don't know. The person didn't leave a card."

"Should I be worried?"

"Maybe," I teased back with a smile.

"Oh, you two stop being so cute!" Maryann cooed.

Both of us gazed towards Maryann and laughed with her. When I asked Eli what he was doing here, he simply answered that he was going to take me somewhere. A little conscious, I was only wearing a simple top and jean shorts, but Eli assured me that I was perfectly fine the way I was.

After bidding Maryann a goodnight, I followed Eli outside. Curious about where we were heading to, Eli was keeping it a surprise from me. Going along with it, I completely forgot that we had both our cars.

Eli shrugged. "That's fine. We can take my car first, and I'll drop you off afterwards."

"You sure?" I blinked.

Eli reached for my hand and mocked my words from Saturday, "Yes, Lana."

Holding his hand back, we both walked over to his car and made our way to the place Eli was being so secretive about. As we passed by familiar buildings and landmarks, I realized we were hitting the shoreline. Were we going to the beach? However, I soon realized we were driving over to the cliff that overlooks the beach. From what I remembered, this place was beautiful and the lush green life occupying the cliff was just one of the many reasons why.

As Eli drove up the cliff, I was excited to come here. It felt like the longest time, and to be with Eli right now definitely made me more awake. We talked about our day in the meantime, but before I knew, Eli was already parking so we could walk towards the cliffside. Cutting the engine off, Eli took off his seatbelt and got out first to open the door for me. Throwing on a grateful grin, Eli smiled back.

"You know those places where you just like to sit and think? Well, this is one of them. I wanted to show it to you," Eli revealed, offering his hand out for me to take.

Blushing, I was a little speechless. Taking his hand, the weather was perfect once I took a step out of the car. Moving closer, the walk was quiet. Every step made my heart to beat a little faster than usual. I smiled unintentionally, being alongside Eli.

Eli happily announced, "Almost there."

Just a few feet away, we finally made it to the fenced off cliffside. Taking in the view left me in amazement. The view overlooks the entire Santa Monica beach and if you look around, several city lights helped light up the night sky. The ocean was literally glowing with the moon's help. It was absolutely beautiful that it left goosebumps in my arms.

"Are you cold? I could get my jacket in the car." Eli must have noticed.

Tearing my attention away from the view back to Eli, I shook my head and complimented, "I remember coming here a lot as a kid. I forgot how nice it is up here. Thanks for taking me here, Eli... and for the bouquet of flowers."

Eli threw on a sideways grin. "How did you know those flowers were from me?" He chuckled. "I'm kidding. I really like it up here. Sometimes, when I need an escape, I find myself here."

"You're lucky... your escape is much prettier than mine." The words escaped from my lips.

"Really?" Eli grew curious. "I doubt that."

I nodded. "It's nothing special, but I do like to think there."

All of a sudden, Eli moved away a strand of my hair that was probably stuck in my face. Sharing gazes with one another, Eli shook his head side to side.

His voice echoed gently in my ears. "I think any place we hold close to our hearts is special. You want to know a little something? This place got more special having you here."

I flushed out red as soon as I heard that. There was something about Eli Wesley that felt so sincere. After a pause, Eli gulped down.

"Lana... I'm going to do something I've been wanting to do for the longest time."

My heart raced.

"What is it?"

I almost couldn't hear the sound of my own voice because the thumping from my heart sounded louder than ever.

But, I ended up not waiting for his answer.

I let my instincts take control. The first time Eli and I did our "catch up" day, he tried kissing me to which I unintentionally slapped him in the face.

Right now, it felt perfect and needed.

Our lips soon touched and sent a shock of happiness from head to toe. The kiss was gentle yet our emotions for one another were vividly expressed through that sweet kiss. Eli managed to make my heart skip a beat, and I was completely breathless. My first kiss was taken away by the boy who easily made me open up to him.

And for a moment, I actually thought the possibility that nothing could ever take this happiness away from me.

Chapter 21

"Is it just me or are you boys looking happier than usual?" Betty approached our usual spot, the corner booth of Chaplin's.

Chaplin's Diner sounded good for dinner, but we always found ourselves here. Betty caught us at the highlight of the conversation. We were talking about Tyler Benson's party towards the end of July. Tyler had given me a call the night I asked Lana to be my girlfriend. Even though I chose to let it ring, he left a voicemail about how pumped he was having all of us together since graduation. I was pretty confused at first, but everything made sense once Preston bought up that he already told the guy we would go to his summer party.

I was relieved that Lana decided to come too. Tyler's party would already be ten times better with her by my side. The reason why we were all laughs was because Coops and Preston joked about having to find dates since Lana was coming. With these two, getting dates wouldn't be a problem for them though.

We were talking about Preston Daniels and Julian Cooper — they weren't my best friends for nothing, you know.

Even so, they liked having Lana's company. We, including Olette, would all go down to the beach, and it was like the fair all over again. Good vibes all over the place. When I was dating Haley, that was another story. But, none of that mattered.

Preston spoke for us, "You know we're always happy to see you, Betty."

Betty's aged face brightened slightly, and she looked like she was about to smack Preston's arm. She hooted. "Charming, but I have a feeling its something else."

Coops lifted his lips into a smile. "We assure you, nothing else."

We laughed as Betty shook her head side to side before joining in. She soon pulled out her order form and clicked the pen.

Scanning through our eyes, Betty said after another chuckle, "You three will never change. What can I get for you?"

After repeating our orders — which Betty pretty much knew it by heart — she soon walked off to let us be. As we waited for the food to come, Preston crossed his arms and leaned towards the cushioned seat.

"Hey Eli, you got plans this weekend?"

I nodded.

Coops raised his eyebrows, a little shocked. "You do?"

Laughing at their reactions, I faked a mad expression. "Wow, you two act like I have no life or something." Once our laughter ended, I continued, "Lana and I are planning to take her family to the OC country."

Preston gasped from disbelief. "What! You serious? You're telling me you get to eat chocolate covered bacon again?"

"I'm probably not. That's your thing, remember?"

"True enough." Preston nodded.

As the guys were talking about whatever plans they were having, I was looking forward to the weekend. I never lost the thought of taking Lana's dad to the fair the moment I noticed the hidden sadness in Lana's eyes when she lightly wished her dad was there to experience the fair.

Coops soon mentioned, "Eli, even though we joke about you and Lana, just know that we're happy for you, bro."

"Thanks guys." I grinned.

I was happy to be with Lana. The days we spent together were seriously the best moments of summer to date. Every time I saw her, we would get closer and closer. The Lana I thought I knew from high school was obviously not her. I was glad that she gave me the chance to see the real side of her. And, hopefully Lana felt the same way.

Before we knew it, the delicious goodness of Chaplin's was placed before our very eyes. After thanking sixteen year old Adam who delivered the food, all of us quickly grabbed our burgers and basket of fries before digging in. For some reason, I was oddly hungry. I couldn't even trace the last time I ate today. Was it breakfast?

"Eli, is that your phone?" Coops had his eyebrow arched upright while I was in the middle of taking a bite out of my burger.

Lowering the burger, Coops was right. Funny how I couldn't even hear that myself. Placing my burger down onto the tray, I grabbed the nearest napkin to wipe my hands shortly before reaching for my pocket. My lips lifted into a smile when I saw Lana's name blinking on the caller ID.

Before even answering, Preston lightly slammed his hand on the table top as if there was an invisible buzzer from a game show. "Lana!"

I rolled my eyes before I nodded my head. The two let out a few chuckles before returning back to eating. Clearing my throat, I clicked the answer button.

"Hey Lana. Did you just get out of work?"

"Eli, is it okay if you come — wait, are you busy right now?"

Why did she sound stressed? Scrunching my eyebrows slightly, I replied, "Hold on... Is something wrong?"

My stomach twisted hearing her reply.

Answering through impulse, I promised, "Yeah, of course. I'll be there."

As soon as I ended the call with Lana, I hastily reached for my wallet and pulled out my share of the bill. Of course, Coops and Preston were completely unaware of the situation. The two were staring at me like a confused student who couldn't understand the concepts of physics — which we still suffered with.

"Dude, everything alright?" Coops' hazel eyes expressed concern.

The two stopped eating and were waiting for a response. Running a hand through my hair, I scooted myself out of booth and threw an apologetic look towards the guys.

"Sorry but, I gotta go." I paused, gulping down. "Lana's dad is in the hospital... and it's pretty serious right now."

To be honest, I was scared as I walked towards my car and drove my way to the hospital. I felt like a robot walking and expressing no emotion. My palms were reaching a sweaty state. I tried shaking that all off once I reached the sliding door of the emergency room.

Sympathy ran through me seeing the stale white room crowded with tons of people sitting and standing. People coughing, kids crying — it was a sight I hated to see.

"Excuse me, how can I help you?" The red headed lady behind the counter called out to me. Her voice was frustrated and tired, and the dark circles under her eyes were evident.

Heading closer to the counter, I asked, "I'm looking for Liam Clarke."

The lady checked the computer screen before settling her brown eyes back to me. "He was moved not too long ago. Are you family?"

"Well, his daughter is my girlfriend." I tried to reason.

The lady nodded knowingly. "Oh, Lana."

Were the Clarke's pretty well-known around this hospital?

Telling her I got it all covered, I soon dialed Lana's phone again, but there was no answer.

"Eli!"

Turning around, I found Landon by the entrance way. He was waving before I gave him my complete attention. I returned a short wave back to Landon and approached his side.

I gulped. "How's everything?"

Though Landon threw on a grin and said that things were okay, I could see right past his eyes. There were definitely hiding something. When I asked where Lana was, Landon soon instructed me to head up on the roof top.

A little stunned, I wondered if I heard things right. I thought something was wrong with Lana's father? Seeing my perplexed expression, Landon soon waved his arms around and insisted for me to just listen.

"My sister needs you. Go to her, okay?"

And I didn't have to think twice about doing so.

Once Landon told me the exact place to go, I couldn't shake off the feeling that I was committing a crime. Wasn't the roof private property? Well, I was sure Lana wouldn't go up there if it was. Going up the stairs, I found a metal door swung open, and I figured that was door to the roof. Peeking out, the rooftop was invaded with machines that probably dealt with electricity or the air conditioning.

Fully surveying the roof, the entire area was silent with the sounds of cars from the streets down below. The sun had fully set, making it slightly ominous. There were even goosebumps on my arms. This probably seemed like a perfect scene for a horror movie, but the atmosphere felt oddly relaxing.

Especially when I found Lana.

She was looking out from the edge side with her arms on top of the brick-made barrier. Lana wore a simple blue top with light demin jeans and appeared lost in her thoughts.

As I called out her name, her head slowly gazed my direction and seeing those delicate blue eyes made my heart thump. Lana's expression was lifeless for a moment, but soon transitioned as she stepped closer towards me. Meeting her halfway, I knew she was bothered.

I tried to lighten up the mood and confessed, "I didn't believe Landon when he said you were here."

Lana softly chuckled before I reached out to hold her hand. It was cold which contrasted mine.

"Sorry. I go here a lot when I need to think... this is my escape, Eli."

The two of us walked together to observe the scenery from the sky to the quiet streets down below.

Breaking the silence, I commented, "You were wrong, you know." Once Lana turned to face me, I smiled at her. "Your escape is special."

Lana broke into a heartfelt grin. "It's not as pretty as yours, that's for sure."

"You sure? This rooftop becomes a lot prettier with you here." I cracked a grin.

She stared at me momentarily while holding in a giggle.

"So, how's your — "

"Thanks for — "

Our voices collided with one another causing us to break our sentences. Lana's cheeks flushed out slightly, and we shared a laugh. When I told her to go on, it was a short battle of who goes first.

Finally, Lana gave in. "Thank you for being here, Eli. I'm probably being ridiculous, but I didn't want to deal with anyone right now. You being here... puts me at ease."

Instantly, I pulled her into a hug. Lana didn't have to tell me anything. Whatever was happening to Mr. Clarke, I knew it was serious, and it was scaring Lana. As I held her close, I could feel Lana trying to stop herself from crying. I closed my eyes and hoped that everything would get better. I didn't want to see Lana like this. Never.

When we broke away, I carefully wiped her tears away before kissing Lana lightly on the forehead. Giving her a confident grin, I stared into her eyes.

"He's going to make it through. Your dad's a strong man."

Even though Lana nodded her head slightly, doubt still resided in her.

Lana pulled all the strength to explain, "I'm worried, Eli. This time, it feels serious. Landon called me after work and said that Dad was having an attack. It was the first time this ever happened to him. My dad... he just collapsed."

Lana swiftly turned away to stare at the building ahead of us, but I soon motioned her to face me once again.

"I know it's easier said than done, but let's try to rid those negative thoughts. Right now, all we need to give your dad is our strength. We need to give him our best fighting attitude, so he can fight back as well."

Taking in my words, Lana soon expressed a tiny smile. Her eyes deemed hopeful, and she nodded her head more confidently than before. She shook her head side to side, letting out a short chuckle as she wiped her eyes.

"You're right. I don't know why it gets to me like this. Thank you."

Lana soon kissed me on the lips, and I felt tingly all over. It was different when we kissed. This sensation would run through me like never before. Being with her made me genuinely happy. After returning the kiss, we kept each other close.

Lana announced through a hint of disappointment, "Our plans this weekend are probably not going to happen. The doctors are having Dad stay in the hospital."

"That's a good thing though. He will get better," I thought as relief seized my nervous heart.

"It's more complicated than you think though." She let out a sigh. "The doctors are worried about his current condition. The treatment is going to happen during the weekend of Tyler's party... I don't think I could go anymore."

Though I was bummed out to hear the news, I understood the situation all the way. Shaking my head, I assured her, "No worries about the party. I'll stay with you that day too."

However, Lana shook her head. "No, Eli. You don't have to because you made plans already. It's going to be okay."

"You and your family are important to me."

Lana held my hand and smiled faintly. "I know that, but I want you to go. I'll tell you how it goes."

I couldn't help but drop into a frown. "It's not going to be the same."

Lana expressed equivalent dismay. Her voice went quiet. "I'm sorry, Eli. But please go to the party, okay?"

Reaching defeat, I nodded along half heartily. When I asked if I could see her dad, Lana nodded, but the expression of sorrow was still on her face which worried me.

Taking a deep breath, Lana revealed, "Eli, I also wanted you here today because this will be the last time you see my dad before he goes into treatment."

My stomach dropped ten floors. What did she mean by that? Noticing my confused expression, Lana forced on a smile, but those ocean blue eyes were telling me another story.

"My dad won't look the same from when you first met him. I don't want you to see him in this condition, I hope you understand."

Though I fell into agreement, sadness grew within me. I had to keep my head up. Even if this wasn't the summer I wanted Lana and her family to experience, helping the Clarke's make it through was the only thing I wanted to happen.

However, I wasn't expecting what was coming for us.

My phone continuously buzzed as I made my way down the stairs of my house. Tonight was the night of Tyler's party. It was crazy how fast time flew. Most of the time, I was with Lana and hoping that her dad was getting better. Preston and Coops were wondering about what was wrong with Mr. Clarke, but I kept my mouth shut and said that it was nothing for Lana's sake. I felt bad for keeping this away from them, but it wasn't my place to say.

Even though I was just going with the guys tonight, it wasn't a problem because fun was the only atmosphere between us three. I just couldn't help but feel a little down since Lana wasn't here, and she was worrying about her dad's condition.

In the back of my mind, I was concerned. Lana's dad was going to get treatment tonight, but here I was, going to a party. Olette would be with Lana with the time being, but I wanted to be there for Lana and her family. Throughout these past few weeks, Lana insisted to attend Tyler's party. Lana would always reason with me that it wasn't fair to leave my friends behind. She was right after all. Preston and Coops had always stuck with me through the thick and thin.

Before I ended the call with Lana an hour ago, I asked her to update me with anything that happens. About to head out, I walked over to the family room where my family was. My parents, the twins and Eian were sitting around the sofa watching a movie on our flat screen T.V. They already knew my plans for tonight, and as I said goodbye to them, Mom called out for me to be safe.

Taking a deep breath, I kept my optimism on a high note as I pulled out my phone to check the text messages. I was picking up Coops and Preston tonight since I told them I'd drive. I figured these two would want to drink tonight, so it wasn't a problem for me to be the designated driver.

As soon as I picked up Preston and Coops, all of us were keeping the mood up, and it wasn't long before we caught sight of Tyler Benson's two acre urban styled mansion with bright lights scattering everywhere.

Did the kid want to attract all of Santa Monica's attention?

However, being extravagant was pretty much Tyler's middle name. Finding parking was already a pain. After a couple tries around the block, we finally found a spot and drove over as fast as I could without being completely reckless.

Preston swung the car door closed and cheered. "Who's ready to party!"

Coops gazed over at me momentarily, but I assured them both I'd be fine. I wasn't going to be a mood killer.

The music bumped loudly as we walked through Tyler's front lawn. Just the lawn itself deemed the size of my own house. Familiar faces and new faces appeared every now and then from the dim lighting. We greeted some of our old classmates and teammates of Coops and Preston. Making our way inside, I wondered if anyone from the swim team was here.

The interior of Tyler's house was already packed with people. The good thing was, his entire lower floor was pretty much open space. Not too surprised, everyone was enjoying as much as they could. Red cups in hand, laughter everywhere, people dancing like they didn't care — the party deemed a success.

People were invading the tables of food and drinks as the three of us walked around. Seeing all these people was making my head hurt a little. I couldn't even pick out which person was calling out to us. However, we soon spotted Tyler and his group of drunk friends. Giving him a quick handshake, Tyler slapped my back.

"Hey! You guys made it! Go, get a drink and party, dude." Tyler's attention only lasted a second before he turned around, calling out to everyone for another round.

The three of us laughed to ourselves before we branched away from Tyler's group and ventured off. After taking in the surroundings, Preston gazed over his shoulder.

"We're going to get some drinks. Want some?" Preston offered through a sly grin.

I answered, waving my hands out, "I'm good."

Coops reminded, "He doesn't drink, remember? Plus, he's our driver for tonight."

Preston clapped his hands. "Good point. I'll be drinking double for you, bro!"

Laughing, I warned lightly, "Just control yourself, okay?"

The two looked at each other before laughing along, but I knew they took it into consideration. As they walked off to join several others, I was stuck in the living room. That moment where you were just standing around, watching.

"Look who I managed to bump into."

Tensing up from surprise, I turned around to find the source of that feminine voice over the obnoxious beats coming from the speakers.

My eyes widened. I was almost unable to speak.

"Ronnie?"

She nodded with a smirk before bringing the red cup in her hand to her lips.

Nothing to freak over about, Veronica Chance or "Ronnie" was one of my teammates from swim.

The reason why I was a little tongue-tied was the fact Ronnie transformed. She used to have thick, curly brown hair that was all over the place. Some of the guys from the team would tease how her hair would never fit into a swim cap, but Ronnie was the type of girl who was tough enough to fight back. Literally.

Her physical appearance made a complete 360. Ronnie's hair was straighter than ever and cut into a short bob. It gave her this matured look. Instead of her usual athletic clothing, Ronnie got more in touch with her girly side.

"Don't stare too long. I was once Medusa." Ronnie laughed.

Shaking my head, I grinned. "Sorry Ronnie. I almost didn't recognize you there."

"You're not the first to tell me, Eli."

When I asked about the change, Ronnie answered honestly, "You can say I needed it, but when you have a roommate who's majoring in fashion... it was pretty unavoidable."

"You look great though. Good to see you," I complimented the old friend.

It was nice to reunite with a teammate. Ronnie was considered second best — after me, of course. Preston once told me Veronica was pretty cute during our last swim meet of senior year. She did have nice green eyes and a friendly smile. I think Preston would be pretty happy to see her again.

Looking at her cup, I alerted jokingly, "That better not be alcohol."

Ronnie threw a glare before she laughed. "Still the same ol' captain, I see. You still swim, right?"

"Not as much, but I haven't lost my touch."

"You haven't changed one bit, Elliot Wesley." Ronnie smirked as I chuckled in return.

"How was school in Europe?" I bought up the fact she was offered that opportunity.

Ronnie gazed around the room of crazed college students before she gave me a smile. "Fun, for the most part. I felt like I took a big step and grew up. I'm done with that though. I managed to transfer to Boston University this fall."

As if the playing cards were on our side, Preston and Coops were coming my way. The two had curious looks on and wondered who the brunette was. Reaching us at a reasonable distance, they had given Ronnie the exact same expression I probably had on — the look where you felt like you had seen that person before.

Ronnie was never the shy type and spoke up, "Julian and Preston, correct?"

Preston's evergreen eyes widened. Immediately, a smirk grew on Coops' face for me to see. We were thinking the same thing. After shaking hands with Ronnie, she let out a laugh.

"First Eli, now you two? Oh man."

"It's just... you look great, Veronica. I had a feeling it was you because of your eyes." Preston sincerely replied.

It was getting to him. There were two sides to Preston Daniels. His most popularized side was where he played that natural player, but this other side appeared when he was completely interested. By that, it meant it impossible to ever think about stopping him.

Veronica Chance was a prime example — and I didn't think about stopping him.

Hearing that, Ronnie's freckled cheeks changed a shade of red before she swiftly turned my direction. That reaction was new. The swim team were pretty close, so I knew she was using me as an escape from embarrassment. Her green eyes pierced me and demanded that I rid the smirk on my face.

I pointed out, "The funny is, Ronnie's going to Boston U this fall. Pretty cool considering you go there too, Preston."

Coops took a sip of his drink and nodded. "You know that place inside and out, Preston. Why don't you help her out?"

Preston ran a hand through his golden-brown hair. His voice was a little unsure. "Well yeah, I go there... so yeah, if you need any help or anything, Veronica... just, you know, let me know."

A smile grew on Ronnie's face and revealed two rows of straight teeth. "Call me Ronnie and yeah, that sounds awesome. Thanks."

"Weren't you going to school in Europe? What brings you here?" Preston mentioned.

So, he has been thinking about her.

"It's summer vacation, dude," Coops teased while I stifled a laugh.

Seeing how the tables turned, it was refreshing that I wasn't the one these two were making fun of whenever I was with Lana.

Despite the joking glare Preston shot us, Ronnie still replied, "These parties aren't really my crowd, but when you're neighbors with the guy for over fifteen years, and he finally notices you... you'd be surprised. Tyler thought I was the long lost 'hot' sister."

The three of us gave a look of disapproval. She rolled her eyes before snorting a laugh. Tyler was an animal — that was never going to change. It was weird to even think how Olette and him were even related.

Preston's jaw tightened. "He's stupid."

Ronnie shook her head. "It's cool, besides I had a feeling I would end up bumping into a few familiar faces." She changed the subject. "Moving along, why aren't you three with any girls?"

Our eyes scattered with one another until Ronnie gasped.

"Oh god, Wesley, tell me you're not with Ms. Haley Jones."

I shook my head, amused. "It was complicated, but we're not anymore."

A look of relief spread across Ronnie's face. "I probably sound like a jerk, but I'm actually happy to hear that. The swim team almost had a breakdown whenever she was there."

Coops added, "Make us all jerks. We're quite happy too."

The three laughed.

I sighed sarcastically, hiding a grin. "Thanks guys, I appreciate it."

"Eli's seeing someone though." Preston mentioned with a small grin.

Ronnie's eyes lit up until she noticed the concerned tone from Preston. He must have thought that Ronnie was interested in me — which she wasn't. He should know better! The brunette kept it casual as she tucked her hair onto her left ear.

She joked, "I don't think I could ever like Eli after he took that scholarship from me. My grandpa enjoys to party more too. Anyways, I'm sure this girl is great. Is she here?"

Despite Ronnie making fun of me, Preston finally got the message and knew that she was completely free. Coops' lips twitched into a grin, and our gazes were literally telling each other that Preston could be so clueless sometimes.

"Hey now." I chuckled. "The scouts couldn't resist this, okay? And she's not... I wish she was, so you could meet her."

Ronnie smiled. "Whatever, Eli. Okay, I'll be here till the end of summer. Make sure you let me meet her, got it?"

Grinning, I then gave Preston a look to make his move. Preston caught it and set his usual antics. Seeing how Preston had Ronnie's completely attention, Coops and I gave them space to let them be.

As Coops and I reconnected with some old classmates, I caught a few girls from across the room who had their eyes stuck towards our direction. I nudged Coops' arm before motioning his options. Coops glanced over.

"One of them is pretty cute. You good here, bro?"

I nodded. "Yeah, go for it, man."

After finishing up some small talk, I was pretty much by myself again. I walked around the entire perimeter and nearly had to push my way through while giving everyone a nod or a smile. Pulling out my phone, I wanted to go outside to give Lana a quick call.

Before I could even take a step towards the front, a hand was slammed onto my shoulder.

It was our "beloved" host. Tyler was red as a tomato. The bottle of straight vodka in hand wasn't a good sign. From past experience, he was a horrible drunk.

"Where you going, Wesley? Party's over here!" He slurred.

His crowd of friends around him started whooping along. Keeping my cool — even though I probably had a broken shoulder — I stared down at Tyler. He was a couple inches shorter than me, but he was bulkier all around.

I grinned carefully. "Just gonna head outside for a while."

Tyler frowned, waving his bottle around. "Aw, don't be such a party pooper, bro!"

Before I could even say anything, Tyler rambled, "So, is it true that you're with that weird girl who's, like, a princess or something?"

My teeth clenched at the fact Tyler said that "weird girl".

Seeing how he wasn't getting any response from me, Tyler guffawed. "Eli, what happened to you? How could you leave a hottie like Haley? Well, she's single now. She was a little messed up after that break up with her boyfriend..."

He cursed before saying, "That weird girl's brother, right?"

The entire time, I told myself that Tyler was just drunk off his mind. I shouldn't let him get to me. Still, I found myself cringing. His mindless friends were laughing along even if they couldn't even understand a word coming out of Tyler's mouth.

"She's not weird. And, she has a name. Lana." I defended sharply.

Tyler's reddened eyes widened. "Are you drunk, dude? Remember, she was that girl who would sit all alone in the corner of the classroom. People didn't even know she was there! She was quiet as heck. That's not normal, man."

Like Tyler Benson would know normal.

This was why knowing Tyler could be a complicated mess.

"Stop talking about her like that," I warned, trying not to snap.

It seemed like Tyler wanted to provoke me. He sneered. "Seriously, Eli? Lana doesn't even act like a regular girl. She doesn't like to party... like legit parties... not for like kids. How lame! I don't even know why my cousin is even friends with her."

I clenched my fists tightly, controlling myself from punching the living lights out of him.

All of a sudden, Tyler inched closer towards me. I backed away as much as I could because the kid was way too close for my liking. The smell of mixed alcohol unwillingly invaded my breathing space. Tyler placed his hand on my shoulder, and his blood shot eyes made their way up towards mine.

He jumbled his words through a murmur, "You're an idiot, Eli. How could you use a girl... and end up liking her? A weird one at that."

A fist was suddenly flung right at his cocky face.

My fist.

I didn't like how Tyler Benson was so close to my face. And I hated how he talked about Lana, the girl I cared about, like that.

No regrets was all that I felt seeing Tyler stumble onto the floor. The crowd around us quieted down as I stood there breathing heavily.

Haley Jones once told me she wouldn't tell Lana herself, but it looked like that didn't stop her mouth from telling others.

Chapter 22

"Dad? Someone's here to see you," I softly called out.

We found Dad lying peacefully on the hospital bed with his eyes shut. A little unsure if this was bad timing, relief soon took over once I saw his eyes gradually open at the sound of my voice. Gazing up at Eli by my right, he grinned with ease. The two of us were more than glad to see Dad awake.

As we stepped closer to Dad's bedside, I hoped that Eli wouldn't be affected by the drastic change of appearance in Dad. Even I was shocked to find Dad much weaker than this morning before I left for work.

Now that I got a full glance at Dad, his skin was paler while his usual bright, blue eyes were now tired. What scared me most was catching his uneven breathing more frequently now. Why was this happening to him? Trying my best to show no fear, I felt Eli gently place his hand on my back shortly. Having Eli here with me helped greatly seeing Dad in this condition.

A smile stretched on Dad's lips as the monitor beside him beeped in rhythm. Dad's voice was filled with as much energy he could express.

"Hey, you two. How are you, Eli?"

Having his attention on Dad, I unconsciously observed the two as they spoke. Despite Dad experiencing problems with his breathing, despite Dad being in a hospital bed, the interaction between Dad and Eli never changed. Both would exchange jokes which made me join in the laughter.

As the two conversed, Eli's deep brown eyes would make their way towards mine every now and then. He gave me a comforting smile which settled my anxious heart.

Being on the rooftop with Eli was what I really needed. When Eli hugged me, that was the best response I could possibly ask for. The way he held me carefully in his arms caused me to let go of all the stress that was building up inside me. Dad's current state was scaring me. Showing my weak side was the last thing I wanted, but I truly felt like I was able to let my guard down in front of Eli.

Eli had placed his hands in his front pockets and gave Dad a motivating grin.

"Mr. Clarke, let's keep fighting, okay?" His voice shifted jokingly, "This was supposed to be a surprise, but there's still that county fair we all got to go to."

Listening, I couldn't help but feel a little disappointed that our plans this weekend were canceled. I was actually counting down the days to when Eli and I were going to surprise my family to the OC County fair. But, this wasn't the time to be thinking about that. The doctors needed Dad to stay in the hospital for a few days, and possibly, weeks.

More than anything though, I wanted Dad to recover.

Dad let out a weak chuckle at Eli's words. A heartwarming expression grew across Dad's face as he replied, "Did you hear that, Lana? Guess I need to get out of here as soon as possible."

The three of us laughed together, filling the room with joy. They never failed to lift the atmosphere. For a moment, everything felt okay. I was really grateful to have Eli here. I probably wouldn't be able to handle the situation alone. Sometimes, my fears and concern would get the best of it. Dad didn't need any of that. Right now, he needed a positive atmosphere.

"Aw, you won't believe it. Visiting hours are coming to a close," a voice suddenly entered in the room.

Eli and I turned around, but I already knew it was Landon.

"Where were you?" I questioned lightly, saddened by the news.

Landon simply answered by lifting a canned drink and water bottles in hand. Landon and Eli greeted one another before he handed us both a water bottle. After thanking Landon, I wasn't too surprised. My brother could never go on about a day without a can of his favorite orange soda. While Landon asked Dad if he needed anything before we leave, Dad shook his head and reassured all of us that he was racing down the highway of recovery.

"Just be safe. All of you." Dad added.

I reached out for his cold hand and held it tightly. We exchanged smiles, and I carefully observed his eyes. There was always this glint that signaled me not to worry about him. As I moved to kiss Dad lightly on the forehead, a soft chuckle escaped his lips. Not sure why he was laughing, I backed away and gave him a curious look.

Dad admitted as he grinned up at me, "Do you remember the days when I used to be the one who would kiss you goodnight?"

Unintentionally turning red, I laughed it off. "Dad, get some rest, okay? I love you."

"Love you too, honey. Drive safe."

Bidding Dad a good night, it was only then a young nurse with her black hair tied into a bun came inside the room and politely instructed us to head out. Landon and I stood around Dad not wanting to leave, yet Dad reassured us he would get a good rest. Landon shared a glance with me as his blue eyes expressed hope. Returning back a smile to my older brother, we said our last farewells and walked out of the room. Releasing a breath, I looked over my shoulder momentarily to gaze at the room Dad was staying in.

Without even noticing, a hand slipped into mine. Looking over to my left, Eli was smiling softly at me. He must have noticed my worry. Smiling back, I thanked him once more as the three of us walked towards the elevator. Eli squeezed the grasp of our hands and shook his head.

"Lana, I'm glad you called me here. We're going to support your dad as much as we can, okay?"

I nodded, and from the corner of my eyes, I saw a grin lifting upon Landon's lips.

How was Eli able to say these words so strongly? Some people would tell Landon and me the same thing, but it was different. To them, it was just routine — like it was necessary to say that. When it came down to Eli, strength and encouragement would always radiant off. There was something about Eli that seemed so confident. His bright aura was something I was so thankful for.

As soon as we walked out of the hospital setting, Landon mentioned that he would head back home first. He did encounter a long day after all. Landon and Eli shared a brief handshake before Landon walked towards the car.

Now that it was just the two of us, I fully faced Eli and took a moment to take in his presence. Everything that happened today seemed to be moving so quickly. It was difficult to keep up. Eli probably caught that, but somehow, he gave me a funny grin.

"Something's on my face, huh?"

"No, you're good." I released a short giggle. "You really don't know how much it means for you to be here."

His tender brown eyes softened in response. "I'm here for you, Lana. Never forget that."

Stepping closer to give Eli a hug, I felt his arms gradually wrap around me. My heart raced as his embrace immediately warmed me up from the mild wind.

As we held each other close, Eli's voice was filled with gratitude. "Thanks for letting me see your dad. You know, I still don't mind missing Tyler's party to stay with you."

Seeing how Eli was trying to talk himself out of it again, it was silly of him to do such a thing. I didn't understand why he didn't think so. To back out from a commitment was the last thing I wanted Eli to do. I didn't want him to choose.

Gently breaking off, I gave him a look and encouraged, "Eli, you and I both know you should go. I'll tell you everything about Dad's treatment."

After a long stare, Eli soon release a sigh. "Fine. You don't mind updating me?"

I replied with a reassuring smile, "You'll be the very first."

Eli's presence changed me. In a good way.

When I opened up to him, Eli didn't turn his back. Instead, he accepted me. During high school, I kept quiet and would always see the star athlete be admired by fellow classmates. Here we were now — no matter what happened during these months — still by each other's side.

Flashing a grin in return, Eli soon pressed his lips against mine which caused the butterflies in my stomach to flutter endlessly. Every time we kissed, I felt myself melting at his touch. For once, it truly seemed like I was living in a fairytale of my own.

Looking past the joyful and untainted moments we shared, there was something I didn't take into consideration.

Did fairytales actually happen, or were they simply a fabrication of happiness?

"Oh Lana! When your dad wakes up to your homemade croissants, I bet you, he's going to get better just like that," Olette chimed as she was busily frosting the cupcakes.

Dad was able to receive treatment tonight, and tomorrow morning, we would hear the results. I still remembered talking to Dad before he went into treatment. The thought sent chills up my spine, but I was confident that Dad was going to get better. He wasn't going to give up, nor were we.

To kill time and the anxiety, Olette and I decided to bake over at my house. Having Olette's company definitely put me at ease. Looking at the time, it was ten at night. I looked over at Olette.

"I hope so. You know, I never baked this late before."

Olette was already in the middle of finishing a chocolate cupcake as she sat in the stool. Her voice was muffled. "Hey, I'm not complaining."

Chuckling as I placed the croissants into the oven, I closed it shut and walked back to Olette. Giving her a grateful look, I grabbed the frosting bag and began piling some buttercream frosting onto the cupcake.

"Thanks for being here, Olette."

"You don't have to thank me, you were the one who kept telling Eli to go to the party," Olette teased after finishing the cupcake. "Besides, I'm more than happy to be here! You know I can't stand Tyler, and it's good you didn't have to deal with him either."

Grabbing a finished cupcake, I decided to eat one myself. Gazing back at my best friend, I forced a smile. "He's still family though."

Olette shook her head and let out an amused laugh. "Don't get me wrong, he is my flesh and blood, but can you tell me a time where Tyler even treated me like family? Don't you remember during sophomore year when he was too embarrassed to introduce me to his awesome football friends?"

Seeing the broken relationship between Olette and Tyler always upset me in a way. I never wanted to see Olette have some disconnection with her family. She was always the kind of person who got along with everyone. But, even I could understand why Olette may dislike Tyler. He was, if this was the best way to put it, different from the people I preferred to surround myself with.

As I took a bite of the cupcake, the warmth and gooey sweetness of the chocolate melted in my mouth. Olette gave me a thumbs-up for making great cupcakes, but I couldn't have done it without her.

Olette soon hopped off the seat to give me a tight hug. "I wouldn't have asked for a better night actually. When was the last time we baked together?"

Suddenly, her green eyes seemed to flicker with interest. "By the way! Any news from Eli? I bet he's missing you at the party!" she cooed in delight, jumping topics.

Jokingly rolling my eyes at her, I swallowed before answering, "A long time actually. And I talked to Eli a few hours before he went to the party. I'm sure he's having fun. I told him not to worry."

Olette shook her head and insisted, "I would say otherwise. He looked pretty bummed for the past few days."

I looked at Olette with playful disbelief. "You're making it sound like I'm not going to see Eli again. It's just for a night. I do miss him, but I want him to have fun too. We've been spending a lot of time together."

"That's because you guys are together." Olette grinned wickedly.

Taking her words into consideration, I nodded. "I guess you have a point."

"And, that's why I'm your best friend." She winked before I heard her sniffing. "Oh! I think the croissants are ready!"

Getting off the bar stool, I stuck my tongue out and countered, "You sure you're not just craving to eat some?"

Olette let out a laugh before I turned around and walked back to the oven. As I was busily tending to the freshly baked pastries, I pulled out the tray and set it to cool. At the same time, I heard a cell phone beeping. It had to be Olette's phone. Her loud ringtone was very distinguishable. Since I had my back towards her, I wasn't able to pay attention to whatever was happening.

Once I faced back, I found Olette with discomfort expressed across her face as she stared at her cell phone screen. Moving closer, I sensed the mood dropping.

I raised an eyebrow and questioned, "Is something wrong?"

Olette knitted her eyebrows and slowly placed her phone back onto the granite countertop. Her voice was soft.

"Something's happened at Tyler's party. One of the girls just texted me that a fight broke out."

"You serious? Are the people okay?"

For a moment, Olette was fighting back her words. I noticed her harshly gulping down. Through all the years I've known Olette, I could tell when she didn't want to speak. Olette would tense up, and her eyes would cloud up so noticeably.

Observing this reaction, I couldn't help but assume. I didn't want to hear his name be mentioned. I hoped that he wasn't involved in this.

"Tyler got into a fight with... Eli."

My stomach flip-flopped. This sensation of panic grew within me. I could feel my eyes widening in shock from the news which resulted into Olette coming towards me. She held both my hands and searched for a response from me. I unintentionally froze before focusing my attention back at Olette. She stared into my eyes with her voice filled with worry.

"Lana? Lana? Look at me. I'm sure Eli is fine. The text just told me there was a fight, but nothing serious. You should call Eli or do you want to go to him?"

Everything seemed like it was going slow motion. This wasn't like me.

All of a sudden, Olette's phone started ringing. Immediately, she reached for it and answered.

"Landon?"

Did something happened to my brother? Or maybe, he was just checking in?

"Yeah... she's here with me. No, we're not at Tyler's party. Why? Did you hear about Eli?"

As I stood there, not knowing what the two were talking about, I needed to see Eli. Was if he was hurt?

"Wait... what? No! That's not true. I can't. Landon, don't. Landon!" Olette soon groaned in frustration, dropping her phone to her side.

I urged, "Olette, what's going on? Why did Landon called?"

Olette wasn't the same Olette from a few minutes ago. Something was definitely wrong. What scared me was how she couldn't answer me.

Walking over to my purse, I was ready to leave the house. I could hear Olette chasing after me, telling me to stay here. Why wasn't she telling me why?

Reaching for my car keys, I turned around once Olette grabbed my hand. I stared at my best friend. Her face looked hurt, and I didn't know how to take it. I needed to see Eli. Whatever was happening to Landon was also spinning in my head. The entire time, I was confused, but I wasn't going to get any answers staying here at home.

Olette pleaded, "Lana, I'll explain it to you! Just stay here, okay?"

I was already making my way out the door as she followed after me. Feeling guilty for ignoring Olette, I paced myself down the front porch until I was pulled to a stop.

Eli was already at my front yard.

I honestly felt like I was just imagining all of this. I couldn't tell if Eli was okay, but relief spread throughout me. As I hurried over to him, a voice suddenly shouted from the dark.

"Get away from her!"

Without being able to even see if Eli was fine, Landon was charging his way towards Eli.

Stopping on my heels, I couldn't believe what I was seeing. Landon attempted to throw a punch at Eli, but Eli quickly dodged it. I gasped. This was the first time I've ever seen Landon this furious.

The faint moonlight showcased an angry expression across my older brother's face. However, my heart stopped when Eli stopped dodging my brother and gave Landon an opportunity to throw his fist across Eli's face. Eli fell back onto the grass.

I ran towards the two and screamed, "Stop it! Landon! Stop!"

Immediately, Preston and Julian came — from who knows where since I wasn't paying attention — and managed to put my brother to a stop. The fallen Eli wiped the cut by his mouth with the back of his hand. My body was shaking as I got closer. Even though the only damage on Eli was the punch from Landon, there was something off about everyone.

Was I just dreaming right now?

Could time just stop this very moment, so I could make sense of what was going on?

Once Landon saw me, he spat out to Eli, "Tell her! Tell her right now."

Preston and Julian both struggled calming Landon down. Everything was just so hard to comprehend. Taking a deep breath, my eyes started to water.

"Landon, why are you acting like this? Why'd you hit Eli?"

Landon managed to pull away from their grasps and began to shake his head. He threw his hands up and gave me a look of disbelief like I was wrong.

"Lana, you don't know him! Why don't you tell her, Eli?"

I slowly frowned at my brother. "What do you mean?"

"Landon, give them space!" The feminine shrill of Olette's voice appeared. An upset Olette approached our circle. She demanded, "Stop it, please."

My eyes riveted back to Eli, who was getting up back on his feet. Ignoring the confusion, I hurried over to Eli. I wanted to make sure he was okay. As I assisted him up, Eli's body was tense, and his eyes momentarily resisted looking up at me.

"Lana." Eli's voice was hoarse.

"Eli." I blinked, not knowing what to do. "What's going on?"

"I made a mistake."

My eyes observed the tint of guilt in Eli's deep brown eyes. His once perfected face was stamped by a fresh bruise, and the cut wasn't a good sign. There was this temptation to reach out and tend to his injuries. Why was this all happening? My heart continued to race unevenly. So many mixed emotions were swirling around me.

"There was something I didn't tell you." Eli gulped down heavily. "I once dated Haley Jones."

As if Eli was speaking a foreign language to me, my ears couldn't interpret his words. I even forced him to repeat what he said again.

I heard right though. Eli dated my brother's ex-girlfriend, Haley.

Eli had been staring at me, hoping he'd get a response from me. I was speechless. My eyes widened once I fully comprehended his words. This weird pang of my heart breaking occurred within me.

Not literally, but the more I thought about it, it all made sense to me.

All the flashbacks of the tension between Eli and Haley hit me.

When Haley asked me to invite Eli to the party, when Eli and Haley acted differently from their usual selves at Haley's birthday party — just about every single time they saw each other or even spoke of one another, I knew something was wrong. But, why? Why didn't I take in the signs?

Right now, I needed to clarify the truth.

However, my voice wasn't as strong as I thought it would be. "Is... that why you came to my work that day?"

Eli's silence caused me to gulp down the lump in my throat.

I wasn't going to cry.

He moved closer to me and explained, "Lana, please listen to me."

Pushing away, I bit my lower lip. "You didn't answer the question."

He released a groan, running a hand through his hair. The injury on Eli's face was distraction. A part of me was upset that Landon punched him, but I wanted to be angry at Eli. I really wanted to be angry. His brown eyes flashed with sorrow.

Eli confessed, "It was at first, but it all changed when I got to know you. Being with you Lana changed everything."

Blinking a few times, I couldn't believe that Eli lied to me. All the times we spent together, all the times Eli managed to make my heart beat, all the times Eli made me feel special — was it all a mask? Was it all to impress Haley Jones? I knew I couldn't stop the hurt I was feeling inside to appear evidently on my face.

I was blinded by being upset, and I didn't want to listen to whatever Eli had to say. The tears unwillingly fell down my cheeks, and that signaled Eli to step towards me in caution. However, I resisted by pushing him away. I soon felt Olette rushing over to my side.

"Please Lana. All of that, the past I had with Haley, doesn't matter. You're the one I care about." Eli tried getting that into my head.

Even though his words felt genuine, I forced myself to not fall for it.

Shaking my head, I countered back harshly, "No. I thought you were different, Eli. How could you do this to me? You made me believe that you... you... actually — You know what? I'm more upset that I was stupid enough to fall for you, for everything!"

From that point on, I found myself bursting out, "Here I was, chasing possibility to be with someone like you. I actually believed that you weren't like the others. We were different, Eli. I opened up to you because it really felt like you cared. But, it turns out that you weren't the person I thought you were."

Once Eli took in my words, I noticed his facial expression dropping. He opened his mouth, ready to say something, but I wasn't going to take it.

Closing my eyes momentarily, I swallowed. "I don't want to see you, Eli."

Eli and everyone weren't budging. I needed to get out of here. I needed time to think. Since I had my car keys in hand, I quickly avoided everyone and ran as fast as I could towards my car.

I could hear the shouts, particularly Eli's, but I tuned all of that out.

Trying to stop myself from crying, I started up the engine and pulled out of the drive way. The last image of that night was seeing Eli's broken expression as he rushed towards to his car. Stepping on the gas, I took a turn to make sure he wouldn't be able to catch up.

Taking a deep breath, I attempted to clear my mind, but the thought of Eli wouldn't leave my mind. I felt betrayed. Focusing my attention on the road momentarily, I quickly parked before making my way into the cemetery. I couldn't even be with Dad right now. I have to see you, Mom.

The moment I reached her grave stone, I forced on a smile.

"M-mom, I need you here. I miss you so much."

However, the strength I thought I had was nonexistent. My lips quivered as I slowly sat by Mom's grave. I couldn't clear the thought that Eli Wesley would do that to me. All of it.

No wonder he came to my work unexpectedly that one day. No wonder he wanted to "catch up". Everything fell into place, and I was ashamed that I didn't see it.

I once told myself this, but I forgot because, for once in my life, it seemed like I found someone who would stay by my side.

The fairytales did end for me the moment the princess parties were over.

Chapter 23

If there was one person who could make me transform into the big, angry, green Hulk in a span of a millisecond, the trophy would go to Tyler Benson.

He was an idiot.

A drunk idiot who needed to learn how to keep his blabbering mouth shut.

The moment I flung my fist at his face, it was like a record scratch echoed throughout his entire mansion. Tyler, being already disoriented, didn't have a chance to even stand ground. He instantly toppled onto the white ceramic tiling which caused shocked gasps — multiply that by 10 or so — to escape from people's mouths. The music was still blasting from the other room, but anyone who was by a close perimeter had their eyes stuck on us.

Tyler was soon helped out by several bystanders, and his brown eyes were fueled by fury. My fists tightened once more watching him breathe harshly like a bull seeing a red flag. I had to keep my cool. The guy already had a nasty bruise on his face.

He screeched a couple vulgar words at me before he threatened, "You want to start a fight, Wesley? Well, guess what? It's on!"

And since no one really knew what exactly sparked my flying fist towards Tyler Benson, the halls were soon bellowing with chants of "Fight! Fight! Fight!"

I grimaced at the entire scene, nor did I feel a slight sign of fear as Tyler waved his fists around. He looked like a shaken jell-o. A red, shaken jell-o since he was flushed from either all that alcohol, or the fact I punched him at his own party. Though it may seem like a jerk-move coming from me, Tyler was asking for it. My blood still curdled as Tyler's words repeated in my head.

Lana was far from weird. In fact, she was the most normal, genuine girl I had ever met.

Of course, Tyler wouldn't know. I felt bad for him. He would be extremely lucky if he ever got to meet a girl like Lana Clarke.

Tyler kept swinging and missing shots at me. As much as the people surrounding us were instigating the fight, I knew better. Tyler wasn't worth tearing up. That simple punch was enough for me.

Because even if I fought Tyler, it wasn't going to change a single bit of the jerk within him.

Immediately, Coops, Preston, and Ronnie were squirming their way through the crowded circle. All of them had worried looks on their faces. It wasn't long before they noticed that it wasn't serious because of Tyler and his out-of-the-loop self.

Once again, Tyler tried bringing me down. With a slight shove in response, he ended up lying back on the floor. Everyone was so amazed by my light action that Tyler was starting to fuel up more energy. Pointless, really. Coops and Preston managed to pull the disoriented idiot away, and that was the end of the "fight".

As the crowd disassembled, I could hear Tyler yelling a few more swear words and demanding us to get out.

Trust me, I was just about to do that.

There were still a few things I needed to straighten out with him. I wanted to know why Haley told him. They were friends in high school, but that didn't mean they were exactly close. The thought was killing me, and Haley Jones just happened to escape the gun because she was still out of town.

"Eli! Slow down. What happened?" I heard Ronnie call from behind.

When I turned around, I found the tiny blonde with widened green eyes. Her face expressed concern, and I set the thought of Haley away. I would deal with her later. Frowning at the sight of Tyler's mansion, realization started to take over. I just punched Tyler at his own party, in his own house.

Remember how there was always something worth talking about Tyler's summer parties every year?

I think I just made the front page.

Even if the last thing I wanted was to make an enemy, it all came down to Tyler and how he insulted Lana. He knew nothing about her. He had no right to talk about her. In a way, I wasn't regretting what I did.

"It's nothing. He's just being a jerk like always."

"Then it's obviously something," Ronnie replied through a sarcastic tone. "Eli, this isn't good. What happened?"

"Just letting you know, your party sucks!" We heard Preston yell as he stormed out of the door.

Ronnie and I soon tore our attention away from each other and watched as Preston and Coops crossed through the lawn towards us. Preston was shaking his head while Coops looked completely upset.

Did something else happen once I left?

I should know better though. This was Tyler we were talking about.

Coops' hazel eyes jumped at mine. His voice was straightforward. "Tyler's being a complete wuss. He called Landon."

"What?" I felt myself burning.

Preston scrunched his eyebrows together and nodded. "Drunk or not, it was like a little kid calling his dad. Bro, this is bad."

My first instinct was to go to Lana. Preston was more than right — this was bad. Why didn't I think about that?

Right. I forgot that Tyler wasn't exactly the "tough guy" he tried to portray himself as.

Taking my car keys out, I told them, "I'm going to her."

The two gave me bizarre looks, but before they could voice their opinion, I was already racing down Tyler's lawn to head to my car. I was positive Tyler tattled like an immature third grader. Landon knew, and I had to let Lana know. I didn't want her to know this from anyone else.

Even if I did though, logic was telling me that it was already too late.

There was this thin string of hope that I tried holding onto.

As I drove off, I noticed that I just left the guys with no ride home. Why was I acting so stupid right now?

My phone buzzed, but I wasn't going to risk checking it. Once I hit a red light, I quickly pulled my phone out of my pocket. A text from Preston said that they were getting a ride from Ronnie. My eyes grew when he mentioned that they were also going to Lana's house. Before I could text back, the light turned green which forced me to drive along.

Within fifteen minutes, I was parking by the curb of Lana's cozy home. Shutting off the engine, I didn't know what I was getting myself into. The whole night escalated so quickly. Was this the right thing to do?

Shaking the doubts, I got out and slammed my car door shut. Walking across Lana's front lawn, my heart jumped when I found Lana coming out of her front door. A voice was shouting her name, and I assumed it was Olette. Lana wasn't exactly paying attention and was rushing down the steps of her front porch.

Staying put, I gulped down. It wasn't long before Lana glanced up, and we shared eye contact.

Seeing her made my heart skip a beat. I longed to hold her in my arms.

Her eyes squinted a little since she probably couldn't see me clearly in the dark. Moving a step closer, I was once again put to a stop when we both were intercepted by a —

"Get away from her!"

Immediately, my head jolted to my left. Right before my eyes, Tyler definitely unleashed the titans. Well, titan.

The once happy-go-lucky lifeguard shifted into the protective, I'm-going-to-disintegrate-you, older brother. Landon was charging right at me.

This wasn't good. At all.

My first instinct was to dodge his fists as much as I could. However, the more I took in his upset expression, I started to feel guilty with myself. If I were in Landon's position, and I heard about what someone was planning to do to my sister, I would be furious. I wouldn't want anyone to hurt my twin sisters.

So, I stopped avoiding his punches and took a full blow on my face.

What was I expecting thinking that I could just avoid the fact I dated Haley Jones? That I was once jealous that Lana's older brother took her away from me? That I expected to get Haley back if I got closer to Lana?

The thing was, I wasn't thinking about that.

I connected with Lana and grew feelings towards her. These feelings I've never experienced before.

Falling onto the ground, I closed my eyes briefly before I heard Lana's voice.

"Stop it! Landon! stop!"

I deserved it. I never felt so ashamed with myself. Lana was so honest with me, and she was already dealing with stress because of her dad. She didn't need any of this. She deserved better.

Once I opened my eyes, I found Coops and Preston trying to hold Landon down. They practically saved me yet again. Landon was breathing heavily as his darkened blue eyes darted right through me. Lana had turned to look at me, and I could feel my lips fall seeing her body shake. Lana's eyes were glassy, and I knew she was trying her best to understand the situation.

Wiping my mouth, a trace of blood was etched on the back of my hand. The pain didn't hurt as much as I was feeling in the inside. That string of hope was evaporating.

Lana and Landon were arguing with one another which was killing me more and more. I was supposed to tell Lana. I never wanted anyone to find out this way. Landon pulled away from my friends' grasps, and even though the two tried holding him back again, Lana made sure Landon would keep his distance from me.

"Lana, you don't know him! Why don't you tell her, Eli?"

I watched Lana scrunch her eyebrows and frown at her older brother. "What do you mean?"

All of a sudden, Olette came into the situation, and she managed to calm her boyfriend down. The world was seriously biting me back, bringing everyone here at this very moment. Lana broke off the conversation with her brother and made her way towards me.

As she helped me up, I couldn't even look at her in the eyes. Lana's concern for me at the time was the last bit of love I would take from her because I knew she would hate me after I told her. Who wouldn't?

And right when I told Lana the truth, I saw everything break through her ocean, blue eyes. She stared at me for the longest time. Lana seemed frozen, and seeing her reaction made me the biggest jerk of them all.

"Is... that why you came to my work that day?"

I couldn't answer because I was obviously ashamed.

I wanted to tell Lana I truly cared for her because I really did.

As I saw the tears falling from her delicate eyes, I couldn't forgive myself. Why didn't I tell Lana the truth earlier? Why couldn't I just meet Lana Clarke like a normal person, without any motives?

"Please Lana. All of that, the past I had with Haley, doesn't matter. You're the one I care about."

I hoped she would know how much she meant to me, but she pushed me away. All of a sudden, Lana told me off with words I would never forget.

"Here I was, chasing possibility to be with someone like you. I actually believed that you weren't like the others. We were different, Eli. I opened up to you because it really felt like you cared. But, it turns out that you weren't the person I thought you were."

Her words affected me because I told Lana that I would protect her, that I would be there for her, that I would pick her right back up when she falls, but instead, I ended up hurting her. She was crying, filled with hurt, because of me.

Within seconds, Lana ran off and left everyone. My mind was still jittery as my ears echoed with her words nonstop. All of us were trying to get Lana to come back, but I soon started to chase after her. I could hear people shouting, but I tuned all my surroundings out.

Hopping into my car, I drove off to find her. Trying to spot her car, it was no where to be found. Lana managed to leave no trace. When we were still at her house, I noticed she didn't have her phone on her, so calling her wouldn't be the best idea.

Pulling into a nearby curb, I slammed my hand against the driving wheel in frustration. Running a hand through my hair, my mind went off again, rewinding back to Lana. My cellphone started to ring causing me to break concentration. Reaching for it, I quickly turned it off. I needed to avoid people right now.

The only person I wanted to see was Lana, but she wouldn't allow me near her even if I tried.

Shaking my head, I was angry with myself. I forgot about Tyler the idiot, Haley Jones, and everyone else — all that was in my mind was Lana. Where was she right now?

Taking a deep breath, I started up my car again and drove to my escape. This was the only place I found sanctuary.

When I reached the top that overlooked the gloomy ocean, I realized that I didn't even apologize to Lana. The words "I'm sorry" never escaped my mouth during the time, even though that should have been the first thing I should have said. I was sorry for being a complete jerk and for hiding this from her.

I was just too happy being with Lana that I forgot about what actually started this. I had to fix everything, but right now, I knew Lana needed time to herself.

Closing my eyes, I used to think this place was so relaxing and beautiful, but it didn't feel like that anymore. Sighing, I placed my hands over my face as I leaned against the railing.

"I'm so sorry, Lana."

There were only two times in my life that I felt at lost. The first was when Grandpa Wesley passed away — but, I bet even he was upset at what I've done. The second was that day because I lost the girl that managed to make me feel like the happiest person on Earth just by being around her.

"Dude, what happened to you! Where are you?"

This was what I woke up to once I finally turned on my phone eight o' clock this morning. Squinting my eyes, I adjusted the seat of my car back into position. My neck was aching probably from the way I slept.

I cleared my throat, answering Coops, "It's not important."

"Not important?" Coops scoffed. "Well, what matters is that we finally got a hold of you. Did you talk to Lana?"

Flashbacks of that night from the party to Lana caused my stomach to twist. I closed my eyes shortly, remembering that I had no clue where Lana was, and she probably wanted to keep it that way. Turning on my car engine, I let the car heat up first.

"I didn't... I'm sure Landon wouldn't let me near her anyways."

Coops sighed. "Just give her some time. It's going to be fine, bro. Your mom called by the way."

Just when I thought things were already bad, I completely forgot about my parents. I should have been home by now, waking up in my bed — not in my car at my escape. My heart raced, thinking of all the possibilities.

Hearing silence from the other line, Coops let out a short chuckle. "Chill, dude. It's cool. I told her that you slept over my place. She wasn't so happy, but I figured it was better than... you know, the other thing."

I nodded several times. "Yeah, yeah. Thanks, man."

All of a sudden, I heard Preston from the other line, "Don't worry about it. Now get your butt over here, hiding isn't gonna change anything."

That was why Coops and Preston were my best friends. No matter what, they always had my back.

After that weekend, there were many things that happened after.

One, when I got home from "sleeping over at Coops' place", I was lectured by Mom and Dad for "my reckless actions of drinking" and questioned about the mysterious bruise on my face.

Somehow, my parents believed me when I said I was just being stupid and ended up hitting something when I was at the party. Maybe because I assured them this was the first and last time. They were also worried that I was being a bother to the Cooper family. Fortunately, Mrs. Cooper mentioned that we were silent and careful that night — only because she thought that all three of us were actually present during the time.

Still, I was grounded. Five days of summer vacation was taken away from me, but I freely accepted the punishment.

Two, I've been trying to see — at least contact — Lana during this past week. Even though I was grounded, I would drive to her work the time no one is home and hope to come across her. I needed to talk to her. It was killing me not being able to see Lana. Maryann wasn't exactly the happiest person whenever she saw me, but I was still determined.

After the fourth day of coming by Lana's work, Maryann suggested that I give Lana space since she's already having a hard time concentrating because of her dad. That's what was bothering me too. How was she and her dad doing? I was the one who was supposed to be by her side right now. Lana wouldn't pick up my phone calls or reply to any of my texts. Coming by her house was a death trap. I was number one on Landon's "Wanted" list, and one step on the Clarke's front lawn would have me disintegrated into pieces.

Taking Maryann's advice into consideration, I had to give them space. As much as I didn't want to, I had to let Lana and Landon cool off. They didn't need more problems.

Three, I had another encounter with Tyler Benson on Friday afternoon - the day I was officially "ungrounded". He rounded up a few of his friends when they came by Chaplin's. Coops, Preston, and I were simply eating until his cocky attitude could be sensed from miles away. For a moment, the three of us thought we'd find ourselves in a fight. Not at Chaplin's though.

However, Tyler just looked at me with a smug grin on his face. The bruise I gave him was still there, but I shouldn't be talking. The bruise Landon gave me was present like a gift under a christmas tree.

He jeered, "We're not here to fight because it looks like Landon took care of you. You don't mess with me, Wesley. Watch yourself."

The guys had to hold me down from getting up my seat and sending another fist at his face. Seeing Tyler already irked me, just imagine hearing him say those meaningless stuff?

The fight between Tyler and I did spread with our old high school classmates. They weren't exactly interested in the back story — which relieved me because that was no one's business in the first place — but more into, why didn't we fight more? That's my generation, folks.

And lastly, today, on this Saturday, I was going to see Haley Jones.

It's been a week since the incident at the party and with Lana. There was some unfinished questions I had with Haley, and since she returned on Tuesday, I figured I would get some answers today.

"Hey Dad, I'll be back soon." I called out, grabbing my car keys from the keys rack.

Instead of Dad replying, I heard one of the twins ask, "How come Lana hasn't stopped by this week?"

Gulping down, I couldn't face my twin sisters with the truth right now. My family still thought I was dating Lana. Turning around, I found both of them with curious faces even though their green eyes glittered with sadness. They did look more happier with Lana's company. Forcing on a smile, I nodded.

"She's going through a lot right now because of work, but knowing her, she'll make time. You two understand though, right?"

Abby and Aly folded their arms until they eventually nodded in agreement. Knowing that they still weren't so happy about the news, I tried my best to show that everything was okay.

Once I said goodbye to my parents and the twins, I was driving down to meet Haley at her beach house. It made me cringe when she replied back to my text saying:

Meet me @ the beach house. It was our secret place, remember?

That wasn't my secret place, nor was it "ours".

Reaching the destination, I took in the presence of the beach house as I shut my car door. I remembered when Haley's birthday party took place here. This was where we officially parted ways. The flowing waves from the ocean could be heard, and even though the sight of the ocean was beautiful, none of that mattered.

"You're here."

Snapping out of it, Haley was standing before me. Her skin was tanner compared to the last time I saw her while her hazel eyes were staring at me with no expression. Haley had her arms folded in an awkward matter as the wind casually moved strands of her blonde hair.

"No one's here. Do you want to go inside?" Haley broke the silence.

I shook my head, keeping my voice stern. "I just came to talk."

Nodding briefly in return, Haley instructed me to follow her. From the direction we were walking in, I realized she was taking me to the patio that faced the ocean. The atmosphere may seem calm and relaxing, but that was far from what I was feeling. I couldn't help but feel fury the moment I saw Haley. This was the girl who I used to like, but none of those feelings existed.

As we took a seat, I sat uncomfortably once I shared eye contact with Haley from across. The last time we properly talked without arguing was hard to recall. A cryptic smile grew on Haley's lips.

"What do you need to talk about?"

There was something twisted about Haley's words that came off like she was mocking me. Haley knew what she caused while she was in the Bahamas. Yet, here she was, playing innocent like always.

"Why did you tell Tyler?"

Her eyes gazed at me shortly until they brightened, remembering. A chuckle escaped from her, thinking that she was the funniest person on the planet. Haley placed her hands on top of the table.

"That's right... Tyler told Landon, didn't he? Tyler shouldn't be provoked when he's drunk."

I glared and repeated, "He's the same person whether he's drunk or not. Why did you tell him?"

That smirk on Haley's lips eventually faded. Her mocking voice shifted. "Why don't you tell me? Landon broke up with me, Eli! I was a mess, okay? Tyler was there for me when I needed someone!"

"That has no relevance," I retorted.

Haley's hazel eyes stared me down as she scowled. "Really, Eli? Because last time I checked, you were dating Landon's sister! You two were so happy together while I was getting dumped."

"So, this was your way of feeling better about the break up? To drag Lana and me into this?"

She snapped, "I'm not done talking! Don't act like the victim. You were playing around with Lana, and you know that! You think it's fair that you can be with Lana when the whole time you were just trying to get me back?"

"Stop!" I shouted back. "That's not true! I got over you, Haley. We went over this a long time ago. Do you realize what you've done?"

She countered bluntly, "I believe you deserve it. Tell me something Eli, would you have told Lana about us?"

At this point, Haley's words got to me. I did deserve what was coming for me. Clenching my fists together, I looked off to the ocean momentarily. All the moments I shared with Lana replayed in my head. I missed her so much. Every single day, I couldn't help but worry about her and pile myself with blame.

"You don't know how it feels to care about a person, Haley. Lana showed me a side of life that caused me to grow out of this immaturity. You're asking me if I would have told her? I never thought about it because you know what? I moved on from it. That part of my life is done. What I regret is not telling Lana because it's never right to hide something, whether it's good or bad. She was honest with me. She is the one who I care about most. I like her, Haley. You don't know what Lana is going through what now. I promised I'll be there for her, but she's not even letting me speak to her. Do you know how that feels, Haley? To be pushed away by someone you care about?" I questioned, releasing my frustration.

As I spoke, that look in Haley's face fell. Her eyes were watering up, but she blinked away. Haley wouldn't look back at me, but I heard her say, "Why do you like her so much, Eli? What does Lana have that I don't have?"

There were many things.

I took a deep breath. "You only care about yourself, Haley. You always have to be the one in the spotlight,"

"Shut up." Haley sniffled. After a few seconds, she screamed, "Do I really mean nothing to you?"

I backed away, stunned by her outburst. "Haley, you broke up with me, remember? I tried so many times asking for another chance, but you never gave it to me. You chose Landon."

"I'm done with Landon. It's just you, Eli! You matter! Only you! Please, Eli."

Haley was becoming hysterical, trying to grab my arm from across the table. Pulling away in response, I stood up from my seat. Haley was always the girl who composed herself. She always had guys going crazy over her. Seeing her like this sent chills up my spine. I shook my head, not wanting to hear her sobbing.

"No, we're done. This isn't right, Haley. I have to go."

As I walked away from the patio, the last thing I heard from Haley was, "Lana won't ever forgive you."

Walking back to my car, I tried to shake off what I just experienced. Haley was wrong.

Suddenly, I felt my phone ringing from my pocket. For a moment, I thought that was Haley, but my eyebrows rose in curiosity seeing how the number calling wasn't registered in my phone. Picking it up as I started up my car, I waited for the person to speak from the other line.

"Hello, is this Elliot Wesley?"

"This is him." I answered, half confused.

"Good afternoon, Mr. Wesley. One of our patients, Mr. Liam Clarke, is requesting to speak with you if you happen to be free today."

Chapter 24

"Did you really think I wouldn't be able to find you?"

Glancing over my shoulder, I sniffled once I spotted Landon there under the moonlight. He wore a smile on his face, hoping it would put me at ease after everything that happened. Even though I thought being alone would be best, having my brother here proved me wrong. Quickly wiping my eyes with the sleeve of my coral colored sweater, I only shook my head in response.

"It's only me, Lana."

I heard Landon's footsteps tread through the soft grass towards me. A wisp of air blew between us once he knelt down beside me. Having a hard time looking at my brother, I didn't want him to see me like this. However, Landon pulled me into an embrace causing me to unintentionally release my tears as I buried my face in his arms.

The last time Landon saw me cry like this was during my high school graduation because I promised him that I would try not to be sad anymore.

Sometimes, it felt more like a mask to make it through the day. I thought I mastered the ability to stop myself from crying. I let myself become vulnerable this summer. Instead of having a simple summer with my family — Olette and my coworkers — I opened up to someone. That was my greatest fear.

Landon patted my back gently and whispered, "Hey, you're my strong little sister. This isn't worth crying about."

My brother was trying to make me feel better, but things just felt so heavy and difficult at the time. Biting my lower lip, I had to forget about Eli right now.

Yet every moment I managed to not think about Eli, the thought of him comes back again seconds later. Did I just overestimate him? I never thought Eli was capable of doing something like that. He was so kind and so considerate to me.

That was why I never assumed he would.

Then again, the more I fell for him, the more easier it would be for him to get back with Haley. There was always this spark in Haley's eyes that was unreadable whenever Eli and I were together. I never thought big of it, but when the truth came crashing down, everything fell into place.

How could I be so foolish into believing all those sweet actions and care?

"Please Lana. All of that, the past I had with Haley, doesn't matter. You're the one I care about."

Despite Eli sounding so sincere, I wanted to blow up when he said that. Why couldn't Eli tell me the truth then? If he was only using me, why couldn't he just tell me instead of making it seem like he had feelings for me?

When people talk about heartbreak, it seemed so cliche and dramatic, but this really did hurt. Just when I opened up to Eli Wesley, he took it to his advantage.

What made it all better was that I had to hear it from Landon. My own brother. My mind was literally going on a thinking rampage. Even though Eli did look upset, he could have just been faking. I was torn. There were just too many things happening that I wasn't able to clearly factor out right from wrong.

Letting out a sigh, I couldn't be weak right now.

"How did you find out?" I quietly asked, yearning for the truth.

Landon took a look at me before wiping my unwanted tears away. He shook his head in disappointment. "From Tyler. He called me from his party. He sounded drunk, but the kid was telling the truth."

"Are you sure?"

There was still that hint of denial in me that just couldn't accept it.

He gritted his teeth together and insisted, "Think about it, Lana. Eli seemed like a good guy, but he fooled all of us. He looked completely guilty! Before I broke up with Haley, she was acting weird whenever I mentioned Eli. I just thought nothing of it. Now, it all makes sense."

It was funny how my brother and I had suspicions, but "never thought any of it". A part of me wanted to believe that everything Eli has done for my family and me was real, but the other half was poking me in the side making me see that it could have been nothing more than just a plan.

As hard as it was to accept, I eventually nodded my head in agreement. We both sat there in silence before I turned to face Mom. She always had this ability to make anyone's day. That was one of the reasons why I couldn't help but miss her every second of my life.

Mom, I really wish you were here so I could ask you why liking someone could be so complicated.

Reminiscing back to what happened this summer with Eli, all the things he did felt like it was coming from his heart. The way he would always smile and how his dimple would appear whenever he'd laugh, grin, or even lift a small part of his lips. My heart thumped remembering how Eli would always be there to comfort me from my fears, and when he asked me to be his girlfriend.

None of that would leave my mind.

Was it wrong of me to just leave and not bother with what Eli had to say?

"You're still thinking about him." Landon interrupted my thinking charade.

Sharing glances with my brother, I confessed, "I can't help it. All of that just happened tonight. It's just... overwhelming."

Landon nodded before he placed his arm around my shoulder. His voice was filled with assurance. "Don't worry. No one is going to hurt you anymore."

"I'm scared, Landon. I don't want to lose anyone."

"Well, if it makes anything better, I'm not going anywhere. Olette's not going anywhere. And even Dad isn't going anywhere."

That was right. We would hear the results with Dad in a couple of hours. I wanted to hear the news as soon as possible. Blinking my eyes, I looked up at my brother.

"Dad's going to be okay, right?"

There was a small pause before Landon managed to answer. Was he thinking otherwise? Before I knew it, Landon nodded several times. He hugged me once more.

From our embrace, I heard him say, "He is. No matter what happens, he's going to okay."

The next morning, my palms were experiencing the worse state of sweat. I never thought my hands could precipitate like that, but I was nervous.

For the most part, I couldn't sleep last night. It was just non-stop tossing and turning in my bed, thinking about Dad and Eli. Just weeks ago, these two would never fail to brighten my day.

Landon took possession of my phone, and I guess it was a good thing. I kind of wanted to isolate myself from everyone. Maryann already gave me the day off today even though I insisted I would be okay to work right after I heard the news. I was sure the treatment would make Dad better. The doctors said it would help his current state.

Once I got out of bed, I didn't even have enough motivation to fix my hair this morning. I simply tied it into a pony tail and threw on a purple zippered hoodie, a white tank and jeans.

Landon and I were sitting on the plastic chairs that were aligned against the hallway. Apparently, we couldn't see Dad just yet which was worrying me even more. We waited for Dr. Hamilton to appear, but these "several minutes" felt like long hours.

"You're tapping your foot like crazy," Landon observed quietly.

When I gazed over to my brother's side, he had this crooked smile on from amusement. Realizing that it was true, I put my shaking leg to a stop.

"Sorry. I can't help —"

My sentence was cut off because I noticed Dr. Hamilton heading towards us. From what I could see, he had his usual cryptic facial expression that made it so difficult to tell if everything was alright or not. Getting up from my seat, Landon rose his eyebrows at me before he proceeded to follow my gaze. Landon realized why and quickly stood up also.

Dr. Hamilton did something that perplexed me though. He asked Landon if he could speak to him first.

Standing there awkwardly, I watched as my brother headed over to the doctor. Why didn't Dr. Hamilton want to talk to the both of us? Landon quickly peeked over his shoulder and gave me a look not to worry. It didn't help. As I observed the two talking, I noticed the shocked and frustrated expression growing on Landon's face. They would occasionally sneak glances at me — like that wasn't so obvious — and continue speaking.

I played with the ends of my hair and sighed heavily. All of a sudden, my ears managed to hear one thing.

"I'm sorry. There's nothing we can really do."

My heart thumped, and I couldn't hold my patience anymore. Dr. Hamilton was supposed to tell us good news. Without even thinking, I marched over there and interrupted their conversation.

Landon tried calming me down. "Lana, it's going to alright."

"Cut it out, Landon." I frowned. Looking over to Dr. Hamilton, I pleaded for the truth, "What happened that you couldn't tell me about?"

Dr. Hamilton's gray eyes made their way towards me and softened. His face fell in sympathy. "I know how much this affects you, but... your father isn't doing so well. Before we started treatment, we found that his cancer rapidly spread making it even more difficult to proceed."

My throat ran dry as I listened to Dr. Hamilton. Blinking my eyes, I breathed. "Dr. Hamilton... does that mean he's not going to get better?"

Dr. Hamilton only replied with sorrowful eyes, "At the moment, we're trying to make your father as comfortable as possible. I'm sorry, Landon and Lana." There was a brief pause. "Would you like to see him?"

Finding myself stuck, I soon felt Landon's arm surround me. He was saying some words to me, but my ears refused to listen. Dad wasn't going to get better. That was Dr. Hamilton's polite way of saying it.

As we walked over to Dad's room, Landon was trying to explain what happened, but I still resisted to listen. All I wanted to know was how come this had to happen to our loved ones? Once we reached Dad's room, we found him silently waiting for our arrival. I tried my best to prevent the tears from falling. Once Dad took in my expression, I noticed his face was breaking into a sadness. It struck me. Heading over to Dad's bedside, he reached for my hand which I tightly clutched onto.

I tried to speak between the broken sobs. "Dad... why is this happening to you?"

Dad's eyes watered slightly, but just like me, we were both trying to pull enough strength not to break down. He carefully answered, "Please don't get mad, sweetheart. This is no one's fault. They really tried their best. Come here."

Instantly, Dad tried to comfort me with a hug. His embrace did help somewhat, but I was so afraid of the outcome. I really did need that day off.

The past three weeks, I've been trying to spend as much time with Dad as possible. Unfortunately, Dad was stuck in the hospital, so the farthest we could go was outside where we would sit in the benches. I wanted to cherish all the moments I had with Dad. No matter how small or how big, as long as I was with him. Sometimes, when I get off work early, the two of us would catch the sun set together.

Dad always had this joyful attitude whenever Landon and I visited him, but he was quietly suffering. Despite the pain and growth of his cancer, Dad acted like he was the most healthiest man in the world which would always make me tear up at the sight of him. I was scared. I couldn't lose Dad.

Not only that, but I've been hearing news about Eli. Apparently, he's been making visits at my work, but my schedule was keeping us from seeing each other. Maybe it was a good thing. I did my best keeping my distance from him during the past weeks. From his phone calls to texts, I literally disconnected myself from him. Good thing Eli was smart because if he showed up in front of the house, I felt that Landon might explode again.

Even so, I still found myself thinking about Eli. I just couldn't help it. These emotions gave me all kinds of mixed signals. Did I still care about him, that's why?

That particular night would never fail to replay in my head especially whenever I tried to fall asleep. Finding out the truth about Eli would make me upset all over again, but I tried everything not to let that spoil my moments with Dad and Landon.

I wanted to scold myself for feeling some kind of sympathy towards Eli Wesley. This silly part of me yearned for him especially since I felt so stressed about the future. He was always showing me support this summer. During that period, I felt completely safe because... Eli was there beside me.

Why did his company feel so real?

That was what was confusing me these past three weeks.

August was already here, and while everyone was probably enjoying their last weeks of summer, I had other things on mind. Whenever I worked, I showed everybody that I was okay even if the feelings were completely opposite. With all the medical bills piling up, I couldn't just shut down and give up. According to Olette and Landon, I did unintentionally close off from others because of all the events that happened.

Every time I got off work, I always found my way going to the hospital to stay with Dad before visiting hours came to a close. Yesterday on my day off, I bought Dad his favorite fresh croissants I made and a deck of bicycle cards.

For some reason, Dad wanted to play a game of cards like how we used to when I was a little kid. Yes, it was a little random, but I didn't mind even if Dad always pulled tricks whenever we played. It was fun nonetheless. Even if Dad was weak, he still joked around and smiled as much as he could.

Once I made it to the fourth floor Dad has been on, I was greeted by passing nurses. It was kind of embarrassing how they knew our faces so well. Giving them a faint smile back, I made my way down the hall and walked over to Dad's room. Carefully coming in, Dad managed to wake up from my movements. He was a very light sleeper nowadays.

A smile stretched on Dad's tired face. "Lana, you're here."

Lightening the mood, I joked. "Where else would I be? Come on, Dad."

He let out a small laugh until he started to cough. Growing worried, Dad managed to put his coughing to a halt. I moved closer towards his bedside and gave him a kiss on the forehead. Looking into Dad's blue eyes, I looked passed the tubing in his nose where the oxygen would help him breath better. I looked passed at all the equipment that was hooked onto him. I looked passed the sudden aged face my dad held.

To me, he was still my handsome, admirable, strong Dad.

"How are you feeling?"

"I'm fine," Dad shifted the topic quickly, "Go take that chair over there and come sit down. Let's talk like we always do."

Giving in, I carefully pulled the nearby chair that still managed to let out a screech against the floor. A smile grew upon Dad's chapped lips. There was a sudden urge to pull out my chap stick from my bag, but Dad was never a fan of chap stick. He always thought the feeling was too greasy for his lips.

Just like Dad wanted, we talked. Well, I did for the most part because it was easier for Dad to listen than speak. I was able to tell Dad about my day even though it wasn't exactly eventful. It was the usual "wake up, get ready, go to work" routine. Sometimes, I wondered if my own dad was bored of hearing about my day, but there was always this interested sheen in Dad's eyes whenever he listened.

When I finished talking, I cleared my throat. "Are you tired, Dad?"

"Nope. I've been sleeping all day." Dad paused shortly. "How about we play cards?"

Following his suggestion, I smiled and reached for my bag to bring out of the deck of cards. This time around though, Dad wanted to play game. Winner would get to ask the loser a question that he or she must answer truthfully. Hearing this caused me to break into laughter.

"Dad! What is this? High school?" I joked.

Dad only grinned and answered slowly, "Doesn't it sound fun? Are you afraid you're going to lose?"

"I'm not afraid! This is a little silly... We're always truthful with each other, right?"

He nodded. "Of course I know that. I just wanted to see you laugh."

In the end, we played a game of cards and went along with Dad's request. The back of my mind was wondering what question was he conjuring up. I already knew what I was going to ask Dad. However, Dad seemed to have the upper hand and won. A triumphant smile beamed across Dad's face, and I was being a good sport about it. Maybe Dad pulled one of his tricks again.

Letting out a playful sigh, I pushed all the cards together back into one stack. Settling my eyes back on Dad, I wondered, "So, what did you want to ask me?"

Dad seemed hesitant for a moment. Once a few seconds passed, Dad gave me his serious stare when he wanted to talk about something important. It wasn't a terrifying look, like I was expecting trouble. This look meant whatever we would talk about during this period was not to be joked around. It was that kind of matter. I gulped down. Even though Dad looked weak, the aura he gave off was still the same.

"I spoke with Landon a few days ago. I've noticed this for a while," Dad stated softly yet kept a stern hold. "He told me about Eli."

A twisted knot stirred in my stomach. There was always someway for Eli to seep into my daily life. Then again, what was I expecting thinking that I could just rid him away? I couldn't. Growing silent for a brief moment, I didn't know how to respond to this.

Coming up with an answer, I looked down at my lap and replied, "I'm sorry, Dad. It just all happened at once. That night and hearing about you... I didn't want to bother you with more trouble. You're already going through with so much. You need to get better and not be worried about me. I'm always going to be okay."

"But sweetheart, answer this. Are you really okay?"

I bit my tongue harshly. Falling into defeat, I muttered, "I'm not. I'm having all these mixed emotions towards Eli. And... I-I'm scared."

"About me?"

I nodded.

Dad then proceeded, reaching for my hand. "Actually, the last thing I want you to worry about is me. What are you planning to do?"

How could I not worry about him? That was like asking me to stop blinking my eyes. Shrugging, I really wished I ended up winning that game of cards. I was so close. I couldn't look at Dad directly.

"I don't have anything in mind. Should I be angry at him? But, how come I feel weird if I am? I don't know how to explain it, Dad. I'm confused with my own head."

Suddenly, I felt Dad's cold fingers tapping the bottom of my chin lightly to get my attention. Gazing at him, he had a warm grin across on his face. Seeing this caused me to smile back.

"It seems like the problem is that you don't know what you really want yet." Dad took a break before continuing on. "What I mean, Lana, is that you're ignoring your heart."

I sighed. "I just can't believe he would do that to me. You saw all the good things he did. Eli made me feel special... but I guess it wasn't really him."

"What caused Eli to first meet you was wrong, and I didn't ever want to see you get hurt. I was disappointed when Landon told me, especially since I couldn't be there."

Shaking my head, I let out a dry laugh. "No Dad. I can't believe I actually cried about that."

Dad soon noted while taking short pauses in between, "I'm not finished yet, sweetie. I just want you to think about this for a moment. If Eli did follow through with this plan, I think if he were still interested, he would have left with Haley the moment Landon and her separated."

I listened as Dad spoke, "I'm not saying that Eli's decision was the right thing to do. His mistake grew through a poor decision. But, in the end, despite all the chances he could have had to get back with Haley, Eli stayed with you. From what I could see, he cares about you."

Having this closed moment with Dad about this topic had me thinking even more.

"I feel torn. I don't want Eli gone, but I feel like I wouldn't be able to look at him the same way." I scrunched my eyebrows. "How can you tell he cares, Dad? He could just be faking."

A knowing look just spread across Dad's face. He patted my hand. "I can also see that you're trying to force yourself to believe that Eli's faking."

My lips fell unintentionally to a frown. "No. I know he was faking."

"I want to offer you a little piece of advice I've learned in my life," Dad remarked politely, "Sometimes, the best way to feel resolved is to forgive. Whether you are the one asking for forgiveness or accepting. Forgiveness doesn't mean moving back to the ways of the past because we bloom from those mistakes. With forgiveness, you will find a new light and from there, you can choose what path to go through."

"What if I... can't forgive him, Dad?"

"Don't be scared. I know you'll know what's best for you, sweetheart." Dad tightened the grip of our hands.

Forgive Eli.

Maybe it was too soon to think about that, but I felt like if I did, I wouldn't be so confused.

Thanking Dad for talking about this with me, I admitted I was embarrassed to even bring this subject up to him. Even though I wished Landon didn't talk about this with Dad, I knew Dad would have never known without Landon. Now, I felt like I had more insight on what to do. This never really happened to me before, but I was considering it. I couldn't figure out when, but I would just let it happen — when it felt right.

What mattered most was being with Dad. Giving him a hug, I looked at him, hoping he could feel how grateful I was to have such an inspiring dad.

Dad soon asked me if he could get a drink of water. Telling him not to worry, I propped myself up from the chair and made my way out the hall. Carrying a pitcher from the nurses, one of the nurses thanked me for delivering it. It caused me laugh. I didn't mind helping my own dad.

Once I entered back to Dad's room, I was so close to dropping the pitcher.

"Dad! What's wrong?"

I panicked, racing over to him as I placed the pitcher harshly onto the table top.

With every breath, Dad was struggling to even his breathing. This wasn't happening. No.

Immediately, I was ready to call to a nurse's attention by running outside. As I turned my body away, Dad took a grasp of my hand.

"Dad, please. I'm going to get help!"

My eyes started to water as Dad was shaking his head with every ounce of strength he had. His struggle eventually ceased, but Dad's breathing pattern was still harsh. My body was shaking at the sight of him. My hand was the only one being somewhat still because Dad held onto it.

Dad's voice was so quiet, so fragile.

"Lana. Just... stay by my side."

My stomach twisted seeing Dad's eyes flutter. Holding onto his hand, I yearned to see those bright blue eyes.

I croaked, "Dad! Don't leave us! Please, please. Don't close your eyes."

At this moment, my cheeks were soaked with tears. The teardrops were landing on Dad's hand. He wouldn't let me go. He wouldn't let me get help. Dad was giving up. And being there was breaking my heart every single second. The entire room was becoming a blur. My attention was only focused on Dad. His chest would elevate as his mouth would release the air. My continuous calls for Dad didn't seem to help. I was reaching a high state of panic.

I couldn't even recognize my voice as I cried out, "Dad, I can't lose you. Landon and I, w-we need you! Dad, look at me. Please. Let's practice breathing together, okay?"

Even though I tried, Dad was reaching that state. Though his eyes barely appeared open, I knew he was looking up at me. He held my hand snugly.

Dad reminded through a smile, "You know how much I love you and Landon, right? Lana, I love you... you have so much ahead of you... and I'm going to be there watching."

Shaking my head, I resisted, "You're going to stay, right Dad? You're not going anywhere, you told us that. W-why? You know how much we need you here, Dad! I can't make it through."

Turned out, I wasn't able to bear anymore pain.

Dad shook his head slightly. He tried to prove me wrong as his voice was gradually disappearing, "You need to stop listening to your fears, and listen to your heart, honey. That heart of yours is golden, and I know you can make it through. Promise me you'll try. Promise me."

As much as it hurted, it was hurting me even more watching Dad suffer like this. He was trying so hard just to make us happy, but he needed to rest.

I nodded, trying to hold back the tears. My lips quivered. "I promise, Dad. I love you. I love you so much, Dad."

A few seconds later, a brightened smile appeared on Dad's face. "Lana, I see... your mother. I'm at the shore where I first saw your mother..."

Biting my lips harshly, I understood where Dad was going. He was going to a better place. No more suffering, and he would finally be with Mom.

The thing was, I wanted to hold onto Dad, but that would be nothing more than selfish of me. Dad needed to be at peace. Wiping my eyes, I gave Dad a smile despite him not seeing it.

I assured him, "Dad, I don't want you to suffer anymore. Don't worry about us, okay? Go to Mom. I'm sure you miss her so much. Thank you for everything, I-I love you so much."

What looked like Dad nodding was the last action I remembered before he let out his last breath. Hearing the flat line bought everything into reality. I was frozen. Dad wasn't breathing anymore. His grip loosed between my hand, and I could no longer see those crystal clear blue eyes.

Letting out a cry, I carefully moved his hand to his side and tried to take in that Dad wasn't with us anymore. Stroking his hair, I then placed my hands over my mouth as the tears unwillingly fell. Once my attention to my surroundings started to kick back in, I could hear the intercom from the hallway that had been ringing for medical help.

Code blue.

Immediately, a nurse came into the room and told me that Dr. Hamilton was coming in. My mind started to spin. Dad was with Mom now, and that was what mattered most. No more pain, Dad.

Dad wasn't gone, he was together with Mom.

Once the nurse saw, she gave me a look of sympathy. I swiftly looked away. I didn't want anyone to see me like this. However, I was already a wreck. Moving away from the nurse, I wanted to head out the door to take a fresh of breath air. Walking towards the door, I wasn't paying attention to where I was going.

I soon found myself crying into someone's sudden embrace.

At the moment, I let that someone hold onto me because I didn't want to break even more.

It was only then that I felt familiarity being in this person's arms.

Eli Wesley.

Chapter 25

I didn't have to think twice about going to the hospital.

After speaking to whoever was on the phone — which I assumed to be some nurse — I already pulled out of the parking lane and zoomed away. This was either a good sign or a bad sign. Either way, it was better than being suffocated in the same perimeter with Haley Jones. As I was driving, texts from Haley would pop up from my cellphone screen. I concluded not to bother. Looking back was not an option.

Once I made it to the hospital and was instructed which floor to go up to, I was soon poking my head slightly from the door where Mr. Clarke was residing. He appeared to be sound asleep on his hospital bed with the monitor beeping in a consistent pace. A clear tubing occupied Mr. Clarke's nose which I assumed assisted him with his breathing. Seeing Lana's dad in this condition caused my stomach to twist uneasily.

The sudden, unconscious fear stated to run within me.

Did Mr. Clarke call me over because he heard what happened to Lana and was upset? My voice involuntarily shook.

"Mr. Clarke?"

I was doing a great job being confident.

As soon as Mr. Clarke heard my call, his eyelids slowly opened. Remembering how Lana wouldn't let me see her dad anymore, I now understood why. Mr. Clarke looked so fragile that it sent chills up my spine. His appearance drastically changed from his sunken cheeks to his tired, blue eyes. Mr. Clarke gazed upon me briefly before acknowledging my presence with a faint grin. The grin was welcoming, but even smiling appeared to be draining the energy out of him.

Taking this as a sign to walk in, my first action was to shove my hands in my front pockets since I thought that it would deem presentable at the time.

"Mr. Clarke, you called? How are you doing?"

His voice sounded slightly strained.

"I'm getting adjusted. Take the seat right here, son."

Following his request, I reached over and lifted the chair to a reasonable distance between Mr. Clarke's bedside. Mr. Clarke was carefully eyeing the injury by my mouth proudly marked by Landon Clarke.

"I hope you've been taking care of your cut. I apologize that my son did that to you."

The bruising did swell down, and all that was really left was the healing cut which my mom continuously forced to put some ointment on. I can say that it wasn't as bad as before, but it was still a marking of my stupidity.

Shaking my head, I reassured him, "It's not his fault, I deserved it. It's getting better though."

As I sat there, it took a lot of strength to face Mr. Clarke and look at him in the eyes because I felt so guilty. I hurt his daughter, my girlfriend, Lana. I couldn't take back what happened. Flashbacks of that moment would scar my sight. I closed my eyes temporarily before bringing myself back to reality.

Instead of Lana's dad speaking, I found myself blurting out of impulse, "Mr. Clarke, I'm sorry. I'm sorry for everything. I didn't mean to hurt Lana. It was never my intention to hurt her. I'm an idiot — I know that, but I never wanted any of this to happen. Lana doesn't deserve it, and I don't deserve someone as remarkable as her. It's all my fault, and I take full blame. But please understand that I do care about her."

I took a deep breath and finished, "I had to get that out. I'm ready for what you need to say."

Mr. Clarke had adjusted his bed upright, so he would be sitting. After listening, he studied me while I tried to hide my clenched fists, wondering what in the world he was thinking about.

He was going to say that he hated me, my guts, all states of matter that spoke and are composed of Elliot Aaron Wesley!

The silence in the room besides the rhythmic beeping noise from the monitor was a definite killer.

"Eli, I know you're sorry," Mr. Clarke finally replied.

My eyes rapidly widened. I was hearing things. That was probably it. I've gone that crazy. My mind was probably making up its own happy ending.

Shaking my head in disbelief, I asked if Mr. Clarke could repeat what he said again. There was a small smile on Mr. Clarke's evidently kind face. His words came out slow yet still easy to understand.

"I wasn't expecting my daughter to meet a perfect boy. Perfection doesn't exist in this world, Eli."

A little stumped, I stared at him blankly and let Lana's dad clarity.

What I didn't understand was, why was he being so nice to me?

"You're still growing up. From what I experience, we're bound to make mistakes. Some more severe than others, but that's what makes us human. Your mistake is something I wouldn't want repeated again, but with every mistake made, a lesson is learned. Through mistakes, we become more knowledgable in life."

"But, what I did was unforgivable, Mr. Clarke. You know that." I jumped in.

Placing my hands over my face, my elbows were on top of my thighs as the words of Lana telling me to leave her alone would repeat over and over again.

Not being able to contact Lana these past few days had me all messed up. I only hoped she would let me redeem myself. However, I was just kidding myself. I didn't deserve it. Luck would be on my side if Lana would even spare half a breath for me. I was the stupid idiot who decided to go along with this plan. I didn't blame anyone but myself.

"Look at me, son." Mr. Clarke broke my thoughts.

Lifting my head up, the trace of happiness on his face urged me to rid the pain that struck me.

"I'm going to be honest with you, as Lana's father, I was disappointed that you would choose to do something like that, but I then reminded myself of the teenage boy I was long ago. I also made mistakes during those years. We tend to make the wrong choices sometimes, but this is an opportunity you can fix. You tell me that what you did was unforgivable, but I will tell you something in return. Forgiveness will happen if you put the effort to make it happen."

Mr. Clarke continued after a brief break to catch his breath. "I didn't call you here to scold you because I can already see how sorry you are about the matter. Eli, it takes a lot in a person to admit their faults, but unlike others, you took it directly in your hands. To see my daughter upset is the last thing any father wants, but if this goes on, she'll never be happy."

Slowly nodding, I thought I understood what he had implied.

"You're right. It would be best if I stay away."

Immediately, Mr. Clarke's eyebrows rose before he started to shake his head. What sounded like a soft, amused laugh filled the once silent room.

Was it something I said?

"I don't seem to understand why you look completely frightened. If you're already scared now, I could only imagine when I'm actually mad."

Hearing his response caused me to grin a little. Mr. Clarke was trying to ease up the mood.

Catching the smile that grew on my face, Mr. Clarke corrected, "It's not in my power to change the course to everyone's favor, but I don't want you to stay away from Lana. My daughter's going to need some time, but she shouldn't be left alone. I know you care about Lana — call it father's intuition, if you will — but we can see good in a gentlemen before us. For the first time in years, Lana has found someone who makes her smile and open up. That someone is you."

Honestly, I wasn't sure how to reply. Mr. Clarke made me sound like some wonderful guy. Why did it feel like his words sounded nothing like me?

"You looked surprised, but you shouldn't be."

After a second, a saddened tint appeared in Mr. Clarke's blue eyes. He tried to sound steady.

"You know about my condition, Eli. I'm not going to be here for very long so —"

"Wait a second, no. You can't say that, Mr. Clarke. Lana needs you," I rushed to interrupt because I was worried about what he would say.

Instead, Mr. Clarke shook his head.

"Unfortunately son, I don't have very much time. You know, there's a saying when someone is gone, there will be another person to help fill that empty gap in someone's heart. I shouldn't be the complete source to Lana's happiness. She will have to find it on her own, and she's going to need someone there to help her along the way. You care about Lana, don't you?"

Nodding sternly, I answered with complete honesty, "Of course I do. She's become a huge part of my life. I never felt this way before..."

It was as if all the doors were finally opened that very moment.

"Everything — I love everything about her. I love your daughter, Mr. Clarke. I love Lana."

Finally, those words were released.

These strong feelings that were once bottled up made me want to shout them out to the world.

More importantly, I wanted to tell Lana.

Mr. Clarke appeared to be at peace from my answer.

"Then, why are you trying to push yourself away? Don't. Don't let my daughter go because even if she tries to deny it, I know she cares about you just as much. I'm here to say that you shouldn't give up."

You know when a little kid gets so pumped up to see Santa Claus, he would run like crazy to give him a hug? That was what I wanted to do at that moment.

"I won't give up," I promised, "Don't give up on us either. You're going to overcome this."

He didn't respond through words, but the calm look upon his face seemed somewhat assuring. Although, I couldn't help but be a guy to worry. When Mr. Clarke mentioned that he didn't have much time left, it confused me a bit. Did people just know when their time was almost up? Shaking those thoughts away, Mr. Clarke wasn't going anywhere.

His breathing got a little uneasy suddenly which caused me to get all jumpy. After a few moments, Mr. Clarke was breathing back to normal. His tired, blue eyes then gazed directly towards me.

"Thank you, Mr. Clarke."

Mr. Clarke shook his head slightly as if it wasn't big deal. Trust me, it was.

I only wished there was a better way to show how thankful I was.

Telling him I would come back to visit, Mr. Clarke said he would appreciate it. It was only then I said my goodbyes to Lana's father and made my way outside the hallway.

However, I wasn't expecting to bump into a particular somebody.

The particular somebody was Landon Clarke.

My stomach twisted in multiple directions. Just looking at the guy caused cryptic messages to fly all over the place. Judging from his attire, Landon looked like he just got out of work from the auto shop. His blue eyes jumped from me to the injury he stamped on my face. Landon's expression was rather blank which made me go into a state of confusion.

Lana's older brother was either gonna throw another punch at me or probably just end it by tearing my head off.

Standing ground, I found myself speechless. I wanted to say something, so it wouldn't be just an awkward staring contest. The tension was unbearable. After a moment, Landon gulped down as he briefly glanced to his left. As soon as he settled his eyes upon me once again, he cleared his throat.

"Do you mind if we talk?"

I shook my head, indicating that it was fine.

We moved further away from Mr. Clarke's room. There were several nurses near us, but all of them were too focused with their own situations. Landon had folded his arms as he leaned against the wall. I was somewhat nearby him, but just enough so I had a good running distance — I was being sarcastic about that last part.

The two of us stood there silently which reminded me of how the conversation between their father and me started out. This time, I cleared my throat.

"Listen Landon, I know I'm the last person you want to see right now, and I don't blame you if you see me as a bad person because it was my fault.

I wasn't thinking about the consequences or any of that... I just went with it, but I never wanted to hurt Lana. Even though all of this happened, I really do genuinely care about her."

While I was talking, I asked myself if I were in Landon's position right now, would I actually believe the guy trying to explain himself? Even if I felt like Landon was highly doubting my words, I did mean every single word, letter, and syllable.

Landon's eyebrows furrowed together in frustration or disgust. Of course, he didn't want to hear any of it. After a moment, Landon's face grew less tense as he sighed.

"I just don't understand how my dad can forgive you like that."

I figured Landon probably overheard the conversation.

Standing quietly, I watched as Landon shook his head. He seemed like he was holding back something, or he was holding an urge to create a mark identical on the other side of my mouth.

Through it all, I wanted to ask Landon how Lana was doing. I didn't have the guts to ask Mr. Clarke. Right now, I should have asked Mr. Clarke instead.

Landon then barked up, "Honestly, I don't want to believe you. That's because I promised myself that I would never let anyone hurt my little sister."

His once piercing blue eyes seemed to have grown sadder which made me feel even worse. The thing was, I understood Landon because I wouldn't want my twin sisters to go through any kind of pain either. That was always the natural role of an older brother.

"When I found out, I kept asking myself why. Why in the world would anyone think of doing this to Lana? Out of everyone, why her?" Landon's voice was toned down. "She's already gone through so much. I'm always worried that one day she'll break, and I won't be able to help her."

He ran a hand through his short brown hair and remarked, "Days after the incident, I wanted to tell you how stupid you were if I ever saw you again. You chose the wrong person to mess with, Eli. It was yesterday when my dad asked me about you and Lana. I don't know how my old man found out since he's been here, but he just knew. I couldn't believe him when he actually said to work things out with you. You. The kid who broke my sister's heart."

As Landon spoke, what struck me was his last words. He saw me as "the kid who broke his sister's heart". No guy, especially me, ever wanted to be classified under that category. Nobody wants to be the bad guy. It was horrible, but I should have expected having this kind of conversation with Landon.

"But, Dad was right. He always is," Landon suddenly explained, "I didn't look at the entire situation. I didn't start at the very beginning. You and Haley were still together when I came in the picture, isn't that right?"

I nodded slowly.

"I didn't know until Haley told me the truth, but I could only imagine what you were going through when you found out about us. It was also unfair to you. We tend to do crazy things when we like someone. The crazy things we do can unintentionally hurt the people around us too, and that ended up being my sister."

His light blue eyes gazed upon me as Landon admitted sincerely, "I wanted to apologize actually. I'm sorry. It wasn't right of me to immediately jump between Lana and you. In a way, I kind of hurt her because I punched the guy she likes without even really knowing what was going on. Everything else is up to my sister, but I hope we can solve somewhat of happened."

For some reason, I couldn't understand why Landon was apologizing to me. I was the one who did his sister wrong, thinking that this plan to get

Haley Jones back as my girlfriend would work in the beginning. Just like Mr. Clarke, why was Landon being so nice to me? He didn't have to say sorry for punching me — I mean, I deserved it.

Even though this didn't completely resolve everything, I was content with calming the fire between Landon. I know that months ago, I proudly proclaimed my complete hate for Landon Clarke, but it turns out that I was just another immature teenager who couldn't get over his ex-girlfriend.

In the end, Haley Jones wasn't worth it, and I had met Lana for the wrong reasons.

Nodding my head, I answered, "I really don't deserve an apology from you, Landon. It was still my fault to decide on something so... unrealistic. I should have just moved on instead of bringing Lana into this."

Landon's mouth twitched as one side of his lips lifted. "As horrible as this sounds, you wouldn't have gotten close to Lana then."

"That's the only thing I don't regret," I confessed freely.

I only wished I reunited with Lana a better way. A kind of reunion that wouldn't lead to this current mess. Maybe, it would have been more smooth if I accidentally ran into her at a children's party. She would be dressed as one of the Disney princesses, and I would be pulled in by her beauty and sweet personality that it was just natural for us to get to know each other.

Of course, things didn't always work out the way we want it to be. We have to try to mend with what we have, and that was what I was going to do.

"I shouldn't have met Lana under those circumstances. But, your sister is amazing. She just has this way to make people feel warm inside and cared about. I care about her just as much. Every moment we spent together was real, and I know you don't believe me, but I didn't have to pretend around her. I felt like myself."

Her brother stared at me briefly, carefully listening. He sighed.

"I understand, Eli. And to be honest, I know you made her feel the same way. A little piece of advice, I don't think right now is a good time to fix things with Lana. I know my sister, and she's not exactly in the right state at the moment."

"What's wrong?"

My concern didn't hesitate to jump out.

Landon's jaw clenched until he ended up shrugging it off.

He replied lightly, "To be frank, what happened between you both wasn't exactly a ray of sunshine, and Lana isn't taking my dad's situation very well."

That was right. Why do I keep dismissing the fact that Lana was obviously hurt by finding out the truth about me the wrong way? What caught my attention was Mr. Clarke's situation — whatever it may be. I decided to keep my mouth shut from questioning Landon more because that was family business.

Running a hand through my hair, I hesitantly nodded, a little disappointed, but I had to understand. I had to give Lana space even if I wanted to be closer.

"You're right. Landon, thanks. I really don't know how to thank you and Mr. Clarke."

He shook his head.

"Don't thank me. I should have had a reasonable conversation before throwing a punch at you." Landon let out a loose chuckle. "Besides, I'm not completely on your side. You look like a mess right now."

A smirk grew on Landon's face which cause me to grin a bit. Even if it was probably true. Landon then pointed towards the room where his dad was with his thumb.

"I better get going. I'll see you around."

I nodded before Landon turned around and walked towards the hospital room.

Taking a deep breath, I couldn't believe how smooth the conversation went. I survived two encounters with Lana's family, and I was still alive. Even if I wasn't on good terms with Lana, I still wasn't going to give up. I reassured myself that I was going to fix the situation. Right now may not exactly be a good time, but I was willing to wait.

As long as I could be able to spend a moment with Lana. Even just a second.

"Hey, Eli."

Not expecting my name to be called, I looked over my shoulder, and it was Landon. His head was peering out from the door of his dad's room. A little confused, I fully turned around. That was when Landon asked for me to come back.

"My dad needs to ask you something."

A little relieved, I was willing to help Mr. Clarke with anything. It was the least I could do after everything he has done. Heading back to the sun lit room, I caught Mr. Clarke waiting for me. Giving him a closed smile, Mr. Clarke had given me a grin in return.

He then politely requested, "Eli, there's just one thing I need you to help me with. Can you do it?"

"Of course, anything."

Looking back, I greatly regretted not being able to hug Lana's dad like I did with mine on those occasions where dads knew best. Mr. Clarke was inspiring and an unforgettable person to talk to.

I figured that was where Lana got it from.

Chapter 26

"Hello? Elliot Wesley? I'm sorry, but Mr. Liam Clarke told us to tell you when something has happened. Please come to the hospital as soon as you can."

It was the kind of moment where your mind exiles everything around it and specifically focuses on this particular goal.

As much as I was being a reckless driver at the time, I had to get to the hospital. Growing frustrated by the traffic and red lights, I already cut off a bunch of people which resulted into getting honked at, cursed at, and all of the above.

Yet miraculously, there were no traces of police sirens.

Rushing into the hospital, I probably showed symptoms of a person running for his life from something as I repeatedly pushed the elevator door button constantly. Maybe I thought the elevator would actually go down faster if I damaged the overused button. Once the elevator doors finally slid open, I hurried in and pressed the button for the fourth floor.

I couldn't stop myself from pacing back and forth in the elevator. Thinking and thinking. This sensation of fear emerged, and for some reason, my gut was telling me this wasn't good.

Ever since my first visit to Mr. Clarke, I had been visiting Lana's dad whenever she was working. I could say we grew closer through that window of time, but as time passed, Mr. Clarke's condition had gradually worsened.

Mr. Clarke would usually set up a time for me to stop by. Today was supposed to be at 5 in the afternoon. It was a quarter until five, but I wasn't expecting a phone call like this from the hospital. The last time I got a phone call from the desk was when Mr. Clarke first requested me to come.

Positive that Lana was at a party, bringing joy to the hearts of young kids and their love for Disney, it worried me that the hospital called me so urgently. I still haven't seen nor spoken to Lana since that night — the night I unfortunately couldn't stop thinking about.

It has been three weeks.

As the days rolled by, each day grew more difficult.

Shaking my head side to side, I tried to persuade myself to dismiss this anxious feeling. My attempt to do so failed miserably.

Once the elevator signaled that I was on the fourth floor with a loud ding and the doors slid open, I wasn't anticipating the floor to be chaos. A bunch of nurses and the main doctor were rushing into the room which almost looked like Mr. Clarke's room from my point of view.

No.

Making myself snap out of it, I literally lunged across the hallway to the room. All of this was real. They were occupying Mr. Clarke's room. Hesitate to walk in, my entire body nearly froze, and I couldn't believe it what I saw.

There was no explanation to this shattered feeling once I saw her.

Lana.

As Lana stood a good distance from the crowd of nurses, she was in complete distraught. Even though she tried to hide it, I could easily see her falling apart. Lana Clarke wasn't the same girl. The girl who walked into her work with a cheerful yet curious expression the first time my friends and I saw her this summer. The girl who I was in love with.

She was breaking.

The words of Landon Clarke crossed my mind: "She's already gone through so much. I'm always worried that one day she'll break, and I won't be able to help her."

My attention gazed away from her for a spilt second to take in what was happening. Everything around me was muffled and frantic. All I really remember was a bunch of nurses and the doctor crowding around Mr. Clarke's hospital bed.

I had promised Lana that I would there for her whenever she fell to a low point. Though I knew she was upset with me, I couldn't let her be. She needed somebody.

As this was all happening, Lana didn't seem to be paying attention to her surroundings. Her body language nearly shouted that she was over-whelmed, and she looked like she wanted to run outside the moment she saw one of the young nurses flash a look of hopelessness at her. It angered me a little. Lana didn't need any of that.

Did people just want to make things worse for her?

Then again, was it a bad idea for me to be here?

Lana paced herself towards where I was standing, staring down at the floor, but I wasn't going to let her fall apart.

Embracing her in my arms, I tore my attention away from the hospital bed and bought myself back to reality. Putting all my attention on Lana as she cried freely and heavily. Unsure if she knew it was me, I was surprised to find Lana grow more relaxed than before. Even if it was just a little bit. Things were always better when somebody was there to comfort from personal experience.

As I glanced down before I held her close, Lana's arms soon wrapped around my back to hug me in return. Her hot tears were staining through my blue shirt, causing me to bite my lips harshly.

Everything was just so hard to take in.

My last visit with Mr. Clarke was three days ago. We shared a few laughs. Now, he was gone. Mr. Clarke was just sleeping, right? He just had to wake up, and Lana wouldn't have to cry anymore.

Even though I wished this wasn't all happening, it was nothing but the truth. My ears could now hear the flat line from the once smoothly beeping monitor. The doctor and nurses were all talking at once.

"He's gone... he's gone now. What will I do now?" Lana's muffled voice weeped.

Carefully wiping her tears away, the tears flowed down endlessly. Seeing her cry made me weak all over. Lana then covered her face with her small hands before I gently embraced her once more.

I quietly encouraged, "Lana, you won't have to go through this alone. Don't you worry. I'll be right here."

Seeing Lana made me think of Mom. It happened when Grandma Helen passed away. I was ten at the time, but I would never forget how Dad held Mom as she fell to the floor. He didn't let go of her until she stopped crying. That was a difficult time, but who was I to say? I never experienced losing a parent. Lana lost her mom and dad. Their family seemed knit tight. Knowing that it was only Landon and her made everything so unfair.

As Lana listened, she didn't push me away or refuse comfort. Instead, she forced a couple nods before she tried stopping herself from crying. It killed me to see her tears fall down and stain her cheeks. My heart pounded sadly because I couldn't do anything.

I wanted to tell her not to cry anymore, and that everything was going to be okay, but it wasn't up to me. To tell someone that everything was going to be okay would be the worst lie to say. I could already recall so many times people would tell me that. Honestly, those words were nothing but a way to finish a conversation with someone in need. No one actually meant it.

No one actually knew when everything was going to be okay for another person. That feeling of contentment was up the person.

Suddenly, the doctor approached us. I never got his name, but he was the doctor that Mr. Clarke would always gratefully talk about. This doctor always did everything he could to help Mr. Clarke. The doctor's gray eyes jumped from mine to Lana. His expression change sorrowfully when he took in the sight of her. He looked at Lana as if she were his own, and his wrinkled hand patted her back softly. The doctor's words came out heartfelt.

"I'm so sorry, Lana."

Nothing how I was by Lana's side, the doctor gave me a brief nod before heading out of the room. The nurses eventually shuffled out behind him one by one. They were probably preparing for the aftermath.

When it was just the two of us, I kept trying to tell Lana that I wouldn't go anywhere, and Landon would be coming soon. Well, I hope he was told. As much as I wanted to make everything okay, the only thing I could do was to help Lana stay in one piece.

Yet, I felt so hopeless.

There was so much difficultly to glance over and see Mr. Clarke. He was already covered with a white blanket placed by one of the nurses. To think that when I was getting ready this afternoon to make a visit, I expected to see Mr. Clarke here, sitting up, and say his welcoming, "Hey there, Eli".

Even though Lana managed to relax a bit, she never lifted her head. Moving the strands of hair that was on her face, I stepped back a bit and met her at eye level. Her blue eyes that were usually cheerful were now clouded with sadness. Noticing that a few tears had still stained her cheeks, I wiped them away. Her soft, pink lips quivered as she hiccuped from her sobbing. I wanted to stay close to Lana, but I wasn't sure if my presence was even helping her.

I decided to speak up, "Lana... I —"

There was an abrupt sound of footsteps that dashed into the room. Glancing over my shoulder, it was Landon. His widened blue eyes were currently stuck on his dad. Landon stood there in the most still position. He could have been mistaken as a statue. It was only moments until he covered his mouth before running a hand through his hair. Just like Lana's reaction, it was upsetting to see the Clarke siblings like this.

Landon soon noticed that I was with his younger sister. I watched as Landon gulped down. His eyes shook with complete concern towards his sister. Knowing how Landon wanted to protect his sister from harm, I didn't even want to imagine what was going through his mind at the moment. When Landon seemed to have snapped out of it, he started to walk towards us. Lana then locked eyes onto her brother while Landon settled his attention onto me.

His voice was lifeless.

"Eli, is it all right if you leave us for a moment?"

That was the last time I saw Lana and Landon that day. I went home after one of the nurses suggested that it was best to give them some time alone. I didn't argue with that.

As I laid in bed that night, I wasn't exactly the happiest person once I got back. The twins commented how I looked like a "dazed raccoon" or something along those lines. I didn't think too much of it because they didn't know what happened. When I didn't comment back, the twins figured that I wasn't in the mood. My parents were curious about my persona, but I didn't have enough strength to talk about it.

I was still in denial of Mr. Clarke's passing.

Turning over to my side, I closed my eyes for a moment. I couldn't stop myself from thinking about Lana. Every time I saw her, she was crying. Lana was going through the hardest time in her life, and I couldn't be there for her. I hoped that Lana and her brother were staying strong. All of this suddenly started to frustrate me. Why did I have to do that to Lana? Why did this have to happen to Mr. Clarke? Why did this all happen at once?

Opening my eyes, I sat up and shook my head.

Sighing heavily, I gazed around my darkened room before I jumped, hearing a surprising beep from my cellphone. The tone indicated that I received a text. Thinking that it was either Coops or Preston since I haven't spoken to either of them all day, my heart stopped once I read Lana's name on my screen.

Lana (3:48 A.M.): I hope I'm not bothering you right now, but I want to thank you for being there for me when I needed someone. Thank you, Eli.

It took ten minutes to register that Lana contacted me, and it took another ten minutes to figure out a reply. Uncertain, I felt like a little kid who couldn't decide what ice cream he wanted from the ice cream truck. Eventually, I managed to conjure up some words.

You don't have to thank me. I'm here for you. Lana, I'm sorry about your dad. If you and Landon need anything or any help, please let me know.

Staying up a bit, Lana didn't reply back. I figured she was dealing with a lot already. Getting this text though managed to make me fall asleep from this long, sleepless night.

Mr. Clarke's funeral was that Saturday. The service for him began at nine in the morning. That weekend was the last weekend before summer ended, and the majority would begin a new school year again. Summer was already ending, but that wasn't what was on everyone's mind.

Including mine.

Practically everyone in our community gathered around for Mr. Clarke's funeral and supported the Clarke siblings. When my family heard the news about Mr. Clarke's passing, Mom was unable to digest what she heard. None of them suspected it, nor spared the thought that Mr. Clarke was battling cancer the entire time.

Mom hesitated to ask me if I was there during Mr. Clarke's final moments at the hospital, but I told her that I came too late. He was already gone. Mom was so torn, especially since she knew that Lana and Landon no longer had their parents. She held the twins and me for the longest time after that, repeating how much she loved us over and over again. I couldn't blame her.

It was hard to shake any of this off because it seemed impossible to.

Even until now.

The guys and I came together for the service, but none of us spoke much. This was the first time we ever fell silent. No laughs, no jokes, no comments were prompted between the three of us. Just a moment to collect.

When we walked in the doors, the chapel of the funeral home was already crowded. What surprised me was finding that Haley Jones and Tyler Benson were there as well. Good vibes didn't exactly trigger between us when I glanced briefly at the both of them, but we all continued to ignore each other. This wasn't the time to argue or linger about the past.

This was about Mr. Clarke and the Clarke family, and more than anything, that was what I cared about..

After finding my family who were already sitting in the third row, I quickly searched for Lana. It wasn't hard to find the Clarke's because they were in the front, accompanied by Olette, near Mr. Clarke's casket. Landon was holding his sister close as people said their condolences.

From afar, their lips were stuck in a tight line, almost like they were holding back the urge to cry. Lana's older brother did most of the talking yet his energy appeared to be completely gone. Turning my attention to Lana caused my stomach to drop ten floors. Seeing her like that, I couldn't help but grow sad. Though Lana nodded gratefully at the people, her mind seemed to be drifting off. Her blue eyes that normally glowed brightly were nonexistent. They were concealed with grief.

Coops caused me to snap out of it by patting my shoulder gently.

"Don't worry. You can talk to her later. We should take a seat cause the service is about to start."

We walked over to the row my family was sitting in. I ended up sitting between Mom and Coops. As I sat down, Mom gave me a sad smile. Even though I returned with a closed grin, I didn't really feel like smiling. Looking down at my attire, the last time I wore a suit was at senior prom. Unfortunately, I never expected the next time would be for Mr. Clarke's funeral.

As the service started, it was bothering me that the girl I loved was sitting exactly two rows in front of me. There was just this pull to be sitting there next to her, holding her, instead of sitting here.

During the service, the clergyman who knew of Mr. Clarke spoke about his journey through life. Sniffling spread across the room as he talked. I admit, it was unbearable which made me take a deep breath a few times. My eyes unintentionally stuck on Lana every now and then, and I noticed that her best friend had her arm around Lana the entire time.

After a while, the clergyman then glanced over at Mr. Clarke's open casket before he announced that Lana was going to do a eulogy for her dad. My stomach churned as I watched Lana slowly walk up to the podium to face everyone. She was wearing a simple black dress with her straight, light brown hair lifted into a ponytail. It was inevitable to notice how exhausted she looked.

Her blue eyes gazed uneasily as she searched the crowds of people. Within seconds, we locked eye contact. Lana didn't bear any change of reaction towards me before she settled her attention back to everyone.

"Good morning. I'm his daughter, Lana Clarke... I want to thank you all who came to see my dad, Liam Clarke."

Her blue eyes gradually wandered to her dad's casket. I felt my fists clench.

Don't make this hard on yourself, Lana.

When it appeared like she was strong enough, Lana continued, "I don't think a eulogy can do my dad enough justice. He's a wonderful person. Actually, wonderful can't even describe the quality my dad has. My dad is my dad. Every single piece of him, from his smile to his bright personality, is easy to love. I'm sure he changed a part of your life, whether big or small, because he definitely changed mine. All the memories I had with him were steps that made me into a better person. I didn't see that until a week ago. My dad had been trying to prepare me for life. To know that whatever life throws at me, I will make it through. His strength and guidance molded me, and I don't think I even got to thank him enough."

"Even if Dad was going through a rough time, he would always make sure Landon and I were fine first. That was the thing about Dad. He always put others before him. Even if he got really sick and experienced all sorts of pain, by the end of the day, he would always make sure that there was a smile on my face."

From there, a tear rolled down Lana's cheek and she cleared her throat. Mom grabbed my hand and held it tightly as she was already wiping her eyes with a tissue. Glancing over, I saw that Abby and Aly were leaning against my parents.

"When we look back at our memories, I don't know about you, but sometimes I wished I whipped out my camera to capture that moment. The last photo I had with my dad was on my birthday. It felt so long ago, and I felt like I took it for granted. We sometimes forget the little things like that. We forget to capture those moments, and all that is left is the memories we keep locked in our mind. To be honest with everyone though, I'm fine with that. I realized I don't need a camera or pictures as proof for all the times I shared with my dad. What matters is the memories I will always remember of him."

Lana was already sobbing through her words. The room became over-powered by constant sniffling, and people attempting to stop themselves from bursting out into tears. As the pain continued to strike me, I inhaled slowly before releasing a breath.

"A few days ago before Dad passed away, he told me before I left that night that he was happy with his life. He said that Landon and I were his greatest accomplishments, and he was so proud of us. But, I'm actually proud of you, Dad. Throughout everything, you always did all you could to be the best dad. I want to tell all of you, and especially my dad, that he is. You are the best dad. Even though it's hard right now, I know you're in a better place. I hope you're doing great with Mom there. We miss and love you both very much. I love... love you so much, Dad. Thank you for being the best dad a daughter could ever ask for."

As soon as Lana finished her eulogy, Landon immediately stood up from the wooden pew to go to his sister. Lana was crying heavily which made me want to get up and go to her side. However, Coops must have noticed my body language and signaled not to. He was right. This wasn't the right time. That moment, I realized that there were a few tears falling from my eyes.

Wiping my tear stained face, I hated crying. I couldn't even remember the last time I did. I wasn't the only one. I caught Preston wiping his eyes secretly, and Coops had hung his head down to avoid the attention. As much as I despised crying, I didn't care about hiding it or not. It didn't really hit me that I was crying because I was more worried about Lana and how she was missing her father.

Before the burial, everyone was allowed to pay their last respects to Mr. Clarke. Rows and rows of people waited their turn, and I couldn't put enough strength to see their expressions. I didn't want to recall back at how people looked during Mr. Clarke's funeral. When I watched my family though, Dad was holding onto Mom as she sobbed quietly into his shoulder. Carefully placing my hand on my mom's back, she turned around to give me a hug in return.

My dad then joined their old co-workers from the auto shop and stood around Mr. Clarke's casket to share a moment of silence. Most of them were wiping their eyes, especially my dad, since the only time he got to reconnect with Mr. Clarke was during the dinner. Unfortunately, some of them never had the chance to.

When it was our turn, I tried to keep a steady face. Seeing a person in a casket always sent chills up my spine, and I never had the thought that it would be Mr. Clarke. I didn't want to remember Lana's father like this.

As we approached his casket, my eyes widened seeing Mr. Clarke sleeping peacefully. He looked different from the last time I visited him. The makeup over his face nearly masked the aged Mr. Clarke. As weird as this sounded, the friendly atmosphere Mr. Clarke gave off felt like it was still present as we stood there.

Coops and Preston both patted my backs before paying their respects to Lana's father. They eventually left me alone for a moment. Glancing at Mr. Clarke, it didn't feel right not being able to see his blue eyes while talking to him. Because Mr. Clarke's appearance looked at peace, it sent some content emotions to fill me.

Mr. Clarke, you're a great man. Thank you for everything. You don't know how much I appreciate it. I know you're watching over us now, but I can't help but miss you. I'm sure Lana and Landon miss you most. Don't leave their side, okay? You're in a better place now with Mrs. Clarke, but you two will always be remembered. I promise to make sure everything works out like you wanted. Thank you for believing in me especially when I couldn't.

The first and last ones to view Mr. Clarke were his children. Lana wept, and her cries could be heard from the front half of the room. I gulped down harshly as I watched Landon hold his sister in his arms, keeping her up from falling down. Her blue eyes were stuck on Mr. Clarke as she bit her lower lip. Soon, she kissed her fingertips before placing them onto the casket. Standing a fair distance from them, I could hear Lana whisper how much she loved him.

Before we knew it, the casket was shut close, and the burial began.

Upon Mr. Clarke's request, I was one of the pall bearers. It was an honor to be a pall bearer, especially to a man like Mr. Clarke. Taking the left side of Mr. Clarke's casket, I glimpsed briefly at the faces who carried the casket as well. There were some familiar ones like Landon and my dad. There were also some of their old co-workers, and I found out that two were Mr. Clarke's close cousins from Washington.

At the beginning, I didn't want to see the people bury Mr. Clarke. I didn't feel like putting a handful of soil in his grave before they filled it up to the top. That was because I was still upset. It was hard to accept that Mr. Clarke was gone. When I reminded myself that Mr. Clarke was in a better place, it still felt unfair.

Unfair to everyone, unfair to Mr. Clarke.

Seeing everyone throw the funeral roses and soil into the grave gradually caused those thoughts to disappear. As much as I didn't want Mr. Clarke gone, I needed to accept it.

Lana and I walked together as we made our way towards his grave. She carried sunflowers and mentioned with a sad smile that it was her dad's favorite flower to look at. After we tossed in the flowers, Lana was still holding back her tears.

Without even realizing it, I reached out to hold her hand as we walked back. It may seem like an offense, but she didn't flinch away. Lana gazed at me, letting me hold her cold, small hand. As we exchanged glances, Lana's blue eyes were like crystal. Glassy and delicate.

"Remember that he's always here."

Her voice was a murmur as she wiped her eyes.

"I know... but it's different."

I reminded, looking into those blue eyes, "As long as you carry him in your heart, nothing will change."

Lana stared at me for what seemed like forever. At first, it confused me until something changed in her expression. There was a sudden shift in her once stressed appearance. Her eyes grew calm, and she nodded her head.

"You're right, Eli. You always know what to say and mean it."

Hearing that made me twitch into a faint grin. She returned with a more lively smile before settling her attention back to the service.

As they began to pour the soil over Mr. Clarke's grave, the world seemed to have stopped. The occasional sniffling would fill the air, but I was surprised to see that Lana was quiet. Sneaking a glance at her, Lana had on this lost gaze like she was having a silent, personal conversation with her dad. Being with my family during this time, the twins were leaning against my sides, and I accompanied my younger sisters close.

After everyone said their goodbyes to the Clarke siblings — I even caught some say the infamous "everything will get better" — our community soon dispersed and headed back home or whatever plans they had afterwards. My family went ahead first.

My parents hugged Lana and Landon tightly, telling them that they would always be there if the two ever needed anything. Lana and Landon thanked my parents through grateful smiles. However, I caught how their eyes were still filled with sadness. The twins were crying as they hugged Lana, but Lana had enough strength to comfort them and tell them that we'll be okay.

For some reason, it felt like the guys, Landon and Olette wanted to give Lana and me some space.

Walking down the hill to our cars after one last collective moment with Mr. Clarke that day, the four of them evidently walked ahead of us. If they were trying to be smooth, it was the complete opposite because Lana and I noticed the moment they all walked five steps ahead of us.

That was my chance to fix something — even if it was just a little.

Even though I wanted to tell Lana how much I loved her, I couldn't. Call me crazy, but it was just too selfish if I did. Lana was going through the death of her dad. The last thing she needed was me trying to butt myself back into her life again. I knew Lana needed time.

It was hard to believe that this was the first time in three weeks we would talk. If the conversation went well. Though the time and place wasn't what I pictured, it was fine with me. Of all things, I just really needed to hear Lana.

As if she read my mind, Lana spoke up, "Eli, I know what happened weeks ago caused us to drift apart, but thank you. Dad was very fond of you, and I appreciate you being there for him and us."

Replying back with a "you're welcome" and reminding her that I would be there for her and her family made our conversation sound so foreign. It was killing me. This wasn't how we were supposed to be with one another.

Noticing how this situation was starting to cause discomfort to Lana as well, her eyes wandered off as the wind blew the loose strands of her light, brown hair away from her face. Lana's eyes were puffed from crying, and it was aching to see.

"I'm sorry, Lana," I admitted with complete honestly.

She blinked her eyes, a little taken back.

"For what?"

I took a deep breath.

"For everything. For what happened that night, for what I did to you, for not telling you the truth, for being so immature, for being a complete idiot... I'm sorry for all of it. Especially with Mr. Clarke, I —"

"Eli, it's alright. It wasn't your fault what happened to my dad. It's no one's fault. You've helped a lot," Lana paused briefly by gulping down until she continued, "and about that, it was really hard to believe that you would do that to me. I understand that we all make the wrong choices every now and then."

Suddenly, Lana bit her lower lip as she glanced up at me. Sorrow seemed to occupy Lana's eyes once more. Her voice became diffident, as if she wanted to resist what she was going to say next.

"But, I want us to stay as we are right now. Like this. I'm sorry if I'm being a bit unfair. It's just that I'm not ready."

Swallowing the harsh lump down my throat, I couldn't complain because Lana had every right to say so.

As much as her words caused my heart to twist, I had to shake my head and indicate that I understood completely. However, my voice sounded more broken than intended.

"Don't be sorry. If anything, it's me who is sorry. If you ever need anyone, I won't be going anywhere."

Though it was clear to me that things weren't going back to what they used to be cause that would be unrealistic even for me, it wasn't going to stop myself from being there for Lana. Even if Lana needed time for herself, I wanted her to keep in mind that I wouldn't leave. We were quiet for a moment, and I grew concerned when Lana didn't say anything.

Instead of a reply, Lana had stepped closer and gave me a hug. A rush of shock ran through me. At the time, I wasn't sure if that was a hug goodbye or a hug in thanks. Raising my arms to hold her back, I missed this feeling so much.

Lana felt perfect in my arms.

We stood there, holding each other, as those summer memories started to flood my mind.

From all the times I heard Lana laugh, watch a bright smile grow on her face, listen to her pour her out heart to me, notice her sweet smelling perfume, held her small hand snugly with mine, kissed her soft pink lips, reminded me that I wouldn't let Lana Clarke go.

Never would I let Lana Clarke go.

Chapter 27

"Hi Dad and Mom. I bought your favorite flowers," I announced with a faint smile on my face.

Admiring the vivid pink tulips and bright sunflowers, I soon knelt down and placed the flowers into the designated cups. Shifting my position so I'd be sitting down, I observed the marble gravestone that etched both my parent's name. They were together now, I would always remind myself whenever I missed them. As much as it made me sad, it also made me to feel happiness. I was positive they were happy together after being separated for so long.

Running my hand across the gravestone, I threw on a bigger smile for them to see.

"How are you today? I really miss you both. Don't worry about Landon and me, we're doing fine. He's starting school this fall, and he's super excited. I'm sure he already told you both. I'm so proud of him too. I know I haven't made a plan yet, but I'm doing okay. Trust me, I'll figure something out. Anyways, I should get going or else I'll be late. Don't want Maryann to stress out again, huh?"

I let out a short chuckle after.

Clearing my throat, I promised, "I'm going to visit again, okay? I love, Dad. I love you, Mom."

Taking a deep breath, I kissed my fingertips before placing them over the gravestone. It was the closet thing I could do. A mild breeze suddenly brushed past me which made me release a happy grin. I wish I was able to hug them back.

As I walked down the hill to my car, I felt my phone buzzing against my demin shorts. The caller ID was blinking Olette's name. Smiling, I picked it up.

"Hey, where are you?" Olette chimed from the other line.

"I just went to visit my parents. I have work in a few."

"Aw, Lana! Did you forget? We were going to have lunch."

My heart sank upon hearing that. Opening my car door, I sat in the driver's seat and let out an uncomfortable laugh.

"I'm really sorry, Olette. I didn't mean to forget."

"Don't beat yourself up for that. We'll have a re-do. After all, it's spring break!"

"I'll make it up to you. Promise. I'll see you after I get off work."

"Of course, can't wait!"

There was a brief pause from the other line.

Olette continued, "You know... Eli's in town. Well, we know he's been in and out of town every weekend, but he's staying in for the whole week."

I wasn't expecting to hear Eli's name in our conversation. Freezing for a moment, what Olette meant by Eli being here every weekend since he started school was true. I didn't know why Eli was always here because I never bothered to ask or see him. Clutching onto my phone, my eyes wandered around the bare road.

"Yeah, he mentioned it through text a week ago."

"You haven't seen him since the funeral, huh?"

"Yeah."

Olette quietly bought up, "I understand. Lana, I can tell the guy's really trying."

Placing the key into the ignition, I had to let those thoughts of Eli Wesley disappear. I changed the subject.

"Olette, I'm about to drive. I'll let you know when I get off. Maybe we can have some dinner over at my place."

There was a hint of sadness in my best friend's voice before she lightened up the atmosphere of our conversation.

"Okay, let me know. I'll probably be over already though."

Releasing a laugh, Olette did bring my mood up.

My brother and Olette have been going strong ever since. I couldn't have asked for a better best friend than Olette. She helped us throughout everything, and I've never seen my brother so in love with a girl before. I was more than happy to see them together. Just wait until they were married. I was kidding, definitely not now.

As we said our goodbyes, I tossed my phone onto the passenger's seat and drove away. Even though Olette spoke of Eli, I didn't want to think much of it. We did still keep in contact - like I called Eli when it was his birthday — but it was all merely through technology. I haven't actually seen Eli Wesley. Then again, I was the one who decided to avoid him. Not because I was still upset with him, but because I needed to get myself back together.

Eli did still worry about me, but I pushed him away as much as I could. I was unsure with what my heart wanted, but I wasn't planning on confusing myself more. Whenever Olette asked what Eli and I "were", I couldn't even answer the question if I asked myself.

I was still unsure.

Even seven months later.

Not being the most attentive person while I was driving, I didn't realize that I was already close to work. Once I parked at my usual spot by the curb, I got off my car and looked forward to the rest of the afternoon.

Even though everyday seemed like a routine, I never grew tired of attending parties. Being surrounded by the kids made me a lot happier. When my car locked, I swung my bag over my shoulder and walked over to the entrance.

Although, I wasn't suspecting someone to call my name.

"Lana! Hey, Lana!"

Looking right then left, it occurred to me to turn around. I couldn't believe it was Preston Daniels who called me. From where I stood, he looked like Preston.

The tall, brown-blonde haired boy was accompanied by a girl sporting a blonde bob cut. Seeing how they were holding hands, they must be boyfriend and girlfriend. I didn't know Preston had one. That was until I reminded myself that it has been a while since I saw or spoke to Preston as well.

Sneaking a glance at the inside of A Fairytale Come True, Maryann was stuck on the phone, and I still had extra time before I had to clock in. Moving my body to face them, I waved before walking over to meet them halfway. Preston was still the same with the cheerful aura he carried along. The couple complimented each other well. The blonde seemed vaguely familiar, but I couldn't pinpoint why. The girl showcased a friendly grin as her green eyes grew with familiarity.

A part of me felt bad since I couldn't reciprocate the same thing. However, I smiled, hoping that it would finally hit me who Preston's mystery girl was.

"Hey, how are you?"

It was actually refreshing to see Preston again.

After all these months, I noticed how much Preston has matured. However, it still didn't prevent him from cracking a joke or two, like always. Preston flashed his famous sideways grin at me.

"Long time no see, Lana! I'm doing great. I also want to introduce you to my girlfriend, Veronica Chance."

That was when the light bulb lit up. She was on the Varsity swim team with Eli.

Veronica reached out to offer her hand.

She returned sincerely, "We've passed by each other in the hallway a couple of times. Nice to finally meet you, Lana. You can call me Ronnie."

Taking her hand back, I chuckled lightly.

"No wonder you looked familiar. Nice to meet you too, Ronnie."

Preston took a good look at me and revealed, "You cut your hair. Looks nice!"

"Yes, I did. Thanks," I admitted with a shy smile.

My long locks of brown hair were getting a little unmanageable once it reached past my stomach. Olette came with me to the salon during the beginning of the year, and I chopped off my hair a couple inches past my collarbones. The rest of my hair was gladly donated while my head felt a lot more lighter. However, my hair was growing faster than I anticipated.

The two of them joined in my laughter before Preston asked through a light tone, "How have you been, Lana?"

Thinking about it for a moment, there were a lot of things I could have said. I was doing a lot better than months ago. I was managing. I still missed my parents. I still had mixed emotions towards his best friend. There were so many possible answers.

Instead, I smiled back.

"I'm great. Thanks for asking."

Both of their green eyes observed me for a moment which worried me at first, until belief overturned their expressions. A breath of fresh air released from my mouth. I was honestly doing better. The two soon asked if I was done working today, but it was kind of the other way around.

When I questioned what they were up to, Ronnie answered with a friendly grin, "We're going to meet up with Julian in a bit. I hope we didn't make you late."

Preston also added, "Apparently, Coops is introducing us to this girl he's gotten quite close to back in San Francisco."

Growing surprised, it turned out that both Preston and Julian had found someone special during these past few months. Seemed like everyone was reuniting this spring break. As I listened, I didn't know why memories of last summer started to hit me again. The bittersweet moments left a temporary pang in my chest before I dismissed those thoughts.

I smiled back.

"That sounds fun. Don't worry Ronnie, I won't be late. Preston... Are you also seeing Eli today?"

Biting my tongue, I wanted to scold myself for mentioning Eli all of sudden. Preston's eyes widened abruptly, maybe because I was the one who decided to bring Eli Wesley up first. Preston pursued his lips shortly before he shook his head.

"Probably not today. He told us he had some plans with his sisters. I'm sure we'll see him some time this week. Maybe we can hang out too?"

Thinking there was no harm in that, I nodded a few times. However, I forgot to take into consideration that Eli might be there. Was I ready to face him again? I remember telling myself several times that there was no longer any tension between us. I thought I believed it. Why did I feel a sense of panic at that moment?

Ronnie beamed in excitement, "You'll let us know when you're free?"

"Of course. Unfortunately, I better get going. It was really nice seeing you both and meeting you, Ronnie."

Both agreed with happy expressions across their faces. Bumping into Preston and Ronnie surprisingly transferred happiness over to me. I couldn't exactly explain it. Guess it was the power of Preston and Ronnie.

Before I left for work, Preston stepped in to give me a hug. A little shocked at first, it was a hug well needed. Despite the events of the past summer which tangled us all in a mess, I wasn't thinking about any of that with them right now. Telling one another we'll see each other soon, I waved good bye before stepping inside the building.

Let me do the countdown in 3... 2... 1...

"There you are, Lana! I thought you were going to be late!" Maryann hollered across the counter.

Letting out a soft chuckle, I handed her my check in card.

"You might want to change the dialogue up a bit. I'm starting to memorize what you're about to say."

Maryann playfully acted like she was going to throw her favorite pen at me.

"You just know me too well. Thanks for coming in today. With Quinn out sick, it's times like this we need our perfect princess to save the day."

I blushed.

"I don't know about perfect, Maryann. Who will I be today?"

"What you are best. Our favorite mermaid, Ariel! You're attending Tiffany's sixth birthday party. Here's the address, honey."

Taking a brief glance at the address, the street name seemed familiar, yet it didn't exactly cross my mind why. I've been to so many places throughout Santa Monica, it was probably just a common street I must have been on or passed by in the past.

Before I knew it, I was whipping my bright, red hair to the side as I drove over to little Tiffany's house. I sang a few notes here and there, just to make sure the princess wouldn't crack during the party. What made me pull into a sudden stop was finally realizing why that street name seemed so familiar.

I was actually driving into Eli's neighborhood. My heart sank a little because of all these flashbacks that appeared unwillingly.

"I'm okay, I'm okay. I'm Ariel right now," I reminded myself.

Shaking my head to regain composure, I spotted rows of cars and knew that was what I needed to follow. Tiffany's house was coated with pink and purple balloons and decorations. The banner of the Disney princesses was the dead giveaway that this was the birthday girl's house.

Cutting the engine off, I checked myself momentarily in the mirror. Or Ariel's reflection. Taking a deep breath, I could already hear the muffled shouts of children from the other side as I stood on the porch. Once I rang the doorbell, a bunch of footsteps shuffled across the floor. Seeing the door knob turn, I quickly cleared my throat and genuinely played my role as The Little Mermaid.

"Ariel!" the little one gasped, "Mom! Ariel's here!"

The one I assumed to be Tiffany screamed through a shrill, excited voice. Giving her a bright smile, I knelt down a bit.

"Are you Tiffany?"

All of a sudden, a bunch of young girls and boys were crowding around me. Tiffany's sky blue eyes lit up, and she started to twirl to showcase her outfit. She was wearing similar clothes as Ariel, along with the bright, red wig. It was always adorable seeing the children dress up.

She screeched, "You know my name? Mom! Ariel knows my name!"

The celebrant's parents soon appeared with cheerful smiles across their faces once they saw their little girl have the time of her life. Cameras were being taken out, and pictures were shot from every direction. Her parents kindly suggested that we all go outside where the main focus of the party was.

Tiffany's party was flourished with all the Disney princess decor one could only imagine. It was no surprise to claim that Ariel was her favorite princess. The entire party gave off a welcoming feeling from the very beginning. I knew right from the start I would enjoy today.

The children and I sang songs from The Little Mermaid and took more pictures which I hoped turned out all right. The young celebrate would stand by me and point out to her guests that she was my twin. Tiffany was absolutely sweet beyond words.

As I busily took pictures with one of the kids attending the party, my attention was suddenly taken away when I noticed little Tiffany skipping towards the entrance gate of her backyard.

I heard her little voice exclaiming how they were here. Who was she referring to?

I thought to myself that she was probably talking about her friends. However, I must have honestly been seeing things because I saw two identical girls who looked like Eli's younger sisters.

Aly and Abby.

Aly was holding a gift while Abby was happily waving to the energetic girl running towards them. Snapping my gaze away from them, I looked down and found a young girl dressed as Belle who had been waiting for a picture.

Giving her a smile, I nodded my head and placed my arm around her. The girl's mother called for our attention and clicked the shutter as the flash appeared. Hugging the young Belle in return, I sneaked a peek again, and it turned out my eyes weren't playing jokes with me at all.

Within seconds, Eli Wesley must have caught up and was walking towards his sisters and Tiffany. My attention immediately tuned out my surroundings.

Eli Wesley was here.

Right now.

I watched as Tiffany's entire glee went towards Eli. There was no way I could make myself blink. Were Eli and Tiffany related?

It has been seven months since I saw Eli in the flesh.

From what I saw, Eli still kept his brown hair the same length, and that dimpled smile of his could be seen from miles aways. Eli wore a pale blue button up shirt with a pair of dark jeans. His dark yet gentle brown eyes were happily glancing down at Tiffany as she hopped up to give him a hug. I wanted to turn away and hoped that they wouldn't see me, but I would be kidding myself.

Soon, Tiffany's parents approached the Wesley siblings and gave them all a hug. I heard Eli's deep, smooth voice explain how his parents were sorry for not being able to make it and something like they would be back in town tomorrow. All of a sudden, I lost complete concentration.

Right when I persuaded myself to simply look away, my ears caught Tiffany proudly announce to Eli how Ariel was at her party. That meant he would have to look my way. He would have to see me. Eli took his gaze off of Tiffany and followed where her tiny finger was directing at.

Just when I thought I had control over the situation, I became lost once Eli and I made eye contact.

As we exchanged glances, it appeared as if Eli suspected it would be me, but just like me, he didn't expect it to be true. Our reactions must have been identical because we both froze the moment we saw each other. There was a cryptic expression on Eli's face that was bothering me to the highest extent only because I couldn't read past it. What was he thinking right now?

It wasn't long before I was sharing looks with the twins as well. Aly and Abby's mouths nearly dropped, but their expressions were much more alive then their older brother.

There was an inner battle circling within me because some part of me liked seeing Eli after so long. When Eli tore his eyes away from me and smiled down at little Tiffany, I remembered all the times his kindness affected me.

As Eli glanced right back at me, I gave them all a smile because one, I cared a lot of Eli's family, and two, there was nothing wrong with Eli and me anymore.

Right?

Tiffany started to drag Eli towards me, and I had to keep myself together. Eli still appeared to be in shock, but we should have known that it wouldn't be long before we ended up bumping into each other. We tended to do that a lot in the past.

Tiffany began to jump up and down.

"Ariel, Ariel! This is Eli! He was my babysitter when I was a little baby. He's the best!"

Eli joked as his dimple reappeared, "You're still little, aren't you?"

Tiffany huffed at the tall boy, "No, I'm not little! I'm a princess now. Just like Ariel. Right?"

Before I knew it, all eyes were on me. Eli fixed his eyes on me, hoping to get some kind of reaction. Instantly, I glanced down at the young princess and nodded my head happily.

"Of course. You're growing up every year, Princess Tiffany."

Tiffany's blue eyes lit up joyfully, and she instantly ran to give me a hug. Tiffany announced how this was her best birthday ever.

Aly and Abby followed along, and the twins mentioned with enthusiasm that Ariel was their favorite princess too. Even if I wasn't 'Lana', seeing the twins made me smile even bigger. I would never forget the time we all had that water fight with the water balloons. The girls all crowded around me as Tiffany's mom took a picture of us.

As this was going on, I couldn't help but look at Eli every now and then. He had wandered off since Tiffany's dad had hung his arm around Eli and suggested to grab some food and eat.

Abby then caught my attention as she noted with a smile, "You're very pretty, Ariel. I'm so happy to see you."

Aly nodded along.

"It feels like a dream."

Feeling my lips pull into a happy grin, I took both their hands and chimed, "It's a pleasure to have the both of you here. Princess Tiffany has such wonderful friends."

Tiffany never looked so happy after she heard me.

"You're my bestest friend, Ariel!"

I gave her a little curtsy and returned, "That would be an honor."

As the party went on, there was never a moment where Eli would glance at me, and I would catch him, or it went the other way around. I did everything I could to keep my composure and hoped that I wouldn't lose character. I told myself that I could handle being around Eli, but it didn't help seeing Eli interact with all the children. They all loved him and would even play jokes on him.

What caught me by surprise was when one of the little boys asked Eli if he thought Ariel was pretty.

All the little kids were eyeing Eli and were anticipating his answer. My heart thumped once Eli looked at me. The way his eyes looked into mine made me hope that I wasn't blushing. After a second, a smile grew on Eli's face, and I didn't know how to react to that smile of his.

Eli nodded.

"Yeah Brandon, she's the prettiest."

All the kids stuck their tongues out and nearly shivered in response because when we were at that age, it was declared that the opposite sex carried cooties. I noticed from the corner of my eyes that Aly and Abby snorted a laugh. I bet they were trying their hardest not to make a joke about their older brother.

Tiffany clapped her hands happily but reminded, "Too bad, Eli! Ariel already has Prince Eric."

Another little boy roared out, "I think Eli can beat Prince Eric!"

"No one can beat Prince Eric! That's Ariel's one true love!" A young Cinderella argued back.

In a matter of seconds, there was a playful argument of whether Eli or Prince Eric could win Ariel's love between the children. Eli and I watched with gaped expressions as one side supported Eli and the other supported Prince Eric.

I heard Tiffany say, "Well... even though Ariel loves Prince Eric, I think Eli can be a good prince for Ariel too."

"But, we can't change the story, Tiffany," one of Tiffany's friend reasoned.

Tiffany shook her head and suggested, "Then, we can make our own story! Prince Eli and Princess Ariel!"

All the young children rejoiced, and I didn't dare to look at Eli's expression. I was embarrassed enough despite me chuckling at the children's enthusiasm. As the birthday girl and her friends came up with a revised version of The Little Mermaid, Tiffany's mom sadly informed everyone that it was time for Ariel to return home. The once brightened expressions of the children immediately fell in disappointment.

"Does Ariel have to leave? I'm having so much fun."

Tiffany's mom fixed her daughter's hair and comforted, "I'm sorry, sweetie, but Ariel needs to head home. She has a long journey."

Understanding the situation, the six year old nodded her head and came over towards me. I didn't even know that it was time for me to go. Tiffany gave me the longest hug and thanked me for coming to her birthday party.

As I hugged her back, I corrected with a smile, "Thank you for inviting me. I had such a good time, Princess Tiffany."

"Promise you'll always remember me?"

I nodded.

"I will always remember you. Happy birthday, Princess Tiffany."

Once I said goodbye to all the guests at the party, the twins gave me a hug as well. Both of them whispered in my ear saying how much they missed me. I managed to slip in that I missed them just as much. Tiffany's parents escorted me to the front door and thanked me for a wonderful time. Thanking them back for having my company, I waved goodbye to Tiffany before they closed the door.

When I turned around, I released a long sigh. I couldn't believe that I managed to survive a birthday party with Eli Wesley there. It was so sudden that I felt numb to even register my thoughts about him. Seeing Eli after so long made me fight a smile, but there was still this unsure feeling about him.

As I walked back to my car, the party became a sudden blur. Were the twins and Eli really there? Was this why Eli couldn't meet with his friends? Did Eli know I was going to be here?

No. Eli looked just as surprised as me.

"Lana."

Thinking that my ears were just hearing things, it eventually became clear to me that they weren't. Hearing Eli call my name sent chills up my spine. I stopped walking and hesitated to look back.

Now that it was only us, I felt vulnerable.

"Hello Eli," I managed to croak out.

Eli had shoved his hands in front pockets. I recalled that it was something Eli did when he was nervous. I couldn't blame him because I was feeling the exact same way. His dark brown eyes didn't look anywhere but at me which caused me to break away. Fiddling with the trimming of my outfit, I waited if he was going to speak up or not.

Eli eventually cleared his throat.

"Hey, it was good seeing you... I didn't expect to see you today."

"Yeah. Me too."

Silence didn't hesitate to appear after that. Gulping down, I soon met my gaze to Eli.

"Are you related to Tiffany?"

He shook his head.

"No, her family is good friends with mine. I babysat her when she was younger."

"Oh."

That was the only thing that managed to escape from my mouth.

After a moment, Eli rubbed the back of his neck with his left hand. He let out an embarrassed chuckle.

"This is getting really awkward. Lana, how have you been?"

I wanted to tell him, you're telling me.

"Okay. I've just been working. How about you?"

"I'm all right. This semester isn't as bad as I thought it would be," he then added, "this is actually the first time I saw you as a princess. You're a great Ariel."

A tiny smile grew on my face as I replied back with thanks. At this rate, I wouldn't be able to handle another minute talking with Eli only because I imagined that a reunion with him would run smooth if I ever saw him again. But, it was nothing but awkward.

"I'm sorry. You probably have some place to be," he murmured.

The way Eli held his voice back after made me catch that there was more Eli wanted to say. I waited in hopes that he would continue on.

"Lana, I was wondering if you were free. I know right now isn't a good time to talk... is tomorrow okay?"

When I thought about it, I actually didn't have work this Wednesday. Should I go meet up with Eli? Or should I just pretend that I had work? I didn't know if I was ready to sit down and have an open conversation about what happened during summer — if that was what Eli wanted to talk about. Snapping out it, I ended up dropping those assumptions and followed with what I assumed my heart was telling me to say.

"Sure, tomorrow is fine."

All of a sudden, a brightened expression reflected upon Eli's brown eyes. A grin immediately grew on Eli's face in relief. Was he thinking that I would immediately say no? My eyes couldn't stop staring at his smile, but I kept my cool. I couldn't have Eli notice.

"Great. I'll pick you up. See you tomorrow then?"

Eli attempted to be hide his excitement, but it was pretty obvious.

I nodded before I smiled in reply.

Behind it all, there was this feeling of worry about what would happen tomorrow. There were just so many possibilities, and I thought I already convinced myself to stop chasing after them.

As I waved goodbye to Eli, I stood there as he turned around to go back to the party. Before he made a turn into the backyard, Eli looked over his shoulder and grinned at me. I reciprocated a similar smile because I would be lying if I said that his smile didn't cause a sudden pull on my heart.

These feelings were so complicated that the only thing I could do at the moment was trust my decision.

As much as I would rather keep myself away, there was always, always something about Eli Wesley that had me coming back.

Epilogue

The way my brother's blue eyes grew in disbelief once he heard my plans for today made me want to second guess my decision.

"You're seeing Eli today?" Landon choked up since he was midway of swallowing his steamed vegetables.

Looking back, I nodded before I picked up a carton of lemonade from the refrigerator. Twisting the lid open, I poured the drink into a glass cup to my liking.

"Yeah, he wanted to meet up. Why are you are so surprised?"

My older brother shrugged in return and continued on eating his lunch. I wasn't buying his simple answer. When I pressed on about the reason for his surprised gesture, Landon gazed back up at me, and a teasing grin surfaced on his face.

"I just wanted to say 'it's about time', but you'd probably throw your spoon at me."

"Probably," I countered as I held in my laughter.

As I sat on the bar stool across from my brother, we sat there silently as we focused on our food and drink. The only sounds were munching or clanking whenever I placed the glass cup down onto the marble stone countertop. Staring down at my cup, I continuously thought about what could possibly happen today.

"Your lemonade isn't going to drink itself," my brother pointed out.

Losing my train of thought, I focused my attention back on Landon who was getting up from his seat to head over to the sink. Landon had his back turned away from me as he washed the dishes.

"Are you going to be okay?" he questioned in a quiet voice.

"What do you mean?"

"Lana..."

I sighed.

"Honestly, I don't know. I haven't seen Eli in months, and now, everything about Eli comes back into my life. It's all so sudden."

Shutting the faucet off, Landon flipped around to face me. He leaned against the counter with folded arms.

"I have a feeling it won't be as bad as you think."

And my brother left it as that.

Landon informed me that he would be getting ready for his afternoon shift at the auto shop, leaving me there in confusion. My brother seemed optimistic about my upcoming day with Eli. Not really looking into that notion, I quickly finished up my glass of lemonade before hopping into the shower to get ready.

Rummaging through my closet to find something to wear, I couldn't decide. It was ridiculous because of my determination to figure out the right outfit. In the end, there was only a pile of clothes and no outfit. Walking back to the pile, I finally settled with a light weight maroon blouse and black jeans. As I was throwing on my blouse, I heard two knocks from my bedroom door.

"Hey, I'm heading out. You'll be okay here?" Landon's muffled voice asked from the closed door.

I laughed a bit.

"Yeah, I'll be safe in my own room. I'll see you later."

I heard him chuckle.

"Okay, Ms. Sarcasm. Tell Eli I said hi. Take care, Lana."

"I learned from the best. You too," I countered with a grin even though he couldn't see it.

Releasing my nearly dried hair from the bun I made earlier, it created soft waves which I was satisfied with. While I attended my mirror, my eyes caught the photo of my parents I taped onto it. Giving them a smile, my fingers grazed the photo of them together. Missing my parents still remained.

Before I knew it, the doorbell rang, making my heart jump in shock.

Peeking from the window, the view didn't reveal much, but it was enough to see a familiar black car parked by the curb of our front lawn. Eli Wesley was here. Grabbing my bag and a beige colored coat in case it got chilly outside, I made my way downstairs and picked up my sandals along the way.

Taking a deep breath, I reached for the doorknob and opened the door.

Don't be afraid, I told myself.

The sun blinded me for a moment which resulted into me squinting my eyes. That must have been presentable.

Once my eyes adjusted, Eli stood before me with a sideways grins on his face. Eli just witnessed my struggle against the sun. What surprised me was when I noticed he was wearing a dark red shirt under his charcoal colored jacket and dark washed jeans. We matched colors again. Recalling back to Haley's birthday party, we both wore blue that even Haley Jones caught that.

Shaking those memories away, I apologized, "Hey, sorry for the wait."

Eli shook his head and grinned. The dimple on his cheek appeared.

"No worries. Your hair looks pretty, by the way," he complimented.

Remembering that Eli only saw me in a bright red wig yesterday, this was the first time Eli saw me without the princess gear. Thanking him, Eli then wondered if Landon was around.

Mentioning that Landon left a while ago for work, Eli nodded before his brown eyes landed on the necklace that hung around my neck. It was the one Eli gave me on my birthday. Until this day, I couldn't go on without wearing it. The heart locket bought memories of mom and even of Eli — whether good or bad. He didn't comment about it, but I could have sworn he was hiding a sad smile.

Eli broke the silence by suggesting that we should head out. Gazing up at Eli's tall stature, I had no clue with what I was getting myself into, but I ended up nodding. As we walked together, the familiar cologne of Eli's wafted to my nose. The scent felt relieving like I actually missed it. Eli politely opened my door, and I returned with a smile in thanks.

During the beginning of the ride, Eli kept things casual by asking how my day was going. The conversation didn't last very long. For the most part, the drive was quiet with the radio playing the current hits in the background. Eli focused on driving, and I caught him tapping his fingers along with the music. However, I was feeling anxious.

Driving to who knows where, I finally summoned enough courage to ask, "What... are we doing today?"

Keeping his eyes on the road, Eli slowly braked when the light ahead was indicating to stop. Once the light turned red, he turned his attention to me. Eli's expression was unreadable even though his brown eyes appeared cheerful.

"It's actually a surprise."

There was something different about Eli. He was more confident than yesterday which may be a good thing because, at least, he wasn't making our situation awkward. Yet, it could be a bad thing because I wasn't sure if I should be worried about Eli's sudden confidence boost.

Catching my look of doubt, Eli sensed that I was freaking out a little. Even though I assured myself I would stay collective, my emotions were betraying me. There was a part of me that was still scared to trust Eli. Before the light turned green, Eli looked at me with an encouraging smile.

"If you give me the chance, I'm going to make things right, Lana."

My stomach dropped when Eli was driving into the plaza of the familiar restaurant we went to last summer. It was Tuscan Bistro.

Memories of that particular day flooded my mind. That day was filled with innocent and humorous memories, but there was a feeling of pain that hovered like a bee. Despite the fact I was clueless with whatever Eli was planning, I came to a decision to go along with his plan.

I wasn't going to stay scared. I would be strong enough.

When Eli handed his car keys over to valet, he had a closed grin on the entire time while he reminded me not to leave anything in the car just in case. Grabbing my purse and coat, I stood alongside Eli until the valet drove his car into the secluded parking.

Fixing his full attention to me, Eli asked again, "Would you give me that chance?"

Knitting my eyebrows, I caught the heartfelt sheen in Eli's brown eyes. He looked so determined that my heart reacted differently than what my head was telling me. Releasing the tensed feeling in my body, I ended up nodding my head. A pleased smile appeared on Eli's face in reply.

If I wasn't already puzzled enough, Eli instructed me to stand there before he walked off the opposite direction. I was left with a dumbfounded expression as I watched him casually turn back around several feet away. However, Eli's eyes didn't meet with mine.

Eli glanced at his surroundings left and right — like he was just taking a stroll — before his brown eyes eventually locked onto mine. His eyes widened with familiarity before a full smile stretched on his face.

"Lana Clarke, is that you?"

Was Eli going crazy?

Not knowing what to do, I didn't reply, but Eli walked up to me. He let out an embarrassed chuckle.

"It's been a long time! Do you remember me?"

Giving him a suspicious stare, I slowly answered, "Yes... you're Elliot Wesley."

"I'm glad," a relieved expression appeared on his face from my remembrance before he continued, "I like it better when people call me Eli."

"Eli," I repeated through a doubting stare.

Eli clarified with a cheesy grin, "Here's the funny part. I decide to walk around the promenade this spring break just for fun, but I don't expect to bump into an old classmate of mine waiting outside by herself. Must be my lucky day, right? I remember her as Lana Clarke. She's beautiful, and it would be wrong of me not to say hi to her. It surprises me seeing her alone, so I should take the chance and ask her for some lunch."

He then pointed at the restaurant and claimed, "I hear this place has pretty good food. Should we try it out?"

From there, I understood now.

What Eli meant by "making things right" was starting over the first time we saw each other since high school. I was in disbelief for a while, but I felt my cheeks unintentionally heated up as Eli spoke. Even though I remembered clearly what I ordered last time we went to Tuscan Bistro, I was amused by Eli's naive personality. My lips twitched into a smile before I went along with it.

Pleased with my agreement, the two of us walked inside. In ten minutes, we were already seated by our waiter. The ambience of Tuscan Bistro replayed a flashback the moment I took the seat across from Eli. Our waiter excused himself to give us some time to look over the menu. Bringing the menu up to glance at the selection, my attention was pulled away when Eli cleared his throat. Lifting my eyes from the menu, his brown eyes had been looking at me. A little surprised, I quickly gazed away.

However, Eli finally decided to disclose what today was about.

"Lana," he started up, "I know you're probably confused right now, but you deserved a better reunion with me. Today, I'm going to make sure it happens."

My lips parted slightly from Eli's words, and I didn't know how to react. As much as I thought moving on was the right decision, I shouldn't stop Eli. No matter how many times I encouraged him that we should go on our separate ways, he still stayed. While I was lost in my thoughts, I eventually snapped out of it since I haven't given him a reply. I cleared up the atmosphere.

"I think we both need it."

For the most part, everything was going well. Our waiter came back to take our orders. When he walked off, it left us back to a party of two.

We talked about what we had been doing during our absence of seeing each other. It contrasted our one sentence replies to each other from yesterday. I couldn't believe that it was just yesterday Eli and I saw each other after so long. At a princess party, on top of that.

While we talked, I couldn't help but notice how much I missed Eli's company. He always tried to hide his shyness, but at the same time, he was confident when he spoke.

"I remember how embarrassed I was telling you about what I wanted to do as a career, but I'm still going down the aerospace path. I also decided to go back into swimming. Not for competitive reasons, but it's nice to be back into the pool."

Now that Eli pointed that out, I did notice how refined his arms had gotten when he took off his jacket earlier. Glad to hear that Eli was doing what he loved, I know my transformation during these seven months wasn't much to talk about, but Eli was still interested nonetheless.

Our orders came — completely different from last time — and we began to eat. Even though it was quiet, the two of us bought some things up, like how my side of loved ones were doing and how his family were doing every now and then.

I revealed, "I don't know if Preston told you yet, but I saw him with Ronnie yesterday."

The knowing look in Eli's brown eyes made it clear that he did speak to his friend. They were best friends after all. A shy expression surfaced on his face before he nodded.

"Yeah, he told me last night. Preston was really excited to see you."

Smiling, I replied back, "It was great seeing them too. Preston and Ronnie make a great couple."

Biting my tongue right after, I realized how awkward that put the both of us. Eli paused briefly once he heard that, but he ended up nodding in agreement. When he returned back to his food, I released a sigh of relief. Focusing back to my almost finished plate of pasta, I shouldn't have bought up the topic of couples. However, Eli broke the silence which I was thankful for.

Eli admitted with a shy grin, "After a good lunch with you, I don't want to say goodbye just yet. So, I think it would be quite chivalrous of me to take you to the pier and win you a prize."

Releasing a soft chuckle from his confession, I jokingly dared, "You're not planning to do that again, are you?"

When Eli flagged down the waiter for the bill, he joined in my laughter before he shrugged out a reply, "I hear second time's a charm."

Eli, you tried more than once that one time, I laughed to myself.

One thing I would never forget about that catch up day was the memory of Eli at the game stand.

The flashback bought a sad smile to my face while we walked around the Santa Monica pier. It was close to sunset, but there were still crowds of tourists and residents along the broad walk who occupied the funnel cake line, multiple rides and game stands. My eyes gazed off to the glittering ocean where the sun was gradually disappearing. The weather was much colder since it was mid March, so Eli and I both wore our jackets.

Eli garnered my attention when he announced, "As we continue on with our day, we walk the pier, and I finally find the game I believe I'm good at."

Following his gaze, it was the same one from before. This time, another person attended the stand. It was an elder women, and she looked more encouraging towards the people who tried shooting the basketball into the far hoop. As a smile crept on my face, I was genuinely enjoying. The way Eli spoke like he was telling a story made it entertaining.

Nodding, I decided to add a bit of my own voice into this revised catch up day.

"And even though I protest that you didn't have to, you still end up going there anyway."

He snapped his fingers and praised, "You're right! I'm surprised that you know, I hope you haven't skipped ahead."

We headed over to the game stand, and I watched as Eli handed a five dollar bill to the stand lady. She gave Eli the basketball before she lightly cheered him a good luck.

Angling his head at the hoop, I fought the grin growing on my face, seeing Eli's similar preparation as before. When Eli unexpectedly turned to look at me, I dropped my grin in surprise before I tossed in words of encouragement of my own. Eli smiled in gratitude, making his dimple even more evident. Before Eli tossed the basketball, he didn't bother to see the hoop and kept his eyes on me.

Once Eli threw the basketball, I ended up breaking my gaze with him and followed the ball's direction.

I heard him say, "You doubt me a little, but there's actually a plot twist..."

To my amazement, Eli shot the ball into the hoop. He wasn't even looking! My jaw dropped, and I could hear the stand lady clap in congratulations.

Eli then finished with a sideways grin on, "... I end up winning that stuffed animal for you."

Stunned, I still couldn't grasp that Eli managed to make it into the hoop without looking. The stand lady then asked me to pick a massive prize of my choice. From the corner of my eyes, I saw the smile on Eli's face as I glanced at the selection of stuffed animals. Indecisive at first, I settled with the stuffed white bear. The bear's fur was very soft once the lady handed it to me.

The stand lady congratulated, "You have quite an arm there, young man."

Eli was humble about it and thanked the lady for the compliment. When we walked away from the game stand, the pier was already lit up with the carnival like lights. The Ferris wheel glowed, making the ocean below glitter various colors. Looking up at Eli, I gave him an appreciated smile as I carried the huge bear.

"Thanks Eli. You didn't have to go out and do that though."

Placing his hands into his front pockets, Eli fixed his eyes on me and grinned back.

"There would be no fun in that then," he soon expressed, "okay, after I win you a stuffed prize, we decide to do something different. I mean, going down to the beach at night seems too 'high school', doesn't it?"

Recalling back to when Eli tried to kiss me and how I slapped him back in response made me chuckle in embarrassment. That would be something I wouldn't want repeated.

"What do you suggest, champ?" I asked through a curious expression.

An amused grin appeared on his face when he heard that old nickname.

Eli then pressed his lips together before he answered, "I'm going to show you my escape."

I raised an eyebrow.

"Isn't it too soon to let a stranger into your escape?"

He shook his head and corrected, "The thing is, I don't think of you as a stranger, and you'll be the only one to know where it is."

Approaching the cliffside of Eli's escape, my sandals crinkled against the rocky ground. The view overlooked the ocean, and I could see the pier that we were once at. It was just like I remembered. Peaceful and stress relieving. Eli was lucky to find a place like this where he could go away whenever he needed time to himself.

Because I wasn't at the hospital anymore, I couldn't go to my escape, the rooftop, anymore. It was fine though because I found myself visiting my parents as an escape from the world. Glancing back, I wondered where Eli was. He told me that he needed to get something in his car, but I didn't expect him to take so long.

The night was relaxing with the faint sounds of the waves crashing, and I took in a breath of fresh air. Gazing up at the night sky, I smiled up at my parents.

The day with Eli was very unexpected, but I was happy with how it was going. I thought that it would be like yesterday where it was nothing but pure awkwardness. Our revised catch up day from that summer ran much smoother, but I was still unsure with my personal feelings towards Eli.

I could see how Eli Wesley cared for me, but I had this inner battle with myself whether or not I should fully let him back into my life. My thoughts were pushed to a halt once I heard another pair of shoes making their way towards where I stood.

Turning back around, Eli finally came back. This time, he was carrying something along with him. Curious with what it was, Eli soon reached me at a reasonable distance. His eyes first observed the view before us, and he released a content grin. He then bought forward what looked like some type of folded material, and we exchanged glances with one another.

"Since it's night and we're up pretty high, it would be pretty cool to light these up," Eli announced, and he revealed what these were.

They were paper lanterns.

Almost expressing a little too much excitement, I had to get a hold of myself as I watched Eli expand the two rectangular lanterns to its full shape. The white lanterns reminded me of the ones from Tangled which grew to be one of my favorite Disney movies. The memory of Eli bringing most of the Disney princess' movies to life replayed in my head. It was the time he asked me to be his girlfriend. Eli then handed one to me and smiled.

I complimented, "These are beautiful."

"Just wait till they're lit," Eli mentioned as he bought a lighter out from his back pocket.

Within seconds, the dull lanterns were lit up by the small fire. The light that emitted from the lanterns casted a luminous glow between Eli and me. Holding the lantern out in front of me, I smiled in awe before I noticed that Eli had been looking my way.

To hide my embarrassment, I suggested, "We should set them free."

Eli nodded in agreement, and it wasn't long before the lanterns were released from our grasp.

Letting out a gasp, the two lanterns lit up the night sky as they danced alongside each other. This moment of silence we shared managed to bring happiness to me. If I was already amazed with two lanterns, I could only imagine how beautiful the sky would look like if there were hundreds lit up just like in Tangled. When the lanterns were no longer in our sight, we both settled our attention back to one another.

Eli's voice was soft.

"Your parents have them now. A piece of your heart."

Blinking my eyes, I couldn't help but feel this overwhelmed emotion from what Eli said. He still thought about my parents even up until now.

During that moment, the only words I could come up with was to thank Eli for today. Throughout these past months we haven't seen each other, I felt like today was allowing me to open up to Eli again.

However, I wasn't expecting a reply from Eli saying that this wasn't the end of our day. Eli gestured to head back to the car because we had one more place to go.

Tilting my head, I couldn't think of what else Eli had in store. I had a feeling I wouldn't get any answers from him until we were actually there.

Even when Eli parked his car at what appeared to be the back parking lot of a row of stores, I was still clueless. Since it was night, the lighting was pretty bad because only one lamppost was working. Getting out of the car, I waited for an explanation, but Eli was fiddling with a few keys on his keychain.

"Eli, what are we doing here?" I asked as I adjusted my coat.

Bringing his attention to me, Eli replied, "I need you to close your eyes."

"I can't," I quickly opposed, "why don't you just tell me?"

Eli gently joked, "You can't close your eyes? How come you're blinking right now?"

Even though I gave Eli a flat stare, I couldn't help but release a short laugh. My answer didn't actually make sense.

"Lana, I promise that this will make you smile. If not, I'll leave you alone."

Taking his words as a risk, I stood there for a moment. Was Eli actually serious about that? As much as I didn't want that to happen, I gave in. Having my world even darker than before, I gulped down and waited.

"I'm going to hold your hand. Is that okay?" I heard him say.

Did I even have a choice?

Signaling Eli with a nod, he then slipped his hand with mine. Just by his warm touch, my heart raced. I exhaled slowly as I blindly followed where Eli was taking me.

From what I heard, keys were jingling, and a door knob was being turned. Still keeping my eyes shut, I knew we walked inside someplace. My heart was excessively beating in anticipation. Once Eli let go of my hand, he must have flicked the lights open because a bright sensation filled my eyelids. After a few seconds, I started to shiver because I had no idea where Eli went off to.

I felt relief when I heard Eli call out, "Okay, you can open your eyes now."

The moment I opened my eyes, I wasn't expecting a single thing.

"Surprise!"

The first thing — or people — I saw were my brother, Olette, Eli's friends and Ronnie. They all had their hands up in the arms with cheerful expressions. What were they doing here? Jumping in shock, I immediately gazed around my surroundings to figure out where Eli had taken me.

There wasn't a proper way to express my surprise and confusion.

"What... is this?"

Everyone let Eli explain as his arm motioned to get a better look, "It's for you. A bakery of your own."

Stopping on the heels of my sandals, I took in the sight. The Tiffany blue painted walls gave this bakery a chic touch along with the white Victorian furniture placed in the front. There were huge glass windows by the entrance, and chandelier light fixtures that brightened the entire place. The bakery looked so cozy from the inspiring wall art to the cute decorations scattered around. Towards the white stone counter were two presentation cases, and the wall behind was inscribed with words that said, "It all starts with something sweet...".

The bakery was the perfect place to grab a pastry or two to eat.

Not being able to react, I was lost for words. Everyone approached my side and were probably expecting me to start jumping up and down in excitement. Even though I was truthfully happy in the inside, I was having such a hard time expressing that. So many questions were flying around my mind.

Olette bought me back to reality with the huge smile stretched across on her face.

"Lana, please breathe," I heard my best friend chuckle out.

I found Preston waving his hand a good distance from my face.

Realizing that I was holding my breath the entire time, I finally exhaled and returned back to a moderate breathing pace. Glancing at all the eyes that had been gazing my way, my eyes eventually landed at Eli. He looked a little concerned by my shocked expression especially since I didn't breathe normally for a while. Trying to let this sink in, I cleared my throat.

"This... this is for me?"

My brother finally spoke up, "Yep. You and Mom love to bake, so it's only right for you to have your own bakery. Why don't you take a look around?"

This was a lot to absorb. However, I followed my brother's suggestion and walked around the bakery. It was perfect.

All the little details in the bakery and the glass cases where I imagined the pastries and cakes already inside made my heart flutter happily. What amazed me was the kitchen in the back. It was already equipped with the best appliances out there. I ran my hands at the Kitchen Aid, the three ovens, and the wood counter where I would be rolling out the handmade dough and bringing Mom's recipes to life.

What did I do to deserve a bakery like this?

Walking back to the front, Eli had been talking to his friends. The four of them all gave me a smile, and I greeted them for coming by. Julian was the only one I haven't seen. He still looked the same, but his jet black hair was much shorter than before. It matured his appearance.

Julian questioned in a friendly tone, "What do you think?"

"I think I'm still dreaming," I answered in an honest tone.

Everyone in the bakery laughed in response before I joined in. Being with everyone again was just like old times. Despite what happened, it was just like when we were all together during my birthday. It wasn't the same without Mom and Dad around, but I was glad to have them here. It made me see how much I missed each one of them. They all made an impact in my life, and we all grew from the events of that summer.

Ronnie then chirped up, "I really can't wait for the grand opening! I hear you're an amazing baker."

Olette nodded her head happily as the boys showcased similar excitement.

I blushed in thanks.

"Thanks Ronnie, but I have to thank my mom for that."

While everyone was busily chatting with one another, I asked Eli if I could talk to him outside. He was fixing the light fixture that wasn't properly working, but he nodded before we walked out. We stood towards the left away from the windows outside the front entrance. The mild breeze sent a cold chill up my spine, but I shook it off. Gazing up at Eli, his warm brown eyes were curious as they looked into mine.

I managed to spill out, "Is this really mine? I-I just don't understand how."

Instead of answering back with words, Eli suddenly reached for his back pocket and pulled out a white envelope. A faint grin surfaced on his face.

"Read this, it's from someone special," Eli chuckled softly before continuing on, "I'm not exactly sure what it says, but it should answer everything."

Hesitant, I doubted to claim that this envelope held the truth.

In the end, I took the envelope because I was eager to find out regardless. As I slowly opened it and grabbed the letter inside, each fold had me anticipating what the contents held. Once I fully unfolded the letter, my heart tightened at the familiar handwriting.

It was Dad's handwriting.

My eyes shook before I weakly looked up at Eli. He had been smiling at me with that dimple on his face. That smile that managed to tug my heart. Eli then nodded which encouraged me that I had enough strength to read what Dad wrote.

Returning my attention back at the letter, I felt my eyes water seeing my name written by him:

Lana,

By the time you get this letter, Eli has shown you my gift. He did a great job bringing it to life, didn't he? I knew he could handle it. This was what I pictured the kind of bakery you and Cathy would have together. Eli even added in a few ideas himself. I know this bakery will bring you all sorts of happiness. With all the pastries and cakes you will create, you will share that love with others, just like you did with me.

Lana, I want to remind you that I am happy. I am so happy to be reunited with your mother. I'm in such a beautiful place, and your mother and I are always watching over you and Landon. We are so proud of you both. I hope you are not upset with me. Please know that I had no regrets about what happened to me during my final moments. My last moments with all of you were something I would never take back. I do not want you to feel the need to miss me, us, all the time. I want you and Landon to explore and love life the way your mother and I has.

I hope you have not and will never close yourself off from the ones you love. I want you to move on from the sadness that burdens your heart because that is the last thing I want my daughter to endure. You deserve to be happy, Lana. That is all I ask for.

There was one person who told me before I left that he would do anything and give his all for you. His intention was never meant to hurt you, I am sure you knew that. That person was very sincere in my eyes and reminded me that we grow from our mistakes. That a mistake can peel and remove a layer off a person and reveal their true self. In this case, a young man who cares about my daughter and truly loves her for everything she is. I think we both know who that person is. Lana, please do not ever ignore what your heart yearns for.

I am always here, whether it would be the wind giving you a kiss on the cheek or greeting you a hello. I promise you I am not going anywhere. Promise me you will remove that tainted smile and replace it with genuine joy. You are strong, my beautiful daughter. Remember, you were not and are never alone in this journey. Make your dreams come true. You are your own fairy tale princess. You deserve your own happy ending, just like the rest.

Thank you Lana for being the greatest daughter a father could ever ask for. Your mother and I love you and Landon forever.

Always,

Dad

P.S. I was thinking of names for the bakery. What do you think about L&C Bakery? You and your mother's initials — my favorite bakers. Of course, it's just an idea. I love you, Lana.

From that point, I couldn't hold back anymore. The tears fell down willingly. The letter Dad wrote me was slightly damped. Dad still wanted to make sure I was happy. He never failed to bring me happiness though. Reading his letter caused contentment to fill me.

Everything made more sense.

I would always be grateful to my parents. They always found a way to guide me to the right path.

"Lana... I'm sorry... what did the letter say?"

Eli's voice was broken, probably because he witnessed my uncontrollable tears.

Remembering that Eli promised me that this surprise would make me smile, my current state answered opposite to that. The thing was, it did make me smile. I just couldn't express that correctly at the time. Shaking my head, I tried to wipe the tears away using the back of my hand. Taking a few breaths, I attempted to speak once I managed to stop crying.

"Eli, why... why did you stay until now?"

His dark brown eyes stared into mine, and compared to earlier, Eli held his voice stern.

"Because... it's because I love you. I know I shouldn't have approached you under those circumstances, but I never regretted the times we spent with each other because I was myself whenever I was with you. I haven't felt this happy and lucky before until I found you. This isn't some kind of crush that goes away. I can't imagine myself with anyone else but you. Even if I knew that you needed time and that there may be a possibility you would never speak to me again, I would continue to stay because you're worth it."

"You know how I said I would leave you alone if this didn't make you smile. I... actually lied. I would keep trying because I can't let you go, Lana. As much as I couldn't be the guy to make you smile, to make you feel happy, I wouldn't give up. That's why I wanted to start over. I wanted to make things right with you. I know it shouldn't be my decision to make, but I had to do it. You mean everything to me, Lana. Seeing you cry right now breaks me because, Lana, you deserve all sorts of happiness."

Eli's face expressed a mixture of sorrow and honesty before a smile occupied his face.

"I love you, Lana."

I wasn't crying anymore because I felt broken. I cried at Eli's sincerity. The way he revealed that he would always love me even though it would have been easier for him to give up and move on.

My heart ached because Dad was right. It did yearn for Eli Wesley.

Eli was the boy I fell in love with. He managed to help me back up whenever I was hitting my lowest point. He showed me that it was okay to be weak sometimes because I would be able to overcome it in the end. Through his mistakes, Eli took full responsibility for it and tried to fix it. Eli never gave up. Even as time passed, his feelings towards me stayed the same.

I was really the lucky one because to have someone who cared about you just as much as you cared about them was rare to find.

I gulped down the harsh lump in my throat before I continued, "You mean everything to me too. I... actually forgave you a long time ago, but

I just needed time to realize it. I'm sorry for doing this to you. You don't deserve it either."

Summoning enough courage to look at him in the eyes, Eli reached in to wipe my tears away. My heart pounded, and the way we looked at each other was different. It was just like those summer nights I would share with Eli.

He shook his head before he returned, "I'm sorry too, Lana."

"Eli..."

"Hm?"

"You were the guy who made me smile, who made me feel happy. No matter what happened, you were still the guy who made me feel that way. You still are," I confessed, "I love you."

The heavy feeling lifted off my chest the moment those words were said. Eli's eyes widened before a full smile stretched on his face. The dimple I loved to see appeared.

"And I love you, Lana Clarke."

After all these months, I found myself in a state of happiness.

The death of my parents and the news about Eli and Haley affected me in ways I didn't want to look back on, but I forgave Eli. I also forgave Haley. I would always miss my parents, but I truly believed that they never left my side. Mom and Dad continued to watch over me even if they weren't physically here, and I smiled at the thought.

I promise I'll be happy, I assured the both of them.

Eli pulled me in closer for a hug and being in his arms again was really all what I needed after months of being separated from one another.

"I've missed you so much, Lana," Eli whispered while we broke off from the embrace.

"You don't know how much I've missed you," I returned.

Gazing up on him, Eli looked at me with a joyful expression on his face. Releasing a smile, I felt myself reciprocating the exact emotion. It felt so natural, so real. Those were the brown eyes I fell in love with. Within seconds, we shared a kiss.

Once our lips touched, it sent waves of happiness as my heart pitter-pattered endlessly. The sweet kiss was filled with emotions of missing each other, loving each other, and promising each other that we were always going to stay.

Holding Eli's hand, we eventually walked back inside the bakery to join everyone again. Before Eli opened the door for me, he settled his gaze on me and grinned.

"Have you decided what you wanted to name the bakery?"

I didn't have to think about it.

"L&C bakery. Has a nice ring to it, doesn't it?"

"You and your mom's name?" he guessed correctly before complimenting, "I already like it."

The moment our family and friends saw us walk in together, knowing grin were on their faces. Despite my teary face, Eli and I let out bashful laughs in response before we smiled at one another.

This catch up day marked a new start. My mom always told me that we should never run away from whatever life threw at us and to face it no matter what because those were possibilities that may take us places we never expected. I thank her for that.

I know you and Mom are watching over us, Dad. I love you both.

I never thought I would find myself here with Elliot Wesley, the one who took my heart away, with the people I loved in a place where I would share my mother's and my passion with everyone.

Smiling and laughing with everyone, we were no longer chasing possibility anymore.